"I'VE TRIED ⋯
FROM YOU ⋯

Isabelle stared at him in mesmeri⋯ ⋯ s his face slowly inched its way to hers. The sight of his lips descending to hers made her heart beat faster with anticipation.

She closed her eyes. Their lips met. His mouth felt warm and gently insistent on hers, and his masculine scent of heather intoxicated her senses.

The feel of his mouth slashing across hers made Isabelle weak. His strong arms encircled her and drew her against the solidness of his body as her arms encircled his neck.

Isabelle reveled in these new and exciting sensations and returned his kiss in kind. . . .

Swept away on wings of yearning, she fell back on the couch. Ever so gently, John rained feathery-light kisses on her temples, her eyelids, her throat. . . .

Isabelle burned with desire. Beyond reason, she molded her young body to his. . . .

Violets in the Snow

Patricia Grasso

A Dell Book

Published by
Dell Publishing
a division of
Bantam Doubleday Dell Publishing Group, Inc.
1540 Broadway
New York, New York 10036

The trademark Dell® is registered in the U.S. Patent and Trademark Office.

ISBN: 0-440-22408-X

Printed in the United States of America

Published simultaneously in Canada

January 1998

10 9 8 7 6 5 4 3 2 1

OPM

For my incredibly talented, exceedingly lovable, and always hilarious advanced creative writing students at Everett High School: Kristina Arvanitis, Nicole Blake, Candie Kane, Phil King, and Allison Quealy.

There will never be another class like you!

Prologue

"God mend your ways," the girl snapped at her stepsisters. In a flash of movement ten-year-old Isabelle Montgomery grabbed her beloved flute out of one sister's hands and her fur-lined cloak out of the other sister's hands. Whirling away, she dashed out the bedchamber door and ran down the corridor.

"Mama said you're supposed to share with us," shrieked twelve-year-old Lobelia.

"We'll tell Mama," eleven-year-old Rue threatened.

"I don't give a rat's arse," Isabelle called over her shoulder without breaking stride.

Isabelle scooted down the narrow stairway and, startling the servants, burst into the kitchen. Ignoring their surprised gasps, she escaped out the door into the April afternoon.

Pausing a moment to catch her breath, Isabelle wrapped her cloak around herself and then started across the manicured lawns toward the woodland where she could evade her stepsisters' greed. She crossed the estate's stately drive built of mellowed plum-red bricks and gray stone dressings and gazed at the bordering masses of blue violets, nodding yellow daffodils, and blooming forsythia.

Joyful spring surrounded Arden Hall. Yet bitter winter gripped her ten-year-old heart and tears welled up in her eyes.

Blinking her tears back, Isabelle stared at the Montgomery family chapel and the graveyard beyond it. They'd buried her father that morning. Who could ever have guessed that her wonderful, healthy father would succumb to the dreaded white-throat disease? Now her dearest papa lay beside her long-dead mother. If only her brother Miles hadn't returned to the university immediately after the funeral.

Isabelle reached up and touched the gold locket she always wore. It contained her mother's miniature, the image of a woman she'd known only in her heart. If her real mother hadn't died, she wouldn't have those two nasty stepsisters or her stepmother, Delphinia.

Squaring her shoulders, Isabelle turned away from the sight of her parents' final resting place and passed through the giant oaks that separated the park from the woodland. She needed to get away from her stepfamily and mourn the loss of her father. Afternoon was fading rapidly into twilight, but the prospect of supping with her stepmother and her stepsisters disturbed her more than being caught in the woodland at night.

With a heavy heart Isabelle walked in the direction of the Avon River. Lilacs mingling with moss scented the air inside the woodland. Here and there she saw the brown and green stripes of jack-in-the-pulpit and the crimson crowns of rock columbine. Delicate white bloodroot blossoms pushed up through downy leaves, and tightly coiled spirals of fiddlehead ferns were just beginning to emerge.

Springtide heralded an active season for nature spirits and flower fairies. Cook had told her so.

Isabelle shook her head at such a fanciful notion and then paused as a sound, fainter than a whisper on a breeze, reached her ears. Someone was playing a flute. The rich tones floated through the air and enticed her to follow them toward the Avon River. With each forward step she took, the flute's song grew louder and clearer. Its hauntingly lonely melody mirrored her mood.

Isabelle quickened her pace. Breaking free of the trees, she stopped short at the sight that greeted her.

A shabbily dressed old woman sat on a tree stump beside the river and played a flute. The gray-haired, wrinkled-faced crone abruptly stopped playing and looked at her.

Suddenly afraid, Isabelle stepped back two paces.

"What's your name?" the woman asked with a smile.

"Isabelle Montgomery," she answered.

Glancing toward the river, Isabelle saw the evening mist beginning to form and swirl. She peered up at the sky. Shades of lavender and mauve streaked the western horizon. Should she leave or stay? Delphinia would be very angry if she returned home after dark.

"Sit down," the old woman invited her.

Isabelle heard the kindness in the woman's voice and responded to it. She crossed the short distance separating them and sat down on the ground beside her.

"I live at Arden Hall," Isabelle announced without preamble.

"Why is a Montgomery living at Arden Hall?" the woman asked.

"My late mother was the heiress of Arden Hall,"

Isabelle told her. "She married Adam Montgomery, my father. We buried him today."

"So young to be orphaned," the woman said, patting her hand in sympathy. "I'm Giselle."

"Elizabeth was my mother's name," Isabelle told her.

"And you loved her very much."

"I never knew her." Isabelle opened the locket of gold and held it out for the woman to inspect the image inside.

"With your pale blond hair and your violet eyes, you certainly have the look of her," Giselle said.

"Thank you. I consider that a compliment."

"So, Belle, what sadness besides your father's passing brings you to my woodland?" Giselle asked.

"How do you know my brother's pet name for me?" Isabelle asked, surprised.

"Sharing troubles always lightens the burden," Giselle answered, ignoring her question. "I've years and years of experience in dealing with problems." The crone shivered suddenly and dropped her gaze to the cloak. "I've been sitting here for a long, long time and I'm very cold. May I borrow your cloak?"

Without hesitation Isabelle removed her cloak and wrapped it around the old woman's shoulders. "Consider it yours," she said, plopping down on the ground again. "To clothe the naked is a corporal work of mercy, and I intend to earn a place in heaven. Then I will finally meet my mother and see my father once more."

Giselle nodded her approval and pulled the cloak tighter around her stooped shoulders. "Child, tell me what else brings you to my woodland."

"Lobelia and Rue, my stepsisters, tried to steal my flute," Isabelle began. "My flute and my locket are my mother's legacy to me. Cook told me that my mother played the flute like a nightingale in song. Delphinia, my stepmother, fired Mrs. Juniper as soon as we buried my father. Juniper loved me the best. That is the real reason she had to go, not because she drank cold tea. And what is wrong with someone preferring cold tea?"

"Who is Juniper?" Giselle asked.

"Juniper was my nanny until today, and she disliked my nasty stepsisters," Isabelle answered. "My brother, Miles, returned to the university after the funeral. I do hope he arrives there safely."

"I'm positive that, wherever he is, Miles is well," Giselle answered.

"Are we friends, then?" Isabelle asked brightly, her eagerness all too apparent in her expression and her voice. "I've never had a friend and don't really want to go home. May I live with you until Miles returns to Arden Hall?"

"Your brother's homecoming may be delayed a long time," Giselle told her. "Who will guard his estates if you live with me in the woods?"

Isabelle shrugged, her hopeful expression drooping.

"What do you want more than anything else in the whole wide world?" the old woman asked, as if she had the power to grant wishes.

"I want to be loved," Isabelle answered, her loneliness apparent in her violet-eyed gaze.

"Listen, child. Don't ask me how, but I know things," Giselle said, reaching out to touch her hand. "Someday a dark prince will rescue you, but only if you return to Arden Hall."

"Rescue me from what?"

"Questioning well-meaning elders is rude in the extreme," Giselle chided her. "Now then, this prince will be the man who believes you are lovelier than a violet in the snow.''

Isabelle gave her an incredulous stare. Even she knew that no one could foretell the future.

''You don't believe me?'' Giselle asked. ''Would you care to see what he is doing this very moment?''

Isabelle gave her a smile filled with sunshine and nodded her head vigorously.

''Come.'' Giselle rose slowly from her perch on the tree stump and held her hand out.

Isabelle looked from the wrinkled face to the gnarled hand. Then she stood, too, and placed her hand in the woman's.

Giselle led her to the river and knelt in the grass at the water's edge, saying, ''Gaze into the water, little one. See what the future brings you.''

Isabelle saw nothing at first, and then a shimmering image formed slowly. An older man, at least twenty years, looked directly at her. His hair and his eyes were darker than a moonless midnight.

''Who is he?'' Isabelle asked without taking her gaze from the image in the water. ''Is he a foreign prince?''

''No foreigners dwell within the kingdom of the heart,'' Giselle said. Her gnarled hand tapped the river, and the prince's image vanished in the rippling of the water. ''It's past time you ran home.''

''Will I see you again?'' Isabelle asked, standing when the woman did. ''How will I find you?''

''I'll find you,'' Giselle told her.

Isabelle looked around. Late afternoon had faded into twilight, and she feared walking alone through the woodland.

''Simply follow the shining whiteness of the birch

tree," Giselle said as if she knew her thoughts, and pointed toward the woodland.

Isabelle's gaze followed the old woman's finger. The shining white of the birch trees lit a path through the woods where there had been only darkness a moment earlier.

"I do hope I'll see you again," Isabelle said. On impulse she planted a kiss on the woman's wizened cheek.

Giselle smiled. "I promise I will visit you often."

Isabelle started down the path through the birch trees. She looked back once but saw only darkness. Ahead was the only way to go.

A friend, Isabelle thought, happiness swelling within her heart as she ran toward Arden Hall. At long last she had a friend in whom she could confide.

Shivering from the evening chill, Isabelle sneaked inside the mansion the same way she'd escaped, through the servants' entrance. She burst into the kitchen, startling the servants again, and then raced up the narrow stairway to the second floor.

Isabelle reached the safety of her bedchamber and bolted the door. Now her stepsisters couldn't bother her. If Delphinia wanted to scold her for sneaking outside, she would need to shout through the locked door.

Intending to fetch a shawl, Isabelle hurried across the chamber. Suddenly, she stopped short and her mouth dropped open in surprise. On her bed lay the fur-lined cloak she'd given the old woman.

Sweet celestial breath, Isabelle thought, a smile of joy lighting her expression. *Giselle is my guardian angel.*

Chapter 1

Thirty-year-old John Saint-Germain, the fifth Duke of Avon, tenth Marquess of Grafton, and twelfth Earl of Kilchurn, relaxed in his favorite chair inside White's Gentlemen's Club on St. James's Street and stared, in turn, at each of his three companions. His twenty-five-year-old brother, Ross, seated in the chair on his left side, cast him a mildly amused smile. Directly opposite him sat his twenty-three-year-old brother, Jamie, who sent him a hopeful look; Miles Montgomery, his youngest brother's bosom friend, sprawled in the chair on his right side but kept his gaze on Jamie.

"Bull's pizzle," John said, his dark gaze returning to his youngest brother, effectively wiping the hopeful expression off his face. "I cannot believe this is the urgent matter that required I leave Scotland earlier than planned."

"We cannot lose the opportunity of a lifetime," Jamie argued with passion. "The profit on this investment will earn us a small fortune."

"I already possess a *large* fortune," John reminded him. He ran a hand through his midnight black hair as he watched a disappointed expression appear on his brother's face.

"How can you be certain this speculation will turn any profit?" John asked, relenting at the sight of the change in his brother.

"Your Grace," Miles Montgomery spoke up, drawing his attention. "Nicholas deJewell, my stepmother's nephew, tipped me off about it. He heard it from a well-placed man at Baring Brothers, which represents the United States' banking interests in England."

"How much is deJewell investing?" John asked.

Miles Montgomery hesitated and then shook his head. "Nicholas is short of funds at the moment. I promised him a share for tipping me off—out of my profits, I assure you."

"Miles and I plan to travel to New York personally," Jamie added, his hopeful expression returning. "I promise we won't leave anything to chance."

"England and the United States are not in accord at the moment, and friction is mounting with each passing day," John replied. "What if war breaks out?"

Jamie shrugged. "So we'll be stranded in New York for longer than we expected."

"What do you have to say about this?" John asked, sliding his dark gaze toward his brother Ross.

"I have no opinion concerning its success or failure," Ross answered. "The required sum isn't enough to bankrupt the Saint-Germains, so I say give Jamie the money."

John studied his youngest brother's eager, hopeful expression. At twenty-three Jamie Saint-Germain was the baby of the family and, until now, had demonstrated no inclination toward anything but social activities. This business venture could be the very thing to transform Jamie into a responsible adult.

"Good evening, Your Grace," said a deep, grating voice.

All four men looked at the tall blond man who stood beside their table. The newcomer stared at them with a decidedly unfriendly expression.

"Grimsby," John said by way of a greeting and inclined his head.

"What a heartwarming picture of family life," Grimsby commented, staring at the Saint-Germain brothers. He shifted his gaze to the only stranger in the group and said, "I don't believe we've met."

"Miles Montgomery is the Earl of Stratford," John said, making the introductions. "Miles, meet William Grimsby, the Earl of Ripon."

Miles Montgomery stood, shook the other man's hand, and then reclaimed his seat. Grimsby cast him a sardonic smile.

"A pleasure to meet you, my lord," Grimsby said. "Take a friendly warning: If you have a sister, keep her away from the Saint-Germains." Without another word William Grimsby walked away.

Miles Montgomery turned in apparent confusion to the others. "What was that about?" he asked.

"My former brother-in-law," John answered.

"Too bad Grimsby isn't your *late* former brother-in-law," muttered Ross.

"You only say that because his pranks have cost our shipping lines a substantial amount of lost profit," John said, casting his brother a sidelong smile.

"How can you remain so calm?" Ross asked. "The man is bent on ruining the Saint-Germains."

John shrugged. "William is upset about his sister's passing."

"Lenore has been dead these past five years," Ross reminded him.

"Brother, let it go for now." John flicked a glance at Montgomery, who was listening to their conversation, and then shifted his gaze to his youngest brother, adding, "I'll loan you the necessary funds, but because of the growing friction between the two countries, you must first travel to Bermuda on one of my ships. From there you can journey via a neutral ship to New York. Agreed?"

Jamie Saint-Germain and Miles Montgomery looked at each other and smiled. At his friend's nod, Jamie turned to John and said, "There is one more thing we need."

Here comes the snag, John thought, cocking a dark brow at his brother. He slid his gaze to his brother's friend when Jamie said, "You explain."

"Your Grace, I have a simple problem," Miles Montgomery began. "I fear my stepmother will neglect my sister while I am out of the country." He paused for a moment as if summoning his courage and cleared his throat before finishing. "I am requesting that you become Isabelle's temporary guardian for the duration of my—"

"No."

"Your Grace, I implore you. Isabelle has brains, heart, and courage," Miles continued, undaunted by the refusal. "She won't be any trouble, she's uncommonly pretty with beautiful blond hair and—"

"I despise blondes," John interrupted. "At the age of forty I plan to remarry the ugliest brunette I can find."

Ross burst out laughing, earning himself a censorious glare from his older brother.

"Isabelle is an accomplished young lady," Jamie interjected.

"Blond-haired, blue-eyed, and accomplished?" John drawled, his voice dripping sarcasm.

"More violet than blue, Your Grace," Miles corrected him.

"I beg your pardon?"

"Isabelle's eyes are a violet shade of blue."

Ross Saint-Germain chuckled at the remark.

After casting his brother a wholly disgusted look, John asked, "And at what is this paragon of womanhood accomplished? Intricate embroidery? The pianoforte?"

"Isabelle plays the flute," Miles told him.

"Divinely," Jamie added.

"Flute playing isn't at all the thing in these modern days," Ross said, earning himself a sour look from his youngest brother.

"She must be accomplished at fashions and gossip," John speculated. "All ladies of quality possess that talent."

"Isabelle prefers to dress simply," Miles replied, shaking his head. "She never engages in gossip."

John hooted with incredulous, derisive laughter. "Show me a woman who doesn't gossip," he said, "and I'll show you a woman who cannot speak. So, my young friend, what are your sister's accomplishments?"

"In addition to playing the flute, Isabelle manages numbers most excellently," Miles answered.

"Numbers?" John echoed. "What do you mean?"

"Isabelle does the bookkeeping on my household and

estate ledgers,'' Miles told him. ''Of course, I check her work quarterly.''

''You actually trust a woman with your finances?''

Miles Montgomery nodded.

John stared at him for a long moment. ''Your sister sounds like an interesting young lady,'' he said, ''but I cannot agree to your request.''

Miles turned to Jamie and said, ''I won't leave Isabelle in Delphinia's custody.''

Jamie turned a pleading look on his oldest brother. In turn John glanced at Ross and sent him a silent plea for help.

Ross grinned and shrugged his shoulders.

''Very well,'' John relented, unwilling to disappoint his youngest brother. ''I will become your sister's temporary guardian and oversee your financial accounts.''

''Thank you, Your Grace.'' Miles glanced at Jamie and then continued, ''There is another tiny favor I need.''

''You're pressing your luck, Montgomery,'' John warned.

''On the first day of May, Isabelle will be eighteen,'' Miles said, giving him an affable smile. ''If I haven't returned by then, do *not* agree to a marriage between Isabelle and Nicholas deJewell. She despises the man. If you have the inclination, marry her yourself, else she needs to make her come-out into society.''

''I will respect your wishes regarding deJewell, but my reputation with the ladies is slightly tarnished,'' John said. ''The girl's reputation will be ruined if I sponsor her.''

''I think that sponsoring the girl is a wonderful idea,'' Ross spoke up.

Surprised, John snapped his head around to stare at

his brother. It was just like Ross to cause trouble for him. How could he extricate himself from this foolishness with his brother recommending the absurd notion?

"Mother never enjoyed the pleasure of raising a daughter," Ross continued. "Aunt Hester and she will relish the opportunity to introduce such an accomplished maiden into society."

"A legal document must be drawn and signed," John said, surrendering to the inevitable. "Bring it to Saint-Germain Court tomorrow afternoon. I have a previous engagement. If you will excuse me?"

Without another word John stood and started to cross the well-appointed chamber toward the club's entrance. He could well imagine the wicked grin gracing Ross's face at that moment.

Behind him, John heard Miles Montgomery whisper loudly, "Do you think he's going to visit his mistress?"

"Which one?" Ross asked.

"Well, I once saw him with an ebony-haired beauty," Miles said. "I believe I heard she was an actress."

"John pensioned Lisette Dupre off several years ago," came his brother's reply.

Passing the newly installed bow window in the middle of the facade, John inclined his head toward Beau Brummell, who had made the celebrated window his own domain. The front door had been moved to the left of the window.

"Your Grace, have yourself a good evening," Brummell called by way of a greeting.

"I've just made other arrangements," John replied, making the renowned dandy smile.

John stepped outside into a moonless night, darker than his own midnight black hair and eyes. Heavy fog swirled around him like a voluminous cloak and appeared especially eerie in the soft glow from the streetlamps.

Spying Gallagher with his coach on the opposite side of St. James's Street, John gestured for the man to remain where he was. There was little sense in manuevering the coach around when his destination was in the other direction.

Silently cursing himself for agreeing to become the Montgomery maiden's guardian, John stepped into the street and started to cross. Suddenly, a coach materialized from nowhere and careened down St. James's Street.

"Watch out!" John heard his coachman shout, and he leapt back in time to save his own life—but not, unfortunately, his evening attire, now splattered with mud.

"Are you injured, Your Grace?" Gallagher asked, reaching his side.

"No, but I'll need to return to Park Lane to change out of this mess," John answered. He touched the coachman's shoulder and added, "Thank you for saving my life."

"It was my pleasure, Your Grace," Gallagher said with a toothy grin. "Besides, your death would mean unemployment for me." The man chuckled at his own wit.

"What I admire about you, Gallagher, is your practicality." John smiled at his longtime coachman and then looked down the deserted street, complaining, "I cannot believe the driver of that vehicle failed to see me."

"He saw you all right, Your Grace," Gallagher replied, opening the coach door for him. "It was as if he was aiming for you."

John sat back inside his coach and pondered his man's words as they drove the short distance to his home on Park Lane. That the driver of the other coach was actually aiming for him was absurd. The only person in England who hated him was William Grimsby, and his former brother-in-law would never be part of an assassination attempt. No, the near-miss was undoubtedly one of those freakish, unexplainable accidents.

Arden Hall, December

"Sweet celestial breath," seventeen-year-old Isabelle Montgomery muttered, tossing her quill down in growing consternation. After pushing several wanton wisps of blond hair off her face, she fingered her gold locket and stared with murderous intent at the recalcitrant column of numbers on page twenty-four of the household ledger book.

"These numbers refuse to be tallied," she said. "Do you know anything about mathematics?"

Isabelle looked across the study at the old woman sitting in the chair in front of the hearth. Giselle still wore the tattered garb she'd been wearing for the past seven years.

"I know nothing about numbers," the old woman answered.

Isabelle felt her irritation rising. At times the old woman's presence in her life felt more like a penance than a blessing, yet she loved her dearly. After all,

Giselle had been her only friend since her father's passing.

"I assumed that celestial beings knew absolutely everything," Isabelle remarked.

"Apparently, you assumed wrong," Giselle replied, casting her a look that said she knew her young charge's thoughts. "When you find the correct answer yourself, the victory will be that much sweeter."

"I haven't the time to waste today," Isabelle complained.

"And what is so pressing?"

Isabelle cast a longing look toward the window where the afternoon sun filtered into the room, its rays beckoning her to escape the drudgery of the ledgers. "I wanted to sit in the garden and play my flute," she answered. "Couldn't you help me this one time?"

"I've heard you say that before," Giselle answered. "My answer hasn't changed. Do it yourself. Suffering is good for the soul, you know."

"I deserve a little enjoyment too," Isabelle countered in an irritated voice.

"Child, patience is a virtue," Giselle replied, unruffled by the outburst.

"Faith, hope, charity, prudence, temperance, justice, and fortitude are the seven virtues," Isabelle informed her, cocking a blond brow at the old woman. "Patience is not numbered among them. How can it be that a guardian angel doesn't know the seven virtues?"

"So, buy me an indulgence," Giselle said with a shrug. "I can list the seven deadly sins. Want to hear them?"

"No, thank you."

"There you are!"

At the sound of that voice Isabelle snapped her head

around to see her stepmother marching across the study toward the desk. Years of practicing self-control kept Isabelle from grimacing at the unwelcome sight. Unconsciously, she touched the golden locket containing her real mother's miniature. The feel of it always calmed her nerves.

"I have had the most wonderful news," Delphinia Montgomery exclaimed, waving a letter in the air.

"Knowing her as I do, someone must have suffered a horrible death."

Isabelle giggled and glanced at Giselle. The old woman was probably correct about that, she thought.

"At what are you laughing?" Delphinia asked, wearing a confused expression. "Why are you looking at the hearth while I speak to you? You aren't going to start talking to yourself again, are you?"

Isabelle silently cursed herself. She'd nearly been caught again. Giselle was so real that she usually forgot others were unable to see or hear her, which did create problems.

"No, I . . . I was thinking about something else." Isabelle managed a smile when her stepmother's expression cleared. "And what wonderful news do you hold in the palm of your hand?"

"Dearest Nicholas will be stopping for a visit on his journey to London," Delphinia answered.

"Damn," Giselle swore.

"Make that a double," Isabelle muttered.

"A double what?" Delphinia asked. "Isabelle, are you ill today?"

"No, merely a little tired."

"Take my advice," Delphinia said. "Look toward Nicholas as a possible husband. My nephew is a prime catch, you know."

"I have no desire to marry anyone at the moment," Isabelle replied, successfully keeping the revulsion she felt off her face. Nicholas deJewell reminded her of a loathsome weasel. "I have household accounts waiting, if you'll excuse me."

Delphinia took the hint and crossed the chamber to the door, but paused before leaving. "Speaking of accounts, I have somehow managed to spend my monthly allowance," she said with an ingratiating smile. "Could I have—"

"No." Isabelle fixed a stern look on her face when she added, "If I gave you extra money today, you'd be looking for more tomorrow. Learning to budget your money would be wise."

"Now, listen to me, young lady—"

"I have no intention of listening to you," Isabelle interrupted. "If your monthly allowance isn't enough, ask my brother to increase it."

"I shall do just that," Delphinia announced and left the study in a huff, slamming the door behind her.

"Why do you always upset her?" Giselle asked.

"She upsets me."

"Would it bankrupt your brother if you slipped her a few extra coins now and then?"

"Delphinia's allowance is more than ample," Isabelle informed the old woman. "My stepmother's pockets have holes in them."

"Remember, child," Giselle said. "Blessed are the generous, for they will be shown generosity."

Isabelle rolled her eyes. "Are you now inventing scripture?"

"Whatever do you mean?"

"Scripture says, 'Blessed are the merciful, for they will be shown mercy.' "

"Oh, my mistake," Giselle said.

"What kind of angel cannot quote scripture correctly?" Isabelle asked.

Before the old woman could reply, the door swung open. Again Isabelle struggled against a grimace as she watched her stepsisters advancing on her. She hoped they hadn't come to beg for money too. When Giselle chuckled, Isabelle cast her a warning look.

"Don't take that attitude with me, child," the old woman scolded her. "You could have saved yourself this sisterly visit by giving Delphinia what she wanted."

I cannot like people who constantly say "I-told-you-so," Isabelle thought.

"*You* always say it," Giselle shot back.

"I do not," Isabelle said out loud.

"Isabelle is talking to herself again," nineteen-year-old Rue whispered to her sister.

"She's crazy," twenty-year-old Lobelia whispered back. "What man will want to marry the sisters of a woman who belongs in Bedlam?"

"At least we aren't blood relatives," Rue replied.

Isabelle stiffened in embarrassed anger, but refused to acknowledge their slurs. After the past ten years she should be accustomed to their insults, yet her stepsisters still held the power to hurt her feelings. Though she couldn't fault them for mistakenly believing her crazy. Having a guardian angel wasn't as wonderful as she had once thought.

"What do you want?" Isabelle asked, giving them her attention.

"Money," Rue blurted out, and then cried "Ouch!" when her sister pinched her.

"I have no money for you," Isabelle told them. "Enjoy the remainder of your day."

"Dearest sister," Lobelia spoke up. "We need new gowns for our spring season in London."

"You ought to dress properly too," Rue added. "You are horribly out of fashion."

Isabelle stared at their gowns. Her stepsisters wore ankle-length muslin dresses with squared necklines and long, full sleeves. Their bodices sported antique frills, and the hemlines had been adorned with bands of embroidery.

Dropping her gaze from their garments, Isabelle noted her own scooped-neck linen blouse and violet wool skirt. Her sisters dressed like fashionable ladies while she appeared like a peasant.

"You are correct," Isabelle said, shifting her gaze to them. "I am out of fashion. Now, if you will excuse me, I have ledgers—"

"You will soon be eighteen and have your come-out into society," Lobelia reminded her. There was a forced gaiety in her voice when she added, "The three of us need new wardrobes in order to secure offers of marriage."

"Won't that be exciting?" Rue cried, obviously attempting to elicit enthusiasm from her.

Isabelle stared first at Lobelia and then at Rue until both young women seemed to squirm beneath her displeased scrutiny. She didn't like to think uncharitable thoughts, but her stepsisters were two of the plainest women she'd ever seen. They would need more than the latest fashions in order to secure offers of marriage.

"Your unkind thoughts mirror mine," Giselle said from where she sat in front of the hearth.

"Go to London if it pleases you," Isabelle said, struggling against the urge to answer the old woman. "Resign yourselves to last year's fashions."

"Your high-handedness is unfair," Lobelia said, stamping her foot in displeasure. "The fortune belongs to your brother, not you."

Rue nodded her head in agreement with her sister.

"Then petition Miles for a new wardrobe," Isabelle replied. "I haven't the authority to purchase you new gowns and gewgaws."

"We'll do just that," Lobelia snapped. "I refuse to die an old maid on the shelf like you. . . . Come, sister."

"Too bad you suffer from freckles," Rue called over her shoulder as they left the room. "Men dislike freckles, you know."

The door clicked shut behind them.

Isabelle reached up and touched the bridge of her nose. She turned a troubled expression on her old friend. "Do these freckles make me ugly?" she asked.

"What freckles?"

Isabelle grinned at her answer.

"Like a fine sprinkling of fairy dust, your freckles make you even more irresistible than you already are," Giselle told her.

"You aren't just saying that?"

"Do angels lie?"

Isabelle shook her head. "You always make me feel better."

A knock on the door drew their attention.

"I wonder who that could be," Isabelle quipped. "My stepfamily never knocks."

Another knock sounded on the door.

"Enter," Isabelle called, and then smiled when Pebbles, the Montgomery majordomo, walked into the study.

"Good afternoon, my lady." Pebbles perched on the

front edge of the desk and winked at her, saying, "Three witches were trampled to death in an unfortunate carriage accident. When they arrived at heaven's gates Saint Peter told them there was no room in heaven and the witches would need to return to earth. They were to jump off a nearby cloud and shout whatever they wished to be called in this second lifetime. The first witch leapt off the cloud and called *Lobelia*."

Isabelle felt her lips twitch with the urge to laugh.

"The second witch jumped off the cloud and yelled *Rue*," the majordomo continued. "The third and oldest of the witches tripped and bellowed *Shit*."

Isabelle burst out laughing and was joined by Giselle.

"I knew I could bring a smile to your face," Pebbles said, passing her a missive. "A courier delivered this from London."

"Thank you." Isabelle watched the majordomo leave and then tore the missive open, saying, "It's from Miles, but I can't imagine why he would hire a private courier."

Isabelle scanned the letter and then frowned, saying, "God mend his ways."

"Bad news, child?"

"Miles has left England on a business trip to America, and—"

"He's gone to the colonies?" Giselle exclaimed.

"America is a colony no longer," Isabelle told her.

The door burst open. Delphinia, Lobelia, and Rue charged like marauding soldiers into the study.

"What's the news from London?" Delphinia asked, unable to contain her excitement.

Isabelle hesitated. She didn't want to tell them the truth, because they would immediately begin to harass her for money. But what else could she do? They'd find out soon enough.

"Miles has gone to America," Isabelle informed her stepmother.

"How can we have our London season without him?" Rue whined.

"Has he left you in charge of the money?" Delphinia asked.

Isabelle stared hard at her stepmother and wondered why she would ask a question when she already knew the answer.

"It would be decidedly unfeminine for you to conduct business, even in an emergency," Delphinia said, then continued without waiting for a reply. "In society's eyes you are still in the schoolroom. We'd be ruined." She turned away, adding, "I must ask Nicholas to take charge of the Montgomery finances."

So that was it, Isabelle decided. Her greedy stepmother wanted to control her brother's fortune. Well, that would never happen. She would never allow Delphinia's spendthrift nephew near the Montgomery fortune.

"That will be unnecessary," Isabelle said, stopping her stepmother in her tracks.

Delphinia turned around, a shocked expression on her face. "You cannot mean to—"

"Apparently, Miles has enlisted the Duke of Avon's assistance," Isabelle told her. "I am to call upon His Grace in the unlikely event of an emergency."

Lobelia and Rue shrieked with excitement and clapped their hands together. "The Duke of Avon is so sophisticated and handsome," Rue gushed.

"Have you met him?" Isabelle asked, cocking a blond brow at her stepsister.

"No, but rumor told me so."

"You mean gossip."

"Whatever."

"Oh, we must definitely have an emergency," Lobelia spoke up. "Then His Grace will visit us at Arden Hall and fall madly in love with me."

"What about me?" Rue asked.

"I am the eldest, so I get the duke," Lobelia informed her sister. "He does have two brothers though."

"Imagine that," Rue said, turning to Isabelle. "There is one Saint-Germain for each of us. We'll be sisters forever."

"That thought is oh-so-tempting," Isabelle said sourly, making Giselle chuckle. She turned to the old woman. "Do not laugh at—" Isabelle clamped her lips together and tried to pretend she hadn't spoken out loud.

"There she goes again," Lobelia sneered. "No Saint-Germain will wish to marry a woman who talks to herself."

"I was merely thinking out loud," Isabelle insisted. She looked at her stepmother and said, "I can manage the Montgomery affairs without need of the duke's assistance."

"Nevertheless, I shall write to His Grace and thank him for being of service to us if we need it," Delphinia announced.

"What a wonderful idea," Isabelle said. "Take Lobelia and Rue with you to help draft the letter."

When her stepfamily had gone, Isabelle sat back in her chair and sighed at her ill luck. Now her stepfamily would harass her for money, gowns, a season in London, and an emergency to bring the Duke of Avon to their door. The last thing she wanted was the Duke of Avon meddling in Montgomery affairs.

"Give them the money, gowns, and London season," Giselle advised. "They'll forget about the duke."

Isabelle cast the old woman an exasperated look.

"Or perhaps they won't forget," Giselle amended herself. "Consider this, child. Adversity is merely the opportunity to prove your worth."

Isabelle rose from her chair and crossed the chamber to sit on the floor in front of the hearth. She rested her head against the old woman's leg.

"I suspect Delphinia will try to force me into marriage with Nicholas," Isabelle said. "Where is that prince you promised would rescue me?"

"Nearer than you think," Giselle answered, stroking her hair lovingly. "Give him time."

"Time is a luxury I don't have now that Miles is across the Atlantic Ocean," Isabelle replied.

"Child, you must work harder to develop patience," the old woman said. "Fate can throw myriad roadblocks down in the blinking of an eye. Perhaps the duke will be your rescuer."

"The Duke of Avon is no prince."

"Angels don't always wear wings or a halo," Giselle said, casting her an ambiguous smile. "And princes don't always wear crowns."

Chapter 2

Princes don't always wear crowns, and witches don't always wear warts on their noses. . . . Some witches looked exactly like her stepmother.

That ridiculous thought echoed within Isabelle's mind as she walked the long length of the second-floor corridor. She'd been summoned to attend Delphinia and had no doubt the topic of their conversation would be money or, even worse, marriage to that odious nephew of hers. For years Delphinia had been angling for a union between their two families.

Reaching her stepmother's sitting room, Isabelle touched the locket containing her mother's miniature, knocked lightly on the door, and then stepped inside. She fixed her violet gaze on Delphinia, who sat in a chair in front of the hearth. Now Isabelle wished she hadn't ordered Giselle not to accompany her.

"Sit over here with me," Delphinia called. "I have tea and sweet biscuits for us."

Yes, some witches did look exactly like her stepmother, Isabelle thought, crossing the chamber. She sat in the chair beside her stepmother's and asked, "What is it you wish to discuss, Delphinia?"

"I will never understand why you've always refused to think of me as your mother," Delphinia said, pasting a hurt look on her face.

Isabelle wasn't fooled for a minute. "It's one of life's mysteries," she replied, staring her stepmother straight in the eye.

"I suppose." Delphinia gave her a faint smile. "Would you care for tea and a biscuit?"

"No, thank you. If this is about—"

"I haven't invited you here to ask for money," Delphinia interrupted, then slid her gaze toward the hearth. "I want to discuss your betrothal to Nicholas."

"I cannot love your nephew and will never marry him," Isabelle said bluntly. She'd refused this proposed match to Nicholas deJewell so many times that she was beginning to wonder if her stepmother knew the meaning of *no*.

Delphinia dismissed her words with a wave of her hand. "Anyone can tell you that marriage has nothing to do with love," she said. "You will grow to love dear Nicholas as I do."

No, I won't, Isabelle thought, but remained silent.

Delphinia stood then and began to pace back and forth as if trying to find the right words. When she spoke, her tone of voice was all business. "I have taken the liberty of having a betrothal contract drawn. When Nicholas arrives, you will sign it."

"No, I won't," Isabelle said firmly.

"I am your guardian now that Miles is abroad," Delphinia said, halting in front of Isabelle's chair. "Nicholas is a handsome and charming baron whom any woman would be proud to call her husband."

"Any woman but me," Isabelle qualified, arching a blond brow at her stepmother. "Nicholas deJewell resembles a weasel. Being in the same room with him sickens my stomach."

Without warning, Delphinia reached out and slapped her. The force of it snapped Isabelle's head to the right.

No one had ever struck her before.

Fighting the urge to strike back, Isabelle stood slowly. She raised her hand to her smarting cheek and narrowed her violet gaze on her stepmother.

"God mend your evil ways," she said in a scathing voice.

Before her stepmother could respond to that, Isabelle turned on her heels and marched across the chamber to the door, muttering loudly, "Only a fool bites the hand that feeds it. She'll never get another half-pence from me though she may beg on her knees for a month." At that she quit the sitting room and retreated down the corridor to her own chamber.

How dare her stepmother strike her! No matter the pressure placed upon her, Isabelle determined never to marry the weasel from Redesdale.

Reaching her own chamber, Isabelle bolted the door behind her. Now if Delphinia wanted to speak to her she would need to shout through the locked door.

"Look what they've done," Giselle cried.

Isabelle whirled around and stared in shock at the shambles in her bedchamber. Her clothing chests were open, and gowns with accessories had been strewn from one end of the chamber to the other. The room looked as if the north wind had swept through it.

"Who did this?" Isabelle asked.

"Lobelia and Rue took what they wanted for themselves and ruined the rest," Giselle told her, shaking her head in obvious disgust. "This never would have happened if you'd agreed to the new gowns they wanted."

Isabelle crossed the chamber and lifted a violet-blue gown off the floor. It was the one her brother had bought for her to wear on Christmas Day. The gown's seams were ripped beyond repairing.

With tears welling up in her eyes, Isabelle clutched the gown and sat on the edge of the bed. Christmas would come and go with no new gown and, more importantly, no Miles. Was she destined to be alone always? Why did the people she loved most—her mother, her father, her brother—die or desert her?

"I'm sorry, child," Giselle said, sitting beside her on the bed. The old woman stroked her blond hair soothingly and added, "I cannot interfere in the actions of others, only advise you."

"The loss of a few gowns matters little." Isabelle sighed in misery. "But why did Miles abandon me again?"

"Your brother will return to you soon enough," Giselle told her.

Isabelle stared through blurred vision at the old woman, who'd been her only friend since the day they'd met at the Avon River. "As my guardian, Delphinia is pressing for a marriage between Nicholas and me. I'm so very tired of being strong. The deed may be done before Miles returns. Oh, where is the dark prince you promised would rescue me?"

"Patience, child. The prince will arrive."

"Who is he?"

Giselle shrugged and stared at the flames in the hearth across the chamber.

"Don't you know?" Isabelle asked, frustrated by the day's disturbing events. "What kind of angel are you?"

Giselle snapped her head around to stare at her. "Only God knows everything, child. Say a good act of contrition, for you've just committed a deadly sin."

"Pride, greed, lust, sloth, anger, gluttony, and envy

are the seven deadly sins," Isabelle informed her guardian angel, the hint of a smile touching the corners of her lips. "Impertinence is not numbered among them."

Giselle winked at her. "So, buy me an indulgence."

Isabelle grinned. "Angel, you are incorrigible."

"I hid this when your stepsisters stormed in here," Giselle said, reaching for the flute beneath the bed. "Let's walk to the river and play."

"Later perhaps." Isabelle rose from her perch on the edge of the bed and lifted the flute from the old woman's hands. "I need to finish yesterday's ledgers. Care to join me in the study?"

Giselle nodded and followed her out of the bedchamber.

Reaching the first-floor foyer, Isabelle turned left to walk down the corridor to the study, but felt an insistent tugging on her sleeve. "What is it?" she asked, looking down at her friend's gnarled hand.

"Do the ledgers later," the old woman said.

"First we work and then we play," Isabelle said, shaking her head. "I need to finish those ledgers in order to keep the Duke of Avon at bay."

"I overheard Lobelia and Rue discussing the duke," Giselle remarked, casting her an ambiguous smile. "I'd like to catch a glimpse of him."

"I have no wish to meet the duke," Isabelle replied. "Go down to the river alone, and I'll finish my ledgers."

"I'll wait for you."

Inside the study Giselle took her usual seat in front of the hearth. Isabelle sat at the desk and opened the ledger book.

"Do you want to know what your stepsisters said about the duke?" Giselle called.

Isabelle looked up at her and shook her head. When she looked back at the ledger, she realized she would need to tally the column of numbers again.

"I heard the duke is incredibly handsome," Giselle called again. "He has midnight-black hair and black eyes."

"That's nice," Isabelle said absently, and then realized her addition was incorrect.

"Women trip over their feet to please him," Giselle called a third time.

Isabelle refused to look up at her, but lost her concentration anyway.

"It's a fact that the duke is England's most eligible widower and richer than the king," Giselle said.

Isabelle slammed the quill down on the desk and glared at her friend. "I cannot tally these numbers if you constantly interrupt."

"Child, you must develop patience," the old woman advised. "It's one of the—"

"Patience is not numbered among the seven virtues," Isabelle snapped.

"Don't get snippy with me," Giselle scolded her. "Patience happens to be a spiritual work of mercy."

Isabelle started to reply, but the door swung open. Pebbles, the Montgomery majordomo, stepped into the study and announced, "A messenger from Avon Park requests an interview with you."

Isabelle sighed in resignation. Apparently, the ledgers would remain unfinished that day.

"Tell him to come inside," she said.

"Come on, man," Pebbles shouted, cupping his mouth with his hands. "Be quick about it, as the lady has work to do."

Isabelle swallowed a giggle at her unorthodox majordomo. How she loved the old man, who always seemed to have her best interests at heart.

"How may I help you?" Isabelle asked when the man stood in front of her desk.

"My lady, the Duke of Avon orders you to appear with the Montgomery ledgers tomorrow afternoon at Avon Park," he said in a haughty voice.

Though irritated almost beyond endurance, Isabelle gave the man her sweetest smile and asked, "What is your name?"

Her question caught the man off guard. He gave her a surprised smile and said, "I beg your pardon?"

"What is your name?" she repeated.

"Gallagher."

"You are His Grace's personal courier?" she asked.

"I'm actually His Grace's coachman," Gallagher told her, "but one of his most trusted retainers."

"Ah, the proverbial jack-of-all-trades," Isabelle said with a smile. "Please inform His Grace that his meddling in Montgomery affairs is unnecessary. He should mind his own business. Good day to you, Mr. Gallagher."

"I can't relay that message," the man groaned.

"Oh, but you must," Isabelle told him. "Those are my words to His Grace."

"As you wish." Gallagher turned and marched back across the study toward the door.

Delphinia, apparently eavesdropping in the corridor, flew past the courier into the study. "How d-dare you!" she sputtered. "Are you mad?"

Unruffled by her stepmother's sudden appearance, Isabelle looked up and asked, "About what are you talking?"

"Your rudeness to the Duke of Avon," Delphinia screeched, her complexion mottling with her anger.

"Oh, that."

"Are you trying to ruin Lobelia's and Rue's chance to find husbands?" her stepmother demanded.

"Of course not."

"The Duke of Avon has entrance into the most exclusive residences in London society," Delphinia said. "His friendship could help us. You will immediately send him a note of apology."

Staring at her stepmother, Isabelle rose from her chair and announced, "I refuse to allow the Duke of Avon to meddle in Montgomery affairs."

"I demand you write him an apology," Delphinia repeated, raising her voice in angry frustration.

Isabelle decided to shock the tirade out of her stepmother. She lifted her flute off the desk and turned toward Giselle, saying, "I'll accomplish no work today. Shall we walk to the river and play until we've calmed?"

"I thought you'd never ask."

Isabelle glanced at her stepmother's horrified expression and then brushed past her toward the door. The last thing she heard was Delphinia calling, "Lobelia and Rue are correct. You *are* crazy."

"What did you say?"

Anger brought John Saint-Germain out of the chair he'd been occupying in his drawing room at Avon Park. Almost nose to nose with his man, John appeared more demon than human. His midnight-black eyes darkened, and a fierce scowl marred his handsome features.

"I-I-I'm only the messenger, Your Grace," Gallagher

sputtered, leaping back a defensive pace. "Mistress Montgomery said—"

"I heard you the first time," John snapped at his man.

Gallagher clamped his lips shut.

"There's no need to intimidate the man for doing his job," a woman said.

"You are dismissed," John said, composing himself.

After watching his man make a hasty retreat, John turned around and looked at the others in the drawing room. His mother was shaking her head, Aunt Hester stared at him in obvious disapproval, and Ross wore the most infuriating smile.

"I refuse to allow that slip of a girl to order me to mind my own business," John said.

Ross's smile became a grin. "How can that be prevented when she's already done it?"

John cast his brother an unamused look. Then he glanced at his mother and his aunt, who instantly wiped the smiles off their faces.

The dowager duchess spoke up. "It reminds me of the time John's father and I—"

"I remember that, Tessa," Aunt Hester interrupted.

The two older women exchanged smiling glances at their shared memory.

John softened his expression on his mother. "And what happened?"

"I do believe that was the night I conceived you," the duchess replied.

"And what happened the night you conceived me?" Ross asked.

The duchess smiled at the distant memory but refused to reply.

John rolled his eyes at their silliness and turned to his

brother, saying, "I am the chit's guardian and responsible for the Montgomery finances."

"Try sending her an invitation instead of an order," Ross suggested.

"I would like to meet this young lady," the duchess said.

"So would I," Aunt Hester agreed.

"She's a blonde," John told them, a bitter edge to his voice. "Need I say more?"

"Not all blondes are Lenore Grimsby," his mother said.

"That remains to be seen," John replied. "The Montgomery girl won't sidestep my guardianship so easily."

"I thought you didn't want the responsibility," Ross drawled.

"I've given my word of honor and intend to see this out to its conclusion," John replied. He marched across the drawing room toward the door, saying, "I'm riding to Arden Hall."

"Care for some company?" Ross asked.

"No, thank you," John called over his shoulder. Within minutes John sat atop his horse, Nemesis, and rode out of the Saint-Germain stable yard.

Early winter wore a serene expression that day. The afternoon sunlight filtered through high, thin clouds, and motes of sun danced across November's golden leaves lying dead on December's winter-brown ground. All around John bare branches of trees etched stark silhouettes against the sky.

With the exception of his annual autumnal retreat in Scotland, John loved this time in the year's cycle best of all. He could return to Avon Park and surround himself with his family instead of the shallow London elite.

He'd always assumed he'd be well married and a father by the age of thirty, but Lenore Grimsby had put an end to that dream.

John followed the Avon River for two miles and then guided Nemesis into the woodland. He halted his horse when an unusual sound reached his ears. Cocking his head to one side, John listened and smiled when he recognized what it was.

Someone—no, two people were playing flutes. The hauntingly lovely melody sounded eerie in the lonely woodland. The lilting notes held a melancholy mood, yet the warm and sensitive tones touched his heart.

John nudged Nemesis forward once again. Remaining in the woodland for this unexpected musicale was not on his agenda for that afternoon. He had a score to settle with the impertinent Montgomery chit and refused to be deterred from his purpose.

When he broke free of the woodland, Arden Hall came into his long view. Built during Elizabethan times, the manor was a product of local materials—timber from the Forest of Arden and blue-gray stone from Wilmcote. The mansion's stately drive had been fashioned of plum-red bricks and gray stone dressings. On one side of Arden Hall was a chapel and a graveyard; on the other side was located its spacious garden, which contained only trees and shrubs at this time of year.

"How may I help you, my lord?" the Montgomery majordomo asked, escorting him into the foyer.

"You may begin by calling me *Your Grace,*" John said in a haughty voice, sliding his gaze toward the man. "I am the Duke of Avon."

"Forgive me, Your Grace," the majordomo apologized, but his expression was decidedly unrepentant.

"Welcome to Arden Hall, Your Grace," said a woman's voice.

"Welcome, Your Grace," two other females said in unison.

John turned in the direction of the female chorus. Three of the plainest-looking women he'd ever seen dropped him curtsies. Apparently, the two younger women had inherited their mother's dismal features. Why, even their gowns fit improperly, as if made for a smaller woman.

The older woman stepped forward to greet him, saying, "Your Grace, we are honored by your presence at Arden Hall."

"Thank you, my lady," John replied.

"Please call me Delphinia," the woman said. "I am the late earl's wife." She gestured to the younger women and added, "These are my daughters, Lobelia and Rue."

Both daughters dropped him a second curtsy. Acknowledging their respectful deference, he inclined his head slightly.

"Your Grace, come into the drawing room and take some refreshment," Delphinia invited him, a gracious smile on her face.

"No, thank you," John said in refusal. "I have business with Isabelle Montgomery. Would you kindly send for her?"

Lobelia and Rue giggled, drawing his attention.

"Isabelle isn't here at the moment," Delphinia explained. "May I—"

"Isabelle is roaming the woods with her invisible friend," Lobelia interrupted, her tone of voice snide.

Rue nodded in agreement. "Isabelle is quite mad, Your Grace."

"That is unkind of you to say," Delphinia scolded her daughters. "Isabelle has been upset about her father's passing."

"The man's been dead almost eight years," Lobelia sneered.

John looked from the daughters to the mother. Apparently, Miles Montgomery had been correct. His stepfamily harbored no fondness for his sister. Suddenly, relief surged through John, and he felt glad that he'd agreed to take charge of the Montgomery affairs.

Delphinia cast him an ingratiating smile and said, "Perhaps I can be of assistance, Your Grace."

"Miles has named me his sister's temporary guardian and given me the management of his businesses and estates," John informed her.

The woman lost her smile. In fact, she seemed damned disappointed.

"I have the necessary documents to verify my words," John continued, reaching into his waistcoat.

Delphinia seemed to recover herself and managed a smile. "That shan't be necessary, Your Grace."

"Good." John gave the woman a polite smile. "I'd like to begin my audit of the Montgomery ledgers and speak with the girl as soon as she returns."

"Pebbles, show His Grace to the earl's study," Delphinia ordered the majordomo.

"Yes, my lady." Pebbles turned to him. "This way, Your Grace."

John followed the majordomo down a long corridor and then into the study. While John made himself comfortable at the earl's desk, the majordomo stoked the fire in the hearth and then opened the draperies behind the desk to allow more sunlight into the chamber.

"Will there be anything else, Your Grace?" the majordomo asked.

"No." John watched the man retreating across the chamber and then called, "Pebbles?"

The majordomo paused and turned. "Yes, Your Grace?"

"Is Isabelle Montgomery mad?"

"The lady is as sane as you or I."

"But she does possess an invisible friend?" John asked.

A wholly disgusted look appeared on the majordomo's face, but was quickly banished. "Your Grace, if you'd grown from childhood to adulthood without a real friend, you'd invent someone too," Pebbles told him.

The hint of a smile touched the corners of John's lips. "I commend your loyalty," he said.

"Thank you, Your Grace," Pebbles drawled. "It's good of you to notice my finer points of character." At that the majordomo left the study and shut the door behind himself.

Blonde or not, Isabelle Montgomery must surely possess a special, redeeming trait in order to inspire loyalty in a servant, thought John. On the other hand, the chit had been particularly impertinent and disrespectful to him. He'd need to make his own judgment as soon as she appeared.

John began his task of auditing the household ledgers. He'd already made arrangements for anything new of a business nature to be sent directly to him.

An hour passed. John began to wonder what was delaying the girl. He hoped nothing had happened on her walk. Should he go in search of her or not?

Afternoon's shadows were already lengthening in the chamber. Where could she have gone? If she didn't return within the next fifteen minutes, he would go looking for her.

Rising from the chair, John wandered to the window and gazed absently at the well-manicured grounds. A movement in the distance caught his attention; as he stared, he realized the figure was a girl crossing the winter-brown lawns toward Arden Hall.

At long last, John thought, this must be the Montgomery girl.

John's hopes for getting this interview completed quickly faded as the girl walked nearer to the manor. She was merely a servant, as evidenced by her coarse gray cloak, and probably destined for Bedlam.

John smiled when he realized the chit was deep in conversation with herself, hand gestures and all. Then he noticed the flute she held and knew that she'd been the one playing in the woods. Finally, the girl disappeared from view.

What a bizarre household, John thought. And what the bloody hell was delaying the Montgomery girl?

Like a cannon exploding, the study door burst open with a loud bang. John whirled around and watched in amazement as the servant girl in the coarse gray cloak marched across the study toward him.

Reaching the desk, the girl pushed the hood off her head to reveal hair the color of spun gold. Then she set her flute down and glared mutinously at him.

"I don't give a rat's arse what Miles wants," she announced. "I forbid you to meddle in Montgomery affairs."

Chapter 3

"Isabelle Montgomery, I presume?"

"No, the Queen of Sheba," Isabelle answered in the most sarcastic tone of voice she could summon. She arched a perfectly shaped blond brow at him and drawled, "The Duke of Avon, I presume?"

"No, the fifteenth Duke of Doom," John told her. "I am also the tenth Marquess of Mean and the twelfth Earl of—" He hesitated as if searching for the correct word.

"The Earl of Egads?" Isabelle supplied, her lips twitching with the urge to laugh in spite of her reluctance to like the man.

"Precisely." The Duke of Avon gave her a wickedly handsome, thoroughly devastating smile. "I see that my reputation precedes me."

"Indeed it does, Your Grace." Isabelle succumbed to the smile she'd been struggling against.

Sweet celestial breath, Isabelle thought, wiping the smile off her face. She'd wanted to insult the man into leaving Arden Hall. She would never have guessed that the duke possessed such an easygoing nature that he'd joke with her in the face of her impertinent provocation.

"What a sly charmer he is."

Isabelle turned her head and looked in the direction of the hearth where her old friend sat. *Does he seem familiar to you?*

Giselle smiled ambiguously and shrugged.

"He seems familiar to me," Isabelle muttered in a voice barely loud enough to hear.

"To whom are you speaking?"

Isabelle whirled back toward the duke and shook her head. "I have a habit of thinking out loud," she tried to explain her odd behavior.

"Who looks familiar?" John asked.

"You do," Isabelle answered. "I feel I've seen you somewhere before."

"If we'd met before," John said, walking around the desk toward her, "I'm certain I would have remembered you." He stopped in front of her, and Isabelle had to tilt her head back in order to meet his gaze. "I watched you walking across the lawns," he added. "You were—"

"Thinking out loud, Your Grace," Isabelle finished for him.

Ever so slowly, the Duke of Avon slid his midnight-black gaze down the length of her body. "Why are you dressed like a servant?" he asked when his gaze returned to hers.

"Have you ridden to Arden Hall to criticize me?" Isabelle challenged him, her gaze fixed on his, every nerve in her body trembling. "If so, you'll need to get in line behind my stepfamily."

The Duke of Avon leaned back against the edge of the desk and folded his arms across his chest. "Do you have an invisible friend?" he asked bluntly.

"Ah, you've had the pleasure of meeting Lobelia and Rue."

That devastating smile of his appeared, confounding her. "If those two were my stepsisters, I'd invent an invisible friend too."

"With all due respect, Your Grace, do not patronize

me." Isabelle unfastened her cloak and tossed it on top of the desk. Then she walked around the desk and sat in her brother's chair in an unspoken challenge that she, not he, was in charge of Montgomery affairs.

The duke turned around to face her, his expression telling her that he knew her ploy. "Call me John," he said in a husky voice.

Isabelle stared down at the top of the desk and refused to spare him even one small glance. "Your Grace, I don't know you well enough to use your given name," she said in refusal.

"You don't like me, do you?" the duke asked baldly.

Isabelle felt the heated blush rising upon her cheeks. Of all the things he could have said, that remark was not the one she'd expected.

"You are a stranger to me, Your Grace," Isabelle replied, refusing to let him embarrass her into meddling in Montgomery affairs. "Like or dislike has no significance to this business between us."

"The handsome devil certainly has you flustered."

Isabelle glared at her old friend.

"What is so interesting about that hearth?"

Isabelle snapped her head around to look at the duke. She blushed and then inwardly cursed herself for letting the man fluster her. She took a calming breath and asked, "What is it you wish to discuss, Your Grace?"

The duke gestured to the chairs in front of the hearth and asked, "Shall we sit down and discuss this gently?"

"I'm already sitting, Your Grace," Isabelle replied, a mulish expression upon her face.

Walking around the desk to stand beside her, he offered her his hand, saying, "Please, Mistress Montgomery, humor an illustrious peer of the realm."

Isabelle looked from his offered hand to his eyes,

blacker than a moonless midnight, and became caught in their fathomless depths. Acting on instinct, she placed her hand in his and rose from her chair. His touch was firm yet gentle as he guided her across the study toward the hearth.

Isabelle sat down in one of the vacant chairs. "Oh, don't sit there," she cried when he moved to sit in the other chair.

John stopped short and stared at her in obvious surprise.

How was she to explain this? The duke couldn't know that he'd been about to sit on her guardian angel.

"I'll move," Giselle said.

Covering her blunder, Isabelle reached out and brushed nonexistent lint from the chair's cushion. "You may sit down now," she said, managing a smile.

Isabelle breathed a sigh of relief when his expression cleared, and he sat down beside her. She nervously fingered her golden locket and hoped her mother's spirit would give her the strength to see her through this difficult interview.

"That's an interesting locket," John remarked, noting her movement. "Is it an heirloom?"

"I carry my mother's miniature inside it," Isabelle told him, dropping her hands to her lap. She certainly didn't want him to realize how nervous she felt.

"Oh, may I see it?" he asked, obviously trying to be pleasant.

"My mother's image is meant only for me," Isabelle said, reaching up to cover the locket with one hand. "Get on with your business."

"Bloody hell, have you no social graces?" the duke asked. "However will I—"

"Your Grace, I really must protest your vocabulary," Isabelle interrupted. "And spoken in anger too."

"A man would need the patience of a saint in order to hold his temper when dealing with you," John shot back.

Feeling unaccountably guilty about her rudeness, Isabelle cast him an unconsciously flirtatious smile and said, "Ah, yes, I hear the clinking of the black stone falling onto your spiritual scale."

"To what do you refer?" he asked.

"The angels drop white or black stones onto a person's opposing scales of spirit in order to keep track of the soul's virtue or sin," Isabelle explained. "You, Your Grace, just earned yourself a black stone, while I earned myself a white stone for warning a sinner."

The duke smiled. "So, will I earn myself a white stone if I wander the streets of London and warn sinners of their folly?"

"Warning the sinner is a spiritual work of mercy," Isabelle told him. "There are thirteen other works of mercy you may perform in order to earn yourself white stones."

"And what would they be?" John asked, stretching his long legs out in front of him.

"Warning the sinner, instructing the ignorant, counseling the doubtful, comforting the sorrowing, bearing wrongs patiently, forgiving all injuries, and praying for the living and the dead," Isabelle informed him. "The corporal works of mercy are feeding the hungry, giving drink to the thirsty, clothing the naked, sheltering the homeless, visiting the imprisoned, and burying the dead."

"How about bedding the frustrated?" he quipped.

"God mend your words," Isabelle gasped, shocked

by his vulgarity. Hearing the old woman's chuckle, she said without thinking, "Lust isn't funny."

"Now the man thinks you're crazy."

How would she explain herself? Isabelle wondered, beginning to panic. Thinking out loud wouldn't do this time.

"I'm sorry," John apologized to her. "You are correct; lust isn't funny. . . . Don't you know enough to look at a man when he is apologizing to you?"

Isabelle looked at him. Thank a merciful God, the man believed she'd turned away because of his vulgarity.

"Will you forgive me?" he asked, the huskiness in his voice returning.

Isabelle nodded. He seemed so contrite and sincere. At that moment she would have agreed to almost anything to keep him from believing that she was crazy.

"I suppose I now have two black stones on that scale?" the duke remarked.

"I'll pray for your soul, Your Grace," Isabelle said with a smile.

"I appreciate your consideration," John said, returning her smile. "Now, shall we get down to business?"

"We have no business, Your Grace."

"Oh, but we do," he disagreed, his voice and his expression pleasant. "Your brother specifically asked me to become your temporary guardian and keep an eye on the Montgomery ledgers, which are fine at the moment. As your guardian I will sponsor your come-out in the spring if Miles hasn't returned by then."

Nervous and angry, Isabelle fingered her golden locket and tried to muster the courage to defy the duke. Inwardly, she rebelled against his announcement, but what could she do about it? She knew for a fact that her stepmother would side with the duke.

Insidious insecurity coiled itself around Isabelle's heart, and she knew, as surely as she was breathing, that she could not make a come-out in the spring. She had no idea how to go about in society. Besides, the world was filled with people like Lobelia and Rue; society would never accept her. She would rather die an old maid on the shelf than put herself through that humiliation.

"Did you hear me?" the duke was asking.

Isabelle focused on him. "I beg your pardon?"

"This document names me your temporary guardian," the duke said, holding up a paper for her perusal. "Believe me, I like the idea less than you; however, I've given your brother my word of honor and intend to keep it."

Isabelle's expression became mulish again. "I am content to live as I have been and refuse to take orders from you."

"Your brother worried about leaving you in your stepmother's care," John argued.

"If he worried that much," Isabelle countered, unable to keep the bitterness out of her voice, "why did Miles abandon me?"

"Abandon?" John echoed, surprised by her choice of words. "Our brothers have taken a business trip and will return as soon as possible."

Isabelle opened her mouth to argue the point, but the door swung open, drawing her attention. Pebbles walked into the study and announced, "Supper is served, Your Grace. My lady insists you join her and her daughters."

John nodded at the man and then glanced at Isabelle. He rose from his chair, saying, "We can finish this conversation later.'' At that he offered his hand to her, and without thinking, Isabelle accepted it.

When they entered the dining hall, Delphinia was already seated at one end of the table, leaving the head of the table for the duke to occupy. On Delphinia's right sat Lobelia and Rue while Isabelle took her place on the duke's right.

Supper consisted of pea soup with bacon and herbs, cornish hens, and potato pudding. Wine, cider, and biscuits with quince jelly completed the fare.

Isabelle hoped her stepsisters wouldn't start insulting her. She didn't give a fig what the duke thought. It was only that—she flicked a surreptitious glance in his direction—he was the handsomest man she'd ever seen.

''Please tell us the gossip circulating in London this year,'' Delphinia was saying.

''I never engage in gossip,'' John said with a polite smile. ''I'm usually the center of such falsehoods. Did I mention that I'll be sponsoring the young ladies' season this spring?''

Lobelia and Rue squealed with delight. Isabelle was somewhat less delighted and rolled her eyes at their behavior.

''My daughters have been looking forward to the season,'' Delphinia said. ''It's time my darlings were married.''

''I know several suitable gentlemen and would be willing to introduce them,'' John replied. ''Let me see. There are Stephen Spewing, the Baron of Barrows; Charles Hancock, the Baron of Keswick; Lord Finch; Lord Somers; and Major Grimase. I do believe the major is a bit too old for them, but very rich.''

''I have nothing to wear,'' Lobelia complained, casting Isabelle a contemptuous look.

"Neither do I," Rue whined.

"Funds for a new wardrobe will be necessary," John told them.

Isabelle thought she might lose her supper when Lobelia and Rue squealed with delight again. She sneaked a glance at the duke and caught him smiling at her. Could he read the mutiny in her expression? Uncomfortably, she dropped her gaze to her plate.

"Isabelle will need more than a new wardrobe to catch herself a husband," Lobelia said snidely.

"No man will want to offer for a woman who talks to herself," Rue added.

"Your stepsister merely thinks out loud," John defended her.

Isabelle felt the embarrassed blush rising upon her cheeks. She absolutely refused to remain here and listen to their insults. Not only that, but the duke's defense offended rather than heartened her. The Duke of Avon was apparently the type of man who wanted others to owe him favors, which was why he was taking her side against her stepsisters.

Isabelle cleared her throat and sent Pebbles a meaningful look. In answer, the majordomo nodded almost imperceptibly. She flicked a quick peek at the duke, who watched her.

"More cider, my lady?" Pebbles inquired, standing beside her chair.

"Yes, please."

Pebbles moved to pour the cider, but spilled half of it on her lap. "My lady, I'm so sorry. How unforgivably clumsy of me."

"No harm done," Isabelle assured the majordomo, rising from her chair. "I'll just change my skirt." Before turning away, Isabelle sent the duke an apologetic look and nearly swooned when she saw his smile, as if he knew her ploy to escape the table.

Whirling away, Isabelle made a hasty retreat out of the dining room. Instead of going upstairs to change, she hurried to the study and retrieved her cloak and her flute. Then she retraced her steps down the corridor. Isabelle paused near the open dining room door and then tiptoed past it.

Stepping outside, Isabelle breathed deeply of the crisp air. The winter's night had been created for romance, with a full moon surrounded by thousands of glittering stars hanging in the black velvet sky. Woodsmoke from Arden Hall scented the air, and the atmosphere was hushed.

As she walked into the garden, Isabelle spied a solitary figure sitting on a stone bench. She smiled, recognizing her old friend, and then advanced on her.

"Are you here too?" Isabelle said by way of a greeting.

"No, I'm a figment of your imagination," Giselle replied.

"Very funny."

"Shall we play?"

Isabelle nodded and sat on the bench beside her. She lifted her flute to her lips and poured all of her feelings into the instrument.

They played a song of infinite beauty, the notes first eerie and lilting, then haunting and reflective. The melody was a soothing bath of sound, reminiscent of a moonlit stroll, rustling leaves, echoing owls calling to each other in the night.

"I'll see you inside." Giselle vanished in an instant.

"Mistress Montgomery?" the Duke of Avon called. "Is that you?"

"Yes, Your Grace." Was she forbidden a few moments of privacy? Isabelle thought mutinously. When the duke stood in front of her, Isabelle tilted her head back to gaze up the long length of him.

"You play divinely," John said. "It sounded as if two people were playing."

Had he heard Giselle's flute? How could that be? No one but her had ever heard the old woman.

"How did you make it sound like a duo?" he was asking.

"Garden acoustics," Isabelle lied.

John nodded, accepting her explanation, and then asked, "May I join you on the bench?"

"Suit yourself, Your Grace," Isabelle answered, sliding over to make room for him.

He sat down beside her, so close his thigh teased the side of her cloak. Glancing down at the close proximity of their bodies, Isabelle felt her cheeks heat with embarrassment and sent up a silent prayer of thanks that the night hid her discomfort.

"I thought I saw someone sitting with you," John remarked, slanting a sidelong glance at her.

Isabelle snapped her head around to stare at him in surprise. Had he seen Giselle? Only she had ever seen the old woman. What did this mean?

"I assure you that I am alone," she told him. "Who would be sitting with me?"

"A friend perhaps?"

"I have no friends."

"Not even an invisible friend?"

"If you saw her, then she wouldn't be invisible, Your Grace," Isabelle countered.

"It's a woman, then?"

"Really, Your Grace, this conversation is ridiculous,'' Isabelle scoffed, trying to steer him away from the subject.

''You are correct,'' he replied, and then stared straight ahead.

A heavy silence descended upon them. Isabelle decided the silence between them was even more uncomfortable than his probing questions.

''You need not have defended me against Lobelia and Rue,'' she told him. ''My stepsisters are henwits.''

''Even henwits can create problems in society,'' John warned, turning his head to look at her, which made her even more uncomfortable than enduring the silence. ''Henwits are the worst purveyors of gossip.''

''You could be correct about that,'' Isabelle replied, tearing her gaze away from his. Lord, but those midnight-black eyes seemed to see to the very depths of her insecure soul.

''I mean no insult,'' John continued, drawing her attention, ''but when you come to London, you must refrain from thinking out loud, or you will never catch a husband.''

''If I want to catch something, I'll go fishing,'' Isabelle shot back, irritated. ''I have no need of a husband.''

''Every woman needs a man to care for her,'' John replied in a quiet voice. ''Any woman who believes otherwise possesses the intelligence of an oyster.''

''I didn't mean that I would never marry,'' Isabelle told him. ''When Miles returns, I will have my come-out and choose a husband.''

''You will have your come-out this spring with or without your brother's presence,'' John corrected her. ''My mother never raised a daughter and is looking forward to introducing you into society. Of course, before that happens you'll need to learn certain rules of propriety."

"I don't give a rat's arse about propriety," Isabelle insisted, aggravated by his haughty attitude.

"Ah, Mistress Montgomery," John drawled, wearing an infuriating smile, "I can hear the ominous clinking of that black stone dropping onto your spiritual scale. On the other hand, I am earning myself a white stone."

"You, earn a white stone?" Isabelle echoed, her voice oozing sarcasm. "Whatever for?"

"Counseling the doubtful," John told her, "and instructing the ignorant."

"Instructing the ignorant?" Isabelle gasped. "Why, Your Grace, I am surprised you even have a mother. Your manners speak of a vile thing that crawled from beneath a rock."

"Be careful, Mistress Montgomery," he warned.

"Or what will you do?" she challenged him. "Refuse to sponsor my come-out?"

John grinned at her. "You'd like that, wouldn't you?"

Isabelle lifted her nose into the air and turned away. She shivered with the evening chill and then regretted it when she heard the duke asking, "Are you cold?" She shook her head and refused to look at him.

John removed his own cloak and wrapped it around her, his fingers lingering longer than necessary on her shoulders. Lord, but this man confounded her. Not that she had any experience with men. She'd never even been alone with one before today.

"Thank you, Your Grace," Isabelle mumbled in embarrassment. She knew she was blushing, but felt certain that he couldn't see her pink cheeks in the darkness.

"Why are you blushing?" he asked.

Isabelle groaned inwardly and grasped at the weather for a suitable topic of conversation. "The night is chilly. Are you certain you won't be cold?"

John shook his head and said, "The night still possesses a tinge of summer."

"Summer?" Isabelle echoed, incredulous, turning her head to stare at him. Oh, Lord, he was smiling at her, his handsome face so close to hers she could have puckered her lips and kissed him.

"By now the snow is probably thigh deep at my estate in the mountains of Scotland," he told her.

Isabelle shivered at the frosty thought and then searched her mind for another topic of conversation. After all, how long could two people discuss the weather conditions?

"Today is the feast of Saint Thomas," she said abruptly.

"Saint Thomas?" John smiled in apparent amusement. "Are you religious, Mistress Montgomery?"

Isabelle nodded. "Though I attend Sunday services only when my family doesn't, I hope to earn myself a place in heaven in order to meet my long-dead mother. I believe the Lord cares more about how we live each day than how many services we attend."

"I have a spot reserved for me someplace else," John quipped.

Isabelle smiled at that. Why, conversing with a man was not as difficult as she had thought.

"Today is the twenty-first of December," John said. "Only a few more days until the Scottish holiday of Hogmanay."

"What's that?"

"New Year's."

"You seem partial to Scotland," Isabelle remarked.

"My oldest title is Scottish," John told her.

"And that is?"

John winked at her. "The Earl of Egads, of course."

Isabelle burst out laughing, a sweet sound as melodious as the music she created with her flute.

"Look up at the sky," he said.

She cast her gaze to the heavens, brilliantly lit by the moon and the stars.

"Those stars return to their same position in the sky every New Year's Eve," John told her. "They've always reminded me of horses returning to their stables after a long, grueling journey."

"I never gave the stars very much thought before, merely admired them from afar," Isabelle admitted. "They do appear to be silent sentinels guarding us."

"Look straight to the south," John ordered, pointing in that direction. "The reddish light is Betelgeuse, which means 'armpit of the sheep.' And dominating the sky over there is Sirius, the brightest star in the heavens."

"I do love the night," Isabelle said. "Sometimes I sit alone outside and play my flute."

"Look at the sky over your shoulder."

Isabelle turned in his direction and gazed at the sky behind them.

"It's Polaris, the ever-constant North Star," John told her, his voice a husky whisper close to her ear.

Isabelle looked at him. His face was very, very close, and his lips hovered above hers. She knew he was going to kiss her, and she knew she was going to let him.

Isabelle closed her eyes as their mouths touched. His lips were warm, gentle, and oh-so-persuasive as he caressed the crease of her mouth with his tongue. His scent of mountain heather intoxicated her senses.

"You smell like violets," John whispered against her lips, breaking the spell he'd cast upon her. "I do believe I've just given a pretty English violet her very first kiss."

His words surprised Isabelle. Supposedly, the dark prince in Giselle's prophecy would believe her lovelier than a violet in the snow. John Saint-Germain was no prince but an infamous rake, and she should never have let him kiss her.

"I shouldn't have done that," John apologized. "When you go about in London, do not be so free with your kisses, or you'll be ruined."

"Free with my kisses?" Isabelle exclaimed, bolting off the bench and rounding on him. "I am no London jade, Your Grace. In the future, refrain from taking advantage of innocents like me." Whirling away, Isabelle said over her shoulder, "Good night, Your Grace." She marched back toward the mansion.

The duke caught up with her at the door. "Mistress Montgomery, I do apologize for casting aspersions on your character. Will you forgive me?"

"Apology accepted," Isabelle said without looking at him as they entered the foyer. "You are not that important."

When she reached the base of the stairs, the duke grasped her forearm and gently forced her to stop and turn around. Isabelle arched a blond brow at him.

In answer John gifted her with a devastating smile and said, "Meeting you was well worth the ride from Avon Park."

Isabelle blushed at his compliment. No man had ever spoken so intimately to her. Most people believed her crazy. How long would it be before the duke caught her talking to herself again?

"Good night, Mistress Montgomery," John said. "May all of your dreams be pleasant."

Isabelle hurried up the stairs and went directly to her own chamber. Leaning against the door, she closed her eyes and tried to calm her rioting nerves.

"Did he kiss you?"

Isabelle opened her eyes and saw Giselle sitting in the chair in front of the hearth. "Lust is one of the seven deadly sins," she told the old woman.

"That is one of the reasons purchasing indulgences has always been so popular," Giselle countered. "Humans sin and purchase forgiveness, which gives Holy Church a fat revenue. Everybody wins, nobody loses."

"You certainly have a lopsided view of sin and forgiveness," Isabelle said, sitting on the floor in front of the old woman. "The duke heard you playing your flute with me."

"Did he now?" Giselle replied. "It would seem John Saint-Germain possesses a special gift."

"Is he the one sent to rescue me?"

"Only time will tell us that, child."

"John Saint-Germain is no prince."

"I told you before that princes don't always wear crowns," Giselle said. "To find the prince, simply follow your heart."

Isabelle rested her head against the old crone's knee and looked up into her angelic blue gaze. "If I follow my heart," she asked, "how do I know where it will lead me?"

"Knowing that is unnecessary, child," Giselle said with a soft smile. "Follow your heart to find true and lasting happiness."

Chapter 4

Isabelle Montgomery smells like violets.

During those hushed moments before dawn John stood at the window in his second-story bedchamber at Avon Park and stared outside at his ancestral domain. The hour was early, much too early even for the servants to rise. Through the stark branches of the winter-barren oaks that separated parkland from woodland, he gazed at the sky's eastern horizon rapidly changing from indigo to muted lavender to fingers of orange light that seemed to reach for the world.

John saw only Isabelle though. Her thick mane of blond hair reminded him of spun gold; in her soft violet eyes he spied a tranquil twilight; the fine freckles across the bridge of her perfect nose were a sprinkling of fairy dust; her flute playing trilled sweetly like nightingales in song. The incredibly enticing feeling of her soft lips pressed against his . . .

"God's knob," John muttered, turning away from the window. He was behaving like a moonstruck schoolboy. He'd assumed that Lenore Grimsby had cured him of all tender emotions. Apparently, no antidote existed for masculine foolishness. What he needed was a long ride in the crisp air of a December morn to clear the cobwebs from his mind.

John dressed and left his chamber. He marched to the

stables, saddled Nemesis, and galloped away from Avon Park as if Satan himself was after him.

For two hours John rode Nemesis hard, but then found himself beside the Avon River. He stared in the direction of Stratford and Arden Hall while the image of his ward danced provocatively across his mind's eye.

"Bull's pizzle," John cursed when he realized what he was doing. Yanking the reins, he turned his horse around and rode toward the safety of Avon Park.

Entering his enormous dining room, John stopped short and stared in surprise at the three people already seated at one end of the mahogany table that dominated the entire chamber. Aunt Hester, Ross, and his mother were eating breakfast, though the hour was unusually early for them. Pausing in their conversation, they gave him their attention.

John realized his family was awaiting a recounting of what had transpired at Arden Hall. After giving them a long look, he sauntered to the sideboard and poured himself a cup of coffee. He stood there a moment and sipped it.

Ignoring their interested gazes, John walked the length of the forty-foot dining table. He took his seat at the head of the table and relaxed in an ornately carved mahogany chair.

Through sheer force of will, John suppressed the urge to smile and nodded at Dobbs to prepare a plate for him. Only then did he gaze down the long length of the table at his mother, his aunt, and his brother.

"Really, Tessa," Aunt Hester spoke first. "I thought you raised your sons to have better manners than this."

"So did I." His mother looked at him and asked, "Well? What do you have to say?"

John waited until Dobbs set a plate of eggs and ham

down in front of him and then remarked, "I do believe the rising sun streaming through that window plays prettily on the chandeliers."

Both Aunt Hester and his mother looked up at the three crystal chandeliers hanging over the dining table and then dropped murderous gazes on him. Ross chuckled at them.

"Do not encourage his perversity," the dowager duchess ordered his brother.

"Perversity?" John drawled, cocking a dark brow at her.

"Sit here beside me," his mother insisted. "If you force me to shout, my throat will be scratchy by noon."

John surrendered to the inevitable. He knew he wouldn't be allowed to leave the dining room until he told his mother and his aunt every word spoken between his ward and him.

"Very well, Mother." John rose from his chair, walked the length of the table, and then sat down opposite his brother. He waited until Dobbs had delivered his untouched plate of eggs and ham and then withdrawn to stand near the sideboard.

"To what can I attribute your early rising?" he asked.

"As if you didn't know," Aunt Hester sniffed.

"We want to know what happened at Arden Hall," his mother said.

Aunt Hester nodded her head vigorously. "Tell us everything, Johnny."

"Where shall I start?" he teased them.

"Start with the Montgomery girl's appearance," his mother suggested.

"Oh, please do, brother," Ross piped up. "I've been on tenterhooks since you left."

John inclined his head at his brother and said, "Mistress Montgomery has banana-yellow hair, eyes like purple grapes, and dozens of dark freckles splattered across the bridge of her nose."

"Freckles?" Aunt Hester exclaimed. "Oh, Tessa, how will we ever marry the girl off?"

"Hush." His mother gave him a look that said she wasn't fooled for a minute. "Continue, son."

"The girl dresses like a servant, talks to herself, and plays the flute."

"Oh, it's worse than I thought," Aunt Hester cried, her hands flying to her bosom. "Flute playing isn't at all the thing. Young ladies of breeding play the pianoforte."

John burst out laughing. Even his mother and his brother smiled. Aunt Hester didn't seem to mind that the girl talked to herself, only that she played the flute.

Flicking a glance at Ross, John noted the speculative look in his brother's expression. "And why are you staring at me like that?" he demanded.

Ross gave him a lazy smile. "I'd bet my last shilling at White's that Mistress Montgomery is the loveliest woman you've seen in years," he drawled.

John frowned at him. "You'd lose, brother."

"I think not, else you wouldn't be working so hard to convince us of her ugliness."

"That thought also crossed my mind," his mother said.

"I dislike blondes," John insisted, "especially impertinent pieces of baggage like Mistress Montgomery."

"Johnny, hatred is love turned inside out," Aunt Hester announced.

Ross shouted with laughter, and the dowager duchess

coughed as if she were covering her merriment. John gave his aunt a wholly disgusted look and started to rise.

"Sit down," his mother ordered. "Tell us the rest."

John sat down again and stared at the wall behind the sideboard. She smells like violets, he thought, and has the softest, most seductively pliant lips I've ever kissed.

"Well?"

John focused on his mother. "Delphinia Montgomery, the stepmother, is a greedy witch who spawned two daughters as nasty as herself," he told them. "They treat the girl so shabbily that she invented an imaginary friend. Not only that, but I felt obliged to promise all three of them a season in order to catch husbands. I couldn't offer one sister a season and ignore the other two. You'll need to send for London's finest dressmakers, because Mistress Montgomery does garb herself in servant clothing, which, I suspect, is her stepmother's doing."

"I see," his mother said.

"The poor child," Aunt Hester added.

"What are you smiling at?" John asked his brother.

Ross shrugged and wiped the smile off his face. "You seem . . . *involved*."

"I am singularly *un*involved," John corrected him. "I am merely aggravated by the prospect of wasting a small fortune to outfit and launch three females into society."

"Miles Montgomery will reimburse you," Ross said.

"If he doesn't lose everything he owns in America," John replied.

"Send Gallagher to Arden Hall to invite the Montgomerys here for Christmas," his mother said.

John gave his mother an incredulous look, saying, "I beg your pardon?"

"We can transport the dressmakers here during the holidays, and all will be ready when we leave for London," his mother reasoned.

"I am planning to pass a peaceful Christmas with my family," John said in refusal. "I refuse to be bothered by Mistress Montgomery and her problems." *Or her fresh violet scent.*

"How uncharitable of you," Aunt Hester spoke up.

John glanced from his brother's smiling face to the disgruntled expressions etched across his mother's and his aunt's faces. "A compromise is in order," he relented. "After Christmas I will personally ride to Arden Hall and invite them for New Year's, while Gallagher fetches the dressmakers from London."

"I can hardly wait for Christmas to be gone," his brother quipped. "I'm dying to meet the slip of a girl who obviously has disturbed you."

"Be careful, brother, or I'll marry you off to one of the stepsisters," John warned him. "And, I must say, I've never seen two plainer brunettes in my entire life."

"Aren't you the one who professed a desire to wed an ugly brunette?" Ross shot back. "Or has Mistress Montgomery persuaded you to prefer blondes?"

"Bloody hell," John muttered. Intending to leave, he rose from his chair and took three steps toward the mahogany double doors, but his aunt's voice stopped him in his tracks.

"Johnny, you haven't been properly excused," she called.

Slowly, John turned around and gave her a thunderous glare.

"Oh, my," Aunt Hester exclaimed. "You are excused."

"Thank you, Aunt," he said in a clipped voice. Without another word John stalked from the dining room.

Six days later John stood in the courtyard at Avon Park and watched Gallagher driving away in the largest of the ducal coaches. His man's destination was London, where he would remain at the ducal residence on Park Lane until the city's finest dressmakers, milliners, glovers, and shoemakers could be gathered and then escorted to Avon Park.

As he waited for Nemesis to be brought up from the stables, John paced back and forth in buckskin breeches that molded perfectly to his muscular thighs and legs. His own destination was Arden Hall, where he would invite the four Montgomery ladies to be his guests at Avon Park during the New Year holiday.

Finally, John left the grounds of Avon Park and turned his horse in the direction of Stratford. Arden Hall lay on the outskirts of that town, less than an hour's ride from Avon Park.

A powdery light blanket of snow, the first of the season, had fallen the previous evening. Now it lay melting beneath the midday sun on an unusually warm winter's day.

John saw few animals in the meadows he passed. Only pawprints revealed their presence as they meandered to unknown destinations. In the nearby woodland, wild roseberries adorned the evergreen hedgerow, and blackberry clusters of false Solomon's seal nodded above the thin snow covering.

Leaving the meadow behind, John guided Nemesis through the woodland to the Avon River. He paused a moment to savor the isolation and the idyllic winter's afternoon.

John rode south along the river for a half hour. Suddenly, he yanked his horse's reins to stop as the sweet sound of musical notes wafted through the air toward him.

Isabelle Montgomery was near. John knew that as surely as he knew he was seated on top of Nemesis.

John sat perfectly still in his saddle and tried to gauge the music's mood. Her trilling song possessed a jaunty tone, bringing to mind the image of crisp air and sparkling water and chirping birds; this faded into a lilting melody that conjured mist and moonlight. All too soon the flute's notes became somber, haunting, and lonely— touching the heartstrings he'd thought severed by his late wife.

She shouldn't be roaming these woods alone, John thought, and nudged his horse forward.

Rounding the river's bend, John halted his horse again. With her eyes closed as if in ecstasy, Isabelle Montgomery perched on a tree stump and played her flute.

A reluctant smile touched John's lips as he studied her perfect profile. She was the image of serene femininity. No casual observer would ever guess the extent to her unladylike impertinence.

John wondered again how she made her flute sound exactly as if two people were playing. Her song died abruptly, and he watched her turn her head and say, "Yes, I do believe he is the handsomest man I've ever seen. A tad authoritarian, don't you think?"

She *is* crazy, John decided. What a waste of great beauty. If only he could manage to keep her from talking to herself, she might be able to snare a husband.

And therein lay his problem. Unaccountably, the thought of Isabelle Montgomery married off to an anonymous nobleman bothered him. Immensely.

"Who is handsome and authoritarian?" John called out, making his presence known.

Isabelle whirled around so quickly that she lost her balance and slipped off the tree stump. Her hands flew to her chest, and her lips formed a perfect *O* of surprise.

John leaped off Nemesis and hurried to her aid. He helped her up and set her on the tree stump again.

"You shouldn't be sneaking up on the unsuspecting," Isabelle said in a disgruntled tone of voice.

"And you shouldn't be roaming these woods alone," John countered. When she opened her mouth to reply, he smiled at her and said, "Merry Christmas, Mistress Montgomery."

Isabelle relaxed visibly and returned his smile. "Merry Christmas to you, Your Grace," she replied.

"My friends call me John," he said. "At least in private."

"Are we friends?" she asked.

"I certainly hope so."

"Very well, Your Grace . . . I mean, John."

John decided he liked the sound of his name upon her lips. "What do your friends call you?" he asked.

Isabelle looked him straight in the eye and said, "I don't have any friends."

"You have me," John reminded her.

Isabelle swept him a look from beneath the thick fringe of her blond lashes and told him, "Miles calls me Belle."

"May I also call you Belle?" he asked.

Isabelle nodded and moved several inches over on the tree stump. "Would you care to join me, John?" she invited him.

"I thought you'd never ask." John sat down beside her, so close his buckskin-clad thigh teased hers. He regretted his decision to join her when the fresh, light scent of violets assailed his senses.

"Are you cold?" he asked, attempting to cover his discomfort with talk. "Perhaps we should ride to Arden Hall."

"Now where did she go?" Isabelle muttered to herself, her gaze scanning the immediate area.

"Who?" John asked.

Isabelle ignored his question. "Would you like a concert?" she asked, holding her flute up.

John nodded, but thought how different her attitude was from what it had been only six days earlier. His ward seemed almost glad to see him. What could possibly have brought about such a sudden change in her?

Isabelle raised the flute to her lips. This time her song was spritely and playful.

When she paused to take a breath, John asked, "How do you make the flute sound as if two people are playing?"

"Woodland acoustics," she answered with an ambiguous smile.

"Woodland acoustics, my arse."

"That vulgarity has just earned you a black stone," Isabelle told him.

"I'll buy myself an indulgence," John replied. "Tell me how you do it."

"Why, my guardian angel plays along with me," she answered, and then winked at him.

John chuckled. "Keep your musical secrets to yourself for now, Belle."

Isabelle searched her mind for something to say. "Two more days until the feast day of the Holy Innocents," she said abruptly.

"It's called Bairns Day in Scotland and the unluckiest day of the year," John told her. "No work should be started on that day because the blood of the Holy Innocents will doom it to failure."

"Are you superstitious?"

"I didn't say I actually believed in such notions."

She stared at him for a long moment and then asked, "If you could have whatever you wished, what would it be?"

A loving wife and children, John thought, but said, "I already possess everything I want."

"How fortunate you are," she remarked.

"For what would you wish?" he asked.

A faraway look appeared in her violet eyes. "Miles's speedy return," she said finally.

"You had something else in mind," John said. "I could see it in your eyes."

"How very perceptive of you," Isabelle replied, raising her gaze to his. "But a lady must save some secrets for herself."

Her hauntingly lovely face was close, irresistibly close. John couldn't resist the invitation in her gaze. He placed his arm around her shoulder and started to lower his lips to hers, but then felt her tremble with the afternoon chill.

"I think we should ride to Arden Hall," he said, drawing back. "I have a surprise for your stepsisters and you."

"I really don't want to go home."

"Why?"

"I'm avoiding my stepmother's nephew, Nicholas deJewell," Isabelle answered. "He's the Baron of Redesdale, you know."

John fixed his dark gaze on her. "Why are you avoiding him?"

"DeJewell is determined to marry me," she told him, "but I loathe the ground upon which he walks."

"You needn't concern yourself with him," John assured her. "I am now your guardian and intend to protect you from those suitors you dislike."

Isabelle stared at him, surprise etching itself across her delicate features. "Since my father's death when I was ten, no one has protected me from my stepfamily's verbal abuse."

That personal revelation confused him. "What about Miles?"

"Miles would have protected me," she said in defense of her brother. "However, he was away at the university."

"Your brother should have protected you from their spiteful tongues." John rose from his perch on the tree stump. "Consider me your knight in shining armor, damsel," he said, offering her his hand.

"Thank you," Isabelle said, placing her hand in his. "Do not judge Miles too harshly. Learning to fight one's own battles is a worthy endeavor."

John lifted her onto Nemesis and then mounted behind her. The ride to Arden Hall was short, but disturbing for John. Her delicate violet scent assailed his senses, and the soft feel of her cuddled in front of him seemed natural, as if she belonged there.

Reaching the courtyard at Arden Hall, John dismounted first and then lifted Isabelle out of the saddle. Together they entered the foyer. A cacophony of noise and off-key singing assaulted their ears.

"The others are gathered in the salon," Pebbles informed them.

"What is that noise?" John asked in a disgusted

whisper as they walked down the corridor toward the salon.

"Someone unleashed the hounds of hell."

Isabelle glanced over her shoulder at Giselle, who strolled along behind them. John stopped walking, looked over his shoulder, and then cast her a puzzled glance.

"What were you saying?" Isabelle asked as they started down the corridor again.

"I wondered what the noise was," he answered. "You said someone had unleashed the hounds of hell."

Isabelle stopped walking and stared at him. Confusion etched itself across her fine features, and she reached up to finger her golden locket.

"You heard the words *someone unleashed the hounds of hell*?" she asked.

"That's what you said, isn't it?"

"Yes, Your Grace. I did make that remark."

"Call me John. Remember?"

Isabelle smiled and reminded him, "Only in private."

John inclined his head. Taking her forearm in his firm but gentle grasp, he escorted her the remaining distance to the salon.

"Lobelia is playing the pianoforte," Isabelle told him. "Rue is the vocalist."

The pianoforte and the off-key singing ceased abruptly when they walked into the salon. Lobelia bolted off the piano bench and dropped a curtsy, saying, "Good afternoon, Your Grace."

"Your Grace," Rue said, following her sister's example.

"Welcome to Arden Hall again, Your Grace," Delphinia was saying as she crossed the salon to greet him. "Allow me to make known to you my nephew, Nicholas deJewell, the Baron of Redesdale."

John turned to the man and shook his hand, instantly taking his measure.

Nicholas deJewell appeared to be about twenty-five, the same age as Ross. The man possessed dark brown hair and beady brown eyes and was short with a slight build. The Baron of Redesdale reminded him of a weasel.

"You must stay for tea," Delphinia said, drawing his attention. "Even better, sup with us this evening."

"I'm afraid I must decline," John said, knowing he couldn't stomach another evening with the woman's cow-eyed daughters. "I've ridden to Arden Hall to invite you to Avon Park during the New Year's holiday. My family and I would like you to stay with us for a week or two. London's finest dressmakers will be arriving, and my mother insists all must be in readiness for the season."

Lobelia and Rue squealed in apparent ecstasy. John slid his gaze to his ward, who appeared decidedly unhappy and began fingering her locket. A nervous habit, to be sure. He wondered what could possibly worry her about having a season. The slight chance that she would be unable to catch a husband?

"Your Grace, I understand that you are now Isabelle's guardian," deJewell spoke up.

John nodded.

"I am formally requesting dear Isabelle's hand in marriage," deJewell announced.

"No," John refused the man's request and slid his dark gaze to his ward, who smiled at him. That smile of hers made him feel as lighthearted as a schoolboy.

"The poor girl is unbalanced," the weasel said, lowering his voice. "Who else will want to offer for her?"

"If that is true," John replied, his dark gaze narrowing on the odious man, "why do you want to marry her?"

The baron shrugged. "Perhaps I feel sorry for her."

"Save your dubious pity for those who truly need it," Isabelle spoke up. "I wouldn't marry you even if you were the last man in England."

"Isabelle Montgomery," Delphinia gasped. "Apologize at once."

"I will not."

"Go to your chamber until you repent of your rudeness to my dear nephew," Delphinia said.

"Actually, I do prefer the solitude of my chamber to your nephew's company," Isabelle replied, and then turned away to leave the salon.

"Mistress Montgomery, you will remain in the salon with us," John ordered. Satisfied when she turned around again and started to walk back to them, he announced, "Isabelle is my ward. From this moment on, she will take orders only from me.

"Baron, I insist you return to Avon Park with me in order to await the ladies' arrival in a day or two," John added, rounding on the weasel.

"Give me a few moments to pack my belongings," deJewell said in a curt voice.

John looked at Isabelle and asked, "Will you wait in the courtyard with me? I'd like to speak privately with you."

Isabelle acquiesced with a nod. She seemed particularly eager to escape from her stepfamily. "Thank you for that," she whispered as they walked down the corridor to the foyer. "But why did you invite him to Avon Park?"

"I don't trust him," John answered when they stood together outside. "Now, tell me why the prospect of a London season frightens you."

"Nothing frightens me," Isabelle insisted. "I'm merely worried."

"About what?"

"I've never been away from Arden Hall," she admitted, her gaze skittering away from his. "I don't actually know how to go about."

"My family and I will stand by your side," John assured her. "Or would you prefer a betrothal to deJewell?"

Isabelle snapped her beautiful violet gaze to his. "That is blackmail, Your Grace."

"I suppose so," John agreed with her. "I do believe I hear the clinking of another black stone falling onto my scale."

"I'll pray for your incorrigible soul," Isabelle said.

John grinned at her and would have spoken, but he heard the door behind them opening for Nicholas deJewell.

Isabelle reached out and lightly touched his forearm, whispering, "Thank you for protecting me."

"Damsel, thank you for allowing me to protect you," John said, covering her hand with his own. "Perhaps there is a place for me in heaven?"

Isabelle gifted him with a smile that could have lit the whole mansion. "Perhaps, Your Grace."

Chapter 5

The twenty-eighth day of December . . . Holy Innocents' Day, the unluckiest day of the year, when no venture should be begun.

Isabelle stood at her bedchamber window and gazed at the winter's day. Trying to clear the insecurities from her mind, she inhaled deeply of the morning's crisp, crystalline air and then closed the ice-etched window.

The first storm of the winter had arrived the evening before. Unlike summer's boisterous storms, this one had come in silence and blanketed the earth with snow.

Frost feathered the evergreen branches of the holly trees, and icicles hung from top to bottom. Nearby, a flock of starlings had gathered on a hackberry tree to dine on its few remaining berries. Beneath the bird feeders she'd ordered erected on the lawns, small tracks in the snow wrote a thank-you note to her.

Isabelle enjoyed this time of quiet contemplation in the year's cycle. She savored her long, solitary evenings sitting with Giselle in front of the hearth in her bedchamber. They'd always spoken of her future and the dark prince who would one day come to rescue her.

The Duke of Avon had ruined all of that. In a few short minutes his coach would arrive to carry her stepfamily and her to Avon Park.

Fingering her golden locket, Isabelle suffered the uncanny feeling that her life would never be the same after that day. Superstition held that this was the unluckiest day in the year for beginning new ventures. Perhaps she could write His Grace a note postponing their visit until tomorrow. No, Delphinia would never allow it.

"Child, what good would it do to delay the inevitable?"

Isabelle whirled around and saw Giselle sitting in one of the chairs in front of the hearth. "God's breath, you startled me. Did I mention that the duke heard you speaking?"

"A dozen times, at least."

"What do you think it means?"

Giselle shrugged.

"If the Duke of Avon is the dark prince, then I don't wish to be rescued," Isabelle announced. "His Grace is too arrogant."

"Child, all men are arrogant," the old woman replied. "Would you prefer marriage to Nicholas deJewell?"

"I would prefer being left alone."

"Oh, that would be unnatural," Giselle said. "A woman needs a man to love and to care for her."

"What do men need?"

"The door swings both ways in that regard," Giselle told her. "A man needs a woman to love and to care for him. Men and women are two halves of a whole. Only when they are joined as one can they reach for infinity."

"My, aren't we the philosophical one today," Isabelle said dryly.

"I *am* a higher being."

"This is a mistake," Isabelle said in a voice no

louder than a whisper. "I don't know how to mingle in society and am certain to make a cake of myself."

"Child, there's no need to worry," Giselle said in a soothing voice, reaching out to touch her arm. "I plan to be with you every step of the way."

"Oh, Lord, I was hoping you wouldn't say that," Isabelle moaned.

"What kind of guardian angel would I be if I didn't accompany you on the greatest adventure of your life?" Giselle asked. "The good Lord would never forgive me for being derelict in my duties."

Someone knocked on the bedchamber door, drawing their attention.

"Lady Isabelle," Pebbles called. "The ducal coach and your stepfamily are waiting."

"I'm coming," Isabelle called, rising from her chair. She turned to the old woman and asked, "Are you ready for my misadventure?"

"God forgive me, but I cannot abide your stepfamily," Giselle said. "I'll meet you there." The old woman promptly vanished.

"Coward," Isabelle called to the empty chamber, and then started for the door.

Slightly less than an hour later Isabelle peered out the window of the ducal coach as it left the road. She couldn't see Avon Park itself, but knew they had entered its grounds.

The ride down the private road to the mansion seemed to take forever. Ignoring her stepsisters' excited chatter, Isabelle studied the sunbeams dancing on top of the crusty snow blanketing the lawns and wondered what awaited her at Avon Park.

The coach crossed a stone bridge over a stream and came to a halt in a circular drive. A Saint-Germain footman hopened the coach's door and then assisted her stepmother and stepsisters down.

Alighting last from the coach, Isabelle caught her first look at Avon Park. Impressive and fantastical, the mansion appeared to have sprung to life from a romantic fairy tale. Made of golden limestone, the house reminded her of a castle; its towers, gables, and ogee caps created a busy skyline.

Isabelle couldn't even begin to guess how many rooms it had, but she knew she wouldn't want to be the housekeeper. The duke definitely needed an army of servants to maintain the house and the grounds in smooth-running order.

Clutching her flute case, Isabelle turned with her stepfamily toward the mansion's double doors just as they opened. A tall, impeccably dressed man with a haughty expression stepped outside. Several liveried footmen followed the man and immediately began unloading their baggage.

"Welcome to Avon Park, my ladies," the duke's majordomo greeted them. "Please follow me."

Walking behind her stepfamily, Isabelle entered the mansion's main foyer. It was three stories high and had a marble staircase that led to the upper floors. Though Avon Park looked like a castle from the outside, the interior appeared to have been completely modernized.

"What an exquisite foyer," Delphinia gushed, unable to mask her envy. "Don't you agree, my darlings?"

"Quite beautiful," Rue said.

"And costly too," Lobelia added.

Now, that's an understatement, Isabelle thought, casting her stepfamily an amused look. Apparently, the Duke of Avon *was* richer than the king, proving at least that idle piece of gossip true. Knowing the amorous schemes her stepsisters would be hatching, Isabelle could almost feel sorry for him.

"Mistress?"

"I beg your pardon?" Isabelle said, realizing the majordomo was speaking to her.

"May I take your case?" the man asked.

"No, thank you." Isabelle clutched her flute case like a mother protecting her baby.

"Very good. The others are waiting in the drawing room."

The majordomo led them down a long corridor to the lavishly decorated drawing room. The chamber had been furnished with a piano, opulent sofas, tables, and chairs. Crimson Spitalfield silk hung on the walls, and the carpet had large octagon patterns of crimson, gold, blue, and brown.

The majordomo announced their arrival. Wearing a polite smile of greeting, the Duke of Avon crossed the room to greet them.

"Welcome to Avon Park, ladies," the duke said.

"It's good of you to invite us," Delphinia said with an ingratiating smile.

"I am so happy to be here, Your Grace," Lobelia gushed.

"Me too," Rue added, and then giggled like an imbecile.

"Are you also happy to be here, Mistress Montgomery?" he asked.

"I am not unhappy to be here, Your Grace," Isabelle lied with a sweet smile.

"Don't you trust my servants?" John asked, his dark gaze dropping to the flute case she clutched in her arms.

His question confused her. "I don't understand," she said.

"I'm certain Dobbs asked to carry your flute," he said. "Apparently, you weren't in the mood to give it up."

"Nobody touches my mother's flute but me," Isabelle told him.

"I suppose we'll need to bury it with her when she passes away," Delphinia remarked.

"I intend to bequeath my mother's flute to my own daughter," Isabelle announced.

"You need to catch a husband first," Lobelia reminded her.

"Who besides Cousin Nicholas would offer for a girl who talks to herself?" Rue asked in a snide voice.

"A deaf man, perhaps?" Isabelle replied, narrowing her violet gaze on her stepsister. "We'll look for a blind man for you."

At that, John burst out laughing.

"Johnny, introduce your guests," called one of the women who were seated on the opposite side of the chamber.

Isabelle looked at the two women who bore an uncanny resemblance to each other. Both had faded blond hair liberally laced with gray and wore kindly but curious expressions.

John escorted them across the drawing room and made the proper introductions to his Aunt Hester and his mother, the dowager duchess. Then he gestured to his majordomo and said, "I'm certain you'll want to settle in and rest awhile. Dobbs will show you to your rooms."

Before leading her girls across the chamber to the majordomo, Delphinia turned to the duke and said, "I'm surprised dear Nicholas isn't here to greet us."

"Your nephew and my brother have gone along to

London," John explained. Then he reached for a sealed missive lying on the sofa table and passed it to her, adding, "The baron asked me to give this to you."

"Thank you, Your Grace," Delphinia said. "We'll see you later." She began ushering her daughters toward the majordomo stationed near the door.

Isabelle followed behind but paused when she heard her name called.

"Mistress Montgomery," the dowager duchess said. "Please remain behind to speak with Lady Montague and me."

The request caught Isabelle off guard. She shifted her gaze to the duke, who also appeared surprised.

"Do *not* disgrace us," Delphinia whispered out of the side of her mouth. And then her stepfamily disappeared out the drawing-room door.

Like a woman going to the gallows, Isabelle crossed the drawing room toward the duchess and her sister. She felt relieved that Giselle hadn't appeared yet. Once those two aristocrats caught her talking to herself, they wouldn't want to be in the same room with her.

"You may return to your office," the dowager duchess said, sliding her gaze to her son. "Hester and I want to become acquainted with Mistress Montgomery. You wouldn't be interested in our conversation."

John nodded, but his expression screamed his reluctance to leave. The door clicked shut behind him.

"Sit down here," the dowager duchess said, patting the sofa beside her. "Mistress Montgomery, we have been hearing a great deal about you."

"Indeed, we have," Lady Montague agreed. "Why, Tessa, the child's freckles enhance her innocent beauty."

Without thinking, Isabelle reached up and touched

the bridge of her nose. Sweet celestial breath, what was she expected to reply to that?

"Johnny was merely teasing us," Lady Montague continued. "Oh, what fun we shall have."

"Hester, please allow me to get a word into this conversation," the dowager duchess said.

Isabelle didn't understand what they were talking about. She flicked a quick glance from one to the other and caught a look that passed between them, as well as a nod from the duchess. What did that mean?

The dowager duchess cleared her throat and began, "Mistress Montgomery—"

"Please, Your Grace, call me Isabelle."

Both women nodded and smiled at her.

"The dressmakers and the others will be arriving right after the first of the year," Lady Montague said. "We have ever so much planning to do."

"With all due respect, this is a terrible mistake," Isabelle said, looking first at the dowager duchess and then at Lady Montague. "I don't know how to go about in society and wouldn't wish to embarrass the Saint-Germains in any way."

"Oh, pish," Lady Montague said, waving her hand in dismissal. "We intend to teach you everything. By the time we're finished you will pass for a duchess."

"When in doubt, bluff your way through a situation," the dowager duchess told her, and then stared at her for a long moment. "You have the look of your mother."

"You knew my mother?" Isabelle asked, surprised.

"I met her more than a few times at social gatherings," the duchess replied.

"What was she really like?"

"Your mother was an exquisitely beautiful woman

and devoted to her husband and children,'' the duchess told her.

Isabelle gave her a smile filled with sunshine. She would have spoken, but heard a familiar voice.

''I like this duchess.''

Isabelle snapped her head toward the hearth. Giselle was relaxing in one of the chairs there.

''Her untimely death saddened me,'' Lady Montague added, drawing Isabelle's attention away from the old woman.

''Perhaps you would like to retire now,'' the duchess suggested. ''We'll speak more about your mother later.''

Isabelle acquiesced with a nod. She knew when she was being dismissed.

''If you step outside into the corridor, you'll find Dobbs awaiting your pleasure,'' the duchess told her.

Isabelle rose from the sofa and curtsied to both women. Still clutching her flute case, she crossed the drawing room, but she felt their eyes upon her. As Isabelle opened the door to leave, Lady Montague's voice drifted to her. ''What do you think, Tessa?''

''I'm optimistic,'' she heard the duchess reply. ''If she's anything like her mother, I believe she'll do rather nicely.''

Wondering what they were talking about, Isabelle glanced over her shoulder and caught them staring at her. They nodded, and she smiled. Then Isabelle stepped outside, and the door clicked shut behind her.

I don't belong here, Isabelle thought, sitting in one of the chairs positioned in front of the hearth.

''What did you say?'' Giselle asked, sitting in the other chair.

Isabelle gestured toward the bedchamber. "I feel horribly out of place in this luxury."

"Mortals can adapt to any situation," Giselle replied.

Isabelle shifted her gaze from the blazing fire in the hearth to the old woman. Then she turned her head and scanned the opulently furnished chamber.

The bedchamber was enormous, at least five times the size of her room at Arden Hall. The canopied bed could comfortably sleep four or five people. It had a mahogany headboard and fluted, carved columns at the bottom. A damask coverlet coordinated with the bed hangings, which kept the cold out. A violet pattern silk that complemented the bed's accoutrements hung on the walls down to the dado, and a woven carpet, obviously imported from some exotic port, covered the wooden floor.

The chamber also sported the little necessities of life. There was a table complete with recesses for toilet articles, a dressing table with mirror, a washstand on tripod feet topped by a porcelain bowl, a bedside commode, a full-length looking glass, and a gigantic tallboy with drawers and wardrobe.

"I am not going downstairs to dinner," Isabelle announced, her voice sounding loud in the hushed chamber. "Without Miles by my side I'll make a complete cake of myself."

"You will be fine," Giselle assured her, wearing a placid smile. "The dowager and her sister already like you."

"I have nothing to wear," Isabelle said. "Lobelia and Rue destroyed my best gowns. Remember?"

"Have you no faith in your guardian angel?" Giselle asked, rising slowly from her chair. She crossed the chamber to one of the trunks and opened it. Reaching inside, the old woman held up a violet gown and said, "You can wear this."

Isabelle bolted out of her chair and hurried across the chamber to the old woman. "That gown does not belong to me," she said. "Where did you get it?"

"Angels perform miracles every day," Giselle told her.

"Can everyone see the gown or only me?" Isabelle asked, narrowing her gaze on her old friend. "I wouldn't care to be like that emperor who walked naked down the road."

Giselle chuckled. "Trust me, child, your stepsisters will drool with envy when they see you in this. Besides, the duke is already too fond of you. Would I let him taste the wine before he's paid for it?"

That remark confused Isabelle. "I don't understand."

"Your understanding is unnecessary." Giselle reached into the trunk again and began removing accessories that matched the violet gown perfectly.

"Where did these come from?" Isabelle asked.

"This ensemble belonged to your mother," the old woman told her. "After she died, your father saved her belongings, because he couldn't bear the finality of giving them away."

Happiness made Isabelle's eyes shine like amethysts. Reverently, she reached out to touch the gown and whispered, "My mother wore this? Yes, I can feel her presence."

"Can you now?" Giselle said, an amused smile flirting with her wizened lips.

"I do love you," Isabelle cried, flinging herself into the old woman's arms.

"Come now," Giselle said after a moment. "Let me help you dress for dinner."

An hour later Isabelle opened her bedchamber door. After pausing to cast her old friend a confident smile, she stepped outside and started down the corridor.

Isabelle wore the violet silk gown with its high waist and puffed shoulder sleeves. On her feet were matching slippers, and around her shoulders she'd artfully draped a matching cashmere shawl. Giselle had parted her blond hair in the middle and woven it into one thick braid knotted at the nape of her neck. She wore no gloves.

Isabelle felt like a princess. She descended the marble staircase to the foyer below and then looked around, wondering where she should go.

"Please follow me," Dobbs said, materializing from nowhere. "The others are awaiting you in the drawing room."

Isabelle nodded and followed the majordomo down the corridor. "Thank you, Mister Dobbs," she said when the man opened the drawing room door for her.

Everyone turned when she walked into the room. Feeling conspicuous, Isabelle hesitated just inside the doorway.

"You're late," Delphinia announced.

"Where did she get that gown?" Rue asked in a whining voice.

"Humph! She's not wearing gloves," Lobelia said.

Ignoring them, Isabelle looked at her guardian. His dark eyes gleamed with obvious appreciation at the change in her appearance.

"How lovely you appear tonight," John complimented her, walking across the room toward her. "I hope you will allow me to escort you to dinner."

Without waiting for her permission, John gently but firmly grasped her forearm and ushered her out of the drawing room. The others followed them to the dining room.

John sat at the head of the long table. On his right sat his mother, Delphinia, and Rue; Isabelle, Aunt Hester, and Lobelia sat on his left side.

Beneath Dobbs's supervision, two footmen began serving supper from the covered, silver platters on the sideboard. First came turtle soup, followed by buttered lobster and peas and potatoes. Baskets of pastry accompanied this main course, and for dessert there was a rich custard.

Isabelle spoke little throughout dinner. She let her stepfamily's inane questions and comments concerning society gossip swirl around her. Sitting in the enormous dining room with its forty-foot-long mahogany table, crystal chandeliers, silver, and china made her feel conspicuously out of place. She'd always assumed that she had every luxury at Arden Hall, and never in her wildest daydream had she imagined that people lived with this opulence.

Her position at the table near the duke inhibited her conversational skills. Isabelle felt the duke's presence with every fiber of her being. To make matters worse, he kept watching her. Moving a forkful of food from her plate to her mouth suddenly became a difficult chore.

"With all due respect, Your Grace," Delphinia said, turning to the dowager, "you'll need infinite patience to instruct my stepdaughter on the niceties of society. Heaven knows how hard I've tried and failed."

"I daresay our stepsister will have a difficult time catching a husband," Rue agreed with her mother.

"She refuses even to wear gloves unless the weather is especially cold," Lobelia added to their list of complaints.

Isabelle focused her violet gaze on her oldest stepsister. "Playing the flute well is impossible while wearing gloves, Lobelia. At least I have enough manners not to speak disparagingly about someone in her very own presence as if she weren't there and couldn't hear."

The duke chuckled. Isabelle flicked a quick glance at him and then at his smiling mother.

"Humph! Correcting me in public is rude in the extreme," Lobelia told her.

"I cannot and will not pretend deafness to your insults," Isabelle replied.

"Bravo, child! It's past time you defended yourself against their jealousy."

Isabelle snapped her head around and spied Giselle standing near the hearth. Without thinking she ordered in an irritated voice, "Be quiet."

"See!" Rue cried. "Isabelle *is* insane."

"Oh, dear," Lady Montague exclaimed softly. "The girl does talk to herself."

Suddenly remembering her audience, Isabelle looked at the others and tried to stammer a plausible explanation, "I-I-I . . ." Her mind remained humiliatingly blank.

"Mistress Montgomery has the most adorable habit of thinking out loud," John spoke up, absolving her of insanity.

"Sometimes I do that myself," the dowager said, also coming to her defense.

Isabelle sent both of them a grateful smile and then looked down the table at Rue, saying, "If you had grown up with a pair of spiteful sisters, then you would also talk to yourself."

John burst out laughing.

"Isabelle Montgomery, that is quite enough," Delphinia scolded.

Rue whined, "She *is* mad, why—"

"I heard she inherited her mother's insanity," Lobelia interrupted her sister.

At the insult to her mother Isabelle leapt out of her chair. She touched her golden locket and threatened, "Never say anything disparaging about my mother, or I'll—" Unable to think of something suitably horrible to say, Isabelle turned on her heels and marched out of the dining room. She heard the duke calling her name, but ignored him. Reaching the foyer, she walked out the front door instead of returning to her chamber upstairs.

Isabelle clutched her shawl tightly around her shoulders and breathed deeply of the crisp night air. She stood there a long moment and tried to calm her rioting nerves. Gazing up at the night sky, Isabelle saw thousands of glittering stars winking at her from their bed of black velvet, but the serene sight did nothing to ease her strained patience.

How dare her stepsister speak so insultingly about her mother, a woman whom none of them had ever known. Why, her stepsister wasn't fit to wipe mud off her mother's slippers.

And then Isabelle felt something warm being wrapped around her shoulders. She looked down and saw a man's voluminous cloak. Glancing to the right, she spied the duke standing beside her. His kindness combined with the pleasing sight of his chiseled profile proved a balm to her nerves.

"If I were a man, I'd challenge each of them to a duel," Isabelle said.

"Dueling is against the law," John told her. "You'll need to say a good act of contrition for your anger, one of the seven deadly sins. If you don't repent you'll regret the error of your ways when those black stones tip your scale."

His warning made her smile. "I do apologize for ruining your dinner," Isabelle said.

"You haven't ruined anything," he assured her. "I could horsewhip Miles for leaving you in their company all these years."

"It isn't his fault," she defended her brother. "Life was different before my father died."

John nodded and asked, "Are you cold?"

Isabelle shook her head.

"Let's take a stroll in the garden," he suggested.

John led her around the side of the mansion, and they slipped through a line of clipped yew trees to enter the garden. Though she was unable to see very much in the dark, Isabelle was certain the garden had to be as lovely as the mansion itself.

"I knew this would never work," she said, as they walked along the path that meandered through the garden. "If you value your reputation, Your Grace, allow me to return to the seclusion of Arden Hall."

"Call me John. Remember?"

Isabelle glanced sidelong at him. She gave him a shy smile and nodded.

"Why do you believe your coming-out will never work?" he asked.

"I don't know how to go about," she admitted, dropping her gaze. "I feel so conspicuous."

Abruptly, John stopped walking and gently forced her to face him. With one finger he tilted her chin up and waited until she lifted her violet gaze to meet his.

"Mingling successfully in society means adopting an

attitude," he told her. "Whenever you feel conspicuous, imagine everyone in the room to be naked."

Isabelle widened her eyes in surprise. "Oh, I couldn't do that," she said, shaking her head.

"Then imagine everyone wearing only their underdrawers," John amended himself. "You can do that, can't you?"

Without thinking, Isabelle dropped her gaze to his muscular body. When she realized what she was doing, she gasped with a horrified giggle and said, "I suppose I could try."

John gave her a devastating smile. "That's my brave girl," he said in a husky whisper.

"Lobelia and Rue will try to make things difficult for me," Isabelle said. "You saw how they behaved at the dinner table."

"We'll worry about your stepsisters later," John said. He winked at her and asked, "Did you know that in the language of flowers *Lobelia* means malevolence and *Rue* means disdain?"

His remark brought a smile to her lips. Apparently, her stepsisters held no attraction for him, and for some unknown reason that fact made Isabelle feel better.

"You must be cold," John said, drawing her close against the side of his body. Before she could protest his familiarity, he pointed toward the sky's southern horizon and asked, "What's that reddish light?"

"Betelgeuse," she answered.

"And over there?"

"Sirius, the brightest star in the heavens."

"You've listened well," he praised her. "What's that over there?"

"Polaris," Isabelle answered. "The ever constant North Star."

John leaned close, so close the warmth of his breath sent delicious shivers dancing down her spine. "I can be as constant as the North Star," he whispered.

His words, his nearness, and his masculine scent flustered Isabelle. She didn't know what to do or to say; no man had ever spoken so intimately to her.

"I would like to retire now," she said without looking at him.

"Your merest wish is my command, Belle," John said, laughter lurking in his voice.

Isabelle felt conspicuously awkward and refused even to steal a peek at him. When he didn't press his suit, she felt relieved, but strangely let down. Instead, he offered her his arm, and together they returned to the mansion.

Reaching the base of the marble staircase, John kissed her hand and said, "Pleasant dreams, Mistress Montgomery." Without another word he turned to walk away.

"Your Grace?" Isabelle called.

He turned around.

"I thank you for your kindness," she said in a soft voice.

"No thank-you's are necessary," John said, gifting her with his devastating smile. "Comforting a beautiful damsel in distress is its own reward."

Isabelle blushed. "Your Grace, I will pray for you."

"Thank you," he replied, and then winked at her. "I dislike overly warm weather."

Gaining her chamber, Isabelle looked around, but Giselle was absent. She changed into her nightgown, brushed her hair, and climbed into the enormous bed. Closing her eyes in a semblance of sleep, she knew that a peaceful rest would elude her that night. Her nerves were rioting from her strange surroundings and her time in the garden with the duke.

A weight settled on the edge of the bed. Isabelle opened her eyes and saw Giselle sitting there.

"The duke harbors a fondness for you," the old woman said.

"His Grace has experience in charming reluctant women," Isabelle disagreed.

"He sounded sincere to me," Giselle said.

"Have you been eavesdropping?"

"I would never do that," the old woman said. "I simply need to fulfill my task of guarding you. . . . Now close your eyes and sleep will come."

Isabelle closed her eyes. A moment later she opened them again, but the old woman had vanished. Isabelle sighed, closed her eyes, and fell into a dreamless sleep.

Wishing the London dressmakers would hurry so that she needn't wear her old gowns, Isabelle brushed her blond hair back and tied it with a ribbon. After inspecting herself in the looking glass, she left her chamber and walked down the corridor to the marble staircase.

How should she behave when she saw the duke? Isabelle wondered, slowing her pace as she reached the staircase. He'd been intimately solicitous of her the previous evening, and she didn't know if she should pretend forgetfulness or acknowledge his interest in her. John was the handsomest man she'd ever seen and chivalrous in spite of his tarnished reputation. Could he possibly be the dark prince destined to rescue her?

As she walked down the staircase, Isabelle noted the flurry of activity in the main foyer below. She wondered what the commotion was about. As if her thoughts had conjured the man, she spied the darkly handsome duke. Dressed for traveling, he was just reaching for his cloak.

"Good morning, Your Grace," Isabelle called.

John whirled around at the sound of her voice. No smile of greeting lit his expression. In fact, he seemed forbidding and distinctly unhappy to see her.

"Mistress Montgomery, the dressmakers have arrived a few days early," he said in a cool voice, marching across the foyer toward her.

Isabelle nodded, acknowledging his words. She dropped her gaze to his cloak.

"I am going to London," John announced, his gaze following hers to his cloak. "I have no fondness for all of this female activity."

"You're leaving before New Year's?" Isabelle asked in surprise.

John nodded.

Isabelle felt her spirits plummet like a nightingale falling from the sky. She forced herself to smile and said, "You won't be here to see those stars of yours return to their stables at midnight on New Year's Eve."

"Wherever I am on New Year's Eve," John said, his dark gaze softening on her, "I will look up at the sky and think of you."

"How kind of you to voice such a thought," Isabelle said.

"I've given my mother orders that you must be in residence at your brother's town house no later than March," John told her, changing the subject abruptly. "Do *not* fail me."

Isabelle remained silent.

"Do you understand, Belle?"

"Perfectly."

Without bidding her farewell John turned and walked out of the foyer.

Isabelle walked to the door and stood beside Dobbs. She watched the duke climb into his coach, and then it began its journey to London.

"The man is trying to escape his feelings for you," Giselle commented.

"I find that exceedingly difficult to believe," Isabelle said.

"What is it you find difficult to believe?" Dobbs asked, looking down his long nose at her.

"Nothing, Mister Dobbs." Isabelle blushed hotly with embarrassment. "I was merely thinking out loud."

"I understand, my lady." The majordomo turned and began walking away.

"I'm sorry," Giselle apologized, wearing an unrepentant smile. "I forgot that others cannot see or hear me."

"I forgive you," Isabelle said. "Please don't do it again."

"Did you say something?" Dobbs asked, whirling around.

Feeling the blood rush to her face, Isabelle shook her head. When the majordomo nodded, she raced up the staircase to her own chamber until she could compose herself. Isabelle only hoped the majordomo didn't tell anyone that he'd caught her talking to herself.

Chapter 6

. . . as constant as the North Star.

Watching the passing scenery from her seat inside her brother's coach, Isabelle recalled the words the Duke of Avon had used to describe himself. She hadn't seen him in the two months since his abrupt departure from Avon Park. Had he gazed at the stars on New Year's Eve and thought of her? Was Giselle correct that he'd left Avon Park because he was trying to escape his feelings for her?

Isabelle doubted it. In fact, she hoped that would not prove true. Traveling to London on that very first day of March was against her better judgment. Society would never accept a young woman who reportedly talked to herself, and she could never snub the only friend she'd ever had for the sake of their acceptance.

"I thank you for your loyalty, child," Giselle said from her perch on the opposite seat.

Isabelle shifted her gaze to the old woman. Leaning forward, she touched the gnarled hand and said, "And I thank you for your loyalty."

"How thoughtful of the duke to send us his own coach," Giselle remarked.

"Yes, his gesture was very kind," Isabelle agreed. "Too bad my stepfamily commandeered it for themselves."

"I'm content to ride without their company," the old woman replied. "Eight hours in a coach with them would have proven unendurable."

"You said you'd meet me in London," Isabelle reminded her.

"Traveling together like this is much more pleasant," Giselle said. "Want to play our flutes?"

"Later perhaps," Isabelle refused, and then gazed out the window.

The March sky was a clear blue, and the days were growing noticeably longer. In the woodland, patches of moss would be growing into a thick, lush green, and flocks of migrating robins would be grazing on the brown grass in the open meadows. All of nature seemed poised for spring.

"Today is the feast of Saint Albinus, whom God gifted with the power of miracles," Isabelle said. "I do hope good fortune secures a miracle for me in easing my passage into society."

"As I recall, the miracle Albinus worked was killing an evil man by breathing into his face," Giselle said.

Isabelle slid her gaze to her guardian angel.

"Strong breath will never ease your way into society," the old woman said, wearing a mischievous smile. "Mark my words, child. Saint-Germain harbors a fondness for you, else he would never have sent his coach."

"I find that a difficult notion to believe."

Isabelle shifted her violet gaze to the window again. The hint of a smile flirted with the corners of her lips as she realized what an amazing picture their entourage presented to the world. Why, they could almost have qualified as a parade. The outriders came first and were followed by the dowager's coach. Behind the coach carrying Isabelle came the ducal coach, in which her stepfamily rode. Several coaches and carts filled with their servants and baggage brought up the rear and were followed by more outriders. The only missing person was Pebbles, who had left for London three weeks earlier in order to supervise preparations for their arrival at Montgomery House.

Soon Isabelle noted the density of the villages and the population as they neared the outskirts of London. In spite of her insecurities Isabelle felt excited by the sights that greeted her. She'd never traveled to London and had never seen so many people in such a hurry.

The afternoon sun was casting long shadows as their entourage traveled down Edgware Road, which brought them to Park Lane along the border of Hyde Park.

The dowager's coach left them at Park Lane and went on to her residence in Grosvenor Square. At Hyde Park Corner their coaches turned left onto Piccadilly and ended their journey at Berkeley Square in Mayfair.

Wearing a welcoming smile, Pebbles opened the front door and stood at the top of the steps as a small army of servants began unloading their baggage. Isabelle alighted from her brother's coach and followed her stepfamily up the stairs to Montgomery House, but her attention was distracted by a shabbily dressed, smudged-faced young girl who walked down the street and called for people to buy her flowers. Isabelle's heart went out to the girl. She never imagined that such poverty existed. Rich and poor alike, people in the countryside took care of each other.

"Has Nicholas stopped by yet?" Isabelle heard her stepmother ask the majordomo.

"No, my lady," Pebbles answered.

"What about the Duke of Avon?"

"No, my lady."

A feeling of relief surged through Isabelle as she followed one of the housemaids up the grand staircase to her bedchamber, located on the third floor. The last room in the rear, her chamber overlooked the sorriest excuse for a garden that she'd ever seen. Naturally, Lobelia and Rue had taken the choicer bedchambers with a view of Berkeley Square. The one good thing about her chamber was its proximity to the servants' stairs in the rear of the town house, in the event she wanted to escape unseen without using the grand staircase.

Their arrival created orderly chaos within Montgomery House. Maids and footmen scurried about delivering baggage to the proper bedchambers and laying fires in the hearths in order to chase away March's chill. In spite of the day's mildness, true spring warmth was still more than a month away.

When the third floor quieted, Isabelle wandered across the room to the window and stared down at the garden and the street beyond the walled area. How foreign this place seemed. She might as well have traveled to the most exotic place on earth. London appeared far different from her beloved Stratford.

The delighted squeals of her stepsisters wafted down the corridor from their chambers to hers. Apparently, Lobelia and Rue had discovered their new wardrobes, gifts from the Duke of Avon.

"I hate this city," Isabelle said to the empty chamber.

"You'll adjust to life here," Giselle said, appearing beside her. "You may even grow to like it once the dark prince arrives."

Isabelle rounded on the old woman. "The prince is in London?"

Giselle nodded. "He's been awaiting the moment to rescue you."

"I don't need rescuing," Isabelle insisted. She would have questioned the old woman more, but her stepsisters' squeals once again reached her ears, grating on her nerves. "I believe I'll fetch a cup of tea and sit outside. Care to join me?"

"I'll meet you there." The old woman vanished faster than an eye could blink.

Isabelle left her bedchamber and walked the length of the corridor to the grand staircase. She descended to the second floor, where the drawing room, gallery, and library were located. Passing the closed library door, she paused when she heard her stepmother's voice and then Nicholas deJewell's voice in answer.

"You'll need to court her," Delphinia was saying. "Make her fall in love with you. You can do that, can't you?"

"The chit despises the very air I breathe," Nicholas replied.

"The duke is her guardian, and I have no legal power over her," Delphinia said. "Nicky, there is no good reason you can't win her over."

Isabelle had no doubt they were speaking about her. In an effort to avoid deJewell she hurried down the length of the corridor to the servants' stairs and then raced down the two flights to the kitchen located in the basement.

Startling the servants, Isabelle burst into the kitchen and scanned its occupants for Pebbles. "May I have a cup of tea?" she asked.

"Lady Isabelle, you needn't have come down here," Pebbles said, rushing forward. "I would have served you in the drawing room."

"I'd prefer to drink my tea outside and . . ." Isabelle hesitated.

". . . avoid the witch's nephew?" Pebbles finished for her.

"Precisely."

The majordomo pulled a chair out from the table and said, "Sit here while I prepare it." He turned to the other servants and ordered, "Continue with your duties. I shall take care of my lady."

Though the kitchen staff instantly returned to work, Isabelle knew that her presence made them uncomfortable. In an effort to ease them she glanced down and saw *The London Times* lying on the table near her arm. She began turning the newspaper's pages until the society page caught her attention.

A whole column of gossip concerned her guardian. The Duke of Avon had been spotted at the opera with a raven-haired beauty; the very next evening he'd been seen at the theater with an exquisite redhead. Reportedly, both widows were not only beautiful but possessed perfect pedigrees. Was England's premier duke finally considering remarriage? If so, to whom?

Isabelle felt the color draining from her face. How incredibly naive she'd been to believe that the duke harbored a fondness for her just because he'd sent his coach to Stratford. The rake probably owned a dozen coaches.

"Pebbles, never mind the tea," Isabelle said, rising from her chair. "I believe I'll just sit in the garden."

"Shall I serve you outside?"

Isabelle shook her head and turned to leave.

"My lady, are you ill?" The man's concern was all too apparent in his voice.

"I'm fine," Isabelle answered, managing a smile for him. "Please do not let Nicholas know where I am."

"My lips are sealed," Pebbles assured her, and then gestured as if buttoning his lips together.

Isabelle walked outside and sat on the first stone bench she saw. How humiliated she felt to have believed that the duke was attracted to her. Why, the man could have his choice of any woman in England. Probably any woman in Europe. Why would he even consider her? No, she was merely his ward. And he was a reluctant guardian at that.

"Is aught wrong, child?"

Isabelle glanced at the old woman sitting on her left. "I see that angels do make mistakes."

"What does that mean?" Giselle asked.

"The duke has several ladies whom he escorts around town."

"So?"

"So, His Grace harbors no tender feeling for me," Isabelle said. "In fact, he probably cannot bear to be in the company of a young and inexperienced woman like me."

"Youthful innocence can be a powerful aphrodisiac," Giselle said. At that, the old woman lifted her flute to her lips and began playing. At first the melody was spritely and playful, but then slowed into a hypnotically sensual tune.

"Welcome to London," someone called.

Isabelle would have recognized that voice anywhere. She whirled around and watched the Duke of Avon descending the steps that led from the street. Dressed completely in black except for his white shirt, the man appeared as enticingly handsome as Lucifer himself. And just as dangerous.

"How did you know I was sitting here?" Isabelle asked by way of a greeting.

John smiled. "I followed the dulcet tones of your flute."

Surprised, Isabelle rounded on Giselle, but the old woman had already vanished. "I don't like your London," she told the duke.

"*My* London?" John echoed, sitting beside her on the bench.

"I do prefer the rustic life in Stratford," she added.

"And how were things in Stratford when you left?" he asked.

"The catkins were hanging from the birch and the hazel trees," Isabelle answered. "The fuzzy buds of the pussy willow were beginning to swell, and crocuses were breaking through the frosty ground."

"How divinely exciting," John drawled.

"The other day I even heard a starling singing a courting song to his mate," she added.

John stretched his long legs out in front of himself. "You may return to those earthly pleasures after the season. Perhaps some handsome young swain will be singing a courting song to you."

Isabelle cast him an unamused, sidelong glance and said primly, "I wonder that you could part from your women long enough to greet me."

John leaned perilously close. The warmth of his breath tickled her neck. "You sound like a jealous wife."

Isabelle refused to dignify that comment with a reply.

"To which women do you refer?" John asked in obvious amusement.

"The merry widows reported upon in *The Times*."

"Oh, *those* women," John said. "Perhaps I'm merely waiting for your come-out so I can sing you a courting song."

"Considering all your women, you'll probably be too hoarse by then," Isabelle replied, her voice oozing sarcasm. Then she began to deliver a lecture on his lack of morality. "Your good reputation is irreplaceable. Once tarnished, it's gone forever. Consorting with numerous women will ruin whatever shred of reputation you still possess."

John stood then, startling her. Apparently irritated by her lecture, he towered over her and said in a clipped voice, "Mistress Montgomery, I am not in the habit of listening to lectures from anyone, never mind a slip of a girl still in the schoolroom. My women are none of your business. I am the guardian here, not you."

Without waiting for her to reply, John turned on his heels and headed for the steps leading to the street. He paused and looked back when he heard her speak.

"I demand you return me to my home," Isabelle said, bolting off the bench.

"You are home, Belle." He gestured toward the mansion. "This is Montgomery House."

"I meant Stratford."

"Your come-out into society will be at my mother's on the fifteenth of March," John said, turning away.

"Where are you going?"

"To pay my respects to your stepmother."

"The door is over there," Isabelle said, pointing toward the kitchen door.

"Am I a servant to enter through the rear?" John asked, clearly appalled by her suggestion.

"Pride goeth before a fall, Your Grace."

"Wise words that you should also live by," John said, staring her straight in the eye. "I'll see you inside."

"I'm going directly to my chamber," Isabelle informed him.

"As you wish, Mistress Montgomery." John bowed from the waist. "Until the fifteenth evening of March."

Isabelle sent him an irritated glare and marched into the kitchen. She hurried up the servants' stairs to the third floor and slammed her bedchamber door.

"Quiet, child," Giselle said from where she sat in front of the hearth. "You'll rouse the dead."

"The duke infuriates me," Isabelle said. "The man is arrogant, overly proud, immoral—" A knock on the door drew her attention. "Yes?"

"Lady Delphinia requests your presence in the drawing room," Pebbles called. "His Grace is here to welcome you to London."

"I have the headache," Isabelle lied. "Send His Grace my regrets."

"Very good, my lady."

"Yes, I know. I'll need to say a good act of contrition for that lie," Isabelle said, glancing at the old woman. She perched on the edge of the bed and added, "His Grace heard your flute playing."

"I know."

"It's strange, don't you think?"

"Quite provoking," Giselle agreed, and gave her an ambiguous smile. "The duke has excellent hearing."

Isabelle gave her a pained look.

"Oh, very well," Giselle said. "His hearing my flute playing means he listens with his heart."

Beware the Ides of March, Isabelle thought as she walked down the third-floor corridor in Duchess Tessa's mansion, where she'd been assigned a chamber in order to prepare for her come-out party. She remembered the lines from one of Shakespeare's plays.

"The soothsayer said it to Julius Caesar."

Isabelle stopped short and snapped her head around to stare at the old woman. "Your presence at my come-out party will create problems," she whispered, her violet gaze scanning the corridor to verify no one was lurking about and listening to her conversation. "Please return to our chamber at once."

"But I've been waiting all these years to see you dance with the dark prince," Giselle complained in an unangelic voice.

"The dark prince is attending my come-out party?" Giselle nodded.

"Then you *must* return to our chamber," Isabelle insisted.

"Oh, very well," Giselle acquiesced. Turning away to walk back down the corridor, the old woman began muttering about ungrateful mortals.

As she reached the top of the stairs, Isabelle paused a moment to compose herself. With a badly shaking hand she smoothed an imagined wrinkle from the skirt of her blue silk ball gown.

The hazy image of the man she'd glimpsed in the Avon River so many years ago flitted across her mind's eye. Would she recognize the prince when she saw him? Would he know they were destined to be together for all of eternity? And, most importantly, was she about to make a fool of herself in front of the ton?

Those unanswerable questions and her insecurity made breathing difficult. Isabelle's legs felt weak, and her knees were beginning to shake as voices from down below drifted up the stairs to her. Now she wished she hadn't sent her guardian angel back to her bedchamber.

Isabelle stared at the Savonnerie carpet beneath her satin-slippered feet. Indecision gripped her and kept her rooted where she stood. *Escape* leapt into her mind. It wasn't too late to return to her chamber and stay hidden behind the locked door. She'd done that numerous times as a child, but she was a child no longer. Running away would be a cowardly action.

"Oh, there you are," said a deep voice.

Isabelle lifted her violet gaze from the carpet to see John Saint-Germain walking up the stairs. The duke appeared darkly handsome, and any young woman of breeding would be ecstatic to have him sponsor her come-out. Any young woman but her.

"Come and meet my brother before the guests arrive," John said, as if he knew her anxiety. He held out his hand in invitation, and when she placed her hand in his, he led her down the staircase to the second floor.

When they entered the ballroom, Isabelle saw that the others had already gathered there and were loosely forming a reception line. Dowager Tessa, Aunt Hester, and Delphinia stood together and chatted while Lobelia and Rue, looking surprisingly pretty, ogled a young man who appeared to be about twenty-five.

Leading her toward the young man, John said, "Mistress Montgomery, I wish to make known to you my brother Ross."

"Nice to meet you," Isabelle said.

"Finally meeting the young lady who has disturbed my brother's peace of mind is a distinct pleasure," Ross Saint-Germain replied. He gifted her with a smile that reminded her of her guardian. Though there was a family resemblance, this brother had none of the dark intensity of the duke.

"Mistress Montgomery, I would be honored if you

would gift me with your first dance tonight," Ross said smoothly.

Isabelle smiled and would have replied, but the duke spoke first, saying, "Mistress Montgomery has already promised her first and last dances to me."

Isabelle snapped her head around to stare at the duke. She had done no such thing. In fact, she'd passed the greater part of the day worrying if anyone would invite her to dance, especially if they caught her talking to herself.

"Then you must promise me your second dance of the evening," Ross Saint-Germain was saying.

"I would love to dance with you, my lord," Isabelle replied.

And then the dowager's majordomo positioned himself at the top of the staircase. Within a few minutes he began announcing their guests as they descended to the ballroom. Everyone's gaze seemed fixed on Isabelle, the young woman who had caught the attention of England's premier widower, the Duke of Avon.

Isabelle spied the first of their guests descending the stairs to the ballroom and panicked. She felt the color draining from her face and took a step backward, but the duke's hand at her elbow prevented her from running and making a fool of herself.

"Simply imagine all of these people standing around in their underdrawers," John reminded her.

His wit helped Isabelle to relax. She gave him a wobbly smile and proceeded to welcome their guests as graciously as a young queen acknowledging her subjects' approval.

Isabelle watched in surprised fascination as two young noblemen tripped over each other to catch her stepsisters' attention. Stephen Spewing, the Baron of

Barrows, insisted that Lobelia dance the first and the last dances with him. Charles Hancock, the Baron of Keswick, nearly begged Rue to dance with him.

"Both men believe your stepsisters possess large dowries," John told her.

"But they don't," Isabelle protested the lie.

"They do now," John said, giving her a sidelong smile. "I'd pay a small fortune to get those witches out of your life forever."

"Lobelia and Rue aren't so bad," Isabelle replied, coming to their defense. "They're just—"

"Shallow and snide?" he supplied.

"Exactly."

And then Lobelia's voice reached Isabelle's ears and made her cringe. "This must be your mother," she heard her stepsister say to a young man.

"I am his wife," the woman replied in a cold voice, and the two of them moved on.

Isabelle flicked the duke an uncomfortable glance. In answer he shrugged his shoulders slightly and managed a smile. There was nothing to be done for her stepsister's stupidity now.

"Oh, how wonderful!" Isabelle heard Rue gushing at a heavyset woman standing in front of her. "You're having a baby. When is the blessed event due?"

"I am not carrying a child," the fat woman said in a frosty voice, then left the reception line without bothering to be introduced to Isabelle.

"*How radiant you look* would have been a more discreet thing to say," John whispered into Isabelle's ear. "Something vague always leaves room for interpretation. Remember that."

Isabelle nodded in understanding.

"Here comes trouble," said a familiar voice.

Isabelle whirled toward it. She forced herself to remain silent.

"Do not even consider talking to yourself," John ordered, a hard edge to his voice.

Isabelle returned her gaze to the receiving line, only to discover Nicholas deJewell and a blond-haired man standing in front of her. She forced herself to smile politely at her stepmother's cousin and successfully squelched the urge to yank her hand back when he lifted it to his lips.

"Isabelle, you are the loveliest woman in attendance," deJewell complimented her.

"Thank you, Nicholas." Isabelle sensed John inching closer.

"I wish to make known to you my friend, William Grimsby, the Earl of Ripon," deJewell continued.

Isabelle shifted her gaze to the attractive blond man and said, "My lord, I am pleased to make your acquaintance."

"I am more than pleased to make your acquaintance," the Earl of Ripon replied. "Dare I hope you'll reserve one of your dances for me?"

"Of course, my lord." Isabelle watched both men turn to greet John. Seeing the exchange of cold looks between her guardian and Grimsby, she realized they disliked each other. The current of hostility that passed between them was as tangible as the floor beneath her feet.

"Good evening, Your Grace," Nicholas spoke first. "I hope you don't mind that I've brought a friend along."

"I don't mind in the least," John replied. He slid his dark gaze to the blonde and asked, "How are you, Grimsby?"

"Hearty as ever, Your Grace," Grimsby replied with a smile that did not reach his blue eyes. He flicked a glance at Isabelle and added, "I see you still have a penchant for blondes."

Isabelle felt John tense beside her and hoped no trouble would result from this uninvited guest. Why did these two men hate each other? And why were most of the guests casting interested glances in their direction?

"Shall we dance?" John said to her before the two men had actually moved on.

Isabelle nodded. She would have agreed to almost anything to escape the tension.

Leaving the reception line, John escorted Isabelle onto the dance floor and, with a flick of his hand, gestured the orchestra to begin their first waltz. He moved with the graceful ease of a man who had waltzed a thousand times, and she followed his every step effortlessly as if she'd been born to be held in his arms.

"It's customary for couples to converse while dancing," John told her.

Isabelle met his dark gaze and after a momentary pause remarked, "Lobelia and Rue look especially lovely tonight, don't you think?"

John nodded, but the hint of a smile made the corners of his lips twitch. "I did need to yank the feathers from their coiffures," he told her.

"You did what?" Isabelle echoed in surprise.

"I told them they needed to attract husbands, not the neighborhood cats."

Isabelle laughed, her gaiety drawing the attention of the couples dancing near them.

"I knew I could wrench a sincere smile out of you," John said. "By the way, you waltz very well."

"When I was a child, I practiced dancing by standing

on top of my father's feet," Isabelle told him. "We would waltz around the hall together every evening. I was very light on my feet."

John smiled at the image. "Perhaps we could try that sometime."

Isabelle danced next with Ross Saint-Germain, who pointed out several young women who'd been angling to become a duchess since the day his brother was widowed. One was a beautiful brunette, Amanda Stanley, and another was Lucy Spencer, a lush redhead. For some unknown reason Isabelle felt the unfamiliar pangs of jealousy at the thought of her guardian marrying either of those two beautiful women.

The next several hours passed in a daze of dancing and conversation. The low point of the evening for Isabelle arrived when she danced with Nicholas deJewell, but she managed to escape from him as soon as the music ended.

Several times Isabelle spied Giselle standing against the wall and watching her. At those moments Isabelle focused hard on her dance partner in an effort to keep the old woman from calling out to her. The strain of trying to keep from making a fool of herself was great.

"You don't seem to be having much fun," Ross Saint-Germain remarked, claiming her for the second-to-the-last dance.

"I'm having the time of my life," Isabelle lied. "I can't remember when I've enjoyed myself so much."

"You are absolutely the worst liar I've ever met," Ross said with a smile.

Isabelle inclined her head and amended herself, saying, "I feel much better now that I'm dancing with you."

"Do you really talk to yourself?" he asked.

Surprise made Isabelle miss a step. "Who have you been—"

"Your stepsisters are telling anyone who will listen that you have been slightly unbalanced since your father's passing."

"My stepsisters fear not being able to find themselves husbands," Isabelle told him. "To answer your question, I do not talk to myself."

"I assumed it was jealous gossip," Ross said.

"I have a guardian angel with whom I speak," Isabelle informed him. "Nobody but me can see or hear her."

Now Ross Saint-Germain missed a step.

Isabelle smiled at his mistake and said, "I share all of my problems with my guardian angel."

Apparently, her smile made him think she was joking. Ross relaxed and replied, "What problems can a beautiful woman have?"

"I have Lobelia and Rue," she reminded him.

Ross laughed and inclined his head at her quick wit.

When the music ended, John appeared to claim her for the last dance. Isabelle gazed up at his dark features and felt there was something vaguely familiar about him, that she'd seen him before that eventful day he'd appeared at Arden Hall. And then she thought of William Grimsby.

"Why does the Earl of Ripon dislike you?" she asked baldly.

John gave her an intense look that said whatever had passed between Grimsby and him was none of her business. "I'll call upon you tomorrow at Montgomery House to see how you are faring," he said, ignoring her question. "Do not forget the Debrett ball is next week."

Isabelle decided to drop the issue. The dance ended,

and as soon as all of their guests had departed, Isabelle returned to Montgomery House with her stepfamily.

The house soon quieted of her stepsisters' excited chatter, and Isabelle sat in front of the hearth with a blanket wrapped around herself. She waited for what seemed like hours before her old friend arrived.

"Child, why aren't you sleeping?" Isabelle heard the familiar voice asking.

Turning her gaze to the right, she saw Giselle sitting in the chair beside hers. "I've been waiting for you."

"I'm here now."

"Where was the dark prince?" Isabelle asked without preamble. "I never saw him."

"That's strange," the old woman remarked. "I saw you dancing with him."

That remark jerked Isabelle into full awareness. "I danced with him? No princes were in attendance."

"I've told you several times, child. Princes don't always wear crowns."

"Well, which man was he?"

Giselle cast her an ambiguous smile. "If you want to know the answer to that, child, you must see with your heart and not with your eyes."

Chapter 7

"Bull's pizzle," John muttered in growing irritation.

His coach, driven by Gallagher, had taken the left turn from Piccadilly into Berkeley Square and then had come to an abrupt halt, nearly toppling him off the seat. Looking out the window, John saw the quagmire of coaches and shouted, "What the bloody hell is happening?"

"Congestion, Your Grace," Gallagher called.

John opened the coach's door and leapt out. "Return to Park Lane," he ordered his man. "I'll walk home."

"Yes, Your Grace."

John started walking down the street toward his destination. In the distance he spied three gentlemen descending the front stairs of Montgomery House. Lords Finch and Somers spoke with Major Grimase for a moment and then went their separate ways to their respective coaches.

The sight of the three gentlemen visitors to Montgomery House made John realize that he had successfully launched his ward and her stepsisters into society. So why didn't that make him feel relieved? Instead, his ward's apparent success made him feel decidedly uncomfortable. The possibility of her actually marrying one of those three shallow men disturbed him. Well, he was her guardian. Whoever wanted to court her would need his permission, and he would never agree to a marriage between Isabelle and one of those fops.

John reached Montgomery House a moment later. He started up the stairs, but heard a voice behind him saying, "Flowers for yer lady, m'lord?"

Turning around, John saw a flower girl. He stared at her bedraggled appearance for a long moment and then dropped his gaze to her basket filled with violets and forget-me-nots.

John despised peddlers. It was one such peddler who had sold Lenore the herb that . . . Shaking off the bad memory, he said in a clipped voice, "No, thank you." Then he turned his back on the girl and walked up the stairs.

"Good afternoon, Your Grace," Pebbles greeted him, stepping away from the door to allow him admittance.

"Good day to you," John said, entering the foyer.

From the floor above, John heard the sound of laughter. Obviously, Isabelle and her stepsisters were enjoying a surge of popularity. Marrying all three of them off shouldn't be too difficult. He had no intention of playing mother hen to three young maidens for very long.

"The others are in the drawing room," Pebbles told him.

John dropped his gaze to the foyer's wall table. Upon it sat a silver tray laden with calling cards. "Why are these calling cards here if the ladies are receiving visitors?" he asked.

"Lady Isabelle suffers the headache," Pebbles informed him. "Several of the visitors wished to be remembered to her."

John reached out and lifted the pile of calling cards. He inspected each one slowly.

"With all due respect, Your Grace, those calling cards are meant for my lady," Pebbles said.

John snapped his dark gaze to the majordomo and asked, "Are you questioning Isabelle's guardian?"

The majordomo's expression cleared. "I'm very sorry, Your Grace. I'd forgotten that—"

"I forgive your lapse in manners and appreciate your loyalty to my ward," John said.

"Thank you, Your Grace. Shall I escort you to the drawing room?"

Instead of answering, John looked at the last three calling cards in his hand. Anger and jealousy—emotions he'd thought long-dead—swelled within his chest. Nicholas deJewell, William Grimsby, and even his own brother Ross had visited Montgomery House to pay their respects to Isabelle.

When the majordomo cleared his throat, John looked at him. "I won't be staying," he told the servant.

"Would you care to leave your calling card, Your Grace?" Pebbles inquired, a sarcastic edge to his cultured voice.

Deciding that the Montgomery majordomo was incorrigible, John looked the older man straight in the eye and inclined his head. "I want this delivered to Isabelle," he said, pressing his own calling card into the man's hand.

After pocketing the other men's calling cards, John shifted his gaze to the surprised majordomo. He stared at him for a long moment in a silent challenge.

The majordomo's lips twitched into a smile. "I've seen the sorry lot of them, Your Grace," Pebbles said. "I applaud your actions."

"I'm so relieved," John drawled.

Reaching the sidewalk outside, John glanced down

the street toward the Piccadilly. A shabby old woman stood several yards away and made a beckoning gesture. Was she calling him to follow her? He looked around, but saw no other pedestrian except for the flower girl.

Again the old woman beckoned him.

John walked toward her. The old woman disappeared down the stairs into the Montgomery garden area. When he stood poised on the top step, John spied Isabelle sitting alone on a bench. Her head was lowered as she concentrated on her knitting.

Wearing an intent expression, Isabelle Montgomery looked like a blond-haired angel. On the other hand, no one knew better than he what could be hidden behind a woman's sweetness.

"Where did the old woman go?" John called, descending the stairs into the area.

Isabelle startled at the sound of his voice. "I beg your pardon?"

"I saw a strange old woman disappear down the stairs," John said, walking toward her. He turned in a circle and scanned the deserted area. "You didn't see her?"

Isabelle dropped her mouth open in apparent surprise. "Was she wearing a tattered black cloak?"

"Yes, she was."

Isabelle shook her head. "I haven't seen her."

"You know what she was wearing, but you haven't seen her?" John said, confused by her answer.

"I've seen her before, of course," Isabelle said with a sheepish smile. "Giselle always wears the same clothing."

"Giselle, is it?"

Isabelle nodded. "Sometimes she visits Montgomery

House to beg a meal and probably slipped into the kitchen without my noticing."

John relaxed, accepting her explanation. "You won't find a prospective husband if you sit alone out here," he said, sitting beside her on the bench.

"I'm not alone. I'm with you," Isabelle replied, and then stared into space for a long moment. Finally, she turned to him and said, "I'm afraid you've found me in a melancholy mood, Your Grace. I keep wondering where Miles is and what he's doing."

"Your brother and mine are in New York by now and, I hope, becoming successful businessmen," John told her. "There is no need for sadness. They will return home this summer."

Isabelle smiled at him. The prospect of her brother's homecoming seemed to brighten her mood.

John had the sudden wish that she—or someone just as sweet—would look forward to his own homecoming. Once a long time ago he'd been foolish enough to think he'd found a love like that. How naively mistaken he'd been. Lenore Grimsby had married him for his title and made his life miserable before she . . .

"What are you doing out here when your drawing room is filled with admirers?" John asked, forcing himself out of his black mood.

"Avoiding them," Isabelle answered with a mischievous smile. "I'm knitting a shawl."

"For whom?"

"The girl who sells flowers in Berkeley Square," Isabelle answered. "I noticed her lack of a warm outer garment. Charity is a virtue."

"You can't save the world, Belle."

"True, but I certainly can chase the chill off one poor child."

"Are you trying to earn yourself a white stone?" John teased. "You'll need more than one stone to offset the lie you uttered last evening about how pretty your stepsisters looked."

"The Lord forgives tiny flaws," she said.

"So, Mistress Montgomery, tell me why *your* lies are tiny flaws," John said, stretching his long legs out in front of himself. He dropped his gaze to her hands, folded primly on top of her yarn. She had slender fingers, and her hands looked soft enough to—

"Is anything wrong?"

"No," John said, lifting his gaze to hers. What could he say? *I was just wondering how those hands would feel caressing me? Would they grasp me tightly in the throes of passion?* Good God, this virgin would swoon dead away if he told her what he'd been thinking.

She was staring at him, a puzzled expression upon her exquisitely lovely face.

"I'm waiting for you to enlighten me about your tiny flaws," John said.

"A bad lie almost always hurts, but a good lie, which is a tiny flaw, keeps someone from becoming angry or upset," Isabelle explained. "In other words, a bad lie causes pain, but a good lie prevents it."

"Mistress Montgomery, it's a relief to know that you are as human as the rest of us," John said, leaning close.

Isabelle blushed. "Of course I'm human. What do you mean by that?"

"Sinners and criminals rationalize their flaws," he teased her. "The truth is that all lying is wrong."

Isabelle cast him a disgruntled look, but her lips twitched with the urge to laugh. "I disagree, Your Grace."

John stood and changed the subject abruptly, asking, "Before I leave, will you promise me something?"

"If it is within my power to do so," Isabelle said, tilting her head to one side.

"Keep your distance from the Earl of Ripon. William Grimsby isn't a suitable prospect for you. Consider anyone but him as a potential husband."

The mulish expression that appeared on her face told John he'd just made a blunder by forbidding her to consider one of the men she'd met the previous evening. She'd expressed no intention of finding a husband; he should have remained quiet about Grimsby's unsuitability.

"I prefer to make my own judgments about people," Isabelle said, giving him a sweet smile. "For obvious reasons I never give credence to gossip."

"Damn it, Belle. I've given you this wonderful season and opportunity to—"

"I never wanted a season in London," she reminded him, rising from her perch on the bench.

"Do not forget the Debrett ball next week," John said, turning to leave.

"I shan't be going."

"You'll be there," John called over his shoulder, and then climbed the stairs that led to the street.

"No, I won't."

John ignored her. He disliked women who needed to have the last word.

Reaching the sidewalk, John glanced to his left and saw the flower girl standing several yards away. He started down the street in the opposite direction toward Piccadilly.

"I can chase the chill off one poor girl." He recalled his ward's idealistic sentiment. Imagine, a lady knitting

a shawl for a flower girl. There was no other lady in the ton he could imagine knitting for a flower girl, and that fact brought a smile to his face.

Suddenly, he stopped short. "Hey!" he called, whirling around. "Come here, girl!"

The disheveled flower girl hurried toward him. "Yes, m'lord?" she asked.

"What's your name, child?"

"Molly."

John reached into his pocket. All he carried was a five-pound note and a ten-pound note, both of which were too much money for the flowers she was selling. He knew he was behaving ridiculously, but the thought of his ward's smile of approval made him pass the girl the five-pound note.

"I'll take all of your flowers," John told the surprised girl. "Keep the change and get yourself something to eat."

Molly scooped up the last of her violets and forget-me-nots into her hand and passed them to him, saying, "God bless and keep ya, m'lord."

"And the same to you, child."

Turning his back on her, John strode briskly down Piccadilly in the direction of his mansion on Park Lane. He could almost hear the clinking of a white stone.

One long, lonely week passed.

Avoiding her gentlemen callers, Isabelle pleaded a headache each day. She hadn't seen her guardian, although *The Times* carried daily accounts of his nightly pursuits. Lady Amanda Stanley had accompanied him to the opera, and Lady Lucy Spencer had danced with him an indecent number of times at the small party she'd

given at her town house. Even worse, Giselle had failed
to make an appearance, leaving Isabelle isolated from
the world and alone with her thoughts.

Isabelle came to a decision about her life. Beginning
with the Debrett ball, she would smile at the world and
flirt with her admirers; she also intended to keep each
one of them at arm's length until Miles returned from
his business trip. Then she would retire to Stratford and
pass several months sitting with Giselle beside the River
Avon. Life had been so sweetly placid until the Duke of
Avon dropped into it. Recuperating from the inner tur-
moil that his nearness caused would take at least six
months.

Exactly one week after her argument with her guardian, Isabelle accompanied Dowager Tessa and Aunt
Hester to the Debrett ball. With them were Delphinia,
Lobelia, and Rue. Isabelle lifted her chin a notch as she
descended the stairs to the Debrett ballroom and determined to win the inner war she waged with her insecurity.

Isabelle had never looked more beautiful. Her gown
had been fashioned in a pale violet India muslin with
gilt spangles. Its squared front sported mere straps over
her shoulders, leaving the flawless ivory skin on her
arms and shoulders exposed. She had dressed her hair in
the antique Roman fashion, with her golden tresses
brought together and confined at the back of her head in
two light knots.

Isabelle knew she appeared as sophisticated as the
other young ladies of the ton. So why did she lack their
confidence? She felt as awkward as the young, mother-
less girl who had sat beside the Avon River and played
her flute.

And then Isabelle knew. Though she could dress up

and pass for one of them, she would never be one of them in her heart.

Isabelle touched her golden locket and hoped her mother's loving spirit would help her through this evening and all of the other evenings until Miles returned. Then she thought of the Duke of Avon. What would he think when he saw her transformation from innocent debutante to sophisticated woman? Why was it so important to her that she please him? After all, the man was an insufferable rake.

Standing beside the duke's mother and aunt, Isabelle scanned the crowded ballroom for him. John hadn't arrived yet. Already Delphinia danced with Major Grimase, while Lobelia and Rue partnered Spewing and Hancock respectively.

"Good evening, Your Grace," said a sultry female voice.

"Lady Montague," another woman said by way of a greeting.

Isabelle turned to see Amanda Stanley and Lucy Spencer smiling at John's mother and Aunt Hester. Though the brunette and the redhead were speaking to the older women, both had their gazes fixed on Isabelle.

"I see the merry widows are hunting tonight," Dowager Tessa drawled.

Both women smiled politely, apparently reluctant to offend the duke's mother.

"Have you met John's ward, Lady Isabelle Montgomery?" Dowager Tessa asked them.

"We haven't been formally introduced," Amanda Stanley answered.

"But we've heard so much about her from her stepsisters," Lucy Spencer added, a snide edge to her voice.

Determined not to be intimidated, Isabelle gave each

a haughty smile and said, "I'm certain that my dearest Lobelia and Rue have greatly exaggerated my finer points of character." She turned her head in a gesture of dismissal and realized that behaving obnoxiously was really rather easy.

And then Isabelle spied Nicholas deJewell slowly wending his way through the crush of people toward her. She'd managed to avoid his almost-daily presence at Montgomery House by pleading a headache. How could she avoid dancing with him tonight? Feeling like a small animal caught in a trap, she nearly groaned at the thought of him touching her as they waltzed around the ballroom.

"Good evening, Your Grace . . . Lady Montague," Nicholas greeted the older women first. "Good evening, Isabelle. I've missed seeing you this past week."

Isabelle managed a smile for him. "I've been suffering from the headache, Nicholas."

"Well, you look fully recovered." He reached for her hand, saying, "Come and dance with me."

Unexpectedly, another hand snatched Isabelle's out of deJewell's grasp. Isabelle looked up in surprise and saw the Earl of Ripon.

"Sorry, Nicky. Mistress Montgomery has promised me this dance," William Grimsby said. He shifted his gaze to hers and asked, "Didn't you, my lady?"

"Yes, I did, Lord Grimsby," Isabelle agreed. She felt relieved to escape from Nicholas and pleased that one of the handsomest men she'd ever seen was inviting her to dance.

"Call me William," the Earl of Ripon said, leading her onto the dance floor.

"You must call me Isabelle," she replied. "Thank

you for saving me from the ordeal of dancing with Nicholas.''

''You don't like deJewell?''

''Not particularly.''

''Why?''

Isabelle smiled mischievously and admitted, ''He reminds me of a weasel.''

The Earl of Ripon chuckled. ''Nicky does appear rather rodentlike. Why not a rat?''

''Nicholas hasn't the rat's intelligence,'' she answered.

Grimsby laughed. ''You, Isabelle, are a refreshing autumn breeze following the summer's heat.''

''I'll take that as a compliment,'' Isabelle said, and then cast him a flirtatious smile. Why, making idle conversation with men was as easy as behaving obnoxiously.

''You waltz divinely,'' Grimsby complimented her, giving her a charming smile. ''By the way, how did you ever become Saint-Germain's ward?''

''My brother asked His Grace to become my temporary guardian while he journeyed to America on a business trip,'' Isabelle told him. ''Once Miles returns this summer, His Grace and I will part company. I do admit, Miles used good judgment. His Grace's presence in my life has kept Nicholas at bay.''

''Then you would never consider deJewell?''

''I'd rather die a spinster on the shelf,'' Isabelle said, making him smile. ''Will you answer a question for me?''

The Earl of Ripon inclined his head.

''Why do John and you dislike each other?'' Isabelle asked.

''Our enmity is of a business nature,'' he answered.

"I see."

"No, you don't see," William said with a smile. "I assure you our differences will soon be settled."

"Blessed are the peacemakers," Isabelle quoted scripture, "for they will be called the children of God."

The Earl of Ripon seemed surprised by her statement. He opened his mouth to reply, but then faltered in a dance step. Isabelle's gaze followed his to the staircase.

Looking like Lucifer himself, the Duke of Avon stood poised at the top of the stairs. His dark gaze was riveted on them.

Isabelle was unable to tear her gaze away from her guardian's forbidding expression. The feeling that she'd betrayed him by dancing with his enemy surged through her.

"My lord, I would like to return to Her Grace," Isabelle said.

"Don't let Saint-Germain intimidate you," William said.

"Please, my lord." The music ended, saving them from negotiating their way through the other dancing couples. Before the orchestra could begin another waltz, Isabelle smiled at the earl and said, "Thank you again, William."

Without waiting for his reply, Isabelle left the dance floor and walked in the direction of Dowager Tessa. She reached the dowager at exactly the same moment her guardian did.

John grasped her hand and led her onto the dance floor. "You're nearly naked," he whispered in a harsh voice.

"My gown is modest compared to several of the other ladies," Isabelle replied. There was a sharp edge to her voice when she added, "Look at Amanda Stanley or Lucy Spencer."

John narrowed his dark gaze on her. "Why were you dancing with Grimsby?"

"He invited me," Isabelle answered, refusing to be intimidated.

"Would you jump off London Bridge if Grimsby invited you?"

"You are ridiculous." Isabelle started to turn away and leave the dance floor.

John tightened his grasp on her hand and silently refused to let her go. "Do not even consider walking off this dance floor."

Isabelle acquiesced with a nod of her head. She couldn't very well create a scandalous scene right there on the dance floor.

"Stay away from Grimsby," John warned. "He isn't the man for you."

"I find William rather charming," Isabelle said, casting him the sweetest of smiles.

"William, is it?" John echoed. "Listen carefully, Mistress Montgomery. Grimsby would love to discredit me before the ton and will not hesitate to use you if it suits his purpose."

"I don't believe you," Isabelle said. "The Earl of Ripon is a gentleman."

Their waltz ended. In an effort to escape her guardian's anger Isabelle told him, "I've promised this next dance to another gentleman."

Isabelle knew she needed another dance partner quickly. Her gaze slid past the slight, brown-haired man who stood against a wall and watched her. For the first time in her life she walked toward the Baron of Redesdale.

"I'm ready now," Isabelle said.

"For what?" asked Nicholas deJewell.

"Our dance, remember?"

DeJewell perked up at her invitation. Taking her hand in his, he led her onto the dance floor.

His touch on her hand repulsed Isabelle, but she forced herself to maintain a placid expression. Dancing as far away from him as she could, Isabelle wondered if facing her guardian's anger would have been less disturbing.

"I must speak with you in private," Nicholas said in an urgent tone of voice, drawing her attention away from troubling thoughts.

"What is it?" Isabelle asked, suspicious.

"I've received a message from your brother," he told her. "Will you walk with me outside?"

Isabelle stared at him for a long moment. The last thing she wanted to do was walk outside with Nicholas deJewell. Then she recalled that Nicholas was her brother's silent partner in this business venture, so he was probably telling her the truth. But why hadn't John received a message from their brothers? He probably had, she decided, but the only moments they'd passed together had been spent in argument.

Scanning the chamber for her guardian, Isabelle saw him dancing with Amanda Stanley. She slid her violet gaze back to Nicholas and nodded.

Leaving the dance floor, Isabelle flicked a sidelong glance at Nicholas, who appeared to nod at someone across the room. Her gaze followed his, and she caught her stepmother inclining her head at them. Were they signaling to each other? If so, why? Something was very wrong here.

Isabelle had a mind not to leave with Nicholas, and

yet . . . Desperation for news of Miles kept her feet moving.

"Are you certain that leaving together is proper?" Isabelle asked worriedly.

Nicholas gave her an encouraging smile. "I guarantee that other couples will be wandering around."

When they stepped outside into the mansion's garden area, Isabelle let her eyes become accustomed to the darkness and then relaxed. Though seeing more than a few feet in front of them was difficult, she spied one couple standing near the stairs that led to the street and decided that she was perfectly safe. Nicholas led her in the opposite direction from the other couple, and when they reached the barrier wall between the Debrett mansion and the adjacent town house, he gave her a weasly smile.

"Well, what news do you have from Miles?" Isabelle demanded.

Unexpectedly, Nicholas grasped her upper arms and yanked her close against his body. Shocked, Isabelle had the absurd thought that he was a lot stronger than she'd imagined.

"Isabelle, I adore you," Nicholas whispered, his lips descending to claim hers.

"Unhand me, you idiot," Isabelle cried, struggling to free herself.

"I love you," he said in a louder voice, his grasp tightening on her. "I want to make you—"

"The lady said to let her go," a voice in the darkness said.

Nicholas dropped his hands, and Isabelle leapt away from him. Whirling around, she saw that her savior was William Grimsby.

"God mend your ways, Nicholas," Isabelle said,

scurrying to her rescuer's side. "William, I'd like to return inside now."

Isabelle and William turned to leave the area, but came face to face with John Saint-Germain. The forbidding expression on her guardian's face frightened Isabelle.

Isabelle tried to explain the situation. "Nicholas lured me outside under false pretenses. William saved me from his advances."

John shifted his dark gaze from her to Grimsby. William nodded once, brushed past them, and disappeared inside Debrett House.

"If you ever engineer my ward into another scandalous position," John warned, sliding his gaze to deJewell, "I will take great pleasure in ending your misbegotten life. Do you understand?"

The Baron of Redesdale bobbed his head up and down and hurried toward the mansion.

"Your stupidity boggles my mind," John said, rounding on her unexpectedly. "Being alone with a man in a dark garden could place you in a compromising position. Your reputation would be ruined, and you would be forced into marriage with the man in question."

Without a word Isabelle whirled away and took one step toward the mansion. John reached out to prevent her escape and gently but firmly forced her to face him again.

"Never walk away from me when I am speaking with you," he growled.

"You are speaking *at* me, Your Grace," she informed him. "I must return inside immediately lest my reputation be tarnished and I am forced to the altar with you. That, I assure you, would be a fate worse than death."

"Your sarcasm is unbecoming," John snapped.

"As is your rudeness."

The anger seemed to rush out of him. "You are correct," John said, surprising her. "I merely want to warn you how dangerous and deceiving men can be."

"You were rude to the Earl of Ripon," Isabelle said. "Why, you never even thanked him for rescuing me."

"Why should I?" John drawled, the hint of a smile tugging at the corners of his lips. "He usurped my duty."

"Your Grace, you are incorrigible."

"Isabelle, listen to me," John said. "Grimsby despises me and will use you if it suits his purpose."

"I cannot believe that," she scoffed. "Why do you dislike each other?"

John looked away. "Grimsby is trying to ruin me financially."

Isabelle stared at him. She sensed he was keeping something from her.

"Look over your marriage prospects and settle on one of them," John ordered. Suddenly, the thought of her married to one of the young swains inside Debrett House troubled him, and that made him feel even more disgruntled. "I want you out of my life as soon as possible," he added. "I'm tired of the responsibility."

"Who the bloody hell asked you to take care of me?" Isabelle said, angry to be a burden on anyone, especially him.

"Your brother," John said in a clipped voice. "Listen, Isabelle. I'm sorry that—"

"I have the headache," Isabelle announced, interrupting his apology. "I am returning to Montgomery House."

"I'll instruct Gallagher to drive you home," John said, offering her his hand.

Isabelle dropped her violet gaze from his face to his offered hand. Lifting her nose into the air, she brushed past him and marched toward the mansion's entrance.

Isabelle refused to forgive the duke's high-handedness until he mended his ways. She vowed to herself not to venture out into society until Giselle reappeared to give her guidance.

Chapter 8

Her stomach growled, protesting the long hours since supper the previous evening. Lord, but she was hungry.

Isabelle looked at herself in the framed, full-length mirror that stood in the corner of her bedchamber. With her thoughts fixed upon the events of the night before, she smoothed the skirt of her white muslin morning dress and turned to leave the chamber.

"Sweet celestial breath," Isabelle exclaimed, surprised to see the old woman sitting in the chair in front of the hearth. "Where have you been for the past week?"

"Here, there, and everywhere," Giselle answered with a nonchalant gesture of her hand. "Were you worried?"

"I missed you," Isabelle said, crossing the bedchamber to sit in the chair beside the old woman's.

"Thank you, child."

"I needed your advice."

"In that case I'm sorry to have been gone for so long," Giselle replied.

"I forgive you."

"To forgive is divine," Giselle said.

"Why were you gone so long?" Isabelle asked. "Do you have other mortals whom you protect?"

"No, child. Every mortal has his or her own guardian angel," Giselle answered. "Why did you need my advice?"

"The Duke of Avon saw you that day in the garden," Isabelle said, lowering her voice to a mere whisper.

"Yes, I know."

"How is that possible? No one has ever seen you before."

The old woman shrugged. "His Grace has a big heart."

"His Grace has no heart."

"Child, how wrong you are," Giselle said. "John Saint-Germain guards his heart against further injury."

"John has been hurt?" Isabelle echoed in surprise. "By whom?"

"His late wife."

"What happened?"

"You know I never indulge in gossip. His Grace must share that with you."

Isabelle gave the old woman a reproachful look.

"You will not persuade me to tell you anything," Giselle said. "If you want to know what happened, then ask him yourself."

"Very well," Isabelle said, then forced herself to change the subject. "When will Miles return?"

"Your brother will be delayed until after the prince and you wed," Giselle told her.

"I have no wish to marry until I fall in love," Isabelle said. "I want to enjoy more days together sitting beside the Avon River."

"I am not of your world and cannot remain with you indefinitely," Giselle said, her voice gentling. "Someday you will sit beside the Avon River again, but your companion will be your own daughter."

Isabelle smiled at the thought of mothering her own child. True, she had no desire to wed at the moment, but she did desire a family of her own one day.

"Accept the Earl of Ripon's invitation to ride with him," Giselle said, drawing her attention.

"The earl hasn't invited me to ride with him," Isabelle told her.

"He will."

"Is William Grimsby the dark prince?"

"Is your vision impaired?" Giselle replied. "William Grimsby is a blond."

Frustrated, Isabelle stood and looked down on her guardian angel, saying, "Oh, you are incorrigible."

"Run along and break your fast," the old woman said with a smile.

Isabelle left her chamber and walked down the corridor. Nearing her stepmother's bedchamber, she heard a familiar voice from within and paused. Revulsion swept through her like a strong gust of wind, but she stepped closer to the door to listen.

"But you told me," Nicholas deJewell was whining.

"I told you to seduce her, not attack her," Delphinia said in a disgusted tone of voice.

"I assumed she'd marry me if I placed her in a compromising position," Nicholas defended himself.

"You assumed incorrectly."

"If it wasn't for that meddling Grimsby I'd have—"

"Nicholas, stop whining," Delphinia ordered. "You sound like an injured dog."

"What are we to do now?" Nicholas asked.

"Stay away from Montgomery House for a week or two," Delphinia told him. "This unfortunate incident shall have been forgotten by that time. You'll need to begin courting her again. And, for God's sake, leave by the servants' stairs; I don't want her to see you.''

Why was Nicholas deJewell so intent upon marrying her when he didn't love her? She was virtually a pauper. Yes, Miles would dower her generously, but why waste time on her when courting an heiress could prove more lucrative?

Isabelle didn't wait to hear more. Wondering about the puzzling conversation, she started down the main staircase. At least she needn't worry about seeing Nicholas for a week or two.

''I'm sorry, my lord,'' she heard Pebbles saying in the foyer below. ''Lady Isabelle hasn't come down yet.''

''I'll leave my card,'' she heard the man reply.

Peering over the banister to the foyer below, Isabelle saw William Grimsby. ''Good day to you, my lord,'' she called, and hurried down the stairs.

Both men turned at the sound of her voice.

The Earl of Ripon smiled. ''You agreed to call me William. Remember?''

Isabelle inclined her head and returned his smile. ''What brings you to Montgomery House?'' she asked.

''I worried for your safety and wished to verify you weren't suffering any ill effects from your experience last evening,'' he told her.

Isabelle blushed. ''I am quite well, but my guardian did give me a stern lecture about being alone with men.''

''For once I agree with Saint-Germain,'' William replied. He raised his brows at her and added, ''I'm positive that my rescuing you failed to lighten his mood.''

''The Duke of Avon is my temporary guardian,'' Isabelle said, ''but he cannot order me about.''

"In that case would you care to ride with me tomorrow morning in Hyde Park?" William asked.

It was just as Giselle had predicted, but Isabelle hesitated before answering. Her guardian would be displeased with her choice of companions, yet the earl had saved her good reputation.

"I see that Saint-Germain's reaction does trouble you," William said.

"I would like very much to ride with you tomorrow." Isabelle accepted his invitation. She gave him her most winsome smile, but appeared more confident than she actually felt.

"Shall we say nine o'clock?"

Isabelle inclined her head. "Nine o'clock will be perfect."

William raised her hand to his lips, murmuring, "It's twenty years until then, my lady."

"Call me Isabelle. Remember?" she said, pleased with his courtly manner.

William grinned. "Until the tomorrow, Isabelle."

After he'd gone, Isabelle stared down at the hand that he'd kissed and regretted her decision. She felt obligated to accept the earl's invitation; he had saved her from her stepmother's nephew. If that wasn't enough, his charming manner attracted her. Most importantly, Giselle had advised her to accept his invitation.

Still, the sinking feeling that she was being disloyal to her guardian overwhelmed her and stole her appetite. She decided to return to her chamber to discuss these new, disturbing emotions with her guardian angel.

Preoccupied with her thoughts, Isabelle crossed the foyer and started to climb the stairs slowly. As if from a great distance she heard the front door's knocker and the majordomo answering it.

"Isabelle!"

The Duke of Avon's voice stopped her in her tracks. His Grace did not sound especially happy.

Isabelle turned around and met his dark gaze. No man ought to be that wickedly handsome, she thought. The duke's dark intensity attracted her as the earl's fair blondness never could.

"Come down here," John ordered. "I want to speak with you."

"Are you planning to apologize for your bad behavior last night?" she asked.

John marched across the foyer to stand at the base of the staircase. "What was Grimsby doing here?" he demanded.

Isabelle stared him straight in the eye and said, "William was concerned for my welfare. . . ." She hesitated, her gaze skittering away from his when she added, "He invited me to ride with him in Hyde Park."

"I forbid you to go anywhere with him."

"You *forbid* me?" Isabelle echoed, incredulous.

"Grimsby is a dangerous man," John told her. "I don't want you to keep company with him."

"I don't give a rat's arse what you want," Isabelle replied. Turning away, she started up the stairs.

Isabelle rose earlier than usual the next morning in order to prepare for her outing in Hyde Park. She wore an ankle-length blue merino gown with high neck and matching, hooded cloak and black kid slippers. Though wearing a hat would have been much more fashionable than a hooded cloak, Isabelle disliked anything sitting on her head, because it made her feel like the limb of a tree playing host to a bird's nest.

All the while Isabelle prepared for her appointment with William Grimsby, the feeling of betraying her guardian grew steadily inside her. She found the guilt oppressive.

"Do you think I should beg off?" Isabelle asked, turning to the old woman, who still sat in the chair in front of the hearth. "I could feign another headache."

"Lying is a terrible sin."

"Yes, but the more one lies, the easier it gets."

"Child, I want you to remember that peacemakers are blessed and will be called children of God," Giselle said, paraphrasing scripture.

"You speak in riddles."

Giselle gave her an ambiguous smile. "Do I?"

Isabelle touched her locket, stared into space, and pondered what the angel was trying to tell her. Suddenly, she rounded on the old woman and said, "I could use this opportunity to make peace between John and William."

"What a wonderful idea," the old woman said.

Isabelle's lips turned up in a rueful smile. "And original too."

"Run along, child. It's already nine of the clock."

Isabelle reached the first floor just as Pebbles was ushering the Earl of Ripon inside. "Good morning, William," she said, wearing a smile of greeting. "I am punctual, as you can see."

"What a delightful departure from the norm," William replied, taking her hand in his.

"What do you mean?"

"Ladies of the ton customarily keep gentlemen waiting," he told her.

Isabelle blushed. "Oh, I didn't know."

"I am glad of that," William said with a smile. "I

guarantee that your radiant beauty will shame the freshness of this exquisite spring morn.''

''Thank you for the pretty compliment,'' Isabelle murmured, pleased. Becoming accustomed to men's flattery could be easy.

''I speak only the truth.'' At that the Earl of Ripon ushered her outside and helped her into his hooded phaeton drawn by two white horses. They started down the road toward Piccadilly.

Isabelle sat back and gazed at her surroundings. She hadn't been up and about like this since leaving Stratford, and she missed her morning walks.

Nature had delivered the clear blue skies of March, month of rebirth and hope. In Stratford, migrating robins would appear this week to graze in the still-brown grass, while amorous starlings would serenade their ladies with courting songs. Crocuses would be breaking free of the thawing earth and opening their petals to the warmth of the sun.

Unexpectedly, a tidal wave of homesickness surged through Isabelle. She sighed with longing for all that was familiar yet forbidden to her until the London season had ended.

''Is something wrong?'' William asked.

Isabelle managed a faint smile for him and shook her head. ''I'm feeling homesick for Stratford.''

''I understand,'' William said, his voice gently sympathetic. ''At times I positively yearn for the solitude of my ancestral home in northern England.''

Isabelle perked up at his words, which mirrored her own emotions. ''We must be kindred souls.''

Reaching the end of Piccadilly, William steered the phaeton right onto Park Lane. From there they drove into Hyde Park.

"Isabelle!" a voice called.

Looking around, Isabelle saw Lobelia riding with Stephen Spewing, the Baron of Barrows. She waved at her stepsister, but the smile of greeting died on her face when she spied the couple on horseback. John Saint-Germain rode with Amanda Stanley.

"Yesterday he rode with Lucy Spencer," William said.

"With whom my guardian rides is of no interest to me," Isabelle lied. "In fact, I can hardly wait for my brother's return so I can be rid of the Duke of Avon."

"I cannot fault you for that," William said.

Blessed are the peacemakers, for they will be called children of God, Isabelle thought. Then she said, "His Grace isn't so bad."

"The devil does possess the power to assume a pleasing shape," William replied, giving her a sidelong glance.

Isabelle turned her violet gaze upon her companion. "Would it be possible for John and you to settle your differences and set aside your anger?"

"What is done cannot be undone," William answered without looking at her.

"What do you mean?"

William halted the phaeton along the side of the lane. Then he stared at her for a long moment.

"John Saint-Germain murdered my sister," he said finally.

Isabelle felt as though she'd been kicked in the stomach. The rosy color drained from her face, and shock made her breathing come in shallow gasps.

"Are you ill?" William asked, leaning close, concern etched across his face.

Isabelle raised her hand in a gesture for him to stay

back. She regained her composure slowly and then defended her guardian.

"My lord, you are mistaken," she began. "His Grace does behave disagreeably at times, but would never—"

"John Saint-Germain married my sister, Lenore, and forced her into an early grave," William said, his eyes gleaming with hatred for her guardian. "I intend to exact my own brand of retribution for her untimely death."

She'd had no idea. Why hadn't John explained the reasons for the animosity between Grimsby and himself?

"I am unwell," Isabelle whispered, shocked by the startling revelation and the unholy gleam in the earl's blue eyes. "Please return me to Montgomery House."

"I never meant to mar our morning," William said, his expression clearing as he regained his own composure.

"I understand, but I need to go home." This time Isabelle's headache was real.

William inclined his head and turned the phaeton the way they had come. They rode in silence the short distance to Berkeley Square. Reaching Montgomery House, William moved to get down and assist her, but she stopped him.

"Don't bother," Isabelle said. Then she leapt in the most unladylike manner out of the phaeton and hurried up the front stairs.

"Isabelle," William called.

Ignoring him, Isabelle flung open the front door and slammed it behind her. Trying to calm her rioting emotions, she closed her eyes and leaned back against the door in an effort to let the solidity of the sturdy oak soothe her nerves.

"My lady, are you ill?" Pebbles asked.

"I am dizzy," Isabelle answered, opening her eyes.

"Let me help you upstairs."

Isabelle shook her head and then regretted the movement. On trembling legs she crossed the foyer and climbed the stairs to the third floor.

"Trying to make peace was the worst thing I could have done," Isabelle cried when she stepped into her bedchamber.

"What is wrong, child?" Giselle asked, looking over her shoulder.

"John Saint-Germain murdered William's sister!"

"At times, child, you astonish me," Giselle said, and then disappeared faster than an eye could blink.

"Don't leave me," Isabelle cried, turning in a circle to see where her angel had vanished. "I need you!"

"You need time alone to think."

She refused to receive visitors for a week.

On the morning of the last day of March, Isabelle sat in one of the chairs in front of the hearth in her bedchamber. Her only companion was her troubled thoughts. She raised her flute to her lips in an effort to banish them, but hadn't the heart to play. If only Giselle hadn't chosen to abandon her in her hour of need.

Isabelle set her flute on the floor beside the chair and took a deep, calming breath. For the past seven days she'd tried to escape those disturbing thoughts. Perhaps she should confront them.

Had William Grimsby spoken truthfully that day in Hyde Park? Did the Duke of Avon murder his wife and then elude justice because of his exalted position in society?

Isabelle couldn't believe John capable of murder. That William Grimsby believed John guilty was the important thing here. In spite of her continuing discord with her guardian, Isabelle knew she owed him a debt for saving her from marriage to her stepmother's nephew. She needed to warn John that Grimsby was plotting revenge against him.

"Now you are thinking more clearly."

Isabelle snapped her head around and saw Giselle sitting in the chair beside hers. "You've finally returned to me," she said, relieved. "Where have you been?"

"Around," Giselle answered with a shrug. "So you believe His Grace incapable of murder?"

"Am I wrong?"

"Never doubt yourself, child."

"Look," Isabelle said, making a sweeping gesture with her hand toward the bedchamber.

The old woman looked around and smiled. The chamber was a garden of violets and forget-me-not bouquets.

"Perhaps that flower girl will knit you a shawl someday," Giselle said dryly.

"What are you talking about?"

Giselle chuckled. "For the past seven days John Saint-Germain has purchased all of that unfortunate girl's flowers and sent them here."

"How do you know where he bought them?"

"I've been watching and listening," the old woman told her.

"I haven't seen you."

"Child, would a guardian angel abandon the mortal she's promised to protect?"

"You've been at Montgomery House for all of this time?" Isabelle asked.

"Does the fact that you can't see me mean I'm gone?" Giselle asked. "You can't see or touch love, yet it exists."

Isabelle nodded in understanding. "As does hatred," she added, thinking of William Grimsby.

"Hatred is such a negative emotion. Peace is found only when you concentrate on love," Giselle told her. "I've appeared today because you are thinking clearly, and I want to advise you about what to do."

Isabelle stared at her expectantly.

"Early tomorrow morning you must go alone to Saint-Germain Court and confront His Grace about what the earl told you," Giselle said.

"I can't do that," Isabelle protested. "Visiting a gentleman is improper and would ruin my reputation."

"No one will see you early in the morning," Giselle argued. "Besides, tomorrow is the first day of April, when misrule is accepted. The fool's festival commences at dawn and ends at noon."

"I don't know," Isabelle said. "What if—"

"Why are you mortals so foolishly inconsistent?" Giselle interrupted, obviously irritated. "When I remain silent, you plead for advice; but when I offer advice, you tell me you can't accept it. Fortune favors the bold. Child, have I ever led you astray?"

Isabelle shook her head and looked contrite. "I apologize for being so difficult and will defer to your divine wisdom."

"Thank God for tiny miracles," Giselle mumbled, rolling her eyes heavenward.

At precisely eight o'clock the following morning, Isabelle opened her bedchamber door a crack and listened for footsteps. All remained silent. She peeked out the door and verified that the corridor was deserted. Glancing back at her old friend, she whispered, "Wish me luck."

"Enjoy your adventure," Giselle replied.

Stepping into the corridor, Isabelle noiselessly closed the door behind her and then hurried toward the servants' stairway in the rear of the mansion. Dressed in a hooded black cloak and black boots, Isabelle looked like a peasant girl on her way to market. She wore a light-weight woolen skirt and a white linen, scooped-neck blouse beneath her cloak. Appearing too rich while walking London's streets could prove dangerous. Or so Giselle had advised her.

Isabelle walked into the kitchen, startling the household staff, and gave them a sunny smile. "I couldn't sleep and decided I need fresh air," she announced, brushing past them.

"Fresh air in London?" she heard one of the scullery maids whisper.

Reaching the area outside, Isabelle pulled the cloak's hood up to cover her blond hair and hurried to the stairs that led to the street. She left Berkeley Square and walked briskly down Piccadilly, which intersected Park Lane, where her guardian lived.

Fifteen minutes later Isabelle stood outside Saint-Germain Court. She glanced around, but the street was deserted. Racing up the front stairs, she reached for the knocker and banged it as hard as she could. She hoped to get inside before any passerby noticed her.

The door swung open to reveal the majordomo.

"Dobbs," she said, relieved.

"Mistress Montgomery, what are you doing here?" the man asked, obviously surprised.

"I must speak with His Grace." Her tone of voice implied urgency.

Dobbs stepped back, allowing her entrance, and said, "Hurry, my lady, lest someone see you." He shut the door behind her.

Isabelle glanced around the foyer, but extreme agitation prevented her from noticing its understated opulence. The only thing she focused on was her good fortune in arriving undetected and, more importantly, what she had come to discuss with the duke.

"His Grace hasn't come down yet," Dobbs informed her. "Would you care to wait in the drawing room?"

Uncertain of what to do, Isabelle worried her full bottom lip with her white teeth. Delaying this interview could result in discovery for her.

"Which chamber is his?" she asked, marching across the foyer toward the marble staircase.

"Mistress Montgomery," Dobbs exclaimed in a scandalized voice.

With her booted foot on the bottom step, Isabelle said over her shoulder, "I must leave in a few minutes lest my absence from Montgomery House be discovered."

"His Grace's apartment is located on the third floor, the first door on the right," Dobbs told her.

Isabelle raced up the stairs and didn't stop until she reached the door. Insecurity and doubt made her pause for a long moment. Through sheer force of will she raised her hand and knocked on the door.

"Enter," she heard the duke call from within.

Isabelle opened the door and stepped inside, but then nearly swooned at the sight that greeted her. Just finishing his morning ablutions, her guardian wore only dark trousers and a black silk bedrobe.

"I thought you already laid out my clothing, Dobbs," John said, wiping soapsuds from his face.

Isabelle stood there and said nothing.

John turned around slowly. Shocked anger registered on his handsome face, and then he tossed the towel on the floor.

"What are you doing here?" John demanded, crossing the chamber toward her. "You must leave at once."

"I have a matter of importance to discuss with you," Isabelle told him, stubborn determination stamped across her delicate features. "I am staying where I am until we speak."

"If anyone knew you were here, your reputation would be ruined beyond repair," he said.

"I don't give a rat's arse about my reputation."

"Then wait for me in the drawing room," John said, the hint of a smile touching his lips as he opened the door for her to leave.

Isabelle shook her head. "My stepmother doesn't know I've left Montgomery House. You are wasting time."

John inclined his head, deferring to her wishes. He gestured toward the elegant Grecian couch perched in front of the hearth. "Let us sit down and discuss what is so important."

Isabelle glanced from her devastatingly handsome guardian to the Grecian couch and then wet her lips, gone dry from sudden nervousness. Squaring her shoulders with determination, she walked past him and sat down on the edge of the couch, but struggled against bolting off it when he sat down beside her.

Gazing at her trembling hands folded in her lap, Isabelle realized he sat so close she could feel the warmth of his thigh against her own. A thousand airy butterflies took wing in the pit of her stomach. Never had she been so intimately close with a man. Why, for God's sake, did he have to be so handsome?

Lifting her gaze to his, Isabelle felt as if she was drowning in the black, fathomless pools of his eyes. She couldn't seem to find her voice. "Thank you for the flowers," she managed finally.

"You are very welcome," he said, giving her an easy smile. "Now, what is so important you need to endanger your reputation?"

"William Grimsby is spreading poisonous gossip about you," Isabelle told him, a frown troubling her features. She hesitated and then pressed on, "He insists you murdered your late wife."

"And do you believe what he says?" John asked, gently taking her hand in his.

"Don't be a pebble brain. You could never harm anyone."

John smiled at that.

"Grimsby's belief endangers you," she warned.

"Do not trouble yourself about William," John replied. "My former brother-in-law is a harmless gossipmonger and inept in his efforts to ruin me."

"The earl wants retribution for his sister's death," Isabelle argued. "I've seen the hatred shining in his eyes when your name is mentioned."

"You risked your reputation to warn me?"

"Something like that," Isabelle murmured, dropping her gaze to her lap.

Unexpectedly, John lifted her hand to his lips and then gently forced her to look at him. "Lenore Grimsby died miscarrying our first child."

"Oh, John, I'm so sorry," Isabelle said, placing the palm of her hand against his cheek.

John turned his head and planted a kiss on the palm of her comforting hand. "Your eyes are the most startling shade of violet. A man could lose himself within their depths,'' he said hoarsely. "I've tried to keep my distance from you.''

Isabelle stared at him in mesmerized fascination as his face slowly inched its way to hers. The sight of his lips descending to hers made her heart beat faster with anticipation.

She closed her eyes. Their lips met. His mouth felt warm and gently insistent on hers, and his masculine scent of mountain heather intoxicated her senses.

The persuasive feel of his mouth slashing across hers made Isabelle weak. His strong arms encircled her and drew her against the solidity of his body as her arms encircled his neck.

Isabelle reveled in these new and exciting sensations and returned his kiss in kind. When he flicked his tongue across the crease of her mouth, she parted her lips for him like a flower blossoming in the heat of the noonday sun. In an instant his tongue invaded her mouth—probing, exploring, tasting its incredible sweetness.

Isabelle shivered within his embrace and surrendered to his possession. Losing herself in his drugging kiss, she followed his lead and stroked his tongue with her own.

Swept away on wings of yearning, Isabelle· fell back on the couch. Ever so gently John rained feathery-light kisses on her temples, her eyelids, her throat.

When his lips returned to hers, Isabelle realized in some distant, still-rational part of her mind that he'd unfastened her cloak and pulled her blouse down to reveal her breasts to his dark gaze. But she didn't care. And then his scorching lips followed his gaze.

Isabelle burned with desire. Beyond reason, she molded her young body to his. . . .

Chapter 9

"John Saint-Germain, unhand that innocent girl!"

Dazed with desire, John turned his head and gazed toward the angry voice. At the same moment he heard the woman beneath him gasp with embarrassment.

God's knob, John cursed inwardly, now fully alert to what was happening. His own mother stood in his bedchamber while he lay on top of his half-naked ward.

"Cover yourself when I move," he whispered against Isabelle's ear.

John rose from the Grecian couch and blocked his mother's view of Isabelle quickly yanking her blouse up. As he faced his mother, John realized the situation was much worse than he'd first thought. His bedchamber seemed more crowded than a Drury Lane performance.

Trying to outface them, John looked in turn at each person. His mother appeared livid with outrage, as did his aunt. Standing in the corridor outside his chamber, Delphinia Montgomery wore a shocked expression. Most infuriating of all was his brother's reaction. Ross stood there grinning like a blinking idiot. Bloody hell, he felt like an errant schoolboy caught in the act with his first woman.

John flicked a glance at Isabelle when she stood beside him a moment later. The poor girl clutched her cloak protectively around herself, and her rosy blush of newly awakened desire had faded into a ghostly white.

"I'm sorry, Your Grace," Dobbs spoke up from where he stood just behind the intruders. "I tried to divert them to the drawing room."

"I appreciate your efforts," John said to his man. "Continue with your regular duties."

The majordomo turned on his heels and left the bed-chamber.

John rounded on the others, intending to order them down to the drawing room, but saw Delphinia Montgomery crossing the chamber toward him. Understanding that the woman was upset at finding her step-daughter in this predicament, he stood in silence as she advanced on him. Instead of confronting him, she stopped in front of Isabelle.

Unexpectedly, Delphinia Montgomery raised her hand to slap Isabelle. Only John's quick reflexes prevented the impact.

"If you ever raise your hand to my affianced wife, I will make you the sorriest woman in England," John threatened, grabbing the woman's wrist in a firm grip.

"Your affianced wife?" Isabelle echoed, surprised.

"Oh, what excellent news," the dowager exclaimed.

Aunt Hester nodded in agreement, saying, "I always knew you raised your sons correctly, Tessa."

John ignored all three of them. Instead, his dark gaze remained fixed on Delphinia. "Do you understand my warning, Lady Montgomery?" he asked.

Delphinia inclined her head. "There's no need to ruin your life," she said. "Nicky will marry the chit."

"I won't marry deJewell," Isabelle cried.

"Her marrying your nephew is out of the question,"

John said. "Belle has promised to marry me. Haven't you, my love?"

Isabelle would have agreed to anything in order to escape marriage with Nicholas deJewell. "Yes, I've accepted His Grace's proposal," she said without hesitation. "I'm positive that Miles will approve when he returns."

"Ross, escort everyone to the drawing room so I can finish dressing," John instructed his brother. "I'll join you there shortly."

"Mistress Montgomery, I insist you allow me to escort you," Ross said as she crossed the chamber to the door. "You won't swoon on me now, will you?"

Isabelle shook her head. John could just imagine the wan smile that probably appeared on her adorable face.

"Well, of course she won't swoon," Aunt Hester was rambling as the others filed out of the chamber. "Dear Isabelle is built of sturdier stuff than that. Don't you think so, Tessa?"

"Most definitely," his mother agreed, walking out of the room. "That's why she's a perfect match for my son."

Ten minutes later John walked into the drawing room and paused. Both Montgomery women looked as if someone had died. Still pale, Isabelle perched on the edge of the red velvet Grecian chaise and leaned heavily against its carved, gilded arm. Her stepmother sat in a chair facing her and shot furious looks at her.

Why would a woman so obviously bent on social climbing protest her stepdaughter's marriage to him? John wondered. He was England's premier duke and considered by all as the decade's finest marriage catch.

"Before we discuss specifics," John said, drawing their attention, "I want to know why all of you chose this precise moment to descend upon Saint-Germain Court.''

Ross spoke first. ''I was returning home after a rather late night when the thought struck me that I should come here without delay.''

''I suffered from the same thought,'' his mother said. ''I felt that either you or Isabelle was in some sort of trouble.''

''I just knew Isabelle was here,'' Delphinia said. ''It was almost as if a voice whispered in my ear.''

''That's it precisely,'' Ross agreed.

''I felt the same sensation,'' the dowager added.

''Do you know anything about this?'' John asked, turning to Isabelle.

''I heard no voice,'' she answered, seemingly surprised by his question.

''Who knew that you were on your way to Saint-Germain Court?'' John asked, a hard edge to his voice.

Isabelle opened her mouth as if to reply, but then closed it again. She shifted her gaze to the opposite side of the drawing room and answered finally, ''Only God knew my destination.''

She's lying, John decided, staring hard at her. He knew that as surely as he knew that she'd just duped him into marrying her. There was no other plausible explanation for the morning's events. She was just like Lenore. Christ, had he learned nothing from his disastrous first marriage?

''A mystery, to be sure. We'll consider that subject closed for the moment and discuss specifics,'' John said, unwilling to accuse Isabelle of lying in front of his mother, who obviously liked the chit. He turned to his mother and said, ''You and Aunt Hester will need to plan the wedding with Lady Montgomery's help. Of course, I shall assume all of the expenses."

"Oh, what fun we shall have," the dowager exclaimed.

"Tessa, I've never actually planned a wedding before," Aunt Hester said.

"There's nothing to it, I'm certain," the dowager replied. "It's like planning a ball."

"The ceremony will take place in Stratford at Holy Trinity Church, with a reception to follow at Avon Park for two hundred," John said. "The twenty-fourth day of June seems like a good day to me."

"That only gives us eleven weeks in which to prepare," his mother protested.

"We'll need eleven months at least," Aunt Hester added.

"Take the eleven weeks," John said in a voice that brooked no argument, "or we'll elope to Gretna Green."

Both older women gasped at the potential scandal. Ross chuckled.

Turning to Delphinia, John said, "I will arrive at Montgomery House this afternoon at five o'clock. Be ready for the signing of the betrothal contract."

Looking decidedly unhappy, Delphinia managed to nod her head once.

"I want no slanderous gossip spread about Isabelle," John said. "As a reward for keeping silent, I will help your daughters win offers of marriage from Spewing and Hancock. I assume those two gentlemen are their intended victims?"

"I wouldn't describe their intentions in exactly those terms," Delphinia said coldly.

"Let's not quibble about semantics, dear stepmother-in-law," John said with a smile that did not quite reach his eyes. "Do we have a bargain?"

"Yes, Your Grace."

"Since everything is settled for the moment, I must ask everyone to excuse me," John said in dismissal. "Ross, linger a moment. I want to speak privately with you."

Dowager Tessa, Aunt Hester, and Delphinia Montgomery rose from their seats. Only Isabelle remained where she was.

"No one asked me what I want," she said in a voice barely louder than a whisper.

John reached out and, taking her hand in his, helped her rise from her perch on the chaise. He gazed into the most disarming violet eyes he'd ever seen.

"My love, you will soon become a duchess," he told her. "What more could you desire?"

Those violet eyes of hers glittered with anger, and her gaze shot daggers at him.

John couldn't credit what he was witnessing. The blond witch from Stratford was behaving as if *she* was the injured party instead of the scheming minx who'd skillfully arranged it all. Too bad she wasn't a man. The government could definitely use her talents.

"I'll see you later today," John said. "You'll be feeling better by then. In the meantime, prepare a list of whom you wish to invite to the wedding."

Dowager Tessa slipped her arm through Isabelle's and led her out of the drawing room. Aunt Hester and Delphinia Montgomery followed behind.

"I thought you despised blondes," Ross said as soon as the ladies had gone.

John gave his brother an unamused look. "I don't

understand how that little witch trapped me," he said. "She couldn't have known that I'd even be home."

"Isabelle Montgomery is no witch," Ross replied. "She's exactly what she appears to be. Your previous marriage colors your judgment, though I don't understand why. Miscarrying a babe and dying in the process was Lenore's fate, not her fault."

"What other explanation do you have for all of you descending upon Saint-Germain Court at that precise moment?" John asked, ignoring his brother's mention of Lenore.

"I have no explanation," Ross answered. "Admit it, brother. You've wanted Isabelle Montgomery since the first moment you set your gaze upon her."

"A man should always be careful for what he wishes," John said, sarcasm lacing his voice.

"If you say so. Brother, I have a feeling you'll never regret marrying Isabelle Montgomery," Ross said. "My regret is that she doesn't have a sister just like her."

"Isabelle has two stepsisters," John said with a smile. "I'm certain I could arrange something."

"Do me no favors."

"Something puzzles me," John told his brother. "Why do you think Delphinia objected to Belle's marrying me?"

Ross shrugged. "Probably she'd entertained hopes that one of her daughters could catch your affections."

"Not bloody likely," John said, a wholly disgusted look appearing on his face. "I don't believe Lady Montgomery had hopes in that direction. What her motives are remain to be seen." He smiled at his brother and asked, "Will you be my best man?"

"I'd be honored," Ross answered. "I wonder what Miles Montgomery will say when he returns."

"The Earl of Stratford did instruct me to marry his sister if I wished," John replied.

Ross chuckled. "I doubt he thought you'd take him up on the offer. Is there anything I can do?"

"Inform *The Times* that the Duke of Avon has decided to remarry and tell them who the young lady is," John answered. "While you do that, I'll need to speak with my solicitor to give him instructions concerning the betrothal agreement, and then I'll need to search London's finest jewelry shops for a betrothal ring."

Ross nodded and started to leave.

"Be at Montgomery House by five o'clock," John called after him. "I'll need a witness for the signing."

After his brother had gone, John sauntered across the drawing room to gaze out the window. He hoped his brother was correct about Isabelle being exactly what she seemed. He intended this marriage to be far different from his first. Yes, Isabelle Montgomery was scheming and devious, but John knew he wanted her. Badly.

"You played me for an April fool."

Standing at the window, Isabelle stared accusingly at the old woman who sat, as usual, in the chair in front of the hearth.

"Child, I don't understand what you mean," Giselle replied, her expression blankly innocent.

"Do you ever do anything except sit in that chair and create problems for me?" Isabelle asked, irritated by the obvious lie. How could one of God's celestial beings lie with a straight face?

"Be careful, or I'll go away," Giselle warned. "Now, what problem have I created for you?"

"Your meddling has placed me in an untenable position," Isabelle told her.

Giselle gifted her with a mischievous smile. "Consider it divine intervention, child. Want to play our flutes?"

"No, I do not want to play my flute," Isabelle answered, her anger apparent in her voice. She walked across the chamber and studied her image in the framed, full-length mirror. "As you can see I am dressed for my betrothal to His Grace, who will be arriving at any moment."

"You look very pretty," the old woman complimented her. "Remember, there are worse things in life than marrying John Saint-Germain."

Ignoring her guardian angel, Isabelle looked at her image in the mirror and, though pleased by what she saw, wondered why the Duke of Avon would want to marry her. Her evening dress had been fashioned in black velvet trimmed with gold cord. Its bodice was squared and had long sleeves. Wishing to keep her appearance simple, she'd woven her golden hair into a knot at the nape of her neck. Her only ornament was her locket of gold with her mother's miniature inside.

"Between the color of that gown and your severe hair, you are decidedly out of fashion," Giselle remarked. "Perhaps you should consider changing into a more festive gown. What will society say when they hear that you wore black to your betrothal?"

"Wearing black is a statement," Isabelle informed her. "If I cared what society thought, I wouldn't be speaking with you."

"A point well taken," Giselle said, the hint of a smile appearing upon her wizened face. "Have you been taking 'nasty lessons' from those stepsisters of yours?''

Isabelle smiled in spite of herself. She crossed the chamber to sit in the chair beside the old crone's. Reaching for the woman's gnarled hand, she said, ''I apologize for my rudeness. But where is the dark prince you promised me?''

Giselle shook her head as if disheartened by her charge's question. ''Child, John Saint-Germain is the dark prince.''

''I cannot believe that.''

''I've said many times that princes don't always wear crowns.''

''John doesn't resemble the man whose image I saw in the river,'' Isabelle argued, unwilling to believe what she was hearing.

''You saw him through a ten-year-old's eyes,'' Giselle said. ''Now you are a woman and were certainly attracted to him this morning.''

Isabelle blushed, embarrassed that her guardian angel might have been in attendance while John and she . . . She forced that disturbing thought out of her mind. A knock on the door drew their attention.

''Yes?'' Isabelle called.

''My lady, everyone has gathered in the drawing room,'' the majordomo informed her.

''Thank you, Mister Pebbles.''

Isabelle left her chamber and walked slowly down the main staircase to the second floor, where the drawing room was located. The door had been left open, but before stepping into view she heard one of her stepsisters complaining.

''I cannot believe Isabelle managed to wring an offer from the duke,'' Rue was whining.

The telltale sound of a slap followed this statement, and then her stepmother's voice, saying, "For once in your life keep those lips shut."

Isabelle touched her locket, squared her shoulders, and marched into the drawing room. She stopped short almost instantly, feeling conspicuous when everyone turned in her direction. She reached up to touch her locket again when the duke's brother chuckled.

"She's wearing black to her own betrothal," Lobelia exclaimed.

Delphinia raised her voice to scold her, saying, "Isabelle Montgomery, I demand that you return upstairs and—"

John held his hand up in a gesture for silence and then crossed the drawing room to her. His dark gaze held hers captive, but Isabelle wasn't in the least afraid. She noted the corners of his lips twitching with a barely suppressed smile.

Surprising her with his lack of anger, John gazed deeply into her eyes. Then he lifted her hand and pressed a kiss on it.

"Belle, you look beautiful," he said in a quiet voice. "I consider myself the most fortunate of men."

Isabelle wondered briefly if he was making fun of her. Whatever his intent, she needed to speak with him privately and offer him the opportunity to back out of this arrangement.

"Your Grace, may I—"

"There's no need for formality after the intimacy we shared this morning," he interrupted, lowering his voice so that only she could hear him.

Isabelle blushed a vivid scarlet.

John placed the palm of his hand against her burning cheek and then held it up, asking her, "Is it scorched?"

Isabelle flicked a glance toward their audience. "I must speak with you before we sign the contract."

John inclined his head in agreement. "We'll return shortly," he told the others. Gesturing to her, he said, "Let's go to your brother's office."

In silence Isabelle led John to the end of the corridor. Every fiber of her being was aware of his masculine presence beside her.

When they entered the study, John closed the door behind them and then dragged the chair in front of the hearth over to the desk. He sat in her brother's chair, leaving her to sit like a supplicant in the other. His gesture of authority was not lost on her.

Isabelle folded her hands in her lap and stared at them lest she lose her courage. "You needn't marry me, you know."

"Are you rejecting your hands or me?" John asked.

Isabelle snapped her gaze to his and amended herself. "I am merely offering you the opportunity to forget this absurd notion of marriage."

"Why do you call it absurd?"

"We scarcely know each other."

John smiled. "Ask me anything."

"Where will we live?" she asked, pouncing on her dislike of London.

"We will live wherever you wish," he answered.

No help there.

"I prefer Stratford to London," Isabelle told him.

"Then we will pass most of the year in Stratford," John said, easily deferring to her wishes.

Sweet celestial breath, Isabelle thought. She'd never seen the duke so agreeable and harmonious.

"Is there anything else that is bothering you?" he asked.

"I want a home filled with children," she answered.

"And so do I, my love."

"You needn't call me *my love* when we are alone," Isabelle said, irritated by his cavalier use of a term of endearment. "As you know, I am deeply religious. I plan to name my daughters after the seven virtues."

"And what would those be?" John asked, dropping the words *my love*.

Isabelle stared at him, surprised by his lack of religious training. "Faith, hope, charity, prudence, temperance, justice, and fortitude are the virtues."

John raised his eyebrows at her. "Fortitude Saint-Germain?"

Isabelle gave him the sweetest smile she could muster and nodded. She thought he might reconsider his offer, but his next statement caught her completely off guard.

"I'm partial to the seven deadly sins, especially sloth," John told her, his expression solemn. "I would like to name our sons after them."

Isabelle stared at him in disbelief. "Sloth Saint-Germain?" she exclaimed.

"It has a nice sound to it." He chuckled, ruining the effect, and said, "I'm teasing you, Belle. Is there anything else?"

Isabelle shook her head. "I have no experience with this marriage business so I don't really know what to ask."

"I understand," John said. "Have you prepared your list of guests?"

"I left it here," Isabelle said, leaning across the desk to retrieve the paper she'd placed there that afternoon. She passed the list to him.

John opened the neatly folded paper and then lifted

his gaze to hers. "You've written only three names here," he said. "Miles, Pebbles, and Juniper."

"Those three are the only people in the world I consider family and friends," she explained.

"What about your stepfamily?" he asked.

"I've never considered them family."

"Why?"

Isabelle dropped her gaze to her lap, certain she'd see pity in his eyes. "They never considered me their family."

"Nevertheless, Delphinia and her daughters need to be invited," John told her.

"Well, I suppose so," she acquiesced. "Let them sit on your side of the church."

John burst out laughing. Isabelle smiled, realizing how foolish she sounded.

"Miles may not have returned by then," John said, looking at her list. "Pebbles is your majordomo. Who is Juniper?"

"Mrs. Juniper was my nanny until the day my father died," Isabelle said. "I consider her family."

"How old were you when your father died?" John asked.

"Ten years."

He snapped his eyebrows together. "Why did Mrs. Juniper leave your service? You probably needed her more than ever in that sad hour."

"Delphinia said she fired Juniper because she drank cold tea. Cold tea or hot tea, what is the difference? No, the real reason is, Juniper loved me and disliked my stepsisters," Isabelle answered.

John appeared to be struggling against a smile, but then lost. "Darling, cold tea is a euphemism for brandy. Apparently, Mrs. Juniper liked her spirits," he told her.

"Could Juniper help us with our children?" Isabelle asked. "I know she'd love to live with us."

"I'll think about it," John said without committing himself.

"Since Miles will be away, I would like Mister Pebbles to give the bride away," Isabelle announced, knowing he would veto her idea.

"I cannot allow that," John said, scowling. "Pebbles is a servant, and his presence at the altar will make us the laughingstock of society."

"Pebbles is family to me," she protested.

"You'll walk down the aisle alone if need be," John told her. "I do grant Pebbles permission to sit with Mrs. Juniper in the front of the church."

"What a noble gesture," Isabelle said, her sarcasm matching his. Trying to aggravate him, she asked, "And what about my guardian angel? Where will she sit?"

"Angels can sit wherever they want," John replied with an infuriating smile. "Is there anything else?"

"No."

John stood, but instead of walking to the door, he knelt on one bended knee in front of her. He gazed into the violet pools of her eyes and took her hands in his, saying, "Isabelle Montgomery, will you do me the honor of becoming my wife and my duchess?"

Surprised and touched by his tenderness, Isabelle smiled and nodded. "Yes, John, I will marry you."

John reached into his pocket and withdrew a small velvet-covered box. He opened its lid and lifted a ring.

"I scoured London until I saw this," he said, slipping the ring onto her finger.

Isabelle looked down at her betrothal ring, the likes of which she'd never seen. Amethyst petals, surrounded by leaves of emeralds, lay on a diamond snowbed.

''The jeweler called it 'violets in the snow,' which is what you remind me of—a lovely violet in the snow,'' John said in a voice suddenly gone husky.

Isabelle raised her gaze to his, and her heart soared with happiness. Her angel's long-ago prophecy was coming true. John Saint-Germain *was* the dark prince she'd once glimpsed in the Avon River.

Chapter 10

Marrying Isabelle Montgomery was a mistake.

That thought crashed into John's consciousness for the hundredth time since becoming betrothed to her five days earlier. He'd already married one flighty woman who had hurt him in the end, and Isabelle seemed even flightier than the first. At least Lenore Grimsby had feigned love at the beginning; Isabelle Montgomery was decidedly reluctant.

So why did he desire a woman who didn't want him? John wondered. Was it her plucky spirit that appealed to him? Or did her exquisite loveliness attract him? Was he destined always to be undone by women?

John stood in his office at Saint-Germain Court and stared out the window at the enormous garden area. He preferred his office in the back of the town house overlooking the garden because there were fewer distractions caused by street traffic. When he tired of his business ledgers and contracts and reports, he could stretch his legs and gaze outside without being bothered by the unwelcome sight of carriages and people. Today the privacy was no friend; it gave him the opportunity to ponder his latest mistake—namely, his engagement to Isabelle Montgomery.

Giving himself a mental shake, John concentrated on the new life emerging in his garden. Yellow daffodils nodded gaily at the forsythia. The ground near the house was a mass of purple violets, reminding him of Isabelle.

"Excuse me, Your Grace."

At the sound of his majordomo's voice, John turned away from the window. "Yes, Dobbs?"

"Baron Barrows has arrived, Your Grace."

"Please send him to me," John instructed, taking his seat behind the mahogany desk.

Dobbs inclined his head and left the room. A moment later the majordomo returned with the baron and, at a glance from his employer, closed the study door to ensure that the two men enjoyed privacy.

"Have a seat, Spewing," John said, gesturing to the chair in front of the desk.

"Thank you, Your Grace." Stephen Spewing sat down and stole a quick peek at the study. "I admire your taste in furnishings, Your Grace."

"I find my office comfortable," John said, reaching for the crystal decanter and two crystal glasses perched on a sterling-silver tray that had been set on his desk. "Care for a whiskey?"

"Yes, Your Grace."

John made a show of pouring two drams of whiskey and passed one to the baron. Then he held his glass up in a salute and said, "To your prosperity and happiness."

"And to yours, Your Grace," the younger man returned the good wishes.

Both men drank their whiskey.

"Congratulations on your forthcoming nuptials, Your Grace," Spewing said.

"Oh, so you've heard the good news?" John asked, leveling his dark gaze on the man.

"Indeed, Your Grace, all of London is talking about

it," the younger man began. Then, as if fearing the duke would be angered by his listening to gossip, he added, "*The Times* printed the announcement."

"Yes, I know," John said with a smile, pouring them another round of whiskey. "However, I haven't invited you here to discuss my marriage. At the moment I'm interested in *your* marriage."

"*My* marriage?" Spewing echoed in surprise. "I don't understand, Your Grace."

"As you know, I am temporary guardian for the Montgomery girls," John said, stretching the truth a bit. "What exactly are your intentions toward Lobelia?"

"Strictly honorable, I assure you," Spewing answered, fidgeting nervously in his chair. "I harbor a deep fondness for Lobelia."

"I thought you did," John replied, relaxing in his chair. "The man who offers for Lobelia will gain a very generous dowry, and as my brother-by-marriage, he will receive an interest—albeit small—in a few of my businesses." John paused for effect and let that bit of information seep into the other man's brain. "I have always held you in the highest esteem and would like very much if you were the gentleman who profited by marriage to Lobelia. I grant you she's not much to look at, but—"

"I find Lobelia to be utterly delightful," Spewing interrupted him. "As they say, beauty is in the eye of the beholder."

John nodded. "So you are considering offering for her?"

"I would like to offer for her right now if I have your permission," Spewing told him.

"You have my approval," John replied. "However, I prefer you propose to her after my betrothal party, which will be held at my mother's residence on the twenty-third of April. Isabelle will be miffed if Lobelia's good news diverts attention away from her. You know how women are.''

''I understand, Your Grace.''

John rose from his chair in a silent signal that their interview was finished. Taking his cue, Spewing also stood.

John walked around his desk and shook the younger man's hand, saying, ''To our prosperous future as brothers-in-law.'' Then he escorted him to the mahogany double doors that led to the corridor.

''I'll name our first daughter Fortuna in honor of the ancient goddess of luck,'' Spewing rambled in obvious excitement. ''I am the most fortunate of men in winning your approval, Your Grace.''

John nodded like a prince accepting his due from a loyal subject. ''We'll discuss business after your betrothal is announced.''

John opened the door for the younger man. Walking down the corridor to his study was his brother Ross.

''Thank you again, Your Grace,'' Spewing said before taking his leave. ''I do appreciate your confidence in me.''

With that Baron Barrows started down the corridor. He nodded to Ross as they passed each other.

Ross walked into his brother's study and sat in the chair vacated by the baron. He poured himself a dram of whiskey and sat back in the chair.

''Your Grace, I do appreciate your confidence in me,'' Ross said in a perfect imitation of the baron's eagerness. ''May I kiss the ground upon which you walk? Would you like me to lick the dirt off your boots?''

John sat down behind his desk. He poured himself a whiskey and raised it in salute to his brother. "I've just neatly trapped my first intended victim. Spewing will offer for Lobelia directly after my betrothal party."

"And what about the other intended victim?" Ross asked.

"I'll wait until I'm married to ensnare Hancock," John told him. "I wouldn't want to appear too obvious in paying for Delphinia's silence. Besides, two such quick offers of marriage for two of the plainest girls I've ever seen will be suspect to society, and I cannot make a laughingstock out of them. If I wait until autumn, Hancock's proposal will seem more of his own doing."

"That's very devious of you," Ross remarked.

"I'll take that as a compliment," John replied.

"My words were intended as high praise."

John smiled. "Now, what can I do for you?"

"Nothing. I'm here to do something for you."

"What a strange change in your behavior. Are you ill?"

"Very funny," Ross said with a smile. "Seriously, I've just left White's, where I saw the most amazing sight."

"What was that?"

"A meeting of the Vanquished Club."

John cocked a dark eyebrow at his brother.

"William Grimsby and Nicholas deJewell sat together and seemed involved in an important conversation," Ross told him. "Their heads were bent close and their voices were low. In short, Grimsby and deJewell appear to have joined forces against a common enemy—namely, you."

"Thank you for the warning, but I'm certain I can handle them," John said, rising from his chair. "If you'll excuse me? I intend to pay a visit to my sweet betrothed."

"Want some company?" Ross asked.

"No, thank you."

Fifteen minutes later John walked into the main foyer at Montgomery House. The faint sound of flute playing wafted through the air.

"Lady Isabelle is in the drawing room, Your Grace," the majordomo said, escorting him to the stairs.

"Don't bother, Pebbles," John said. "I know the way."

The music of her flute playing grew louder as he neared the drawing room. Her melody held a jaunty air, like a bird call in summer or sparkling sunbeams dancing across the top of a crystal blue lake. Yes, his fiancée was definitely in high spirits that day.

John paused in the drawing room's doorway and watched Isabelle. With her hair of spun gold and her pert profile and her gown of pale pink, she appeared almost angelic.

As if she felt his intense stare, Isabelle turned her head and saw him standing there. She stopped playing instantly and gave him a smile that rivaled her hair for brightness.

"Good morning, John," she greeted him.

"I still do not understand how you make your flute sound as if two people were playing," John said, crossing the drawing room to sit beside her on the couch.

Isabelle's eyes sparkled with mischief. "My guardian angel accompanies me. I do admit that she plays better than I."

"Very well, keep your musical secrets to yourself," John said with a smile.

"You don't believe in guardian angels?" Isabelle cast

him an unconsciously flirtatious look. "How about drawing-room acoustics?"

John burst out laughing. She was the most impertinent, charming minx he'd ever met.

"I see you are blessedly alone," he remarked.

"Delphinia and her daughters are making a round of social calls," she told him.

"And that sort of activity holds no appeal for you?" John asked, though he already knew the answer.

"Not in the least."

"I've sent Mrs. Juniper her invitation to our wedding and enough money to purchase a suitable gown to wear," John told her.

"I would have done that," Isabelle said. "Couldn't we wait for Miles to return? I am his only sister."

John hesitated before answering. Friction between England and the United States was growing with each passing day. Hostilities seemed imminent. If their brothers were still in New York when war erupted, they could be delayed for its duration, but that wasn't something he wanted to bother his fiancée about.

"Waiting for our brothers to return is impossible," John said, his tone of voice brooking no argument. He leaned close and inhaled her violet scent, saying, "You smell good enough to eat."

Isabelle blushed. She changed the subject by telling him, "My guardian angel told me a long, long time ago that you would enter my life."

"He knew of my existence before we met?"

"My angel is a *she,* named Giselle, who knows many things that we humans do not," she informed him. "Giselle told me that I would marry a dark prince."

"Giselle, is it?" John echoed, cocking a dark brow at

her. "I'm a duke but thank you for the elevation in rank."

"Princes don't always wear crowns," Isabelle replied. "Or so Giselle says."

"The old girl has common sense," he said with a smile. "Before I forget, would you like to ride with me tomorrow in Hyde Park?"

"I'd love a morning outing."

John leaned close, so close her violet scent teased his senses. He gave her his devastating smile as he lowered his head and claimed her lips in a sweetly sensual kiss.

"Mistress Montgomery, you are a temptation," he murmured, his lips hovering above hers.

"Lust is one of the seven deadly sins, Your Grace," Isabelle informed him, drawing back out of temptation's path.

John smiled and rose from the couch, saying, "Until tomorrow at nine."

"I'll be ready," Isabelle said, walking with him to the drawing-room door. "I do hope the weather cooperates."

"Damsel, I shall order us a day of brilliant sunshine, clear blue skies, and a gentle breeze," John said.

"Could you manage a few fluffy white clouds for decoration?" she asked.

"That could prove difficult," John answered with a boyishly charming smile. "I'll see what I can do."

God's breath, Isabelle thought in amazement when she drew aside the draperies to peer out the window early the next morning.

Bright tentacles of orange light streaked the mauve-colored eastern horizon, promising a perfect morning with radiant sunshine and clear blue skies. The bud-laden branches of the trees in the garden area remained motionless, which meant no biting spring wind with which to contend.

"His Grace must have the ear of God," Isabelle said over her shoulder. "He's managed to conjure the perfect morning for a ride in the park."

"I fixed it for him," Giselle said, her voice low as she stared into the hearth.

"Why are you looking so glum?" Isabelle asked, crossing the chamber to sit on the edge of the opposite chair.

"Saint-Germain has seen and heard me," the old woman complained, "but he still refuses to believe I exist."

"Convincing skeptics can be a frustrating and impossible task," Isabelle said.

"I thought seeing was believing," Giselle replied.

"Only for men named Thomas."

"Very funny."

"Give John time," Isabelle said. "Together we will bolster his faith in the celestial."

"Child, you are beginning to love him," Giselle remarked, turning to look at her.

That comment surprised Isabelle. "Why do you say that?"

"You've just defended him to me by insisting he is not beyond redemption," Giselle explained.

Uncomfortable with the topic of her growing fondness for the duke, Isabelle rose from her chair, saying, "It's early yet. I think I'll go back to bed."

"Would you like me to play for you until you fall asleep?" Giselle asked. "I always did when you were a child. Remember?"

"I'd like that very much."

Isabelle climbed into bed and pulled the coverlet up. The old woman sat on the edge of the bed and played a lullaby until her charge fell into a deep, dreamless sleep.

Three hours later Isabelle had washed and dressed in preparation for her outing in Hyde Park. She wore a peacock-blue silk and wool gown that was as light as sarcenet but warmer. Over this she donned the Wellington mantle and the Wellington boots that were all the rage in fashionable London. As usual she'd left her head bare. After brushing her blond hair off her face, she'd woven it into one thick braid and knotted the braid at the nape of her neck.

Isabelle took one last peek at herself in the framed mirror and then turned to leave the chamber. She looked toward the hearth for her angel's approval, but Giselle had vanished.

"I'm leaving, Giselle," Isabelle called softly. "Wherever you are."

She started for the door, but paused when she heard the voice say, "Enjoy yourself, child."

Isabelle whirled around, but the chamber was empty. A smile touched her lips at her angel's antics, and she left the chamber in a good mood.

With her spirits high, Isabelle walked briskly down the main staircase to the foyer on the ground floor. John was already waiting. He looked up as she descended the final five steps. His smile of greeting made her feel warm.

Is this really love? she wondered. Or am I becoming ill?

"Your punctuality heartens me," John said, when she stood before him. "I detest tardiness in anyone."

"I am always punctual," Isabelle replied. "I've been

told that timeliness is out of fashion with London's society ladies.''

"Never change, Belle," John said, escorting her toward the door. "I like you exactly the way you are."

The perfection of the day was a rarity for early April. The sun shone radiantly against the sky's clear blue backdrop, and from the west blew a gentle breeze.

Isabelle paused when John held out his hand to assist her into his carriage. Shielding her eyes with one hand, she gazed at the blanket of blue above their heads.

"What are you doing?" he asked.

"Searching for those fluffy white clouds I ordered," she answered, and then turned her head to see him smiling at her.

John and Isabelle sat close together in his curricle drawn by matching, dapple-gray geldings. Taking the reins in hand, John drove the coach to Piccadilly. From there they rode down Park Lane and entered Hyde Park.

The park was glorious on that brilliant April morn, and throngs of London's elite crowded its lanes. Most waved or called greetings to the Duke of Avon and his fiancée, and Isabelle was astonished by the number of people who knew and seemed to respect her husband-to-be.

"I never realized those people knew who I was," Isabelle said after a coach with a small group of older ladies waved at her.

"My mother's cronies," John replied. "They attended your come-out party."

"They only accept me for your sake," Isabelle remarked without thinking.

"You need to bolster your confidence," he said, turning to look at her. "You aren't afraid of those people, are you?"

She shrugged.

"Trust me, darling," John said. "Those people are more concerned with the possibility that you might find them unacceptable."

"Only because of you," Isabelle insisted. Discouraging further comment, she inhaled deeply of spring's delicate fragrance and changed the subject, saying, "What a wonderful day you've managed to conjure for me."

"God answered my prayers."

"Do you pray, Your Grace?"

"In my own fashion," John answered with a smile that made her insides warm pleasurably. "I do believe the world's most interesting characters will be enjoying a rather warm hereafter. By the way, how is your guardian angel?"

"As a matter of fact, she's irritated that you refuse to accept her existence," Isabelle told him.

"I guess I'm a skeptic to the end."

Isabelle didn't respond to his teasing. Instead, her gaze fixed on the couple on horseback who were riding in their direction. She felt a strange sinking sensation in the pit of her stomach when she recognized William Grimsby. Riding with him was a raven-haired beauty whom she'd never seen before.

Had the Earl of Ripon heard about her engagement to the Duke of Avon? she wondered. How foolish of her to think he hadn't. All of London knew of their betrothal. It had been announced in *The Times*.

"Is something wrong?" John asked.

"William Grimsby is riding toward us," Isabelle told him. She placed her hand on his forearm and added, "I do hope the two of you won't have words."

John turned his head and saw the couple who were nearly upon them. His placid expression darkened into a forbidding frown. Surprisingly, he was staring at the beautiful dark-haired woman instead of the earl.

William Grimsby nodded as he and his lady friend came abreast of their curricle. Unexpectedly, the raven-haired beauty reined her horse to a stop beside them.

"Good morning, Your Grace," the woman said, her smile feline.

"Lisette, how are you?" John replied politely, yet his expression remained forbidding and positively screamed his displeasure at the woman's appearance.

"I am simply fantastic," Lisette replied. "But you already knew that, Your Grace." She slid her gaze to Isabelle, who squirmed mentally beneath the thorough inspection the woman gave her.

"Is this your fiancée?" Lisette asked.

John nodded, saying, "Isabelle, I would like to make Lisette Dupre known to you."

Isabelle could have managed a smile for the woman, but William Grimsby's chuckle distracted her. Something was going on here, and she was the only one present who was ignorant of what it was. The tension in the air was as tangible as the curricle in which she rode.

"You've just committed a shocking breach of etiquette, Your Grace," Grimsby said in a sardonic voice.

Isabelle decided that she'd been wrong about the Earl of Ripon's character. He was not a nice man at all. The meaning of his words was lost on her though, and that was something she disliked.

"Seeing you with Grimsby is quite a surprise," John was saying to the woman.

"Even bigger surprises await you, Your Grace." At that Lisette Dupre yanked on her horse's reins and rode away with the earl.

Isabelle stared at her betrothed's angry expression

and wondered what had just transpired. Then she flicked a glance around and noticed that gentlemen and ladies in several carriages were watching. When her gaze touched them, they quickly turned their heads away and pretended an interest elsewhere.

"What was that about?" she asked.

"Nothing."

Isabelle knew he was lying. *Nothing* was making the muscle in his cheek twitch with anger.

"I've had enough of Hyde Park for one day," John said, steering the curricle toward the park's exit. They rode in silence back to Montgomery House. John left immediately after escorting her inside, leaving Isabelle to wonder about their chance meeting in Hyde Park.

For days Isabelle pondered the reason for John's swift change in mood at the sight of William Grimsby and Lisette Dupre. Was it the Earl of Ripon who disturbed him? Or was it Lisette Dupre? Or, more importantly, was it the sight of Grimsby with the raven-haired beauty that had troubled him? Had John been in love with Lisette Dupre? Was it jealousy that had consumed him? And why hadn't she met Lisette Dupre at any of the social gatherings she'd attended?

Other puzzling questions about that morning occurred to her. What had Grimsby meant when he'd accused John of a breach in etiquette? What other surprises did Lisette have for John?

Isabelle knew she could always ask someone about these things, but in her deepest heart she feared the answers. Even Giselle remained strangely silent on the subject.

Then, as the days passed one into another, Isabelle became caught in the excitement of her Saint George's Day betrothal party. During the quiet moments she gazed at her violets-in-the-snow betrothal ring and gained strength from it, much as her golden locket containing her mother's image gave her strength.

Giselle had told her that John was the dark prince of prophecy. Isabelle decided that no matter how distant he'd seemed since that day in Hyde Park, the duke was her destiny. They were meant for each other. Only together could either of them find a true and lasting happiness. Maybe she was beginning to fall in love with him, and she had forgiven Giselle for her April Fool's Day prank. Her one regret was her brother's absence. If only Miles could attend her wedding and walk her down the aisle. Instead, she would walk down the aisle as she had walked through her first eighteen years—*alone*.

On the evening of her betrothal party Isabelle hurried down the third-floor corridor toward the grand staircase. Excitement coursed through her and colored her cheeks with a high blush.

An ice-blue silk gown with its deep *V* front draped her body, molding tightly to her figure. On her feet she wore satin slippers suitable for dancing.

With her Wellington mantle hanging over one arm, Isabelle struggled to slip on her white kid gloves without dropping the circular fan she carried. The upstairs corridor was unusually quiet, her stepfamily having already left for the dowager's mansion.

Isabelle paused to regain her composure before starting down the stairs. She only hoped John wouldn't be too angry with her tardiness. After all, a girl didn't become engaged to be married every day.

Slowly, Isabelle descended the grand staircase to the main foyer on the ground level. John was pacing back and forth across the foyer while Pebbles watched him. He whirled around when he heard her approach. She saw his expression of mild irritation transform into admiration mingled with a gleam of possession.

"The wait was worthwhile," John said, dropping a courtly kiss on her gloved hand. "You are exquisitely lovely."

Isabelle smiled at his words. In turn, she inspected his formal attire, which made him even more devilishly appealing than he already was. "You look very nice too," she said. As he guided her toward the door she said, "How embarrassing to be late for one's own betrothal party. I'm certain Delphinia will have some unpleasant words for me."

"Mother's residence isn't far," John said.

Hand in hand, John and Isabelle stepped outside into the moonless and foggy night. He helped her into his barouche and shouted instructions to Gallagher.

A scant fifteen minutes later John and Isabelle poised on the balcony overlooking the dowager's ballroom. Two hundred people milled below them. An orchestra consisting of a cornet, a piano, a cello, and two violins stood at the far end of the ballroom.

"No flutes, Your Grace?" Isabelle said, feigning disappointment.

John smiled at her. "How remiss of Mother to forget our favorite musical instrument."

"We are the last to arrive," she said, frowning.

"Be careful, or your face will freeze like that," he replied, making her smile. "Count your blessings, darling, we've missed the reception line."

Before she could reply, the majordomo announced in a loud voice, "His Grace, the Duke of Avon, and Lady Isabelle Montgomery."

Two hundred people—a small gathering by most standards—turned toward the balcony and looked up at them. Isabelle felt like swooning at the sight of all of those watching people.

"Don't move," John said. "Here comes my brother."

Smiling broadly, Ross Saint-Germain bounded up the stairs to greet them. He shook his brother's hand and then kissed Isabelle's. Finally, Ross said, "Mother got the obligatory quadrille out of the way, but held back on the waltzes." He turned to their audience and said in a voice loud enough to carry below to them, "I wish to announce officially the Duke of Avon's engagement to Lady Isabelle Montgomery."

Everyone below clapped.

"Let's go," John said, escorting her down the stairs as the orchestra began its first waltz. Instead of greeting their guests, John led Isabelle onto the dance floor. Soon other couples joined them.

"You dance divinely," John said, and winked at her.

"My guardian angel and I have been practicing most diligently," Isabelle returned his teasing.

"Darling, you are incorrigible," John told her. "I do hope you make a better wife than a ward, and I pray you can control our future children better than I've been able to control you."

"I'll take that as a compliment," Isabelle said, her smile jaunty.

"I pray our daughter is as lovely as her mother and our son inherits my patience," John added.

"You mean Sloth Saint-Germain?"

John threw back his head and laughed. Their apparent happiness drew approving smiles from everyone who watched.

"Lobelia and Spewing are spending a good deal of time together," Isabelle remarked when her gaze fell on her stepsister. "I wouldn't be surprised if he offers for her."

"Is that so?" John said. "I hadn't noticed."

A moment later Isabelle spied Charles Hancock dancing with one of the pretty young ladies in attendance. She scanned the hall along the wall for her stepsister until she saw Rue standing with Delphinia.

"What's wrong?" John asked.

Isabelle tipped her head toward the wall where her stepsister stood. "I feel sorry for Rue. She's developed a crush on Hancock."

"No one can predict the future," John said. "You seem remarkably relaxed tonight. Why, I haven't seen you reach for your locket once."

"I have you to thank for that," Isabelle said, her violet eyes gleaming like amethysts. She lowered her voice as if divulging a secret and added, "While we were standing on the balcony, I pictured everyone in their underdrawers."

John burst out laughing. "What a naughty chit you are."

Isabelle nodded in agreement. "I have a wonderful teacher."

"Thank you for the compliment, darling."

Three waltzes later John and Isabelle left the dance floor. While he went to the refreshment room to fetch her a glass of champagne, she walked over to her stepsister.

"Why so sad, Rue?" Isabelle asked, drawing her aside.

"Charles hasn't invited me to dance this evening," Rue complained, perilously close to tears. "Spewing hasn't left Lobelia's side once."

"No one can predict the future," Isabelle repeated

John's words to her. "This evening could have a happy ending for you."

"That's so easy for you to say," Rue replied. "You'll be married to a duke in two months."

"Now that I think of it," Isabelle said, ignoring her sister's meanspiritedness, "there is a way to predict the future."

"What do you mean?"

"Do you remember how superstitious old Cook was?"

Rue nodded.

"Today is the twenty-third of April, which means tomorrow is Saint Mark's Eve," Isabelle said. "Tomorrow evening you must fast beginning at sunset. During the night, bake a cake containing an eggshellful of salt, wheatmeal, and barley meal. Then open the door of the kitchen. Your future lover will come inside and turn the cake."

"I think I'll try it," Rue said, brightening.

"It couldn't hurt."

"What if no one comes inside?" Rue asked, her face paling at the thought.

"Don't be a goose," Isabelle replied. "Everyone has a future lover. Though you may not like who you see."

"I'm certain someone wonderful will walk in," Rue said, happy again.

Several hours later, after supper had been eaten and the final ten waltzes danced, the party dwindled into quiet conversation with the few remaining guests in the cardroom. Isabelle struggled against a yawn and lost.

"I'm taking you home," John said with an indulgent smile.

"Several of our guests still linger," Isabelle protested.

"They'll leave when we leave," he told her.

Donning her Wellington mantle, Isabelle allowed John to lead her away from the others. His mother's majordomo opened the front door for them, and they started down the front stairs.

Gallagher had parked the barouche on the opposite side of the street. Seeing them emerge from the dowager's house, he lifted the reins in order to turn the coach around, but John gestured for him to remain where he was. They stepped into the street, but stopped when a woman shouted to them.

"Isabelle!"

John and Isabelle whirled around and took three steps toward Lobelia and Spewing, who stood poised on the dowager's front stairs.

"Stephen has asked me to marry him," Lobelia cried in obvious excitement. "Come back, and we'll—"

A gunshot rang out suddenly.

John grabbed Isabelle and shoved her down on the sidewalk, shielding her with his body. Another shot sounded, and a lone horseman rode at breakneck speed down the street and vanished into the fog.

"Are you injured?" John asked, helping her up.

Trembling with fear, Isabelle shook her head. "Are you?"

"No." The angry twitch in his cheek muscle appeared.

Lobelia stood on the front stairs and screamed as if she were being murdered, while Spewing appeared torn between quieting her and dashing over to them to make certain they hadn't been hit. Gallagher was at their side in three seconds. Ross Saint-Germain and the remaining guests streamed out of the mansion to discover what the commotion was about.

"What happened?" Ross asked.

"Someone took a shot at us." John turned to his man and ordered, "Gallagher, fetch the Bow Street runners here."

"You'll spend the night here," John said, ushering Isabelle up the stairs of his mother's mansion. "Tomorrow you'll return to Montgomery House and pack all of your belongings. I want you out of London as soon as possible."

Inside the foyer, John turned to his mother, saying, "I want her safely ensconced at Avon Park from tomorrow until the wedding."

"I understand," the dowager said.

"Never fear," Aunt Hester added. "We will protect her with our lives."

Isabelle didn't know whether to laugh or to cry. She couldn't imagine how two old ladies could possibly protect her. Besides, she didn't need protecting. Whoever had fired that gun hadn't been aiming for her; she'd stake her life on it. She opened her mouth to protest leaving him in London when he so obviously needed her there.

John flicked a glance at her and told his mother, "If she gives you an argument, lock her in her chamber."

Isabelle clamped her mouth shut.

"Take her upstairs and put her to bed," he ordered his mother.

"But you are in danger," Isabelle cried, unable to hold her silence. "I cannot leave you in your hour of need."

"Thank you for worrying," John said in a low voice, "but the villain won't try to harm me again tonight." He planted a kiss on her lips. "I'll be with my brother here in my mother's study trying to figure this thing out.''

"But tomorrow—"

"Tomorrow you must go to Avon Park," he told her. "I cannot protect myself if I am distracted with worry about your safety."

"I understand," Isabelle said. "I don't like it, but I will go. Promise me you'll be careful."

Putting his arm around her, John escorted her to the grand staircase. He leaned close and whispered in her ear, teasing, "If anything happens, you won't have to marry me. Two weeks ago you would have relished the idea."

"I wish no harm to befall anyone," Isabelle said. Imitating him, she leaned close and whispered in his ear, "If anything happens to you, I'll be forced into marriage with Nicholas deJewell. Please take care of yourself."

Chapter 11

Isabelle worried for eight long weeks.

Would John be safe in London? Who had tried to assassinate him? Nicholas deJewell, bent on marrying her, popped into her mind and then popped out just as quickly. Nicholas was a cowardly weasel who hadn't the intelligence of a rat.

William Grimsby seemed a more likely candidate with a better motive for revenge. He blamed John for his sister's untimely death. That Lenore Grimsby died miscarrying her child was no fault of the babe's father. These unfortunate occurrences happened in this imperfect life.

Isabelle longed to be with John in London, but knew he was correct about her being a distraction to his safety. Never would she wish to compromise his welfare.

She loved him.

Apparently, absence did make the heart grow fonder. No other man had ever attracted her like the Duke of Avon. Of course, she hadn't a great deal of experience with men; in fact, she'd never had a gentleman caller. Except Nicholas deJewell, but her stepmother's nephew hardly qualified as a man.

The puzzling aspect of this betrothal was the duke's feelings for her. Why would a handsome, wealthy nobleman, who could have any woman in Europe for the asking, stoop to marry a penniless, unloved country girl who talked to herself?

Those eight weeks passed excruciatingly slowly. Isabelle counted the passage of time by Mother Nature's changing expression.

April's ending saw brilliant daffodils and forsythia fading into purple violets. And then May arrived with its infinite variety of colors and shapes in the woodland outside the giant oaks that bordered Avon Park. Lilac bushes became laden with perfumed purple blossoms.

The beauty of her beloved Stratford had been diminished by John's absence. Even arguing with him was infinitely more enjoyable than being alone. She'd never felt more alive than when she was with him. How had she survived all of those long, lonely years without him?

Anticipation swelled within Isabelle's breast when the heavenly perfection of May surrendered to the warm, dry breezes and sunny days of June. Finally, her wedding day arrived.

Isabelle waited nervously in the nave of Holy Trinity Church. Now the previous eight weeks seemed to have passed faster than a lightning flash, and her worries for her betrothed's safety became concerns for their married life together. She was the young woman whom everyone believed would never be accepted into his sophisticated world. Once married, she would become an embarrassment. John would grow to hate her for that.

And then she would be alone. Again.

"I cannot believe my little girl is a grown woman," a kindly voice beside her said. "What a beautiful bride you make."

Isabelle banished her disturbing thoughts and focused on Mrs. Juniper, who had arrived at Avon Park a week earlier. She smiled at her former nanny and felt the intervening years of their separation melt away. Juniper had always cherished and protected her, until she'd been sent away. Now graying and pudgy, the older woman still possessed the ability to make her feel loved and accepted and special.

"How I've missed you," Isabelle said, reaching out to touch the older woman's hand. "I do hope you'll agree to remain at Avon Park and help me with whatever children come along."

"Thank you for making me feel needed again," Juniper replied. Overcome by emotion, she dabbed the moisture from beneath her eyes with her handkerchief. "You don't think I'm too old? His Grace—"

"Don't bother yourself about His Grace," Isabelle interrupted. "I can handle him. Besides, you are family to me. What young mother wouldn't wish for a grandmother to care for the little ones?"

"You always did possess a kind heart," Juniper said with a grateful smile.

"If you don't mind, I would like a few moments before I walk down that aisle," Isabelle said.

Juniper nodded. "I'll go find Pebbles and we'll take our places." At that, she disappeared into the church.

Alone with her thoughts, Isabelle worried her bottom lip with her teeth. Today was her wedding day, a moment that every young girl dreamed of for years. Her husband-to-be was England's premier duke; after the ceremony she would be a duchess. In a few moments she would walk alone down that aisle in front of two hundred of England's elite. She only hoped her stepsisters' malicious gossip hadn't reached their ears.

"Child, no frowning is allowed on this day."

"I haven't seen you this week," Isabelle said, rounding on Giselle, who still wore her tattered clothing. "I feared you wouldn't be here."

"I remained hidden in the shadows while you prepared for today," the old woman told her.

"Thoughts of my parents have filled my mind this week," Isabelle said.

"Child, trust me. Your parents are watching you this very moment."

Isabelle brightened at her words. "Do you really think so?"

Giselle nodded. "Love does not die with a person's passing," she said. "Your father and your mother are with you in spirit."

Isabelle closed her eyes and touched her golden locket, trying to feel her mother's spirit near her. "Thank you for all of those years of loyalty," she said to the old woman.

"Child, I was with you before you came into this world, and I'll be with you long after you go out of it," Giselle said. "The problem is, you mortals have short memories."

"So I am never alone, even when I feel so?" Isabelle asked.

Giselle nodded and asked, "Do you believe that John Saint-Germain is the dark prince?"

"I certainly hope so," Isabelle answered, giving the old crone a rueful smile. "If not, I'll be marrying the wrong man."

Giselle laughed and then reached out to touch her hand. "My blessings upon you, child. The moment has arrived for the greatest adventure of your life." The old woman vanished in a blinking of an eye.

Leaving the nave, Isabelle positioned herself at the end of the long aisle. Her wedding gown had been cre-

ated in ivory satin and lace and adorned with hundreds
of seed pearls. Its high-waisted bodice had a squared
neckline and short, puffed sleeves. Her hair of spun gold
cascaded down her back to her waist, and her veil was
the sheerest ivory lace, which had once belonged to her
own mother. In her hands she carried the traditional orange blossoms. The fragrant white flowers proclaimed
her virginity and served as a fertility charm, because the
blossom and the fruit appear simultaneously on the orange tree.

Isabelle caught her first glimpse of the church. Hundreds of candles lit the chapel, casting eerie shadows on
its muraled walls, stained-glass windows, and ornate
sculptures. At the end of the aisle was the altar where
John and she would kneel in front of the Bishop of
Coventry, who had journeyed to Stratford to marry
them. Bouquets of blue forget-me-nots, purple violets,
and white lilies adorned the altar.

The organist began playing. The wedding guests rose
from the mahogany pews and faced the center aisle.

Ignoring the sea of unfamiliar faces, Isabelle gazed
down the long length of the aisle to the handsome man
who awaited her at the altar. Formally attired in black,
John Saint-Germain was the prince she'd once glimpsed
in the Avon River, and she gave him a smile filled with
love. His darkly intense gaze on her held the promise of
love and acceptance, giving her the courage to start
down the aisle to him.

Almost there, Isabelle thought when she reached the
midpoint of the long aisle. John's gaze never left hers,
and she suffered the almost overwhelming urge to run
the remaining distance.

And then Isabelle heard the vibrating notes of a flute
emanating from the choir loft behind her. The flutist's

melody held a poignant, sensitive tone that touched her heart.

Peering over her shoulder, Isabelle sent Giselle a smile that rivaled the flute's song of infinite beauty. She returned her gaze to John's and then realized that he heard the celestial melody too. Wearing a puzzled expression, he stared at the choir loft for another long moment before offering her his hand as she reached the altar.

Hand in hand, John and Isabelle followed the bishop inside the sanctuary.

"I never ordered a flute to accompany the organist," he whispered. "Did you?"

"Giselle is playing for us."

"I always believed that angels played harps."

"Angels can play whatever they wish," Isabelle said, casting him a sidelong smile.

Thankfully, the wedding ceremony lasted less than thirty minutes. Isabelle's heart warmed when John pressed his lips to hers, their first kiss as husband and wife.

Isabelle gifted him with a smile. Perhaps their marriage would work in spite of all the odds against it. With her angel's blessing, it was a union made in heaven.

Leaving the sanctuary, John escorted Isabelle down the aisle. On impulse Isabelle passed the orange-blossom bouquet to Lobelia, surprising her oldest stepsister. "You'll be next," she said.

"What about me?" Rue whined. And then, "Ouch! Mother, you needn't pinch me."

John guided Isabelle down the aisle and outside into the bright sunshine. Even the summer's breeze whispered success for their marriage. The largest and most luxurious of the ducal coaches awaited them.

Sitting close beside him on the leather seat, Isabelle felt suddenly shy. The incredibly handsome man beside her was now her husband, and in a matter of hours they would share his bed. She peeked at him from beneath the thick fringe of her blond lashes and saw him watching her.

As if he knew her thoughts, John lifted her left hand and kissed it, and then told her, "The scroll on your wedding band is actually my wish for our marriage, written in old French. It says *joy sans fyn*—joy without end."

"My sentiments match yours," Isabelle replied. "My only regret is that Miles—"

"No regrets are allowed on our wedding day," John told her, leaning close to kiss her.

His lips were warmly insistent, and his fresh scent of mountain heather assailed her senses until she felt as though he was casting a spell on her. His drugging kiss held a possessiveness that hadn't been present before.

"I hope this isn't midsummer madness," John whispered.

"Your Grace, I would bet my last shilling that you have never encountered a spontaneous moment in your life," Isabelle teased.

"You would lose, Your Grace," John returned her teasing.

Isabelle suddenly became serious, asking, "Have your investigators learned any information about that night in front of your mother's town house?"

"I want no discussions about that today," John said with a smile. "I want our wedding day filled only with happiness. How do you like being a duchess?"

Isabelle cast him a rueful smile. "I feel the same as I did yesterday when I was Mistress Nobody."

John chuckled. "I wouldn't want the mantle of greatness to give you a haughty attitude."

"No, indeed. That would make two of us with the same attitude."

Within the hour John and Isabelle stood beside his mother and his brother to greet their guests in Avon Park's candlelit and flower-adorned Great Banqueting Hall. The head table had been set along one of the rectangular room's short walls, with two long tables large enough to sit one hundred people at each side poised perpendicular to it. More than an hour passed before the last guest in the receiving line stepped in front of John and Isabelle.

"Best wishes, Your Grace," Major Grimase greeted her, kissing her hand.

"Thank you, Major," Isabelle replied. Lord, but her face was beginning to hurt from smiling for nearly two hours.

"Congratulations, Your Grace," Major Grimase said to John, shaking his hand. "High time you took yourself a wife."

"Emulating my actions might be a good thing," John said.

"To tell you the truth, I do believe a young bride would kill me now," Major Grimase replied. "What a quandary. I'm too young for an old bride and too old for a young one."

"I don't believe a young woman would ever consider murdering someone as nice as you," Isabelle piped up, making both men smile.

"I see that you have your work cut out for you," the major said.

John nodded. "It would appear so."

"By the way, Saint-Germain, what do you think of

the war?'' Major Grimase asked, seemingly intent on talking longer than necessary. ''How long do you think it will be before the King's navy puts those colonials in their place?''

Isabelle sensed a change in her husband's demeanor. She turned to look at him.

''I wouldn't care to hazard a guess,'' John said to the major, losing his affability.

''We'll show them this time,'' Major Grimase said, his voice rising with his excitement. ''Too bad about your brother, though. He'll probably be delayed until the war is over.''

''You never can tell what the future will bring,'' John said noncommittally.

At that Major Grimase moved away to find his place at one of the long tables.

Isabelle realized that her husband and the major were discussing war between England and America. Miles and Jamie were still in New York.

Anger swept through Isabelle like a sudden gust of wind. Her husband had known all along and kept it a secret from her. How could he be so callous? He knew how worried she was about Miles. Their ''joy without end'' had lasted less than two hours.

''Our guests are waiting for dinner,'' John said, gently grasping her elbow to lead her to the head table. ''Shall we take our places?''

Isabelle rounded on him. Only a blind man could have failed to see her anger.

''God mend your lying ways,'' Isabelle said.

John snapped his brows together. ''What are you talking about?''

''The war.''

"I never lied about that," John said smoothly. "I merely—"

"It was a lie of omission," Isabelle interrupted him.

"Listen to me, Isabelle," John said, lowering his voice. "We have two hundred guests waiting to share our wedding dinner."

"Your lies have stolen my appetite," Isabelle said, lifting her nose into the air.

"Anger is one of the seven deadly sins," he reminded her.

"Is this the devil quoting scripture?" she asked.

John burst out laughing. Isabelle failed to see the humor in what she'd said.

"Do not humiliate both of us in front of all of these people," John said. Then he added, "Please, Belle."

Isabelle looked from him to their guests and then back again. Finally, she nodded and said, "We will discuss this as soon as they're gone."

"Thank you," he said, surprising her.

As the violinists began circulating through the hall, John escorted Isabelle to the head table, where their families were already seated. Once the toasts were finished, John fed Isabelle the requisite quince, which represented female fertility. Blushing, Isabelle ate the yellow apple to the loud applause of their guests.

With that tradition done, the Saint-Germain servants entered with their wedding feast, the likes of which Isabelle had never seen. First came the turtle soup, followed by the main course of poached salmon steaks with anchovy essence, duck with horseradish, rump of beef, stuffed artichokes, asparagus in cream, and tomato stuffed with mushrooms. The second course contained raspberry cream, gooseberry cream, baked custards, and walnut pudding with chocolate sauce. Finally the traditional wedding cake arrived.

Giddy with the small amount of champagne she'd drunk, Isabelle ate lightly of the soup, poached salmon, and the vegetable medley. She noted her husband's long fingers on the delicate stem of the crystal goblet and then imagined those fingers caressing her naked body. Blushing hotly at the tantalizing thought, she sneaked a peek at him and caught him smiling at her as if he knew her thoughts.

Isabelle watched him shift his gaze toward their guests, and then his devastating smile became a dark scowl. The angry twitch in his cheek muscle had returned.

Isabelle turned her head to follow his gaze. Advancing on them through the two rows of tables was Lisette Dupre, the raven-haired beauty from Hyde Park. Clutching Lisette's hand was a young girl, four or five years old, who looked exactly like Lisette. The child held a small satchel and a doll in her free hand.

An awkward hush fell over the wedding guests. With her head held high, Lisette ignored their stares and fixed her gaze on the head table.

John started to rise when Lisette finally stood in front of them. Isabelle placed her hand on his forearm and stopped him.

"Your Graces, I've brought you a wedding gift," Lisette said, dropping them a curtsy. She released the little girl's hand and gestured to her, saying, "I give you our daughter."

With those parting words Lisette Dupre whirled away and hurried out of the Banqueting Hall, leaving the little girl behind.

Several things happened simultaneously.

"Lisette, don't leave me," the little girl screeched in a panic.

"Bloody hell," John cursed, bolting out of his chair.

"Sweet celestial breath," Isabelle exclaimed, rising from her own chair, her heart breaking at the sight of the abandoned child.

John dashed out of the Banqueting Hall in an effort to catch Lisette Dupre. Two steps behind him raced his brother Ross.

With her gaze fixed on the weeping child, Isabelle left the head table and hurried toward her. The wedding guests watched in scandalized silence, the only sounds coming from her new in-laws.

"Oh, my Lord, whatever shall we do?" Aunt Hester was exclaiming.

"Hester, do not even consider swooning," the dowager duchess ordered in a stern voice.

"A bit of cold tea will revive her," Juniper called from where she sat.

Ignoring them, Isabelle crouched down on one bended knee in front of the girl in order to be eye level with her. She gifted the child with a smile filled with sunshine. The girl sniffled and gave her a wobbly smile in return.

"My name is Isabelle," she told the child. "What's yours?"

"Lily." She dropped the satchel on the floor and held the doll up. "This is Charlotte."

"Lily, you are among friends here," Isabelle said, gazing into her disarming green eyes. "There is no need to be frightened."

"Are you a princess?" Lily asked.

Isabelle smiled. "No, merely a duchess."

"Who is your duke?"

"Your papa is my duke," Isabelle told her.

"I don't have any papa," the girl said.

"It appears that you do."

"I always prayed for a papa," Lily said, smiling. "I suppose God does answer prayers sometimes."

"Indeed, sometimes He does," Isabelle agreed.

"Which man is my papa?" Lily asked, gazing at the wedding guests.

"The duke just stepped outside for a moment," Isabelle told her. "I'll introduce you when he returns."

"You mean the angry man?"

Isabelle nodded. "Your papa is the fifth Duke of Doom, the tenth Marquess of Mean, and the twelfth Earl of . . . *Egads!*"

Lily giggled. "I like you."

"I like you too," Isabelle said. "Are you feeling better now?"

Lily nodded and then glanced at the watching guests. When she looked at Isabelle again, her expression was worried.

"Where's Lisette?" she asked. "I need her."

Isabelle felt her heart wrenching at the lost expression on the child's face. She saw her own insecure childhood in the little girl standing there.

"Lisette had important business that needed tending," Isabelle lied. "So she's brought you here to visit with me. Do you think you'll like that? I know lots of games to play."

Lily brightened at the prospect of playing games. "What kind of games?"

"Let's see," Isabelle said, placing one finger across her lips as if thinking. "In the summer I lay on my back outside and watch the clouds make pictures. When I tire of doing that, I roll down the side of a grassy hill. Have you ever tried that?''

Lily shook her head.

"When autumn arrives, I toss the fallen leaves into the air and shout *hooray,*" Isabelle continued, desperately trying to keep the child calm. "During the winter I make angels in the snow. Springtime is my favorite because I walk in the woodland and play with the flower fairies."

Lily's green eyes grew large with wonder. No child could resist the magical.

"When the rains come, I enjoy tea parties and sitting in front of the hearth to play my flute," Isabelle added as an afterthought, covering all eventualities. "Like my mother before me, I'm an excellent flutist, you know."

"No, I didn't know."

"Sometimes I sit outside and gaze at the stars in the night sky," Isabelle continued. "Do any of those activities interest you?"

Lily nodded, her smile eager.

"Then you'll stay here and visit with me?" Isabelle asked.

"Well, I'll need to ask Myrtle what she wants to do," Lily said.

"Who's Myrtle?"

"Myrtle is my special friend," Lily explained. "No one but me can see or hear her."

"I have a special friend too," Isabelle said. "Her name is Giselle."

"She's very old," Lily whispered.

Her remark surprised Isabelle. "How do you know she's old?"

"She's standing there," Lily answered, pointing her finger to the right.

Isabelle turned her head and instantly recognized the tattered skirt her old friend always wore. How could this child whom she'd never met see her guardian angel? She would ask Giselle about it later. At that moment Lily's arrival had already given two hundred members of the ton enough to gossip about; she needn't add herself as another topic for their drawing rooms.

"We've created enough scandal today to make the regent look like a priest," Giselle said. "Take the child upstairs away from these people."

"Are you hungry?" Isabelle asked the girl.

Lily shrugged as if she hadn't quite decided if she was going to stay.

Isabelle stood then and offered the girl her hand. "Will you come with me?" she asked.

Lily bit her bottom lip in indecision.

"I bet you would like to wear my veil," Isabelle said, removing the headpiece and gently setting it on top of the girl's raven tresses. "There now, you look exactly like a princess."

Lily smiled and placed her hand in Isabelle's, asking, "Can Myrtle come with us?"

"Well, of course, Myrtle can accompany us," Isabelle said with a smile. "I wouldn't dream of abandoning Myrtle in this crowd. . . . Dobbs!"

Her husband's majordomo materialized from nowhere.

"Please bring a platter of beef, an artichoke, and walnut pudding to my chamber," Isabelle instructed the man. "And don't forget a wedge of the wedding cake."

"Yes, Your Grace," Dobbs said, and turned away to do his lady's bidding.

Next Isabelle gestured to Juniper, who was at her side

in an instant. She could tell by the older woman's expression how pleased she was to be needed again.

Lowering her voice so that no one could hear her, Isabelle instructed, "Take my guest's satchel upstairs and prepare a chamber for her."

"Yes, Your Grace," Juniper said, starting to drop a curtsy.

Isabelle reached out and stopped her old nanny from curtsying to her. "Drop the *Your Grace*."

The longtime Montgomery nanny left the hall immediately. Isabelle, holding the girl's hand, started to follow Juniper out, but heard the murmurs of gossip racing through the assembled guests. She knew how shockingly scandalous it was for the new bride to shelter her husband's mistress's child, but the alternative was tossing the little girl out. Her choice was actually no choice at all.

Realizing she should say something, Isabelle turned around and faced their guests. "I thank all of you for attending my wedding," she said in a strong, clear voice that carried to the far corners of the hall. "I know you'll understand that I consider this child more important than celebrating at the moment."

At that, Isabelle and Lily left the Banqueting Hall. Gaining the main foyer, they met John and Ross returning. Apparently, they'd had no success in catching Lisette, which, in Isabelle's mind, was just as well. She wouldn't wish to give the little girl over to a woman who had deserted her.

"I'm sorry Lisette ruined our wedding day," John apologized, but his dark gaze never left the little girl's face.

"We'll discuss this later," Isabelle told him. "Send the wedding guests home."

•

"There is no need for that," John replied, reaching for the child's hand. "Gallagher will drive her back to London and drop her off at her mother's town house."

Isabelle stepped in front of Lily and prevented her husband from taking hold of the girl. She stared him straight in the eye and announced, "I'm keeping her."

Shock registered on her husband's face. "You cannot possibly keep—"

"The Duchess of Avon can do anything she damned well pleases," Isabelle interrupted, her violet gaze fixed on his, challenging him to refute her.

Ross Saint-Germain burst out laughing. With all the haughtiness of a young queen, Isabelle gave her brother-in-law a quelling look.

"Isabelle . . ." John's voice held a warning note.

"We'll discuss this later," she told him.

Isabelle turned away and started to climb the stairs with the little girl in tow, saying loud enough for the men to hear, "Sometimes your papa behaves like a rat's arse."

"Oh, I didn't know," Lily said. "Thank you for telling me."

Chapter 12

Bull's pizzle, John thought, shoving his hands in his trouser pockets. His dark gaze followed his bride up the stairs until she and the child disappeared from view, and then he cast his brother a sour glance.

"Now I must perform the unenviable task of sending the wedding guests home," John said.

"Don't bother," Ross replied. "I'll do that for you."

"This is my wedding and my scandal," John refused, shaking his head. "Once I've made the announcement, I would appreciate your seeing them off."

"Of course."

Together, the Saint-Germain brothers walked down the corridor to the Banqueting Hall. John never loved his brother more than he did at that moment when Ross elected to stand by his side.

Before stepping into the hall John felt his brother's hand on his arm and turned to face him, asking, "Yes?"

"Is the child yours?" Ross asked, staring him in the eye.

"I don't know."

John and Ross walked into the Banqueting Hall and paused inside the doorway. Within seconds a hush fell over the wedding guests.

"Relatives and friends, I thank you for attending my

wedding,'' John announced in a strong voice that carried throughout the hall. ''Due to these unexpected circumstances, the wedding celebration is indefinitely postponed.''

Seeing the uncomfortable expressions on many faces, John realized that they were more embarrassed than he was. In an effort to break the tension in the hall, he managed a rueful smile and added, ''All of you will be invited here to celebrate our first anniversary . . . if my wife doesn't divorce me after this.''

Smothered pockets of chuckles erupted along the tables. The women still wore furious expressions, but there was nothing to be done for that. Most of the gentlemen were smiling sympathetically and probably thanking a merciful God that it was the Duke of Avon who'd been caught siring a bastard on his mistress.

''Please finish your meals,'' John added. ''After which Ross will see you out.''

''Well done, brother,'' Ross whispered.

John nodded at him and headed for the door, gesturing his majordomo to follow him. His man was there in an instant.

''Your Grace?''

''Tell Her Grace to bring the child to my office after the last of our guests have gone,'' John instructed him.

''Yes, Your Grace,'' Dobbs said, and hurried down the hall in the direction of the grand staircase.

Using the servants' staircase at the opposite end of the corridor, John walked up one flight to his office on the second floor. He poured himself a whiskey, downed it in one gulp, and then poured himself another. Sitting in his leather chair, he stretched his legs out and put his feet on top of his desk.

John closed his eyes and pondered the day's strange

turn of events. He felt more angry than embarrassed. That little scene with Lisette had been William Grimsby's wedding gift to him. He knew that as surely as he knew he was sitting in his office and drinking Scotland's finest whiskey.

He didn't care for himself that the wedding reception had been ruined, but Isabelle deserved better. His bride was the sweetest, most caring woman he'd ever met.

How humiliating for her to be faced with his former mistress on the day of their wedding. What horrible opinion did she now have of him?

And then there was the not-so-minor matter of his withholding the news of England's war with America. He'd intended only to make her wedding day as happy as possible and would have told her about the war in a few days.

Would Isabelle ever forgive him? Suddenly, her opinion of him was the most important thing in the world.

He loved her.

He loved her in spite of her eccentricities. Or perhaps because of them. His Mistress Nobody from Stratford was the only woman he'd ever known who hadn't wanted to marry him for his money or his title. Hell, she hadn't wanted to marry him at all. He had better keep his love for her hidden, or she might use it to her own best advantage. Letting his bride get the upper hand wouldn't do at all.

And then John's thoughts turned to the little girl. Could she actually be his daughter? He couldn't believe that she was. Lisette had never contacted him about a child. What better way to get money from a wealthy man than to give birth to his child? The girl had to be an impostor, an innocent being used by Grimsby and Lisette for their own nefarious plans.

Even if the girl was his child, she couldn't live with him at Avon Park. No respectable gentleman invited his bastard to live with his legitimate family. The byproduct of a tawdry affair, the girl would never be accepted by society.

An hour passed. And then another.

Finally, John heard the sound of knocking on the door. Before he could call out, the door swung open to reveal his mother.

Automatically, John bolted to his feet when she walked into the study. His mother didn't appear to be especially pleased with him, and he couldn't blame her. No real scandal had ever been attached to the Saint-Germain name, and the last thing she needed at her age was a scandal of epic proportions.

His mother sat in the chair across the desk from him. John sat when she sat.

She stared at him for what seemed like a long time and then asked, "Is the child yours?"

"I don't know," John answered honestly. "Lisette was my mistress, but I'm almost positive that this is one of Grimsby's schemes to exact revenge for Lenore's death."

"William Grimsby is an ass," the dowager announced. "Lenore died miscarrying a child, an unfortunate but relatively common occurrence. I never did care much for the Grimsby family. They lack intelligence."

"This fiasco certainly proves it," John replied.

"Delphinia Montgomery has taken the overnight guests to Arden Hall," his mother told him. "The others have also gone."

John nodded. "I never would have thought Delphinia Montgomery intelligent enough to think of that."

"She didn't; I did," the dowager said, making him

smile. "Hester and I will return to London in the morning and try to stifle the gossip."

"For once, Mother, you are destined for failure," John replied. "Society loves nothing better than scandal."

"Humph! We'll see about that."

"Ross will travel to London with you," John said. "I want him to investigate the girl's parentage while I mend the damage done to my marriage."

The dowager rose from the chair and stared at him for a moment. She shook her head sadly and said, "Will you men never learn to keep your pizzles tucked inside your trousers?"

John burst out laughing.

"Ah, well," his mother said with a smile. "I suppose that's the way the world wags. No pun intended." At that, she left the study.

A few minutes later another knock sounded on the door.

"Enter," John called.

The door opened to reveal Isabelle with the little girl in tow.

She's changed out of her wedding gown, John thought, rising from his chair. He hoped that wasn't a bad omen.

"Come inside and close the door," he said. "I want to speak with both of you."

Isabelle started forward, but the little girl remained rooted where she stood.

"Come inside," Isabelle said, trying to coax the child with a smile.

"Myrtle doesn't want to go in there," the girl said, shaking her head.

"Who is Myrtle?" John asked.

Isabelle threw him a smile. "Myrtle is Lily's invisible friend."

God's knob, John thought, rolling his eyes heavenward. Was he now harboring two females who insisted they had invisible friends? Well, the younger female would soon be gone from Avon Park, and his well-ordered life could resume.

"Why doesn't Myrtle want to come inside?" Isabelle asked the child.

"She's afraid."

John watched his bride gesture toward the study and say, "I promise there's nothing dangerous here."

"The Duke of Doom frightens her," Lily said, pointing her finger at him.

Isabelle laughed. "His Grace is sweeter than a bowl of walnut pudding with chocolate sauce."

"You said he behaves like a rat's—"

"His Grace would never be cruel to a little girl," Isabelle interrupted her. "Would you, Your Grace?"

"No," John answered, frowning.

"His Grace isn't happy," Lily said, her gaze fixed on him.

"His Grace is thrilled that you've come to meet him," Isabelle said. "You do trust me, don't you?"

Lily nodded.

Watching them, John marveled at his wife's patient skill in handling the child. She'd make an excellent mother for his children.

Realizing the girl was staring at him, John forced himself to smile and say in a well-modulated voice, "Lily, is it?"

She nodded.

"Won't you come inside and sit down?" John invited her. "I'd like to become acquainted with you."

Lily let Isabelle lead her into the study. The two of them sat in the chairs across the desk from him.

"John, I wish to make Lily, your long-lost daughter, known to you," Isabelle said. "Lily, this is your papa."

"May I call him Papa?" Lily asked, her startlingly green gaze riveted on him.

"No," John said in a clipped voice.

Bloody hell, he thought in the next instant. The girl was going to cry. How could he question her if she did?

Isabelle cast him a disgruntled look. She reached out and grasped the girl's hand comfortingly and explained, "His Grace means that he would prefer to become acquainted before you share familiar names. Isn't that correct, Your Grace?"

"Yes, quite correct." John shifted his dark gaze to the child, saying, "Now, then, Lily, I'd like to ask—"

"Mistress Dupre, if you please," the girl interrupted him.

In spite of the situation John struggled against a shout of laughter. The girl had pluck. She reminded him of Isabelle, who was smiling at him.

"Mistress Dupre, I do apologize," John said, inclining his head. "Who brought you to Avon Park?"

"Lisette."

"What relation is Lisette to you?"

"My mother."

"Why don't you call her Mama?" John asked.

"She prefers Lisette," Lily told him. "Mama makes her feel old."

How like Lisette's vanity to deprive her only child of calling her Mama, John thought. "Who brought Lisette and you to my home?" he asked.

"Earl."

"Earl who?"

Lily shrugged. "I don't know."

"Can you tell me what Earl looks like?" John asked.

Lily nodded. "He's a man, like you."

Isabelle giggled, and John cast her an unamused look. Then he returned his dark gaze to the child and asked, "What color hair does Earl have?"

"Yellow."

Now he was getting somewhere, John thought. Grimsby had plotted this for revenge. Purposefully, he stared hard at the little girl until she squirmed uncomfortably in her chair.

"Who is your father?" John asked, his gaze fixed on the child.

"You are, but I mustn't call you Papa," Lily answered. She turned to Isabelle and said, "Please, I want to leave now."

With battle etched across her fine features, Isabelle said, "Lily, step outside while I speak privately with His Grace."

"Myrtle doesn't want to be alone," the little girl whined. "She's afraid."

"Very well, sweetheart," Isabelle said. "Sit across the chamber in that chair in front of the hearth and block your ears."

"How do I do that?"

"Simply cover your ears with your hands like this," Isabelle said, demonstrating.

Lily raced across the study, climbed onto the chair, and blocked her ears.

"Can you hear me?" Isabelle asked in a normal tone of voice.

"No," Lily answered.

Isabelle bit her bottom lip to keep from laughing. She needed to retain her righteous anger in order to prevent her husband from hurting his child and himself beyond repair.

"How dare you speak so coldly to a child," Isabelle said in a harsh whisper, rounding on her husband. "True greatness knows gentleness."

"I am trying to learn the truth of the matter," John defended himself.

"I don't give a rat's arse for your truth," Isabelle told him. "That child has been abandoned by her own mother. I won't allow you to badger her, nor will I allow you to speak about her as if she couldn't hear you."

"For God's sake—"

"If you take the time to become acquainted with her, you will learn your precious truth," Isabelle interrupted. "I will not allow Lily to be deposited on that unnatural woman's doorstep."

"Do not try to force the waif on me," John said. "Even if she is my daughter, her living beneath the same roof as us is a shocking breach of propriety."

"You should have considered propriety before you bedded her mother." Isabelle gave him a contemptuous, wholly disgusted look. "You are mistaken if you believe I care about society's opinion."

At that, Isabelle whirled away. She crossed the chamber and tapped Lily on the shoulder. Hand in hand, they left the study.

John stared at the closed door through which they'd disappeared. Though irritated, he couldn't suppress the soft smile that touched his lips. His bride had never looked more beautiful than when she was championing the little girl.

Suddenly, his smile became a scowl. How dare his bride march into his study and dictate to him. He'd tolerate no mutiny in this marriage. At first opportunity he would set her straight about who was the master at Avon Park.

How dare her husband dictate to her, Isabelle fumed as she sat with Lily on the window seat in her bedchamber. Yes, John Saint-Germain was the Duke of Avon, and only hours ago she'd sworn to love, honor, and obey. However, Isabelle had no intention of obeying orders based on insensitivity and erroneous beliefs. She had a mind of her own and intended to use it. At the moment she was thinking more clearly than he. Apparently, she needed to save her husband from his own pigheadedness.

"He doesn't like me," Lily said, her expression glum.

Drawn from her mutinous thoughts, Isabelle focused on the little girl and said, "I beg your pardon?"

"The Duke of Doom doesn't like me."

"His Grace loves you," Isabelle told her, cupping the child's chin in one hand. "He just doesn't know it yet."

Lily smiled, and the thought of her father's loving her made her eyes sparkle like emeralds. "When will he know?" she asked.

"Only God knows the answer to that," Isabelle answered, and then realized how much she sounded like Giselle.

"Why is His Grace so mean?" Lily asked.

Isabelle paused before answering and tried to think of something plausible other than the truth. Finally, she dropped her voice to a mere whisper and said, "His Grace suffers from a bowel problem. It isn't serious, but it affects his mood."

"Oh." Lily was silent for a few minutes while she

considered that bit of information. Suddenly, she cried, "Look at the sun."

Isabelle gazed out the window at the western horizon. The dying sun was a red ball of fire. She dropped her gaze to the gardens below and thought of the wonderful times she and Lily could enjoy outside.

"If you walk through the sitting room over there and go into my dressing room," Isabelle told her, "you can see the sun rising in the east."

"Let's go see," Lily said.

Isabelle laughed. "Like people, the sun rises in the morning."

"What's that?" Lily asked, pointing her tiny finger.

Isabelle followed the little girl's gaze. On the distant, rolling hills, fires blazed and seemed to reach for the darkening sky.

"Today is Midsummer's Day," Isabelle explained. "The country folk celebrate by lighting bonfires built of fir and oak and then dancing around them."

"Let's go dance with them," the little girl said, excitement shining in her emerald eyes.

"We can't this time. Perhaps next year His Grace will be feeling better." Noting the child's disappointed expression, Isabelle added, "Tomorrow we'll play outside in the garden. Or perhaps we'll walk through those giant oaks over there and go to the river. I'll bring my flute. Won't that be fun?"

In answer, Lily clapped her hands together.

A knock on the door drew their attention, and Isabelle called out, "Enter."

Dobbs walked into the room. The majordomo smiled at Lily and then said to Isabelle, "His Grace wishes to know if you are supping with him."

"Please tell His Grace I suffer from the headache," Isabelle replied.

"Yes, Your Grace." The majordomo turned to leave.

"Mister Dobbs, tell His Grace that Mistress Dupre hopes his bowels feel better," Lily called out.

"Bowels?" Dobbs echoed, whirling around in surprise. The little girl's words broke the man's usually haughty demeanor. He struggled against a shout of laughter and lost.

"Problem bowels are not funny," Lily scolded, shaking her finger at him.

Several moments later, when Dobbs had finally regained control of himself, he said in a dry tone of voice, "I do apologize and will definitely deliver your sympathy to His Grace."

The majordomo retreated across the chamber to the door. Isabelle noted that the man's shoulders shook with silent laughter.

Another knock on the door drew their attention. Before Isabelle could call out, the door opened and Juniper walked in.

"I've prepared a chamber at the other end of the corridor," the woman reported.

"Go with Mrs. Juniper now," Isabelle instructed the girl. "She'll tell you a story and put you to bed."

"Myrtle doesn't want to leave you," Lily cried, throwing herself into Isabelle's arms and clinging to her as if she'd never let go. "Myrtle is afraid."

Isabelle gazed down at the child and read the insecurity couched in her disarming emerald eyes. She couldn't blame the child for being afraid. Her mother had abandoned her in a crowd of two hundred people, and now she was about to pass the night in a strange house.

"You must sleep in your own chamber," Isabelle said in a gentle voice. "Myrtle doesn't need to be afraid, because Mrs. Juniper will be with her. Did you know that Juniper took care of me when I was a little girl?"

"She did?"

Isabelle smiled and nodded.

"Then I'll stay with Juniper too," Lily agreed. "Will you come with us?"

"Yes, and I'll play you a lullaby," Isabelle said, reaching for her flute.

Together the three of them walked the length of the corridor and entered the last chamber on the left. Isabelle and Juniper undressed the child down to her chemise and tucked her into bed. Juniper sat in the chair near the hearth.

Isabelle sat on the edge of the bed and pressed the girl back on the pillow, saying, "Close your eyes, little one. Listen to my song and feel it in your body."

Lifting the flute to her lips, Isabelle began her song, a melody that her guardian angel had played for her through the years, one that always persuaded her to sleep. The lilting notes vibrated throughout the chamber, bringing peace to the girl, whose eyes closed. The tune was hauntingly hypnotic, a soothing bath of warm notes that conjured a spring twilight and then the rhythmic turning of the tides.

Glancing down at Lily, Isabelle realized that her breathing had evened and she slept with a smile on her face. So young to be abandoned by her mother. So young to be rejected by her father. So young to be alone.

At least Giselle had come into her life on the day her father's passing, Isabelle thought. How fortun she'd been, though she hadn't realized it at the tim

Isabelle rose from her perch on the edge of the

She mouthed the words *thank you* to Mrs. Juniper and left the chamber.

Isabelle changed hurriedly into the nightgown that had been created for this special night. Scooped-necked and sleeveless, the gown was made of silk and nearly transparent.

"Inflaming a man's passion is the gown's intent."

Surprised by the voice, Isabelle whirled around and saw Giselle sitting in the chair in front of the hearth. "And what do you know about a man's passion?" she asked the old woman.

Giselle gave her an ambiguous smile, but said nothing.

"Is Lily my husband's daughter?" Isabelle asked.

Giselle shrugged. "Does it matter?"

Isabelle shook her head. "Is Myrtle an angel like you?"

Giselle smiled. "Myrtle is the girl's imaginary friend."

"People have always believed that you are imaginary because they can't see or hear you," Isabelle said.

"Alas, the world is filled with skeptics," Giselle replied. "Your prince has arrived."

A knock on the connecting door between her chamber and her husband's drew Isabelle's attention. She glanced at Giselle, but the old woman had vanished.

Isabelle rose from her chair and crossed the chamber to the door. At least Lily's arrival had kept her from worrying about what was going to happen in a few mintes.

Isabelle opened the connecting door and got her first at of her husband. Appearing incredibly handsome, wore a black silk bed robe that tied at the waist sash. Her gaze slid to the robe's opening, which revealed a muscular chest covered with a mat of black hair.

Faced with her husband's virility, Isabelle lost her confidence. She lifted her violet gaze and found that his gaze was riveted on her body, almost completely visible through her transparent night shift.

Sweet celestial breath, her husband had the intensely hungry expression of a man who hadn't eaten for days.

"Is our wedding night canceled?" John asked.

Isabelle shook her head.

"You've recovered from your headache?"

"Completely recovered," she answered.

John shifted his gaze to her chamber, then looked at her again, asking, "Where is she?"

"Lily and Juniper are sleeping in the chamber at the end of the corridor," Isabelle told him.

John inclined his head. Apparently, his bride had the good sense to put the issue of Lily off until the morning. "I have champagne chilling," he said, offering her his hand to escort her into his chamber. "Will you share a glass with me?"

For one awful moment John thought Isabelle was going to refuse, but then she placed her hand in his.

His wife looked like a woman on her way to the gallows.

John saw that as they crossed the chamber to the chaise in front of the hearth. Anxiety had etched itself across her delicate features and paled her complexion, emphasizing the fine sprinkling of freckles across the bridge of her nose.

Bull's pizzle, John swore inwardly. His experience in breaching blushing virgins was limited to Lenore Grimsby, and that night had proved less than enjoyable. He would need to proceed slowly and gently with her, for whatever happened between them on this night would color their marriage for the next forty years or so.

John looked from her pale face to her white-knuckled hands clutched together in a death grip. He dropped his gaze to her body, barely hidden beneath her sheer nightgown. God, she looked too beautiful to be real.

Without sparing her another glance, John opened the champagne and filled a crystal goblet. "Let's sit on the chaise and share the champagne while we talk," he said.

"You only want to talk?" Isabelle echoed in surprise.

John couldn't tell if she was disappointed or relieved. When he turned toward her a frantic expression appeared on her face, and he struggled against the laughter he felt bubbling up.

"Sit on my lap," John invited her, sitting down on the chaise.

"There's no need for that," she said. "The chaise is big enough for two."

"I want to be close to you," he replied. "Please."

That one *please* worked a tiny miracle. She nodded and sat on his lap.

Putting his left arm around her, John gently drew her close until she rested against his chest. "Drink," he said, lifting the goblet to her lips.

Isabelle took a sip and swallowed. "The champagne tickles my nose," she said with a smile.

John returned her smile. After taking a sip of the champagne, he set the goblet on the floor and drew her down until her head rested against his shoulder.

"Are you comfortable?" he asked, his hand on her shoulder beginning a slow caress.

"Yes." Isabelle gazed up at him from beneath the thick fringe of her blond lashes.

"Darling, you have nothing to fear. Lovemaking is a

natural expression between a man and his wife and binds their—" John hesitated, catching himself before he uttered the word *love*. "Lovemaking binds their vows for all time. Without this physical joining those sacred vows are empty, meaningless words. Do you understand?"

"I think so."

"Will you share my bed?" he asked.

Isabelle looked at him through enormous violet eyes. She paused so long before answering that John feared she would refuse. And then what would he do?

Isabelle slipped out of his embrace and rose from the chaise. "Yes, I will share your bed," she said in a voice barely louder than a whisper.

John stood then and held his hand out in invitation as if he were asking her to waltz. Isabelle dropped her gaze from his dark eyes to his outstretched hand. When she raised her gaze to his again, John saw that the anxiety had crept back into her expression.

"I'll stop whenever you say," he promised. "Trust me?"

In an unconsciously sensual gesture Isabelle flicked her tongue out and wet her lips, gone dry from nervousness. Then she reached out and placed her hand in his. Together they walked to the bed.

John reached out with both hands and slid the straps of her nightgown off her shoulders. The gown fluttered to the floor in a pool of silk.

Ignoring her furious blush, John worshiped her with his eyes. He dropped his gaze from her face to her perfectly formed breasts, her tiny waist, her enticingly rounded hips, and her dainty feet. When his scorching gaze returned to hers, John unfastened the bed robe's belt and shrugged out of it. His robe mingled on the floor with her nightgown, even as their bodies were about to mingle.

Isabelle silently refused to drop her gaze below his neck, and John suffered the urge to laugh, but controlled himself. "Look at me, Belle," he said. "Please?"

Again that word worked its magic.

Slowly, Isabelle slid her gaze from his broad shoulders to his chest covered with a mat of black hair. Her gaze dipped lower to his tapered waist and then lower.

John stepped a hairbreadth closer. With one hand he reached out and caressed her silken cheek, then glided his fingertips down the column of her neck to her shoulders.

Allowing her no time to think, John drew her into his embrace and captured her mouth in a lingering kiss that stole her breath away. Then he scooped her into his arms, gently placed her on the bed, and lay down beside her.

For the first time in her life Isabelle experienced the incredible sensation of masculine hardness touching her female softness. And she liked it.

John lowered his head and sought her lips in a slow, soul-stealing kiss that seemed to last forever. When she returned his kiss in kind, he sprinkled dozens of feathery-light kisses on her temples, her eyelids, and the bridge of her nose.

"I love your freckles," he murmured.

"What freckles?" she whispered, dazed with awakening desire.

John smiled and let his gaze roam from her hauntingly lovely face to her softly rounded breasts. "Exquisite," he said, gliding his hand from the column of her throat to the juncture of her thighs.

His lips followed the path his hand had taken, from

the column of her throat to her breasts. He paused there to suckle upon her pink-tipped nipples, igniting a heat between her thighs that banished all coherent thought.

"Spread your legs for me," John ordered, his voice thick with desire.

Isabelle heard his voice and obeyed without hesitation. John kissed her again and then, watching her face, inserted one long finger inside her.

Isabelle opened her mouth to cry out, but John was faster. He covered her lips with his own, the urgency of his kiss drugging her senses.

"Be easy, darling," he coaxed her, inserting a second finger inside her. "I want to make you ready to receive me."

John dipped his head to suckle upon her nipples and began to move his fingers seductively inside her. And then Isabelle began to move her hips, enticing his fingers deeper inside her writhing body.

Moaning with need, she moved her hips faster and faster. And then his fingers were gone.

"Darling, look at me," John said, kneeling between her thighs, his manhood poised to pierce.

Isabelle opened her eyes and stared at him in a daze of desire.

"One moment of pain," he promised.

With one powerful thrust John pushed himself inside her and buried himself deep within her trembling body. Clutching him, she cried out in surprise as he broke through her virgin's barrier.

John lay still for several long moments and allowed her to accustom herself to the feel of him inside her. Then he began to move, enticing her to move with him.

Innocence vanished and primal instinct surfaced.

Caught in the midst of swirling passion, Isabelle

wrapped her legs around his waist and, moving with him, met each of his powerful thrusts with her own. And then she exploded, as wave after wave of exquisite sensation carried her to paradise.

Knowing she'd found fulfillment, John unleashed his powerful need. He groaned and shuddered and poured his seed deep inside her.

They lay still for several long moments, their labored breathing the only sound in the chamber. Finally, John rolled to one side and pulled her with him into his embrace. He gazed at her expression of wonder and recognized her heart shining in her amethyst eyes.

John gave her a lazy smile and pulled her across his chest. "I apologize for failing to tell you about the war," he said. "I only wanted our wedding day to be perfect and would have told you in the morning."

"Thank you for your thoughtfulness," Isabelle said, smiling at him. "Now, about Lily—"

"May we please save the subject of Lily for the morning?" John asked.

"I suppose so."

John gently drew her down and kissed the top of her head. "We'll be thinking more clearly then."

"I'm keeping her, though."

John smiled down at her. "Go to sleep, wife."

Isabelle closed her eyes. When her breathing evened, John knew that she slept and joined her in a deep, dreamless sleep.

Chapter 13

Good Christ, she's talking to herself again.
John stood at the window in his office and watched Isabelle sitting alone on a stone bench in his garden the following morning.

His bride looked like an angel destined for Bedlam. Provocatively innocent in her white muslin morning gown, Isabelle wore a wreath of oak leaves and violets on top of her blond head and carried on an animated conversation, complete with hand gestures, with the vacant spot beside her on the bench. But where was the child?

John tore his gaze from his bride and scanned the area until he spied the girl at the far end of the garden. Wearing a wreath of oak leaves and violets, the girl gamboled around and around as if life held no greater joy than frollicking beneath the summer's sun in his garden.

The girl's joy was contagious, and John was unable to suppress a smile. Had he ever been that enamored of the simple joys in life? Perhaps once, a long time ago, before Lenore Grimsby had shattered—

The door opening behind him drew his attention. Ross, followed by Dobbs carrying a breakfast tray, walked into the room. While the majordomo set the tray on the desk, his brother sauntered across the room to him.

"What a charming picture," Ross said, gazing out the window.

John cast him a sidelong glance, but said nothing.

"To whom is Isabelle speaking?" Ross asked.

"She's speaking to the little girl over there," John lied.

"The child isn't listening," Ross said.

"Many children don't listen when an adult speaks," John replied.

"Well, they do make a fetching picture," Ross remarked, and then turned away from the window.

John relaxed. He didn't want his brother to think that Isabelle possessed the peculiar habit of talking to herself.

After the door clicked shut behind the majordomo, the two brothers sat at the desk. John poured his brother a cup of coffee and then filled one for himself.

"So, how goes the married life?" Ross asked.

John scowled at him.

"That good, huh?"

"The girl's arrival almost cost me my wedding night," John said. "And that was after Grimase dropped the news of England's war with America."

"You hadn't told Isabelle about it?" Ross asked.

John shook his head. "After failing to tell her that, I thought she would place the girl's need above mine."

Ross grew serious. "She's an adorable child, but I've never seen a sadder, more bewildered expression on anyone."

"Mistress Dupre, as she insists on being called, passed the night with Juniper," John said.

"Shall I return her to Lisette?" Ross asked.

"Isabelle won't allow it," John answered. "Mistress Dupre will remain at Avon Park until you finish investigating her paternity."

"And if someone else sired her?"

"I will not accept a child who isn't mine."

"And if she is yours?"

John shrugged. "Her mere presence here is a scandal. I don't know what I'll do if she is mine." He stood then and crossed the chamber to gaze outside, asking, "What time are you leaving for London?"

"Mother says that Hester and she need a couple of hours," Ross answered. "Then we'll be off."

John fixed his dark gaze on his wife, who now sat quietly on the bench and watched the girl prancing about. Isabelle rose from the bench and started across the lawns toward the girl. Lily stood beneath one of the giant oaks separating parkland from woodland. The child was pointing at something in the tree, and his wife looked up as if trying to discern what was up there.

Isabelle stared up at the oak's branch. She smiled at what she saw.

"What is it, Your Grace?" Lily asked.

Surprised by the girl's use of the title, Isabelle whirled around and asked, "Why did you call me that?"

"Juniper said I mustn't be too familiar," Lily explained. "She told me to call you Your Grace."

Isabelle crouched down to be eye level with her, saying, "My friends call me Belle."

Lily grinned. "Are we friends, then?"

"I certainly hope so," Isabelle answered.

"I wouldn't wish to make Juniper unhappy," Lily told her.

"Call me Lady Belle."

Lily nodded in agreement. "What is in that tree, Lady Belle?"

"A bird's nest."

While they watched, a robin landed on the oak's branch and the tiny chirping nestlings appeared. Their mother dipped her head toward each one of them in turn.

"What is she doing?" Lily asked.

"Feeding them insects."

Lily grimaced. "Yuck, yuck!"

Isabelle laughed at her expression. "Let's sit on that bench, and I'll play my flute for you."

Lily grabbed her hand, and the two strolled across the garden. Isabelle inhaled deeply and sighed with contentment. Honeysuckle and roses scented the breeze, and sweet birdsong filled the air. Avon Park appeared like a paradise on earth.

"The Duke of Doom's mother visited me this morning," Lily said in a conspiratorial whisper.

Isabelle looked at her in surprise. "She did?"

Lily nodded. "Juniper was helping me dress."

"What did the dowager say?"

" 'I've seen enough.' "

"How provoking. Did she smile?"

"Yes, and she nodded her head."

Sitting down on the stone bench, Isabelle reached for her flute case, which she'd left there. Lily sat down beside her.

Isabelle lifted the flute out of the case and asked conversationally, "What do you want more than anything else in the whole wide world?"

"I want to be loved," Lily answered without hesitation.

Isabelle snapped her head around to stare at the girl.

Lily wanted what she had wanted all of those long years ago when she'd met her guardian angel.

Leaning close, Isabelle whispered, "I love you."

"Oh, I am so very happy that Lisette brought me to you," Lily exclaimed, clapping her hands together.

Isabelle lifted the flute to her lips and began playing. Her melody was as jaunty as a brisk morning walk. Sweet trills, rich notes, and liquid phrases like a nightingale's song filled the air in the garden.

"Your Grace?"

Isabelle immediately stopped playing. Lily and she turned toward the voice.

"I apologize for interrupting," her husband's major-domo said. "The dowager wishes to see you and the child as soon as possible."

"Thank you, Dobbs." Isabelle returned her flute to its case and turned to the girl, asking, "Shall we go inside?"

Lily's expression screamed disappointment.

"Do you know how butterflies kiss?" Isabelle asked.

"No."

"Come close and shut your eyes." When Lily did as she was told, Isabelle fluttered her eyelashes against her cheek, making her giggle.

Together the woman and the child stood and walked toward the mansion. Before going inside, Lily whirled around and shouted, "Farewell, garden. I'll see you later."

Reaching the dowager's apartments, Isabelle knocked on the door. The dowager's personal maid answered and ushered them toward the sitting room. Aunt Hester was with the dowager.

"Dearest Isabelle, we are leaving for London shortly," the dowager greeted her.

"Oh, don't leave simply because the wedding is over," Isabelle protested.

"John and you need time to sort this unfortunate incident out," Dowager Tessa said. "Do you think you can forgive him?"

"There's nothing to forgive," Isabelle told her. "What is done is past and has nothing to do with me."

"How relieved we are to hear that," Aunt Hester piped up. "Any other young lady of breeding would—" She shut her mouth abruptly when the dowager cast her a warning look.

"I can see that you've already become attached to the child," the dowager said with a smile. She turned to Lily and asked, "Do you know who I am?"

Lily nodded. "The Duke of Doom's mother."

The dowager chuckled. "Do you know what that means?"

Lily shook her head.

"I am your grandmama," the dowager announced.

Isabelle beamed with approval, thinking that at least one Saint-Germain had sense. With an expression of awe appearing on her face, Lily stared at the older woman.

"Tessa, you do not know that for sure," Hester said.

"Hush," the dowager silenced her. "The child is my granddaughter."

"How do you know?" Isabelle asked, puzzled.

"A woman always recognizes her own flesh and blood."

"And what do I call you?" Lily asked in a loud voice.

"Grandmama."

With a smile that could have lit the whole mansion,

Lily threw herself into the old woman's arms and asked, "Do you really have to leave?"

"Your papa and you need time together to become acquainted," the dowager said, giving her a hug. "Will you do something for me?"

Lily nodded.

"Be patient with your papa."

"I promise, Grandmama," the little girl said solemnly.

"Good. I'll see you again in London." The dowager turned to Isabelle, who mouthed the words *thank you.* "I'm depending on you to take good care of them and help them through this."

Isabelle smiled and nodded, saying, "Of course I will."

"As you know, my son can be irritatingly stubborn, a miserable trait he inherited from his father," the dowager continued. "Don't give up on him. Promise me you'll keep him from making the worst mistake of his life by refusing to accept her."

"I promise," Isabelle said as solemnly as Lily had.

Joy without end.

Isabelle gazed at her wedding band and thought about the sentiment it carried. If only those words could prove true.

Something wonderful had happened yesterday. Her life had changed the moment she'd become John's wife.

Isabelle closed her eyes and conjured her husband's image as he had appeared the previous evening. Again she saw the magnificent sight of his broad shoulders tapering to a narrow waist, his perfectly rounded buttocks, his well-muscled thighs. Again she felt his lips on hers, his hand caressing her body intimately, the weight of him as he covered her and shared his love.

Isabelle flushed hotly. She knew she'd enjoyed her duty as his wife, and somehow that seemed sinful.

Isabelle gave herself a mental shake. If she went down to supper with flushed cheeks, John would know what she'd been thinking about. How embarrassing that would be.

Supper's success or failure depended upon her husband. Unfortunately, John had been especially stern with Lily the previous day. And yet Isabelle knew her husband was not a stern man. He was merely protecting himself from further emotional injury.

Isabelle touched her golden locket for luck and then squared her shoulders with determination. She would force her husband to acknowledge and accept his daughter. In the end he would thank her for not giving up on him.

In spite of her worries Isabelle felt exhilarated. Another of her wishes was about to come true. For the first time in many lonely years she would be part of a real family supper.

Wanting to look her best, Isabelle inspected herself in the framed, full-length mirror. She wore a pastel lavender silk dress with a squared neckline and short, puffed sleeves. Her blond hair had been tied back with a matching lavender ribbon.

"Enter," Isabelle called when she heard the knock on her bedchamber door.

"You look like a princess," Lily exclaimed, dashing across the chamber to her. Behind the child stood Mrs. Juniper.

"Thank you." Isabelle smiled at the little girl and said, "You look very pretty too."

Lily looked like an angel in a white muslin dress. The white contrasted becomingly with her raven hair, which Juniper had woven into one thick braid.

Isabelle made a mental note to take Lily into Stratford at the first opportunity. The child desperately needed a complete wardrobe. If need be, she'd use her own money to purchase it.

"Are you hungry?" Isabelle asked her.

Lily nodded eagerly.

"Are you ready to sup with your papa?"

Lily's expression drooped, and a worried frown creased her forehead.

"Tell me what bothers you," Isabelle said.

"What if His Grace growls at me again?" she asked.

"Then growl back at him."

Lily stared at her in obvious surprise.

"If His Grace bites you, then bite him back," Isabelle said. "And if His Grace tickles you, tickle him back. Like this . . ." She tickled the girl and made her giggle.

Isabelle offered Lily her hand, and she accepted it. Turning to the nanny, she said, "Have your own supper now, Mrs. Juniper."

"Don't forget," Lily reminded the older woman. "You promised to tell me a story."

"I haven't forgotten, dear," Juniper replied.

Hand in hand, Isabelle and Lily walked the length of the corridor to the grand staircase. Descending to the first-floor foyer, they met the duke's majordomo.

"Good evening, Your Grace," the man greeted them. "And a very good evening to you, Mistress Dupre."

"Thank you, Dobbs," Isabelle said.

"Thank you, Dobbs," Lily imitated her.

Isabelle escorted the little girl toward the dining

room. She paused in the doorway when she spied John with his back to them and staring out the window.

"What a big table!" Lily exclaimed.

Hearing the girl, John turned around and smiled at Isabelle. When he shifted his gaze to the child, a frown appeared on his face. To his credit he banished it quickly.

"Good evening, Your Grace," Lily called to him.

John inclined his head. "And a good evening to you, Mistress Dupre."

Thank God for tiny miracles, Isabelle thought in relief. Her husband had gentled his approach to the child.

The three of them sat down at one end of the long mahogany dining table. John sat at the head of the table, while Isabelle and Lily sat on either side of him.

Beneath the majordomo's supervision the footmen began serving them from the sideboard—cucumber and tomato salad, split-pea soup with bacon and herbs, asparagus in French rolls, roasted chicken, and raspberry cream for dessert.

An uncomfortable silence descended upon them as they began eating. Isabelle peeked at John, who cast speculative glances at Lily. Only the little girl ate with gusto, but even she threw an occasional cautious glance at the duke.

Isabelle tried to think of something witty to say that would warm the atmosphere in the dining room. Unfortunately, her mind remained humiliatingly blank. In the end Lily saved the meal from being a dismal failure.

"Oops," Lily exclaimed when a bit of chicken fell on her lap. She reached to pick it up, but the chicken landed on the carpet.

"Don't bother about it," John said.

Ignoring him, Lily pushed her chair back. She knelt on the floor to search for the chicken.

"Dobbs will retrieve it when we've finished the meal," John said.

"Dobbs is an old man," Lily shouted from somewhere under the table. "I can bend down better."

At that, Lily reappeared and held the piece of chicken up for their perusal. Dobbs started forward to take it from her, as Isabelle opened her mouth to tell her to put it down on top of the table.

Lily popped it into her mouth and began chewing, which made the duke smile. After she'd swallowed the bit of chicken, she held her hand up and said, "All gone."

John burst out laughing, and Lily gave him an innocently flirtatious smile.

Isabelle beamed at the byplay between them. Perhaps persuading him to accept his daughter wouldn't be as difficult as she'd assumed.

Reclaiming her seat, Lily rested her chin on her hand and leaned closer to John, asking in a voice loud enough for the servants to hear, "How are your bowels today?"

Isabelle felt a bubble of laughter rising in her throat. She glanced at the majordomo standing near the sideboard. Dobbs had turned his back on them, but his shoulders shook with silent laughter.

John stared at the little girl in surprise. "I beg your pardon?"

"Lady Belle told me about your bowel problem," Lily said. "That's why you frown at me. But you must be feeling better today, because you laughed."

John flicked a sidelong glance at Isabelle and then said, "What remarkable powers of deduction you have, Mistress Dupre."

"Thank you." Lily smiled, obviously pleased with herself.

Isabelle would have bet her last shilling that the little girl had no idea what he was talking about.

"What else did Lady Belle tell you?" John asked, leaning close to the child.

"If you growl at me," Lily warned, pointing a tiny finger at him, "I'm going to growl back at you. If you bite me, I'll bite back. If you tickle me, then I'll—"

"Tickle me back?" John interrupted.

Lily nodded.

"Then I will remain on my best behavior," John said, reaching out to tap the tip of her small nose playfully.

Watching them, Isabelle felt her heart soar with her success. Lily was a sweet child, and only a man with no heart could possibly resist her.

"Being tickled makes me laugh," Lily was telling him. "I like it."

"What else do you like?" John asked her.

"I like Lady Belle," Lily answered, "and I like you too."

Isabelle felt tears welling up in her eyes. She glanced at her husband and saw him swallowing as if he struggled with his emotions too.

"And I like you," Isabelle told the little girl.

"Do you like sitting outside in the garden on warm summer evenings?" John asked.

"I bet I would," Lily said, her eagerness apparent.

John glanced at Isabelle. "Shall we?"

The three of them rose from the table and left the dining room. With Lily in the lead, John and Isabelle walked down the corridor to the door that opened onto the garden.

Like a real family, Isabelle thought, her spirits soaring.

A warm breeze caressed them when they stepped outside. The fragrant scents of honeysuckle and roses mingled with new-mown hay and wafted through the air.

Taking Lily's hand in hers, Isabelle led her to one edge of the garden that overlooked a meadow. Sparkling lights flickered and died among the tall grasses in the distance.

"What is it?" Lily asked in an awed whisper.

"Fireflies," John answered. "They light up while ascending."

"Wishes whispered to those fireflies will come true," Isabelle told her. "Those glittering creatures will carry your wish to God and His angels."

Lily instantly snapped her eyes shut. Her lips moved silently as she whispered her wish to the fireflies.

"What did you wish for?" John asked.

Lily looked up at him with her enormous emerald eyes, then lifted her chin a notch, saying, "I shan't tell you, because then my wish won't come true."

They started walking toward the mansion and stopped to sit on the stone bench. Beside the bench someone had set a bowl of water.

"What's that?" Lily asked.

"I've left water for the garden toad," Isabelle told her. "If we sit here very still, he just might appear."

Lily sat down on the bench between them. For ten long minutes the three of them sat in silence. Isabelle stole a peek at John, who was watching her as if she were the most interesting sight in the world. She blushed and smiled at him, and then gave the little girl her attention.

"A toad seeking your companionship is considered

the sign of a special favor," Isabelle told her. "Do not be disappointed if he doesn't come out to meet you tonight, because toads are shy creatures. He needs to become accustomed to your presence."

"What will you do when Mister Toad does come out to meet you?" John asked her.

"I'll catch him and give him a kiss on the lips," Lily said.

John chuckled and then ordered, "Look up at the sky." When she did, he said, "Very soon now the sky will light up with stars. Did you know there are three twilights?"

Lily looked at him and shook her head.

"Civil twilight arrives as soon as the sun sets in the west, but we still have enough natural light by which to read," John told her. "The civil twilight deepens into nautical twilight, when the horizon and the sky become one. Astronomical twilight is when the stars emerge in the sky."

"I want to see the stars," Lily said, gazing up at the darkening sky.

"The light is still hiding them," he told her.

"Can we wait here until they come out?" Lily asked.

John shook his head. "Perhaps another night. I have important work to do on my ledgers."

"What's a ledger?" she asked.

"My ledger is the book where I keep accounts of my businesses," he answered.

"What are accounts and businesses?" Lily asked, making Isabelle smile.

"I'll tell you tomorrow," John said. "Now is the time for little girls to go to their beds."

When they returned to the mansion, Mrs. Juniper was waiting to take Lily upstairs. The girl gave Isabelle a kiss and then turned to John, asking, "Would you like a kiss too, Your Grace?"

John looked decidedly uncomfortable, and Isabelle held her breath. The most marvelous thing happened then. John nodded and crouched down to receive his kiss from Lily.

"I'll pray for your bowels," the little girl told him.

John grinned. "On behalf of my bowels, I appreciate your prayers."

Hand in hand, Juniper and Lily started up the stairs, but their voices drifted back to Isabelle and John.

"What are bowels?" the little girl asked.

"Do you want to hear a story about a princess, or do you want to know about His Grace's bowels?" the nanny asked.

"I want the princess. . . ."

Smiling, Isabelle turned to her husband, but he wasn't smiling at her. Instead, a forbidding scowl had etched itself across his face.

"I want to speak with you in my office now," John said curtly.

Isabelle nodded and followed him up one flight of stairs to his office. Forcing herself to remain calm, she looked at him expectantly when he closed the door behind them.

"I have two things to say to you," John said in a clipped voice.

Isabelle knew he wasn't going to thank her for reuniting him with his long-lost daughter.

"Cease talking to yourself when you are alone," he ordered.

Isabelle opened her mouth to protest, but John held his hand up for silence.

"I glanced out that window this morning and caught

you sitting in the garden having a conversation with yourself," he told her. "Please do not insult my intelligence by prattling about guardian angels."

Again Isabelle opened her mouth. She intended to set him straight about a number of things, beginning with his lack of faith in the invisible. But her husband didn't give her a chance to speak.

"Do *not* force that child upon me," John said, his expression pinched with anger. "Accepting her is beyond my capability. Even in the unlikely event she is mine, Lily is illegitimate issue and belongs with Lisette."

"God mend your words," Isabelle gasped, finally finding her voice. "Let me tell you something, Your Grace. I am keeping Lily and will never send her back to the woman who abandoned her. Do I make myself clear?"

"You cannot keep a child who belongs to another woman," John told her, his voice rising in anger. "She does not belong at Avon Park."

With battle etched across her features, Isabelle glared at him. "Then I'll take her to Arden Hall."

"I am your husband and refuse to allow it."

"You won't be my husband if I divorce you."

"Over my dead body," John shot back.

Isabelle stared him straight in the eye and said, "So be it, Your Grace, and may your blackened soul rest in peace." At that Isabelle whirled away and marched to the door. Before leaving she called over her shoulder in an angry voice, "Thank you for showing kindness to her this evening."

Muttering about her husband's pigheadedness, Isabelle slammed the door shut behind her. She marched down the corridor to the grand staircase and then climbed the stairs to find refuge in her own chamber.

Isabelle sat in one of the chairs in front of the hearth and felt the fight rushing out of her, leaving her depleted of energy. She sighed. Performing her wifely duty was out of the question for that night. After all, she couldn't very well threaten her husband with a divorce and then slip into his bed.

Isabelle gazed at her wedding band. Joy without end? Those were empty words, expressing a meaningless sentiment from a man who had no heart.

Chapter 14

What else could he have expected from a lady who knitted a shawl for a flower girl?

John stood in his office the next afternoon and watched from the window as his bride sat in the garden and played her flute. His alleged daughter gamboled around and around like a garden sprite.

He didn't know what to do about the two new women in his life. Having passed a sleepless night alone in his own chamber, John now understood how his wife's mind worked. Isabelle saw her own lonely childhood in the girl and was determined to shower the child with love. Apparently, saving the girl from a lonely childhood would somehow heal her own emotional scars.

And if he refused to accept the girl as his own? A divorce was out of the question. He would never allow it. Neither would he accept a miserable marriage.

God, but he wanted Isabelle back in his bed.

He loved her. Her threat to leave him had made him even more aware of that fact, but he could never let her know his feelings. Lenore had used his love against him, and John intended never to allow that to happen again.

True, Isabelle's and his union had been no love match in the usual sense. On the other hand, if he hadn't loved her just a little, no amount of pressure from his angry mother could have persuaded him to marry her.

A smile touched John's lips. Isabelle couldn't resist adopting any stray who wandered across her path. Would he have wanted her if she were any other way? *No,* an inner voice answered. His wife was perfection.

He wanted a wife who cared deeply for others, not just herself, and that brought him back to his problem. What course of action should he take regarding his alleged daughter? Whatever he chose to do could color his relationship with Isabelle.

John lifted the parchment off his desk and read the missive from his brother. Ross had wasted no time in beginning his investigation. London society was buzzing about the Duke of Avon's scandalous wedding reception disaster. Lisette Dupre had conveniently disappeared, leaving no evidence of her daughter's birth certificate.

So what was he to do? John wondered. He couldn't accept a child who wasn't his, yet his bride threatened to leave him if he didn't acknowledge the child. He'd been caught in a no-win situation.

John decided he needed to keep an open mind regarding the girl, which wouldn't be too difficult. Lily Dupre was a delightful child.

With that settled in his mind, John turned his attention to bedding his wife again. She might resist him now that she'd threatened to divorce him, but Isabelle didn't stand a fighting chance against his superior sophistication and considerable charm. He would need to proceed slowly, though.

What he needed to ensure success was a change in scenery. His wife would let her guard down once she'd left the usual details of everyday life behind. Not only that, but they would be free from the threat of his would-be assassin.

Scotland. He would take her to his estate in the

mountains of Argyll, where London society did not exist.

John sat down at his desk and penned two missives. The first was to his brother and explained where they'd gone. The second was bound for his Liverpool office, instructing them to prepare one of his ships to sail to Scotland on the evening of the twenty-eighth.

John rose from his chair and tugged on the bell pull. A few minutes later the door opened, and his majordomo appeared.

"Yes, Your Grace?"

"I want two groomsmen to deliver these," John said, passing him the missives. "Then inform Her Grace I want to speak with her in my office."

"Yes, Your Grace." Dobbs left the room and closed the door behind himself.

For fifteen minutes John paced back and forth behind his desk. "Enter," he called when he heard his wife's knock.

The door swung open to reveal Isabelle. Determination had etched itself across her fine features as she marched across the study toward him, ready to do battle. Her violet eyes glittered with her anger.

"I meant what I said last night," Isabelle announced, without giving him a chance to speak.

John gifted her with his devastating smile, meant to confound her, and was pleased to see surprised bewilderment replace the anger in her expression. "We're leaving in the morning for my estate in Scotland," he told her. "Please make the necessary preparations."

"I am not leaving England," Isabelle insisted, the battle returning to her expression.

John had expected that sort of reply and nearly laughed out loud at her wonderful predictability.

"Please sit down and we'll discuss this gently," he invited her.

Isabelle lifted her chin a notch and told him in a haughty voice, "I prefer to stand."

"I said *sit*," John ordered in a stern voice, unused to having his wishes thwarted.

Isabelle sent him a murderous glare and then sat in the chair in front of his desk. She said nothing, but her gaze shot daggers at him.

Righteous anger becomes her, John thought. Her stubborn determination was admirable—but not when directed against him.

John walked around his desk and perched on its front edge so he would be perilously close to her. He smiled at her again, but she refused to meet his gaze. Her lap had suddenly become the most interesting feature in his study.

"Anger is one of the seven deadly sins," John reminded her.

That certainly got her attention. Isabelle snapped her violet gaze to his. Her expression told him she was not amused.

"Within the past two days I've managed to acquire a wife and a child," John began, not giving her a chance to argue. "I believe whoever tried to assassinate me may try to get to me through my new family."

Worry replaced the anger in her eyes. "Do you really think so?" she asked.

"It's a possibility," John answered. "We'll be safer in Scotland until I hear from my investigators. Ross is the only person who will know where we've gone. Do you see the sense in what I'm saying?"

Isabelle nodded and then asked, "Will Lily accompany us?"

Her question surprised him. "Do you actually believe I'd leave her behind?" he said. "Dobbs and Juniper will also travel with us."

"Very well; I agree." Isabelle smiled for the first time since walking into his study.

"You have an enchanting smile and should use it more often," John remarked, and then saw a becoming blush stain her cheeks. "Pack your oldest gowns, darling. Summer in the Highlands is a casual affair."

"I'll begin the preparations immediately," Isabelle said, rising from her chair.

John allowed himself the pleasure of a wolfish grin as he admired the natural sway of her hips as she crossed the study to the door. His wife had agreed to go to Scotland without giving him too much difficulty. Away from society's constraints, she would be more vulnerable to his seduction. Getting her into his bed again could prove easier than falling out of a tree . . .

. . . Getting her husband to accept and acknowledge his daughter could prove easier than falling out of a tree, Isabelle decided as she lifted the flute case off the table the following morning. Away from society's constraints, John would find becoming acquainted with Lily much easier. She was a sweet child, and he would become irrevocably attached to her.

"I knew His Grace would soften toward the child."

Isabelle whirled around at the sound of the old woman's voice. "He hasn't acknowledged her yet," she said.

"Simple creatures that they are, men need time to become accustomed to fatherhood," Giselle told her.

That brought a smile to Isabelle's lips. "Will you be joining us in Scotland?"

"The Highlands are closer to heaven," Giselle answered. "I'll meet you there." She crooked a gnarled finger at Isabelle, who stepped closer. "Remember this, child. Happiness is found in the journeying, not at the end of the road." With those parting words, the old woman vanished as if she'd never been there.

Isabelle shook her head. At times the old woman's advice puzzled her.

Leaving her chamber, Isabelle hurried down the grand staircase to the main foyer and then stepped outside into the circular drive. Brilliant sunshine greeted her, and Isabelle couldn't help but think that this trip would prove auspicious for all of them. John would accept his daughter, which meant that she could resume her wifely duties.

There were two ducal carriages awaiting them. Gallagher drove one and a second groomsman drove the other. A third ducal retainer sat on the seat of the cart that carried their belongings.

When Lily waved at her from the window of the second carriage, Isabelle realized she would be riding alone with her husband. "Lily belongs with us," she said.

"She preferred riding with Juniper and Dobbs," John told her. "I believe Juniper promised to tell her an interesting story about a princess and a frog."

Isabelle smiled as she made herself comfortable in the carriage, but couldn't help feeling disappointed by the girl's defection. Not only did she sincerely like Lily, but the girl's presence would have proved a distraction and given her several conversational topics. Now, she would be alone with her husband. They had nothing in common. Yes, she was a married lady, but had almost no experience with men. Sweet celestial breath, whatever would she talk about for all of those long hours looming in front of her?

John smiled at her from his seat directly opposite her. Isabelle felt herself blushing. Out of habit, she touched her golden locket and then turned her head to gaze out the window as they began their journey.

"How long will it take to get to Scotland?" she asked.

"Approximately two days."

"Only two days to travel to Scotland?"

"Traveling by sea is faster than traveling by land," John told her. "Tomorrow afternoon we'll reach Liverpool, where one of my ships is waiting. The morning after that we'll arrive in Oban, which is a two-hour ride by coach to my estate."

Silence descended upon them. The lapse in conversation made Isabelle feel uncomfortable, and she tried to think of something to say. Finally, she settled upon the weather.

"We certainly have a wonderful day for a ride," Isabelle said, gazing out the window.

"Yes, we do," came his reply.

"It isn't too hot or too cold."

"Yes, the day is comfortably tepid."

Was that laughter lurking in his voice? she wondered.

"Isabelle, look at me," John ordered, and when she did he asked, "What's bothering you?"

"Bothering me?"

John inclined his head.

"We haven't been alone much," Isabelle began, but then hesitated. She dropped her gaze and confessed to her hands folded primly in her lap, "I'm feeling uncomfortable."

John snapped his dark brows together. "I make you feel uncomfortable?"

"You misunderstand," Isabelle said, shaking her head. "Being alone together makes me feel uncomfortable. What shall we talk about all the way to Scotland?"

"We can discuss anything you wish or nothing at all," John answered with a smile of understanding. "Sometimes silence is welcome. Unless there is something else you'd like to say about the weather?"

Isabelle smiled with relief. "I think I've said everything there is to say about that."

"I have something I'd like to discuss," he said.

"What is it?"

John surprised her by rising from his seat and joining her on hers. He placed his arm around her shoulders and then lifted her left hand to his lips.

"I would like to apologize again for not telling you about the war," John said. "I foolishly thought that by keeping it from you I could make our wedding day perfect. Instead, my good intentions made things worse."

Isabelle softened her gaze on him and forgot about her nervousness. "I understand and appreciate your consideration."

"Thank you, darling." John planted a kiss on her cheek, sending a delicious chill down her spine.

"Do you think our brothers are in danger?" she asked.

"Civilians are usually safe," he told her. "Jamie and Miles may even have begun their journey home already."

"Why can't everyone, including countries, just be friends?"

"Most people and countries do not possess your wisdom." John winked at her and added, "Friendship begins at home, you know."

"You mean charity begins at home."

"I stand corrected." John stretched his long legs out and relaxed against the leather seat.

"Do my ears deceive me?" Isabelle teased him. "I thought I heard you admit to being wrong about something."

"Ah, my sweet Belle, how divinely naive you are," John said. "Men never admit to being wrong about anything."

"I swear never to tell another soul," Isabelle replied, casting him an unconsciously flirtatious smile.

His expression became serious when he said, "I have a favor to ask of you."

Isabelle looked at him expectantly and waited.

"Will you share my bedchamber at the inn and at my estate in Scotland?" John asked. "To do otherwise would be an embarrassment to me. The Scots are quite old-fashioned about such things."

Isabelle felt the heated blush rising upon her cheeks. She couldn't very well say no to his request. He was her husband, the man who had saved her from marriage with Nicholas deJewell. Perhaps sharing his bed each night would give her the opportunity to persuade him to accept and acknowledge his daughter. Their close proximity each night would encourage that wifely duty she'd enjoyed performing.

"Yes, I will share your bedchamber," Isabelle answered.

"Thank you," he said simply, as if she were doing him a great favor.

Isabelle felt her spirits soaring at her progress, and suddenly, making coversation wasn't difficult at all. She pointed out the reddish-purple bull thistle and bright blue chicory along the roadside. Passing an open meadow, she spotted the rich yellow flowers of Aaron's rod, and when their coach crossed a bridge over a stream, she had him looking for blue irises.

Arriving in Stafford at the supper hour, they stopped for the night at the Purple Peacock Inn. John, Isabelle, and Lily sat at one table, while Dobbs and Juniper sat at another. Gallagher and his two groomsmen had sidled up to the bar after bedding the horses down for the night.

Supper consisted of roasted beef, savory pudding, and gingerbread with clotted cream. Lily ate two helpings of the gingerbread, and soon her eyelids began to droop.

When Isabelle gestured to Juniper that Lily's bedtime had arrived, John said, "Go with them, and I'll join you later."

Relief surged through Isabelle, who'd begun to feel awkward about undressing in front of him. Saying she would share his chamber was easier than actually doing it.

After bidding good night to Lily and Juniper, Isabelle went to her own chamber. The room was clean and comfortable, though a far cry from the luxury of Avon Park.

Before undressing, Isabelle perched on the edge of the bed and worried her bottom lip with her teeth. She felt more nervous than the evening of her debut into society. Would her husband want her to resume her nightly duty that evening?

Isabelle realized he would soon be returning to their chamber. She leapt off the bed and undressed hurriedly. Leaving only the one candle burning on the table, she went to bed and yanked the coverlet up to her chin.

Lying alone in the dimly lit chamber, Isabelle stared wide-eyed at the ceiling and clutched the coverlet tightly until she heard the door creaking open. Instantly, she snapped her eyelids shut and willed her hands to relax their death grip on the coverlet.

When Isabelle heard the faint rustling sounds of her husband undressing, curiosity almost got the best of her, but she summoned her reserves of inner strength and refused herself even one quick peek. She nearly cried out in surprise when the bed creaked, protesting his weight as he slid into bed beside her.

Isabelle felt him roll onto his side away from her. Apparently, her husband did not intend to exercise his conjugal rights that night. She didn't know whether to be relieved or disappointed.

"Pleasant dreams, wife," John said in a voice that sounded loud within the quietness of their chamber.

"How did you know I was awake?" Isabelle asked.

The bed creaked as John rolled over and gazed down into her face. Sweet celestial breath, her husband was barechested. Making matters worse, the dim light from the candle across the room accentuated his magnificent virility.

John gave her a lazy smile. Almost nose to nose with her, he said, "Sleep etches peace across a person's expression, not anxiety."

"I have no worries," Isabelle replied, staring him straight in the eye.

"Correct, darling. I would never force you into lovemaking," John said, and then dropped a kiss on her lips. "I'm positive you'll let me know when you've changed your mind about that. For now I am content to sleep beside you."

His topic of conversation heated her cheeks.

"You need not blush."

"I am not blushing," Isabelle insisted, and realized how ridiculous she sounded. The man could see the telltale stain on her cheeks, and now he was smiling at her lie.

"Traveling has wearied me," he said. "I would only embarrass myself tonight."

Isabelle had no idea what he referred to. Instead of replying, she said, "Pleasant dreams, then."

John turned his back on her and said over his shoulder, "Sleep, Isabelle. We leave at dawn."

The morning came too quickly.

As if she were sleepwalking, Isabelle splashed water onto her face and changed into her traveling gown. She was too damned tired to care if her husband saw her bare flesh, though she did perk up a little after breakfasting with Lily. The little girl's excitement was contagious.

Again Lily insisted on riding with Juniper and Dobbs. Isabelle was glad that the child and her new nanny were getting along so well, but couldn't understand why she didn't want to ride for a little while with them.

"I didn't realize that Juniper and Lily had become such good friends," Isabelle remarked, unable to keep the hurt tone out of her voice as she made herself comfortable in the coach.

"I heard Juniper say she knew a story about a princess and a pea," John said, sitting beside her.

"A pea, did you say?" Isabelle stifled a yawn. "I never heard that one. Perhaps, I should ride with—"

"Do not even consider leaving this coach." John put his arm around her and gently drew her against his body, saying, "Lean against me and sleep."

Too tired to argue, Isabelle did as she was told. With

her head resting against his shoulder, the rocking of the coach lulled her into a deep, dreamless sleep.

Their entourage reached Liverpool as the afternoon sun was casting long shadows across the road. Though impressed by the sight of her husband's ship, Isabelle was too tired from traveling to inspect it. She, Juniper, and Lily ate a light meal and then retired to their respective cabins.

Before dusk the ship slipped from its moorings and began its journey north. While Isabelle slept, her husband's ship entered the Irish Sea. Bypassing the Isle of Man, the ship sailed into the North Channel, sneaked through the Sound of Jura, and glided into the Firth of Lorne to Oban.

The Saint-Germain ship had docked by noon. Isabelle and the others waited while John gave his captain instructions and then walked down the gangplank to the ducal coach sent to meet them.

"I want Harmony," Lily demanded, looking at John, when the coachman opened the door for her.

"All of us desire harmony in our lives," John said.

Isabelle smiled at his misunderstanding. Apparently, her husband had no experience with children. She had no experience either, but some things in life came instinctively with women.

"Who is Harmony?" she asked.

"My pony."

Isabelle smiled. "Sweetheart, you don't own a pony."

"His Grace promised to buy me one if I rode in the coach with Juniper and Dobbs," the little girl told her.

Ignoring the smiles of Juniper and Dobbs, Isabelle rounded on her husband. "Your conniving has earned you a black stone."

John shrugged and gifted her with one of his wickedly devastating grins.

"I'll pray for your soul," Lily piped up. "If you buy me a pony."

"I always keep my promises to little girls," John said, crouching down to be eye level with her. "When we return home to England, I'll send to Dartmoor for one of their finest ponies. Will you trust me until then?"

Lily nodded.

"Let's seal the bargain with a hug," he said.

At that Lily threw herself into his arms and held him close. Before breaking the embrace, she gave him a wet kiss on his cheek.

Since there was only the one coach, John elected to sit with the driver. Isabelle, Lily, Juniper, and Dobbs made themselves comfortable inside the coach.

While Lily napped against her side, Isabelle gazed with interest out the coach's window, and her spirits soared at what she saw. The horizon was a carpet of purple heather; breathtaking mountains, painted green by a thick blanket of trees, rose spectacularly in the distance.

A land of lonely majesty, Isabelle thought. This world appeared more suitable for her than the crowded, dirty lanes of London.

Two hours later Isabelle and the others alighted from the coach. Kilchurn Castle sat on a small promontory that jutted into Loch Awe. Protectively surrounding the castle and the loch rose magnificent mountains. In the distance toward the northwest Pass of Brander stood Ben Cruachan, easily the tallest of all the mountains in the area.

"Look at the big hills," Lily cried in excitement.

John smiled. "Those are mountains, not hills."

Isabelle turned in a circle to gaze at the view from all directions, saying, "I do believe I'll enjoy summering here."

A late dinner awaited them in the dining room: vegetable mulligatawny soup, grilled trout, steamed asparagus topped with melted butter, and custard tarts.

Lily yawned loudly after she'd eaten. Gesturing at Juniper, Isabelle started to rise, but John stopped her.

"I'll take them upstairs," he said. "Wait here, and we'll walk to the loch."

"I'd like that."

John held his hand out to Lily, but she shook her head.

"I'm too tired to walk up the stairs," she said, looking up at him through half-closed eyes.

"Then I'll carry you." John lifted the little girl into his arms and left the dining room. Mrs. Juniper followed behind him.

Watching them, Isabelle smiled inwardly. Her decision to accompany him to Scotland had been wise. Her husband seemed to be warming to his daughter. It would be only a matter of time before he accepted her. And then she could resume her wifely duty.

A few minutes later John returned, and the two of them walked outside. The day was a Highland rarity of blue skies and brilliant sunshine. Protected by the surrounding mountains, Loch Awe and the glen looked like paradise to Isabelle.

"Summer in the mountains is much cooler than at home," she remarked.

"Are you chilled?" John asked. "I can go back for a shawl."

Isabelle shook her head. "How clear the water is," she exclaimed when they reached the loch's shore.

"Scotland's lochs are nothing like England's tired rivers." John picked up a stone and tossed it, skimming it across the top of the water before it disappeared.

At the water's edge, Isabelle plopped herself down to remove her shoes and stockings. She stood then, hiked her skirts up, and waded a few inches into the water.

"It's cold," she squealed.

John laughed. "Be careful," he warned, "or the monster will get you."

Isabelle leapt back out of the water. Excited, she looked around at him through violet eyes that gleamed like amethysts. "What monster?"

"Sit over here with me, and I'll tell you."

Side by side, John and Isabelle sat on the grass several yards away from the loch's shoreline. When she looked at him expectantly, he tapped the tip of her upturned nose.

"The monster is called the Big Beast of Loch Awe, but no two people can agree what it looks like," John began. "Some say it's like a horse, but others insist it's a great eel with twelve legs. During the winter, cracks and rumblings are heard from beneath the loch's frozen surface, and many locals believe it is Big Beast breaking the ice."

"I don't believe there is a monster," Isabelle said.

"As I always say, it's better to be safe than sorry," John replied.

Isabelle giggled. "I've never heard you say that."

John put his arm around her shoulder and drew her close. Looking up at him, Isabelle became caught in the dark intensity of his gaze. She saw his face inching closer and closed her eyes, surrendering to the pleasurable feeling of his warm lips upon hers.

Isabelle sighed against his mouth when she felt his

free hand caress the side of her cheek. He gave her another kiss and then drew away.

"Lass, you are lovelier than a violet in the snow," he said in a husky voice, gazing down into her eyes.

Isabelle stared at him. Once more his words echoed Giselle's prophecy. John Saint-Germain was undoubtedly the dark prince whose image she'd once glimpsed in the Avon River.

"This changes nothing," she told him.

"What do you mean?" he asked, obviously puzzled.

"I'm keeping Lily."

"My kiss was not intended to change your mind about anything," he told her. "Our discussion of the child can wait until summer's end. Let's relax and enjoy the moment."

Isabelle lay back on the grass and smiled up at him.

"What are you doing?" John asked.

"Enjoying the moment."

John lay on his side next to her and leaned his head against his left hand. "As boys, my brothers and I summered here every year. We'd ride into the upper pastures when the herdsmen and their families drove the cattle there for summer grazing."

"What special childhood memories you have," she said.

"And you do not," he replied, leaning close to plant a kiss on her lips. "I could cheerfully strangle your brother for leaving you at your stepfamily's mercy."

"My childhood wasn't that bad," Isabelle said. "I didn't know you had Scottish blood in you."

"Should I walk around saying, 'Hoot, mon'?" John asked.

Isabelle giggled. She closed her eyes and breathed

deeply of the crisp mountain air. "I do believe I could be happy in the Highlands," she said dreamily.

"Happiness is found in the journeying, not at the end of the road."

Surprised by his sentiment, Isabelle opened her eyes and stared at him. Without thinking she said, "You sound exactly like Giselle."

John shook his head. "Are we back to that again?"

"For your lack of faith, John Saint-Germain," Isabelle scolded him, "consider your soul one black stone heavier."

John laughed. He stood then and offered her his hand to help her up, saying, "You are incorrigible, Your Grace."

"How comforting to know we do have something in common," Isabelle replied with an impish grin. She lifted her skirts and cried, "I'll race you home." At that she started running toward the castle.

Isabelle hadn't run more than ten steps when her husband caught up with her. Instead of racing past her, he lifted her into his arms and tossed her over his shoulder like a bag of barley.

"Put me down," Isabelle cried, and then began laughing.

"Nay, lassie," John said, imitating the Scottish burr. " 'Tis Highland tradition for a mon to carry his woman home like this. Hoot, mon, hoot."

Chapter 15

Isabelle opened her eyes and knew from the chamber's dim light that the hour was still early.

She almost never awakened with the dawn and, with this mountainous altitude tiring her, had slept later than usual since arriving in Argyll.

Rolling toward the window, Isabelle realized her husband's side of the bed was empty. A noise drew her attention, and she raised her head off the pillow to see what he was doing.

With his back turned toward her, John splashed water onto his face from the porcelain bowl sitting on top of the tripod-footed washstand. Filtered light from the newly risen sun played across the muscles of his upper back and shoulders as he moved.

Slowly, Isabelle slid her gaze from the sinewy muscles of his upper back to his tapered waist. Her husband was naked except for black silk underdrawers.

Watching him through heavy-lidded eyes, Isabelle slid her gaze lower to his lean hips and thickly muscled thighs. A fiery-hot melting sensation ignited in the pit of her stomach and spread throughout her body. A primitive feeling of being the only man and woman in the world overwhelmed her senses, and she yearned for . . . *him*.

Isabelle knew she loved her husband. And now she knew desire.

John reached for the towel to dry his face and broke the spell his maleness had cast upon her. Isabelle snapped her eyes shut. She didn't want him to catch her peeking at him.

Isabelle heard the muffled sounds of him dressing and then felt the bed creak as he perched on the edge. She opened her eyes and smiled at him, but couldn't control the blush heating her cheeks.

"Why are you blushing?" John asked, giving her a puzzled look.

"I didn't know you wore black silk underdrawers," Isabelle said.

John raised his brows at her. "Were you peeking at me while I dressed?"

"No, I peeked while you washed."

Her admission brought a smile to his lips. "I hope you enjoyed the entertainment," he said. "I'm going for a ride. I'll see you for breakfast later."

Isabelle pulled the coverlet up and returned to sleep. This time her rest was not so deep and peaceful as before. Wearing black silk underdrawers and flexing his sinewy muscles, her husband paraded through her dreams.

She felt his lips covering hers.

She felt his hands caressing her flesh.

She felt his thickly muscled thighs pressing her down.

Isabelle awakened with a start. Finding herself alone was a disappointment, and in that moment she realized she needed to accept her husband whether or not he accepted his daughter.

"Make him gallop, Your Grace," she heard Lily's voice.

"Only experienced riders are allowed to gallop," John answered the little girl.

Isabelle rose from the bed and, without bothering to don a robe, padded on bare feet across the chamber to the window. Leaning against its sill, she spied her husband and his daughter outside. Seated atop a black pony, Lily held on to the reins while John used a lead rein to escort them around the grassy area.

Happiness and hope swelled within Isabelle's breast. In spite of what he said, her husband was warming to his daughter.

"Lady Belle, look at me riding," Lily called, spying her in the window.

"Good morning, Your Grace," John called, halting the pony and gazing up at her. "I hope all of your dreams were pleasant."

Isabelle leaned forward, giving him a spectacular view of her breasts. "You appeared in each of my dreams," she called.

John smiled at that.

"Did you dream about me too?" Lily asked.

"Yes, sweetheart, I did."

"What was I doing?"

"You were riding a pony," Isabelle lied.

"What was *I* doing?" John asked.

Isabelle blushed at his question, which made him chuckle.

"I can make your dreams come true," he said.

Isabelle closed her eyes against her embarrassment and then changed the subject, saying, "You said Lily had to wait for her pony until we returned to England."

"She does," John answered. "But I own several

Shetlands that she can use for learning how to ride while we're here."

"Lily, promise me you won't try to ride unless His Grace is with you," Isabelle called to the little girl.

"I promise." Lily looked at John and asked, "Will you buy Myrtle a pony too?"

"Do you really think Myrtle wants a pony?" he asked. "Tell me the truth now."

Lily cast him a flirtatious smile. "Myrtle would prefer a monkey."

"No monkey." John looked toward the window and asked, "Would my two ladies like to learn how to tickle a trout?"

"Yes," Lily exclaimed, clapping her hands together.

"I thought you'd never ask," Isabelle said. "I'll bring my flute, and we'll picnic at the loch. I'll be down in a little while."

Isabelle turned away from the window. She took one step toward the washstand, but the little girl's voice drifted back to her.

"Your Grace, you are more fun than Myrtle," Lily was saying.

"Thank you for the compliment," John replied.

After washing, Isabelle chose a lightweight, black woolen skirt and scooped-neck linen blouse to wear. She brushed her hair back away from her face and then grabbed her shawl.

"I told you he'd come around."

Startled, Isabelle whirled toward the familiar voice. Giselle sat in the chair across the chamber. "Where have you been?" she asked the old woman.

Giselle shrugged. "Here, there, everywhere."

"Will you be joining us for the picnic?" Isabelle asked.

Giselle shook her head. "Run along and enjoy your new family."

Isabelle walked across the chamber and knelt on one bended knee beside the old woman. Lifting the gnarled hand, she planted a kiss on it. "You will always be part of my family," she told her.

"Child, we will always be together here," Giselle said, placing her hand over her heart. "At the moment the man and the girl need you to bond them together. Whenever you need me, I will be with you faster than an eye can blink."

"You know where to find us if you change your mind," Isabelle said, and leaned close to plant a kiss on the old woman's wrinkled cheek.

An hour later John, Isabelle, and Lily left the castle behind and walked to the loch. John carried their picnic basket, and Isabelle carried her flute case. Obviously excited by their outing, Lily fairly danced down the path and sang a song off-key.

Brilliant sunshine ruled the day. Summer's lush wildflowers grew in abundance as far as the eye could see.

Reaching the shoreline, John removed his boots and his socks and then rolled his trousers over his knees. He started to wade into the clear loch water.

"Look, His Grace has hairy legs," Lily cried.

Isabelle laughed.

"Do you want to learn how to tickle a trout?" John asked, standing up to his knees in water. "Or do you want to admire my legs?"

"Tickle a trout," Lily shouted, and instantly removed her shoes and stockings.

Isabelle helped her to hike her skirt up and said, "Go on. I'll wait for my turn here."

Lily waded out to John and looked at him expectantly.

"Stand perfectly still," John instructed her. "Ever so slowly, submerge your hand in the water . . . like this."

Lily imitated him, and John continued, "Fish are curious creatures, like little girls. When one swims close to investigate, you stroke its belly with one finger. Once it is paralyzed with pleasure, flip him onto the shore."

"And then what happens?"

"You cook him up and eat him."

"You tickle him to death?" Lily asked, her green eyes large with horror.

"In a manner of speaking."

"I don't want to tickle a trout," Lily cried, and she backed away. She lost her balance, plopped into the water, and began to cry.

John lifted her into his arms and carried her to shore, saying, "You're safe now."

"Thank you for rescuing me, Your Grace," Lily said, wiping the tears from her eyes with the sleeve of her blouse.

"Let's get her out of that wet skirt," Isabelle said. "Do you have anything we can wrap around her?"

"I brought an extra blanket," John said.

Isabelle quickly removed the little girl's skirt and underdrawers. She reached for the blanket and started to wrap it around Lily, but John stopped her.

"Look at that," he said, pointing to the child's derriere. One of her cheeks had a small birthmark in the shape of a heart.

"Yes, I've seen it," Isabelle said, wrapping the blanket around the child.

"No peeking, Your Grace," Lily scolded.

"I'm terribly sorry," John apologized. "Someday in the distant future that pretty mark will be a wonderful conversation piece."

"That's a terrible thing to say."

"I meant with her husband," John said. "Do you want to learn to tickle a trout?"

Isabelle shook her head. "I think I'll pass too."

"You ate grilled trout the other night," John said.

"Please don't remind me," Lily replied in a dramatic tone of voice. "I fear I'll take ill."

John burst out laughing. Isabelle joined in the merriment, and Lily giggled because they were laughing.

"The water warms once the dog days are upon us," John said, sitting beside the girl on the blanket that Isabelle had spread out for them. "I'll teach you to swim then."

"What are the dog days?" Lily asked.

"Sirius is the Dog Star and rules the hottest part of the year," he explained.

"We need music," Isabelle said, lifting her flute to her lips to play.

Her melody contained a jaunty air. Then its tempo changed into spring's tranquillity, summer's birdcalls, and autumn's rustling leaves.

When her concert ended, John asked, "Can you play a waltz for us?"

Isabelle inclined her head. "I can try."

Again Isabelle lifted the flute to her lips. At first haltingly and then more confidently, her flute vibrated with the smooth, rhythmic tempo of a waltz.

John stood and bowed to the girl, asking, "Mistress Dupre, will you honor me with this dance?"

"I don't know how," she told him.

"Anyone can learn to waltz," John said, dismissing

her refusal with a casual wave of his arm. "I'll teach you."

Lily's emerald eyes glittered with happiness as she leapt off the blanket. Holding his hands, she tried to follow his lead, but her tiny feet kept going the wrong way.

"Place your feet on top of mine and hold on," John ordered. When she did, the two of them waltzed gracefully around in the grass.

Watching them, Isabelle felt an insistent tugging on her heart and thought of her long-dead father. She and her father had danced together like that. Now John was doing the same with Lily. By slow degrees her husband seemed to be accepting his daughter.

By the time the waltz ended, John and Lily were laughing. He bowed to her again and said, "Mistress Dupre, that waltz was undoubtedly the best of my life."

"I liked it too," Lily said, smiling up at him.

"What shall we do now?" Isabelle asked when they joined her on the blanket.

"Eat," Lily answered.

"Let's see what Cook prepared for us," John said, peeking beneath the cloth covering the food basket. "Why, I believe it's grilled trout."

"I'm not hungry," Lily said.

"Neither am I," Isabelle added. "Besides, I'd feel as if I were eating a friend."

"I'm teasing." John took a platter of cold roasted chicken from the basket.

"Do you have a drumstick for me?" Lily asked.

"I certainly do," John said, passing her the drumstick.

Lily took a bite, but as she broke a piece off with her

tiny teeth, the chicken flew out of her hand and landed on the grass. "Oops," she said, reaching for it.

John was faster and scooped it up, saying, "I don't want you to eat dirt."

"I don't give a rat's arse about dirt," Lily told him.

John turned his dark gaze on Isabelle. "I never imagined she would imitate me," she said by way of an apology.

Passing Lily another piece of chicken, John asked, "What would you like to do before we return home?"

"Let's catch frogs," she answered.

"Frogs?" Isabelle echoed.

"Juniper told me if I kiss a frog, he'll turn into a handsome prince," Lily said. "Do you want to kiss one too?"

"I'd rather tickle a trout," Isabelle replied. "I have a wonderful idea. I'll play my flute while you lie back on the blanket and watch the clouds make pictures."

Lily nodded and lay back on the blanket between Isabelle and John, who also lay back with his arms behind his head.

Isabelle played a lullaby, and within minutes the girl was asleep. She shifted her gaze to her husband and smiled. John was asleep too.

A week passed. During those seven idyllic days Isabelle savored the family life for which she'd always yearned.

Pony-riding lessons, picking early berries, wading in the loch's shallows, watching the cloud formations, and rolling down the sides of hills filled the sunny days. Rainy days passed quickly because of Isabelle's flute playing and John's tales of wild Highland adventures and local ghost stories.

On the tenth morning in the Highlands, Isabelle stood

in front of the looking glass in her dressing room and inspected herself. Excitement flushed her cheeks a rosy hue and brought the glitter to her violet gaze. She'd just finished plaiting her blond hair into two thick braids, and she wore her oldest clothing—a lightweight woolen skirt and scooped-neck blouse. Over her arm she'd slung a hooded cloak.

Lifting her hands, Isabelle stared at the two rings her husband had given her. On her right hand she wore her violets-in-the-snow betrothal ring, its sentiment signifying that he was the dark prince of prophecy. She shifted her gaze to her scrolled wedding band. Its heartening message—*joy without end*—tempted her to trust him.

John Saint-Germain, the fifth Duke of Avon, the tenth Marquess of Grafton, and the twelfth Earl of Kilchurn, was her lawful husband. For better or for worse. They had exchanged their sacred vows before God.

Isabelle loved him.

She desired him.

And she intended to seduce him.

During those first ten days in Scotland, Isabelle had realized that she needed to accept her husband as she expected him to accept the little girl. True, John had apparently warmed to the idea of being Lily's father and had even begun to treat the little girl as if she belonged to him.

No matter the final outcome, John Saint-Germain was her husband. When he invited her to ride alone with him to his hunting lodge to pass a few days together, Isabelle had accepted his invitation.

Now that the moment of their departure had arrived, Isabelle felt uncertain as she stared down at her wedding ring. Was she doing the right thing? What if he rejected

Lily in the end? Yes, she loved him, but could she forgive him if he hurt that lonely child?

"His Grace loves you, child."

Isabelle whirled around and saw Giselle sitting in the chair in front of the hearth. She crossed the chamber, sat in the opposite chair, and said, "John does not love me. He's never told me so."

"Listen with your heart and hear what his true feelings are," Giselle replied.

"But how do I—"

The door opened, drawing their attention. Seeing her husband, Isabelle flicked a quick glance at the old woman, but she wasn't there.

"I hope you're ready," John said, smiling as he crossed the chamber. "Why are you sitting there alone?"

"I'm counting my blessings," Isabelle answered, returning his smile.

In spite of her worry, Isabelle couldn't help but admire her husband. She could well understand the reason so many women found him irresistible. How much inner strength could a woman possess? Hence, his tarnished reputation with the ladies.

"I want to go too," Lily cried, running into the chamber and straight into Isabelle's arms. "Myrtle is afraid you won't come back."

"How could we stay away from you?" Isabelle asked, her heart wrenching at the girl's stricken expression. The poor child feared being abandoned again.

Isabelle looked for help to John, who sat in the chair vacated by Giselle. "Come and sit on my lap," he invited the child.

Lily crossed the distance between them and sat on his

lap. John put his arm around her and gave her an encouraging smile.

"The day you arrived to live with Lady Belle and me was our wedding day," John explained. "So we haven't had any time to enjoy a honeymoon like all married couples do. Can you understand that?"

Lily nodded.

"Lady Belle and I are riding to my hunting lodge to enjoy a short honeymoon," John continued. "I promise we'll return to Kilchurn in a few days. Have I ever broken a promise to you?"

Lily shook her head.

"Will you trust me about this?"

Lily nodded.

"How about an I'll-see-you-in-a-few-days kiss?" John asked.

Lily giggled and wrapped her arms around his neck. Then she planted a noisy, wet kiss on each of his cheeks.

"Mistress Dupre, I will forever cherish your kiss," John teased her. "Give Lady Belle a kiss."

The little girl scooted over to Isabelle and threw her arms around her. She kissed each of Isabelle's cheeks and then gazed into her eyes, announcing, "I love you, Lady Belle."

"I love you more," Isabelle told her.

Leaving Lily in the main foyer with Mrs. Juniper, John and Isabelle walked outside into the bright sunlight. Two saddled horses awaited them, while a third carried saddlebags and baskets filled with supplies.

"Are you ready?" John asked, reaching out to tug gently on one of her braids.

Isabelle laughed at his boyish gesture, so incongruous with the darkly sophisticated man. "I'm ready," she answered.

John and Isabelle rode at a leisurely pace down the path that would eventually lead them into the upper pastures. The rich blue of the sky and the lush green of the trees dominated the area, and the various hues of wild-flowers garnished the whole scene.

Isabelle felt optimism swelling within her soul. Her husband, the dark prince of prophecy, had warmed to his daughter, and she would resume her most enjoyable wifely duty. Together the three of them would live happily ever after, and all of Isabelle's lonely girlhood dreams would become reality.

At the far end of the moors, the trees grew taller and thicker. Rabbits scampered across the road, and grouse whirred away before their approaching horses.

John and Isabelle passed through the glades and entered a forest of pine, spruce, birch, and larch. Ancient beeches reached out with their gnarled branches over beds of bracken.

"We're here," John said, halting his horse when they reached a clearing in the woodland.

A small lodge and a stable stood in the clearing. A stone well perched on the opposite side of the area between the two buildings, saving the occupants from walking to a stream.

"After settling in, we'll walk down that path to the valley of Glen Aray," John said, helping her out of her saddle. "Come, I'll show you the lodge."

John unlocked the lodge's door and then, surprising her, scooped her into his arms to carry her across the threshold. After setting her down on her feet inside the doorway, he said, "Highland tradition requires that the man carry his bride across the threshold. Doing so ensures them a happy marriage."

"I hope that proves true," Isabelle said with a jaunty smile.

"Joy without end, darling," he murmured, lifting her hand to press a kiss on its palm, sending a delicious shiver racing down her spine.

The first floor of the lodge was one enormous chamber. An unmade bed, the most commanding presence in the room, stood along the wall on her right. Linens and a fur throw had been slung across it. Between the bed and the wall a stairway led to a second level.

"What's up there?" Isabelle asked.

"A loft of bedchambers," John answered. "I prefer sleeping down here though."

Isabelle continued inspecting her surroundings. A privacy screen stood in the corner to the right of the bed. Pots and pans hung on the wall to the left of the hearth, which was built into the wall facing the door. An oak table stood along the wall on the left side of the chamber, and shelves on that wall contained an ample supply of crockery as well as unperishable supplies.

"Give me a few minutes to bring the supplies inside," John said, turning away. "Then we'll put the bed in order."

As soon as he left, Isabelle shook the linens out and started to make the bed. Did her husband think she was incapable of menial chores? Is so, he had a surprise coming his way. True, she was an earl's daughter, but a friendless young girl sought companionship with whomever she could, including an aging majordomo, a superstitious cook, and kindly maids who'd taught her to do minor tasks.

The door opened. Laden like a pack horse, John walked in and set the satchels down in the center of the floor and the baskets on top of the table. Then he walked across the room to help her.

Standing on opposite sides of the bed, John and Isabelle touched each other with their gazes. Mesmerized by the tender expression in his eyes, Isabelle felt a melting sensation in the pit of her stomach.

Would John want to make love immediately? she wondered. Or would he wait until evening?

"Cook packed us a pot of stew, but we'll save it for supper," John said. "I'd like to show you the glen if you're not too tired."

"I'm fine," Isabelle replied. "What about the horses?"

"We'll take care of them before we go."

After their horses had been fed and watered, John and Isabelle started down the path to the glen. With her spirits soaring, Isabelle fairly skipped along beside him. She was young and in love and alone with her exceedingly handsome husband.

They walked into the silent grandeur of Glen Aray surrounded by massive peaks. The afternoon sun sparkled across the top of a serene pool of water formed by two mingling streams. All around them summer's lushness colored the valley.

"What are those?" Isabelle asked, pointing at the yellow flowers with red tendrils.

"Glenside sundew," John answered. "The sweet-smelling tendrils attract and then ensnare insects, which the plant eats."

Isabelle grimaced. "That's worse than tickling a trout to death."

When they reached the pool, Isabelle plopped down on the ground and promptly removed her boots and her stockings. Then she hiked her skirt up and dipped her toes into the water.

"Oh, it's cold," she exclaimed.

"The water will warm as the summer progresses," John told her.

Isabelle sat on a large boulder and gazed at the awe-inspiring scenery. Stealing a peek at her husband, Isabelle found him watching her as if she were more interesting than the spectacular setting. His gaze on her brought a blush to her cheeks.

"The solitude of these mountains always rejuvenates me," John told her. "I feel more human away from London society."

"I feel the same way about Stratford and my beloved Avon River," Isabelle replied.

"Stratford is cosmopolitan when compared with this," John said, making a sweeping gesture with his arm.

"I agree." Isabelle pointed toward the water, saying, "Look, two streams form the pool."

"Sorrow and Care—the Campbells' names for those streams—mingle in the pool and then separate again to continue their journeys to Loch Fyne and Inverary Castle," John told her. "Inverary belongs to my cousin, the Duke of Argyll."

"Did I meet him at our wedding?" Isabelle asked.

"He sent his regrets, but his son attended."

"Which one was he?"

John chuckled and playfully tapped the tip of her nose. "You are shockingly ignorant of London's elite. His son is the Marquess of Inverary." He pointed to the tiny hovels of stone and turf dotting the sides of the hills around them. "In the olden days before the Clearances, the Campbell women and the children would pass the summer in this valley. They'd sleep in those hovels while their men slept outside in their plaids.''

"How sad that people should lose their ancestral homes," Isabelle said.

"The world's ways can be cruel," John agreed, and then gave her one of his devastating smiles. "Next month we'll return here with Lily. For a few days each year during August, showers of falling stars race across the night sky.''

"Lily will love it." That her husband was beginning to think of Lily as part of their family pleased Isabelle immensely.

"Put on your boots," John said, rising from his perch on the boulder. "Let's go home and eat.''

Making its descent in the west, the sun cast long shadows as John and Isabelle retraced their steps through the glen. The forest was noticeably cooler without the sun's strong rays directly overhead.

Inside the lodge Isabelle watched John start the fire in the hearth, and she marveled that a man at ease in London's most exclusive drawing rooms would apparently relish menial chores like lighting fires and tending horses. She stopped him when he pulled the covered pot from one of the baskets and turned to retrace his steps toward the hearth.

"I can do that." Isabelle lifted the pot out of his hands. "Fetch us a couple of buckets of water.''

"Are you certain?" he asked, a doubtful expression appearing on his face.

"I promise I won't poison you.''

He inclined his head. "The kitchen is yours.''

Isabelle set the pot of stew on the hook over the hearth and stirred it with a ladle. Then she crossed the chamber to the crockery shelves. Lifting two bowls, she used the bottom edge of her skirt to wipe the dust from them and then searched the food baskets for bread. She placed the loaf of bread down on the table between their bowls. After stirring the stew again so it wouldn't burn, she began unpacking their belongings from the satchels.

"It smells delicious," John said, walking into the lodge. He set the buckets of water down near the hearth.

Isabelle ladled stew into their bowls and set them down on the table. "Your Grace, I give you the first meal I *almost* cooked for you," she said with a rueful smile.

"I do believe that warming counts the same as cooking," he said with an answering smile.

"Is warming the extent of your culinary skills?" she asked.

"Actually, no," he answered, surprising her. "Usually I fend for myself up here. Though I'd never consider myself a culinary artist. What about you?"

"Old Cook taught me everything she knew." Seeing his incredulous expression, Isabelle amended herself. "Oh, very well. I know enough to keep myself from starving."

John smiled at her confession. "Anything more is unnecessary, like icing on a cake."

Isabelle rose from her chair and carried their empty bowls to the water buckets. Then she returned to clear the table.

"You'll need a lady's maid when we return to London," John told her.

Surprised by the idea, Isabelle stopped and looked at him. "Whatever for?"

"All ladies of breeding have a personal maid," he said. "Don't forget. You are a duchess now."

"I don't feel like a duchess," she admitted. "I feel like me."

"Nevertheless, you will employ a lady's maid," he told her. "To do otherwise would be an embarrassment to me. Mother will help you with the interviews."

Isabelle returned to sit across from him at the table. "What about Molly?" she asked.

"Who?"

"You know, the girl who sells flowers in Berkeley Square," she reminded him.

John shook his head. "Molly would be inappropriate."

"Your mother will help me train her," Isabelle argued.

"We'll see." John smiled at her. "I'd bet my last shilling Molly is missing your business."

"And you would lose, Your Grace," Isabelle said, her violet eyes gleaming like amethysts. "I left enough money with Pebbles to purchase her flowers every day until the first of October."

Her husband looked stunned. "You did what?"

"I said I left enough—"

"I heard you the first time," John said, cutting her words off. Too surprised to be angry, he added, "Isabelle Saint-Germain, you are a constant source of amazement."

Isabelle smiled. *Isabelle Saint-Germain.* She definitely liked the sound of those words.

John stood then and said, "I'm going to bed the horses down for the night. Use this time for your private needs."

Isabelle blushed, embarrassed that he would speak so intimately with her. True, they'd been sharing a bed for a couple of weeks, but he'd always returned to their bedchamber after she'd retired for the night and had left the chamber in the morning before she awakened. Except for the morning she'd caught him wearing his black silk underdrawers.

"Lord, what a blusher you are," John said with laughter lurking in his voice.

Isabelle saw the tender amusement in his dark gaze when he leaned close to caress her cheek with one hand. John pulled her out of the chair and into his embrace. His lips swooped down to capture her mouth in a lingering kiss that held the sweet promise of love.

"I do love kissing you," he murmured in a husky voice.

"More than eating early berries?" she asked.

His lips twitched as if itching to smile, but his expression remained solemn when he said, "Even more than rolling down the sides of hills."

Chapter 16

His wife wanted him as much as he wanted her.

John saw that as soon as he opened the door and stepped inside the lodge. Isabelle had changed into the ridiculously sheer nightgown that she'd worn on their wedding night. The gown had been designed to entice, and John was so damned enticed he thought he might embarrass himself.

John decided to proceed slowly. He intended for them to savor this evening and each other.

After closing the door and dropping the latch into place, John gave her his most charming smile. Then he sauntered across the chamber and set a bucket on the table.

"What do you have there?" Isabelle asked, crossing the chamber to stand beside him.

"I've kept a bottle of champagne chilling at the bottom of the well," John answered.

"Your ingenuity is amazing," she said.

"May we still amaze each other forty years from now," he replied, opening the bottle and pouring champagne into a mug.

John lifted it to her lips, and she took a sip. He drank from the same spot on the mug that her lips had touched.

After setting the mug on the table, John fixed his dark gaze on hers and began to undress. First he yanked his boots and socks off and tossed them aside. Then he removed his shirt and trousers, until he stood in front of her wearing only his black silk underdrawers.

"Shall we go to bed?" John asked, holding out his hand in invitation.

Isabelle smiled and without hesitation placed her hand in his. Instead of escorting her across the chamber, John scooped her into his arms and carried her to the bed.

"Wait," Isabelle said before he placed her on the bed.

John set her down on her feet. For one awful moment he thought she'd changed her mind.

Surprising him, Isabelle reached up and slid the straps of her nightgown off her shoulders. It fluttered to the floor at her feet. All she wore was her glorious mane of spun-gold hair.

John worshiped her with his eyes. His gaze drifted from her lovely face to her pink-tipped breasts and then traveled down to her tiny waist, her slim yet curvaceous hips, and finally her dainty feet.

Isabelle gave him a soft smile when he raised his dark gaze to hers. And her unspoken invitation was irresistible.

Stepping closer, Isabelle entwined her arms around his neck and pressed her body against his. She drew his head down and kissed him lingeringly.

"You are beautiful," John said in a husky voice.

Leaving her lips, John rained feathery kisses down the slender column of her throat. He dropped his lips lower and suckled upon her aroused nipples.

Isabelle moaned at the incredible sensation he was creating.

John knelt in front of her, and his tongue slashed her

moist female's crevice in a tender assault. When she gasped in surprise and instinctively tried to pull away, he cupped her buttocks and held her captive.

Up and down John flicked his tongue, licking and nipping her female button. She cried out as waves of throbbing pleasure washed over her.

John stood then and would have scooped her into his arms, but Isabelle surprised him again when she slid her hand down his chest to his nipples. Her lips followed her hand, and John's breath caught raggedly in his throat.

Following his lead, Isabelle dropped to her knees in front of him and pressed her face against his groin. She reached up and slid his black silk drawers down, leaving him naked to her gaze.

Taking his manhood in her mouth, Isabelle sucked until it grew too big. Then she licked the long length of it, flicking her tongue this way and that, suckling upon its ruby knob.

Unable to bear any more, John drew her up. He kissed her slowly and lingeringly, then gently laid her on the bed.

Isabelle looked at him through eyes glazed with passion and held her arms out in invitation. John spread her thighs and mounted her, riding her in a wild frenzy.

Isabelle cried out at his entry. Mewling sounds welled up in her throat, urging him to thrust deeper and deeper. She arched her body and met each of his thrusts with her own.

John groaned loudly and exploded with his wife. He shuddered as his seed flooded the deepest part of her.

Only their labored breathing broke the silence inside the lodge. Finally, John rolled to one side, pulling her with him. He planted a kiss on her forehead and gazed with love at her wondrous expression.

With her heart shining in her eyes, Isabelle looked up at him and said, "I love this wifely duty."

John laughed. He'd heard sexual relations called a lot of things, but *wifely duty* wasn't one of them.

"This particular 'husbandly duty' does bring me pleasure," John agreed, gently drawing her head down to rest against his chest. "Sleep now."

Isabelle closed her eyes and promptly fell asleep. Unfortunately, in spite of his contentment John lay awake with his thoughts.

His wife was one problem solved, John thought. And that left Lily Dupre. What should he do about her? Isabelle had become deeply attached to the girl, and if the truth were told, so had he. His thoughts traveled the long distance to London, and he wondered if Ross had learned anything new concerning Lily's parentage.

And then there was the matter of who had tried to kill him. He couldn't believe that William Grimsby hated him enough to see him dead, and deJewell was too much of a weasel even to consider. Why, he must have dozens of enemies, businessmen who'd lost profits due to his success. Here in the Highlands he was beyond anyone's reach. He would worry about the assassin when he returned to England.

Sated and content, John closed his eyes and joined his wife in sleep.

"Wake up, darling."

Isabelle heard the voice, but kept her eyes closed for another moment. The husky sound of her husband's voice warmed her all over, and the faintest of smiles touched her lips.

Opening her eyes, Isabelle blinked at the blinding

sunshine streaming into the lodge through the window beside the bed. She looked at her husband, who perched on the edge of the bed.

"Good morning," John said, holding up a bowl of something that smelled delicious. "I've made you oatmeal porridge."

Isabelle sat up and leaned back against the headboard. Holding the blanket up to cover her nakedness, she pushed several recalcitrant wisps of spun-gold hair off her face.

Bare-chested, John wore only his black trousers. Isabelle felt a melting sensation in the pit of her stomach at the intimacy they'd shared the previous night.

"It's hunger," John said dryly, as if he could read her thoughts.

Isabelle blushed and reached out with one hand for the bowl. When she lifted the spoon to her mouth, the blanket slipped to her waist.

Her blush deepened to a vibrant scarlet. Before she could yank the blanket up, John reached out and caressed her breasts. Her nipples hardened in arousal, and she sucked in her breath.

"Darling, there'll be time for that later," John teased her. "Do you want to learn how to make bannocks?"

Isabelle nodded. "Where's my nightgown?"

John looked around. His black silk bed robe was closer, so he lifted it off the floor, saying, "Wear this." At that he rose from his perch on the edge of the bed and headed for the door. "I'll feed and water the horses first."

Setting the bowl of porridge aside, Isabelle stood and slipped into his robe. She paused for a moment to inhale his scent of mountain heather and then, realizing he'd be returning, washed her hands and face from the bucket of cold water. By the time her husband returned she was sitting at the table and eating her porridge.

"People learn by doing," John told her. "So follow my instructions carefully."

Isabelle nodded. "Very well."

"I've already begun heating the griddle, that cast-iron plate over there," he said. "Check its temperature, but never—"

Isabelle ran over to the griddle and touched it with her finger. She screeched in pain.

John walked over to her, grabbed her hand, and plunged it into the bucket of cold water. "I was about to say not to touch it. Always leave an inch of empty space between your hand and the griddle." Lifting her hand out of the water and inspecting it, he said, "I'll make the bannocks. Watch what I do."

Isabelle watched in amazement as her husband cooked the bannocks. Who could have guessed that the illustrious Duke of Avon would be at home in a kitchen? Or that he wore black silk underdrawers?

"You know, I'm beginning to miss Lily's chatter," John said as they sat at the table eating his bannocks.

Isabelle smiled, pleased with her husband's progress in accepting his daughter. "I miss her too," she said. "Do you want to go home and see her?"

"Juniper will take good care of her until we return," he said in refusal. "Come here."

When she stood and walked around the table, John pulled her down on his lap and kissed her. "And what would you like to do today?" he asked. "Pick early berries? Roll down the sides of hills?"

Isabelle shifted her gaze to the unmade bed.

"We can do that too," he said with a smile.

That week of marital bliss passed much too quickly

for John and Isabelle. They savored each moment together. By far Isabelle's favorite day was the one that rained. She especially liked the indoor games that she and her husband played.

Both John and Isabelle were loath to leave on the day of their departure and lingered in bed all morning long. They set out for Kilchurn Castle long after the sun had reached its highest point in the sky. First they rode through the magnificent forest with its century old beeches and beautiful beds of bracken. The trees thinned out all too soon, heralding the moor with its enlarging carpet of purple heather.

Reaching the crest of the moor, the breathtaking spectacle of Loch Awe burst into view. Dotted with islets and overhung by Ben Cruachan, Loch Awe appeared like an earthly paradise and Kilchurn Castle like an enchanted castle.

Isabelle felt as though she'd come home. For the first time in her life she had a loving family around her. Isabelle could hardly wait to see Lily, Giselle, Juniper, and even Dobbs.

A small army of groomsmen materialized from nowhere as soon as John and Isabelle halted their horses. John dismounted and then helped Isabelle off her horse.

"You're home!"

Isabelle turned around to see Lily running toward her. She bent down and opened her arms for the little girl, who hugged her as if she'd never let her go.

"Oh, I was so afraid you wouldn't come back to me," Lily cried.

"I would never leave you," Isabelle assured her, holding her close. "Did you really miss us?"

Lily nodded. Leaning closer, she added in a loud whisper, "Dobbs and Juniper know nothing about riding ponies. They insisted I keep my two feet planted on the ground.''

John and Isabelle exchanged smiles.

"Welcome home, Your Graces," Dobbs greeted them.

"Welcome home," Juniper added.

"Thank you, it's good to be home," Isabelle said. She looked at Lily, saying, "His Grace and I are very hungry. I hope you haven't eaten our supper."

"No, we saved it for you," the little girl said.

With Lily between them John and Isabelle walked inside and went directly to the dining room. Dobbs and Juniper followed behind, but left them in the foyer in order to continue with their household tasks.

Several footmen served them fried strips of veal and seasonal vegetable medley in a basil vinegar. Scottish burnt cream was for dessert.

"Did you have fun?" Lily asked, unable to keep her gaze off them for even one moment.

"We certainly did," Isabelle answered. "Next month His Grace is going to take *both* of us to his lodge."

Lily clapped her hands together in excitement and then turned to John, asking, "What did you do at the lodge?"

John cast his wife a sidelong smile before answering, "We did lots and lots of fun things."

"Lady Belle, you must be sick," Lily said. "Your face is red."

John chuckled at that, and Isabelle sent him an unamused look. "I'm only tired," she told the little girl. "You better go to bed."

"That's what made her tired," John said dryly.

"Bull's pizzle," Lily scoffed. "Going to bed doesn't make people tired."

Now Isabelle turned her head to stare accusingly at her husband. In answer John shrugged and raised his eyebrows.

Much later Isabelle escorted Lily to her chamber and then went directly to her own bedchamber. Lord, but she was tired. And happy. She changed into her nightgown and, without bothering to brush her hair, slipped into bed.

"So your honeymoon was better than a daydream," Giselle said, materializing from nowhere to perch on the edge of the bed. "Does His Grace know about the baby?"

Isabelle stared at her in blank confusion. "What baby?"

"Come the spring you will deliver your own baby," the old woman told her.

"That is too incredible for belief," Isabelle replied.

"Have I ever lied to you?"

Isabelle shook her head.

"Have I ever been wrong about anything I've told you?"

Again Isabelle shook her head.

"Trust me, child," Giselle said. "A year from now you will have become a mother."

Isabelle smiled at the prospect of having her own baby. A year from now she'd be the mother of two: Lily and— "Is it a boy or a girl?"

Giselle shrugged.

"You know what it is," Isabelle said. "Don't play games with me."

"Guessing what the babe will be is part of the fun," the old woman told her. "I would never deprive you of that."

"Thank you, I think," Isabelle said dryly.

"Here comes your prince." With those words Giselle disappeared.

The bedchamber door opened, and John walked in. First he went to the bed and gave Isabelle a chaste kiss on the lips. She knew she must have looked disappointed, because he smiled and teased, "I'm only a man and need to take my clothing off."

Isabelle blushed. Her embarrassment didn't prevent her from watching her husband strip down to his black silk underdrawers.

"Whenever I look at Lily, I imagine you as a young girl," John said, slipping into bed. "You know, I couldn't love her more if I was in truth her father."

"I love her too," Isabelle said, gazing up at him through gleaming amethyst eyes. "How could Lisette abandon her like that?"

John caressed her cheek. "I've decided to adopt Lily when we return to London so that no one—not even Lisette—can ever take her away from us."

Isabelle rose up on her elbow to look down on him. She lowered her lips to his and poured all of her blossoming love into a single, stirring kiss.

"Go to sleep, my lovely violet in the snow," John said, when she drew back and smiled with love at him.

"I don't want to go to sleep."

"But I do," he said. "Christ, I never realized how draining happiness can be."

Isabelle slid the palm of her hand down the length of his body to his groin. "Could you manage to stay awake for just a little while longer?" she asked, slipping her fingers beneath the black silk underdrawers to stroke him.

Ever so gently, John flipped her onto her back. Nose to nose with her he said, "I think I can manage that."

* * *

John awakened with the dawn. Intending to go for an early ride, he rose from the bed, dressed in silence, and left the chamber.

Reaching the first floor, John cut down the corridor that led to the rear of the castle, where the stables were located. Clad in her bed robe, Mrs. Juniper stood midway down the long corridor outside the chapel room. Her presence there surprised him, but as he approached, the nanny put a finger across her lips in a signal for silence and gestured toward the chapel's open door.

John peered inside and saw Lily. The little girl had just reached the altar at the end of the aisle and was kneeling.

"What is she doing?" John asked, lowering his voice.

"Lily insisted she needed to talk to God," Juniper whispered.

John rolled his eyes and stood poised in the doorway. He was about to turn away, leaving Juniper to wait for her, when he heard her speak.

"God?" Lily called, her voice sounding loud in the quietness of the chapel. "Are You there, God?"

John felt his lips twitch with the urge to laugh. He stepped inside the chapel to listen.

"It's me, Lily."

Silence.

"Lily Dupre!"

John bit his bottom lip to keep from laughing. The girl was more entertaining than a Drury Lane production.

"I know what You're thinking, God, but I haven't come to ask for anything." Then she amended herself.

"Yes, a pony would be nice, but I could live without one
. . . *if necessary*. I came here to thank You for answering one of my prayers. Do You remember all of those
nights I asked You to send me a father?"

John lost his smile and, on silent feet, started down
the aisle. He stopped before he reached the altar.

"Thank You, God, for sending me a wonderful father—even though I must call him Your Grace." Lily
held her hands up, saying, "I'm not complaining,
but—" She hesitated as if reluctant to ask for anything
more.

Drawing her attention, John closed the short distance
between them. He knelt beside her at the altar, but did
not look at her, though he felt her gaze upon him.

"God, are You listening?" John called, and then
waited.

Lily leaned close and whispered, "Don't worry, Your
Grace. He hears you."

John nodded solemnly and continued, "God, I'm
here to thank You for sending me my wonderful daughter—only I wish she would call me Papa."

Lily squealed with delight and, as he turned to her,
threw herself into his embrace. "My papa," she said,
placing the palm of her hand against his cheek.

John grinned. "May I call you Lily?"

"Yes, you may," she answered, nodding her head.
"Do you think Lady Belle will let me call her Mama?"

"Yes, you may." The voice came from the rear of the
chapel room.

Lily whirled toward Isabelle. Releasing her father,
she ran down the aisle and hugged her. A sudden frown
marred the child's expression, and Lily asked worriedly,
"What about Lisette?"

"You'll have two mothers," Isabelle answered. "Come and sit with me." She led the little girl into the last row of pews and sat down. "When we return to London, your papa is going to adopt you. That means you'll share the same name."

"Your name will be Lily?" she asked him.

John laughed and then explained, "No, sweetheart, your name will become Lily Saint-Germain, because my name is John Saint-Germain."

Lily looked confused. "Where does Dupre go?"

"Your mother will explain everything after breakfast," John told her. He looked at Isabelle and asked, "What brought you here this morning?"

"An angel told me to hurry to the chapel if I wanted to witness a miracle," Isabelle answered.

"An angel, huh?" John rolled his eyes heavenward.

"Lily, your papa is a skeptic," Isabelle told the little girl.

"What's that?"

"He doesn't believe in angels."

"That really is too bad of you," Lily said, wagging her finger at him.

"I apologize," John said with laughter lurking in his voice. "I promise to try harder to acquire a belief in the absurd."

"What does that mean?" Lily asked.

"It means that he has less intelligence than a rat's arse," Isabelle answered.

"God mend your words," John said, borrowing one of her pet phrases.

Isabelle smiled at him. "This angel also told me that I will deliver a baby next spring."

John smiled, and his dark eyes gleamed with a mixture of happiness and amused disbelief. Leaning over the pew, he planted a kiss on her lips and said, "If that proves true, darling, I'll never doubt the existence of angels."

Chapter 17

Rising early on that September morning, John stood in his office at Saint-Germain Court and gazed out the window at the garden area below. He smiled to think that his wife's oft-quoted Old Cook would probably say that the flower and tree fairies danced with glee around his garden.

Autumn had painted vivid colors within the setting of his London garden. Besides nature's orange-, gold-, and red-leafed trees, his gardener had landscaped the area into an earthly paradise where his two angels—Isabelle and Lily—could play in secure privacy.

John let his thoughts travel up one flight of stairs to his pregnant wife and wondered for the hundredth time if she did have a guardian angel. Her prediction that she was carrying his child had proved true. After his disastrous marriage with Lenore, he'd never imagined that any woman could be happy about carrying a child, but Isabelle was proving him wrong.

He loved her for that. And she loved him. Her love was there in every word, every glance, every touch.

Isabelle needed and deserved to hear words of love from him. After Juniper had taken Lily upstairs to bed that night, he would tell his wife that he loved her, and then he would take her to bed and show her how much.

Joy sans fyn, my love, John thought. *Joy without end.*

"Good morning, Your Grace."

John turned around at the sound of his brother's voice. Ross looked like a bedraggled tomcat after a night on the prowl. He'd slung his black evening jacket over his shoulder, untied his neckcloth, and unbuttoned his shirt at the throat. Apparently, his brother had not gone home the previous evening.

John looked his brother up and down. "I hope she was worth ruining your health," he said dryly.

"The lady was well worth every moment she's stolen from my life span," Ross replied with a smile. He sat down in the chair on the opposite side of the desk, poured himself a dram of whiskey, raised it in salute, and then gulped it down in one swig.

"Don't you think the hour is a little early for that?" John asked.

"Since I haven't been to bed, the hour is quite late." Ross grinned suddenly like a mischievous boy and amended himself, saying, "Ah, let me rephrase that: I've been to bed, but not to sleep."

John smiled at that. "How did you know I'd returned to London?"

"I met Lord Pennick at White's last night," Ross told him. "He happened to be driving down Park Lane as your entourage was disembarking."

"Have you had any word from Jamie and Miles?"

"No, but I believe they must be en route, else we would have heard from them by now," Ross replied.

"I agree with you," John said. "I wonder about Montgomery's reaction to my marrying his sister."

Ross shrugged and then drawled, "I'm certain Montgomery will welcome you into the family with open arms."

"Montgomery will be forced to welcome me into the

family, since I am the father of his sister's expected child," John said, and then grinned at his brother's surprised expression.

"Congratulations," Ross said, rising to reach across the desk to shake his brother's hand. He poured two drams of whiskey, handed one to his brother, and then raised his glass in salute, saying, "To my new nephew or niece. May he or she be healthy, happy, and prosperous."

John raised his glass and then drank. "Now, then, brother, have the investigators discovered any information concerning the attempt on my life?"

"One of the investigators will be reporting to me later this morning. I'll let you know what he's discovered."

"What's been happening in London during my absence?"

"I'll start with your inconsequential in-laws," Ross said. "Lobelia is planning her wedding, but Hancock wavers from day to day in his affection for Rue."

"I've sent a note to Hancock asking him to come around later," John told him. "I guarantee Rue will be receiving a marriage proposal by this evening."

"Nicholas deJewell has been a live-in guest at Montgomery House since your wedding," Ross continued.

"The man is a weasel," John remarked. "What has been happening with William Grimsby?"

"He's been keeping a low profile," Ross said. "Though I occasionally see deJewell and him with their heads together at White's."

John smiled. "The Vanquished Club?"

"Their camaraderie should be no laughing matter," Ross warned him. "I'd bet my last shilling they're hatching some scheme against the Saint-Germains."

John dismissed the danger with a casual wave of his hand.

"Lisette has returned to London," Ross said.

John sat up straight. "And?"

"I paid the bitch five hundred pounds to get a look at the girl's birth certificate," Ross told him, "but Lisette named no one as the father."

"Good, that means she can be bought."

Ross gave him a blank look. "I don't understand."

"I've decided to adopt Lily," John told him. "Lisette's cooperation will expedite matters."

"But you don't know if you are the girl's father," Ross argued.

"Lily is my daughter, whether or not I sired her," John replied, his dark gaze on his brother becoming cold.

"Well, I'll be damned," Ross said and burst out laughing. "I fully support your decision and will extend—Lily, is it?—all the affection that should be accorded her as my niece."

"Thank you, brother. Now go home and sleep." John rose from his chair. "I've promised my family a morning carriage ride in Hyde Park, part of Isabelle's assault on society to gain acceptance for Lily."

Ross stood and walked to the door with his brother. "I'll return this afternoon and let you know what the investigator reported."

John nodded. Together the Saint-Germain brothers left the study. They reached the foyer just as Isabelle and Lily, dressed for their outing, walked down the stairs.

"Good morning," Isabelle called.

"Good morning," Lily called, imitating her.

"Congratulations," Ross said, lifting Isabelle's hand to his lips. "I just heard the good news about the baby."

Isabelle smiled. "Thank you, my lord."

Ross dropped his gaze to the little girl, asking, "Do you remember me?"

Lily shook her head.

"I am your Uncle Ross," he told her.

"Oh, I'm so lucky," Lily gushed, clapping her hands together in her excitement. "I have an uncle."

Ross smiled. "You have two uncles."

"Three uncles," Isabelle corrected him.

"You also have two stepaunts, one great-aunt, one grandmother, a stepgrandmother, and hundreds of cousins," John added.

"Good God, this foyer is becoming crowded," Ross exclaimed.

Lily laughed and then told him, "Next spring I'm going to have a brother and a sister."

"No, sweetie, a brother *or* a sister," Isabelle corrected her.

"What's the difference?" Lily asked.

The three adults laughed.

"I also have Juniper and Dobbs," Lily told Ross.

"What about me?"

Surprising the two men, both Isabelle and Lily snapped their heads around to gaze at the stairway as if someone had called to them.

"I have Giselle too," Lily corrected herself, turning back to Ross, "but you can't see her sitting on the stairs over there because she's an angel."

"That's better," said Giselle.

At the little girl's words John stared hard at Isabelle, who pointedly refused to meet his gaze. Apparently, his wife was infecting Lily with her eccentricities. The girl would have a difficult enough time being accepted into society. She didn't need the added burden of talking to angels.

"Are you ready for our carriage ride through the park?" Isabelle asked the little girl, changing the subject.

Lily nodded.

"Deftly done, sister-in-law," Ross said. He looked at the little girl, saying, "Meeting you was a distinct pleasure, and I promise to visit you again very soon."

"And what do I call you?" Lily asked him.

"Uncle Ross, of course." With those words Ross left Saint-Germain Court.

"Gallagher brought the coach around," John said. "Shall we go?"

"I cannot believe what a big family I have," Lily said as they walked outside. "The only thing missing is—"

"Is what, sweetheart?" John asked.

"A pony."

"Can I tell you a secret?" he asked.

"I love secrets," Lily exclaimed.

"Most women do," John replied, flicking a glance at his wife. "While we are here in London, your pony is being delivered to Avon Park and will be waiting for you when we go home."

"Let's go home now," the little girl demanded.

John laughed. "I need to have some very important papers signed. Can you wait a few more days?"

Lily smiled and nodded.

Autumn wore a serene expression that morning. The sky was a blanket of blue with a couple of fluffy fairweather clouds breaking the monotony. The sun's rays were warm, and the park was landscaped into a variety of vibrant colors.

"William the Third had three hundred lamps hung from the trees along *route du roi,* the road upon which we are riding," John told them. "Rotten Row became the first road lighted at night in the whole country."

"I didn't know that," Isabelle said.

"Neither did I," Lily spoke up, making them smile.

"The king intended the lighting to deter highwaymen," John continued.

"What's that?" Lily asked.

"Highwaymen are robbers," John told her. "I bet you didn't know that hundreds of duels have been fought in this park."

"What's a duel?" Lily asked.

"Sometimes gentlemen have disagreements," John began. "When that happens, they bring their pistols to the park and—"

"This topic is inappropriate for a young child," Isabelle interrupted him. "I cannot understand why men resort to violence to solve their problems. Women never do."

John gave her an amused look and said, "That's because you women are—"

"Superior?" Isabelle interrupted.

"Good morning, Your Grace," said a voice beside them. "What a perfect portrait of family life the three of you paint."

John turned his head to see William Grimsby perched on top of his horse beside their carriage. He glanced at his wife, who was glaring at the blond-haired earl. He almost laughed out loud at the thought of all the good deeds she'd feel the need to do in order to overcome the black stone her anger was earning for her.

"And whom do we have here?" Grimsby asked, shifting his blue gaze to the little girl.

"Good morning to you, William," John said, pasting an insincere smile on his face, playing along with the other man's feigned ignorance. "This is Lily, my soon-to-be-adopted daughter."

Grimsby's forced smile vanished, and an irritated frown replaced it. Apparently, the man couldn't bear to see him enjoy an ounce of happiness.

"When we go home, my father is giving me a pony," Lily said, her youthful exuberance uncontrollable. "Come next spring my mother is giving me a brother and a sister."

"A baby brother *or* a sister," Isabelle corrected her again. "Remember?"

Grimsby snapped his gaze to Isabelle, who gave him a sunny smile and said, "I am happy beyond belief."

"Congratulations, Your Grace," Grimsby said, looking at John. He tugged on his horse's reins and told Isabelle, "Your husband killed my sister in the same way." At that Grimsby galloped away.

"I'll pauper him for that," John said, watching the other man ride away. How dare he frighten his pregnant wife!

"Calm yourself, husband," Isabelle said, reaching around the little girl to touch his shoulder. "Grimsby is an unhappy man with a poisonous tongue, but no real threat to us."

Slowly, by degrees, John composed himself. Finally, he turned to Isabelle and nodded.

"I don't like Earl," Lily said.

"Was that the man who delivered you to Avon Park?" John asked.

Lily shook her head. "No, he brought me to you."

John burst out laughing. Putting his arm around the

child, he planted a kiss on the top of her head. "Lily, you are an original."

Lily beamed with pleasure. "Thank you, Papa."

"What about me?" Isabelle asked.

John grinned. "You, darling, are an incomparable."

"Thank you, husband."

"You are welcome, wife."

"Please be seated, Baron Keswick," John said, gesturing to the chair in front of his desk.

"Thank you, Your Grace." Charles Hancock sat down and gazed with nervous expectation at him.

"Would you care for a whiskey?" John asked, reaching for the crystal decanter and two crystal glasses perched on the sterling silver tray that had been set on his desk.

"Yes, Your Grace. That is, if you are."

This one is more of a blockhead than Spewing, John thought. He poured two drams of whiskey and passed one to the baron. "To your prosperity," he said, holding his glass up in a salute.

"And to yours, Your Grace."

"I would like to know what your intentions are regarding Rue," John said, and then fixed his most intense gaze on the younger man, almost pinning him to the chair.

"I-I harbor a respectful f-fondness for Rue," Hancock stammered, fidgeting in his chair.

"The man who offers for her will receive a generous dowry, including a small interest in several of my businesses," John said, relaxing in his chair without taking his darkly intense gaze off the nervous man. "Since I've always held you in high regard—"

"You have?" the younger man interrupted, obviously surprised that one of England's premier dukes had noticed him.

John struggled against the almost overpowering urge to laugh; he managed to control himself. "I would like you to be the man who profits by marriage to her. Rue might be considered plain by today's standards of beauty, but—"

"Rue is simply perfection," Hancock exclaimed. "I would like to offer for her today if you give me your permission."

"You have my approval," John replied, nodding. "But what about the lady's feelings for you?"

"I believe she harbors a fondness for me," Hancock answered. "I will propose marriage to her this evening."

John smiled with satisfaction. He had no doubt that Rue would accept Hancock's proposal. Lobelia's and Rue's happy betrothals should keep their jealous tongues from hurting his wife's feelings. And if that didn't work, their prospective husbands would keep them quiet or answer to him.

Signaling that the interview was finished, John rose from his chair and walked around the desk. Hancock stood when he did.

"To a bright future as brothers-in-law," John said, shaking the other man's hand and then escorting him to the mahogany double doors.

"Your Grace, I swear you will never regret your confidence in me," Hancock vowed. At that Baron Keswick left the study and walked with a spritely step down the corridor.

Poor bastard, John thought, closing the door behind the baron. Though John considered himself a brave man, the idea of marrying Rue or Lobelia was enough to give him a severe case of the hives.

Before returning to his desk, John wandered across the study to the window and gazed into the garden area below. A smile touched his lips as he spied Lily gamboling around and around, apparently pretending to be riding her pony. He scanned the area for his wife and saw her sitting on a bench in the far corner of the garden. Beside her sat a wizened old woman.

John couldn't credit what he was seeing. He snapped his eyes closed and opened them again. What he saw confused him even more. Now Isabelle sat alone on the bench and talked to someone who wasn't there.

Giving himself a mental shake, John told himself that the idea of his wife actually having a guardian angel was too absurd for consideration. And yet—his belief that he could never love again had been shattered by his wife's presence in his life.

"Your Grace?"

John turned around slowly.

"Both Mr. Matthews and your brother are here," Dobbs said.

"Send them in."

A moment later the two men walked into the study. Ross sat down in one of the chairs in front of his brother's desk. Mr. Matthews, one of the Saint-Germain solicitors, shook his employer's hand and, at the ducal gesture, sat in the vacant chair beside Ross.

John looked at his brother first and asked, "Have you discovered anything new about the assassin?"

Ross shook his head.

"Mr. Matthews, I've asked you here because I want to adopt my natural daughter," John said, turning to the solicitor. "The problem is, the child's mother failed to name a sire on the birth certificate."

"How do you know the child is yours?" Matthews asked.

"Lily is my daughter because I say it is so," John replied, his voice coldly authoritarian.

"Then it must be true," Matthews agreed. "I assume you want me to draw up a legal petition to present to the magistrate."

John inclined his head. "I also want a legal document for the mother to sign, relinquishing custodial care to—"

With no warning knock, the door swung open. The three men turned in surprise to look at the majordomo.

"Lisette Dupre wishes an interview," Dobbs announced in a hushed tone of voice.

Though surprised, John managed to retain his calm expression. Perhaps he could contrive to get her to sign an adoption paper. With that in mind, John instructed his majordomo, "Escort her to me. Gentlemen, wait outside. This won't take long."

Dobbs left the study. Ross and Mr. Matthews followed behind the majordomo. A few seconds later Lisette Dupre walked into the room.

Unfastening her cloak before he could stop her, his former mistress wore a gown meant to seduce. The Circassian wrapper dress, the latest rage among London's fashionmongers, looked exactly like a night chemise. Its front, composed entirely of lace, was shaped to her bosom.

There had been a time not too long ago when he had considered her one of the most beautiful women in the world. Now John stared at her display with insulting indifference.

John lifted his dark gaze to her face. Set off by that luxurious ebony mane, Lisette's startling emerald eyes reminded him of Lily's. Yet Lily and Lisette were as different as day and night. He wondered briefly if Lisette had ever been an innocent child.

"John, I'm so happy to see you," Lisette said in her husky voice, her hips swaying provocatively as she closed the distance between them.

"Call me Your Grace," John said.

Her back stiffened at his rebuke, but her feline smile never wavered. "You don't find me attractive?" she asked.

"Actually, I'm wondering what attracted me to you in the first place," he said in a cold voice. "What do you want?"

"My daughter, of course."

"I'm keeping her."

"You cannot keep a child who doesn't belong to you," Lisette argued.

"Lily belongs to me," John told her. "I have two hundred witnesses who can testify that you abandoned *our* daughter to me."

"Lily is no daughter of yours," Lisette insisted.

"Who sired her is insignificant," John countered. "I am adopting her."

"Lily needs her mother."

"She's found another."

"No one can replace me in her affections," Lisette said with confidence.

"I wouldn't bet on that."

"You can have her for one hundred thousand pounds."

"I've already got her," John replied. "You have nothing with which to negotiate."

"The law is on my side," Lisette cried, raising her voice in frustrated anger.

"Get out of here now," John warned, "before I lose my temper."

The sultry-eyed beauty leveled a murderous glare on him. Whirling away, she stormed out of the study and slammed the door behind her.

John stared at the door in disgust. Why had he ever been attracted to such a mercenary bitch? The only good and fine thing to come out of that liaison had been Lily.

While John was confronting Lisette, Isabelle and Lily enjoyed the garden just below the study's window. Isabelle played her flute, and Lily danced to the vibrating melody that sounded like the rustling of falling leaves.

As she ended her dance, Lily tossed a handful of leaves into the air and shouted, "Hooray!" Spying something unusual on the lawn, Lily scooped it into her hand and marched across the garden to Isabelle.

"What's this?" she asked, holding the green elongated object up.

"See that maple tree over there?" Isabelle said, pointing toward the tree and then lifting the object out of the girl's hand. "These are the maple's winged seeds, called keys. Keys always come in pairs. See?" She broke the winged seed into two halves and continued, "If we open this inner part, we'll find sticky liquid inside. I like to stick it on top of my nose, like this." Isabelle demonstrated by sticking the opened winged seed on the tip of her nose.

Lily giggled. "Open mine for me."

Isabelle opened the maple's keys and stuck one half on the little girl's nose. The two of them laughed uproariously.

"I want to walk around the house and knock on the

front door," Lily said. "When Dobbs opens the door, he'll scream in fright."

"Very well, but I'll wait here," Isabelle said. "Go directly to the front door and don't speak to any strangers."

Lily nodded.

Isabelle watched her climb the area's stairs and then disappear around the house in the direction of the front door.

"Go after her," Giselle said, appearing on the bench beside her.

"I beg your pardon?"

"Hurry, child," Giselle warned. "Danger is near."

Panicking, Isabelle leapt off the bench and ran toward the area's stairs. "Mama, save me," she heard Lily shriek.

Isabelle raced around the corner of the house onto Park Lane. Lisette Dupre was dragging a struggling Lily into a waiting coach.

"Help! She's stealing my daughter," Isabelle cried, running down the street.

Too late! The carriage moved forward into traffic just as Isabelle reached it. She leapt back to save herself from being run over and landed on her backside.

John raced down the front stairs. His brother and his solicitor followed two steps behind him.

"Lisette grabbed Lily," Isabelle shouted from where she sat on the ground.

"Matthews, help my wife," John ordered without breaking stride. He started to run down the street after Lisette's coach, but Ross caught him from behind.

"Release me," John shouted, trying to shrug his brother off.

Ross held on tightly, and John watched the coach disappear from sight.

"What the bloody hell are you doing?" John demanded when his brother released him. A muscle in his left cheek twitched angrily. "The bitch stole my daughter."

"Were you planning on chasing the coach to Lisette's?" Ross asked. "How many hundreds of witnesses could she call into court to testify to the fact that you're mad and unfit to care for Lily?"

Isabelle kept her gaze fixed on her husband. Though she wanted Lily returned to her immediately, she breathed a sigh of relief when he nodded at his brother. She'd feared that in his agitated emotional state her husband would strike Lisette. Or worse. And then what would they do?

"Are you hurt?" John asked, putting his arm around her and drawing her close.

"I'm fine," Isabelle assured him.

John allowed his brother and his solicitor to lead them inside the town house. The four of them stood in the foyer to discuss what should be done.

"We must retrieve your daughter by legal means," Matthews said.

"I don't give a damn for legalities," John snapped. "Let's pay the bitch what she wants and have done with it."

"Lisette will come back for more when the money is gone," Ross said.

"Two hundred wedding guests witnessed Lisette Dupre's announcement and abandonment of the child," Matthews said. "We'll go to the magistrate, present him with the facts, and ask for temporary custody. I can almost guarantee that your daughter will be home tonight. Once she's returned, I'll negotiate with Lisette for permanent custody.''

John nodded in agreement and then turned to Isabelle. ''We'll be back as soon as we fetch Lily,'' he said, and then kissed her forehead

Isabelle worried her bottom lip as she watched them leave. Ignoring Dobbs and Juniper, who stood nearby, she climbed the stairs and sought the privacy of her bedchamber.

Gaining her chamber, Isabelle locked the door behind her. Then she leaned back against its comforting solidness and took a deep calming breath.

Disturbing thoughts raced through her mind. So many things could go wrong. What if the magistrate was busy? What if he refused to grant them temporary custody? What if Lily was not returned home by nightfall?

''*Whenever you need me I will be with you faster than an eye can blink. . . .*''

''Giselle,'' Isabelle said. ''Are you here?''

Silence.

''Giselle,'' Isabelle called in desperation. ''I need you!''

Chapter 18

"Lower your voice, child. You'll rouse the dead."

Isabelle looked across the chamber and saw the old woman sitting in her favorite chair in front of the hearth. Hurrying over to her, she knelt on the floor beside the chair.

"Lisette abducted Lily," Isabelle told her, touching the old crone's gnarled hand, desperation tinging her voice. "My husband has gone to get a magistrate's order for temporary custody, but I cannot wait. What if the magistrate refuses? Lily will believe that we abandoned her too. Will you help me?"

"Yes, I'll help," Giselle said, patting her hand. She turned her head to stare into the darkened hearth as if she needed time to think.

Isabelle watched her in silence and, as the moments ticked by, grew increasingly nervous. If only John had gone after Lisette, Lily would be home with them at that very moment. And if only she hadn't allowed Lily to walk alone to the front door . . . What if Giselle couldn't formulate a plan?

"Have you so little faith in me?" Giselle asked, giving her a sidelong glance.

Isabelle blushed at having been caught thinking unkind thoughts. "I am sorry for my lapse in faith."

"I forgive you," Giselle said. Her blue eyes sparkled with mischief when she added, "I have a plan."

"I knew you would think of something," Isabelle said, brightening. "What should I do?"

"Go as quickly as you can to Grosvenor Square," Giselle instructed her.

"Grosvenor Square?" Isabelle echoed in confusion.

Giselle nodded. "You cannot confront Lisette Dupre alone. The dowager and her sister will accompany you."

"The dowager is an old woman," Isabelle exclaimed in surprise. "How can she help?"

"Never denigrate the aged," the old woman told her. "Experience can outsmart youth any day of the week."

"I cannot involve my husband's mother in this," Isabelle refused, shaking her head.

"I've said this many times before—you humans are a tiresome lot," Giselle snapped at her in unangelic irritation. "You snivel and whine and plead for divine guidance, but do you ever follow it?"

Isabelle was determined not to involve others in what was technically illegal. "I'm sorry, but the dowager cannot—"

"The dowager has vast experience and myriad tricks at her disposal," Giselle interrupted. "Trust me, child. Her ingenuity will surprise you."

"What do you know about the dowager?" Isabelle asked, narrowing her violet gaze on the old woman.

Giselle gave her an ambiguous smile. "Are you going to sit there all evening?" she asked. "Or were you planning on rescuing your adopted daughter?"

"Very well, I'll trust you on this," Isabelle said, standing. "Are you coming along?"

"I wouldn't miss the fun for all the harp music in

heaven," Giselle answered. With those words the old woman vanished as if she'd never been there.

Isabelle hurried across the chamber and grabbed her black hooded cloak. Pressing her ear to the door, she listened for activity in the corridor. There was none. She opened it a crack and peered outside. No servant was about. Isabelle stepped into the corridor and closed the door.

Noiselessly, Isabelle glided down the corridor to the servants' staircase in the rear of the mansion and then descended to the ground level. She would need to cut through the kitchen. At the bottom of the stairs, the noise from inside the kitchen was louder as her husband's staff prepared for supper.

Steeling herself with a deep breath, Isabelle pasted a serene expression onto her face and stepped inside the kitchen. Instantly, all conversation ceased, and surprised gazes turned to her.

"Continue with your duties," Isabelle said as she marched through the kitchen, dismissing the staff with a casual wave of her hand.

Escaping out the door that led to the garden area, Isabelle stepped out of sight of any curious servants who might be watching. She paused to lean back against the side of the house. Her heart pounded frantically within her chest and breathing was difficult.

It's the babe mingled with my guilt, Isabelle told herself. Lord, but she would never make a competent criminal. Sneaking around like this made her nervous.

"Are we going to rescue Lily or not?"

Isabelle gasped in surprise, and her hands flew to her chest. She raised a finger to shush the old woman, who burst out laughing at the gesture.

"No one can hear me but you," Giselle reminded her.

Isabelle nodded at her old friend and scurried across the area to the stairs. Reaching the street, she pulled the hood of her cloak up to cover her blond hair. She didn't want to be recognized by any passersby.

Autumn's late-afternoon sun cast lengthening shadows, and Isabelle gazed up at the sky to judge the hour. The sun would be setting in no more than two hours, and she wanted Lily back before nightfall.

Grosvenor Square lay only two blocks to the east. Ten minutes later Isabelle stood outside her mother-in-law's mansion. Without hesitation she hurried up the front stairs and banged on the door.

When the door opened a moment later, Randolph, the dowager's majordomo, stood there. Isabelle brushed past him into the foyer.

"Just a minute, miss—"

Isabelle whirled around and flicked the hood off her head. "Yes, Randolph?"

"I am sorry, Your Grace," the man apologized. "I didn't recognize you." He glanced out the open door and asked, "Where is your carriage?"

"I walked," Isabelle told him. "Where is Her Grace?"

"I believe Her Grace and Lady Montague are in the drawing room," the man answered.

Isabelle dashed up the grand staircase to the second floor and then down the corridor. "I need your help," she cried, bursting into the drawing room. "Lisette has abducted Lily."

The two older women turned to stare at her in surprised confusion. Finally, the dowager said, "Calm yourself, Isabelle."

"Extreme agitation isn't good for the baby," Hester added.

"You don't understand," Isabelle said, hurrying across the room toward them.

"Sit down," the dowager ordered, pointing to a chair. "Tell us what happened."

"Lisette Dupre came to Saint-Germain Court and abducted Lily," Isabelle told them, perching on the edge of the chair. "John and his solicitor have gone to the magistrate's to procure temporary custody, but I cannot leave Lily in that woman's care for even one night." At that she burst into tears.

"Control yourself," the dowager ordered, waving a handkerchief in front of Isabelle's face. "We cannot solve this problem if you insist on weeping."

"Weeping isn't good for the baby," Hester added.

The dowager rounded on her sister and said, "Silence, you peagoose."

"That isn't a very nice thing to call your only sister," Hester reprimanded her.

The dowager rolled her eyes. "I apologize."

"I forgive you."

Wiping her tears, Isabelle sniffled and smiled at their byplay. She loved these two elderly aristocrats. Aunt Hester's wonderful simplicity always tickled her emotions.

The dowager rose from her chair and crossed the room to tug on the bellpull. A moment later a footman walked into the drawing room.

"Jeeves, tell Randolph to fetch me my *big* reticule," the dowager ordered. "Then have my carriage brought around."

"Yes, Your Grace."

"I want my *big* reticule too," Aunt Hester called.

Jeeves turned around and nodded in acknowledgment of the second order.

After the man had left, Isabelle turned to her mother-in-law and asked, "His name is really Jeeves?"

"I call all of my footmen Jeeves," the dowager told her. "It's easier to remember. Shall we go and fetch Lily?"

Isabelle rose from her chair, and together the three of them left the drawing room. They reached the main foyer, where Randolph was waiting with two of the biggest reticules Isabelle had ever seen.

"Be careful, Your Grace," the man said, opening the door for them.

"Thank you, Randolph," the dowager replied. "I will be as careful as I am skillful."

"Very good, Your Grace."

Isabelle looked blankly from the majordomo to the dowager. She had no idea what they were talking about. The man had no knowledge of where they were going. Why would he tell his lady to be careful?

Isabelle banished that puzzling thought from her mind. Lily was the most important thing at the moment, and they were on their way to rescue her from that woman.

"Where does Lisette live?" the dowager asked once they were seated in the carriage.

Isabelle gazed blankly at her mother-in-law. How could she have been so stupid to forget she needed the woman's address?

"Fifteen Soho Square, child," Giselle prompted.

"Fifteen Soho Square," Isabelle answered.

The dowager turned to the waiting coachman, who said, "I know the street, Your Grace."

Fifteen minutes later the dowager's coach halted in

front of Lisette's house. The coachman opened the door and, in turn, assisted each of them down.

Isabelle started up the front steps, but the dowager's hand on her arm stopped her. "Walk behind me," the dowager ordered. "I'll handle this matter."

Isabelle inclined her head and deferred to her husband's mother. She fell into step behind her, and Aunt Hester followed. Giselle had advised her to trust the dowager's vast experience, and so she would.

The dowager grabbed the door knocker and banged loudly, as if demanding entrance. The door opened a moment later to reveal a middle-aged woman, obviously the housekeeper.

"May I help you?" the woman asked.

Without bothering to answer, the dowager brushed past the woman. Isabelle and Hester slipped inside behind her.

"What do you think you're doing?" the woman asked in an angry voice. "This is private property."

The dowager whirled around and arched a brow at the woman's impertinence, reminding Isabelle of her husband. "Where is your mistress?" the dowager demanded.

"State your business," the woman said.

"Do you know who we are?" the dowager asked, narrowing her gaze on the servant. "I am the dowager Duchess of Avon." She gestured to Isabelle and Hester, adding, "This is the Duchess of Avon and Lady Montague, widow of the late earl. Now, where is Lisette?"

"I apologize, Your Grace," the woman said, flustered. "Lisette is—"

"I'm here."

Isabelle saw Lisette Dupre, ravishingly beautiful, slowly descending the stairs to the foyer. Watching her,

Isabelle felt a tinge of jealousy that John had once been involved with her.

"Alice, open the door for them," Lisette said, crossing the foyer toward them. "The ladies won't be staying."

"Where is Lily?" Isabelle demanded.

Lisette glared at her. "*My* daughter is in her bedchamber. If you—"

"Alice, fetch the child," the dowager interrupted.

"Stay where you are, Alice," Lisette countermanded the order. She dropped her emerald gaze to their enormous reticules, adding, "Unless John has sent you here with what I want."

Isabelle watched her mother-in-law fix a frigid smile on Lisette. The dowager lifted her reticule and opened it. Instead of money, the old aristocrat pulled out a pistol and pointed it at Lisette.

"What are you doing?" Isabelle cried, appalled by the prospect of the dowager actually doing violence to another. And then she noticed Aunt Hester's pistol trained on the ebony-haired beauty.

"Do you want Lily or not?" the dowager asked her.

"Of course I want her," Isabelle answered.

"Then kindly let me handle this," the dowager said. She ordered, "Alice, fetch the child here."

Alice glanced at her mistress. Lisette glared at the dowager, but then nodded at her servant.

"This is beyond absurd," Lisette said. "Abduction is illegal."

"The aristocracy has always been privileged enough to stretch the law a bit," the dowager replied in a haughty tone of voice.

Lisette smirked, then asked, "Do you even know how to use that thing?"

"Care to find out?" the dowager countered, cocking the pistol's trigger. "No? How unfortunate."

"The late duke taught Her Grace everything he knew about pistols," Aunt Hester piped up. "And she taught me everything she learned."

"Mama," Lily cried, appearing at the top of the stairs. She ran down the stairs, nearly tripping in the process, and threw herself into Isabelle's waiting arms. "I knew you'd come for me."

"Sweetheart, I'll never let you go," Isabelle assured her, stroking her back soothingly. "You belong with me."

"She belongs with *me*," Lisette said. "I'll file suit, and the magistrate will agree with me." She glared at Lily, adding, "You little ingrate, I'm the one who gave you life."

In a small voice that echoed with truth, Lily looked at Lisette and told her, "Mama Belle gives me love, and I love her."

Isabelle stood then and, taking Lily's hand in hers, left the town house. Aunt Hester followed her out.

"I apologize for intruding upon your leisure," the dowager said, turning to leave. "Have a good evening." At that she walked out of the house.

As the coach started out into the traffic, Isabelle breathed a sigh of relief. Lily leaned against her and held her hand as if she'd never let her go.

Now she would need to deal with her husband, Isabelle thought. The day's events had taken a toll on her. At the moment she didn't have the strength to argue with him about involving his mother in this. And then an idea came to her that could gain her a couple of hours reprieve from her husband's ire.

"Lily and I will be going to Montgomery House," Isabelle told her mother-in-law.

"I beg your pardon?"

"I would like to give John an hour or two in which to calm down," Isabelle explained.

The dowager nodded. "I understand completely."

"Well, I don't," Aunt Hester said.

"Tell John that he can fetch Lily and me at Montgomery House," Isabelle said.

"Is she leaving Johnny?" Aunt Hester asked.

Ignoring her, the dowager called to the coachman, "Drive us to Berkeley Square." She looked at Isabelle and said, "I'll wait until he stops shouting before I tell him where to find you."

"Thank you," Isabelle replied. "Don't tell him until his cheek muscle stops twitching."

When the coach halted in front of Montgomery House, Isabelle reached out and touched the dowager's hand, saying, "I can never repay what you did for Lily and me today."

"Intimidating that woman was my pleasure," the dowager replied. "Besides, being part of a family means being able to depend on others."

Isabelle smiled. "Thank you for including me in your family."

Hand in hand Isabelle and Lily climbed the front steps of Montgomery House. Before reaching for the door knocker Isabelle stared up at the mansion's facade. Saint-Germain Court seemed more like home to her than Montgomery House. Was that true because she'd passed her whole life at Arden Hall in Stratford? Or was it because John lived at Saint-Germain Court and not here?

"Your Grace, so good of you to visit us," Pebbles greeted her when he opened the door.

Isabelle managed a sunny smile for her old friend. "I've come home to hide from my husband for a few hours."

The old majordomo stared at her in obvious bewilderment.

"You heard me correctly. My husband and I are not in accord," Isabelle told him. "Do you remember *my daughter* Lily from the wedding?"

Pebbles gave the little girl a warm smile and said, "I've known your mother since she was younger than you."

Lily giggled.

"Where is Delphinia?" Isabelle asked.

"I believe your stepmother is in the drawing room," Pebbles answered.

"Lily, Pebbles will take you to supper," Isabelle said to the little girl. "I'll join you in a few minutes. Will you go with him, or is Myrtle afraid?"

"Since I met you, I don't play with Myrtle anymore," Lily told her. She looked at the majordomo, asking, "Will you tell me the story about when my mother was a little girl?"

"I cannot think of anything else I'd rather do," he answered.

"Is that a yes or a no?"

"That is a definite yes."

Lily accepted the man's hand and walked away with him. Isabelle watched them until they disappeared from sight and then walked up the stairs to the drawing room.

Pausing in the open doorway, Isabelle hesitated when she saw who was visiting her stepmother. She mustered her courage and advanced on that unholy trinity: Delphinia, Nicholas deJewell, and William Grimsby.

"My daughter and I may be passing the night here," Isabelle informed her stepmother, ignoring the two men.

"Your daughter?" Delphinia echoed in apparent confusion.

"Lily Dupre . . . I'm keeping her."

Delphinia rounded on Grimsby and deJewell. The three of them exchanged smiles, their obvious satisfaction reminding Isabelle of three cats that had just cornered a mouse.

It was then that Isabelle felt the first stirrings of fear.

Coming here had been a terrible blunder, Isabelle thought, backing away. "Actually, I think John may be concerned about my whereabouts and angry enough to go looking for me," she said, hoping to gain courage by invoking her husband's name.

Their reaction wasn't what she'd expected. Their smiles broadened into grins, and Isabelle stared at them in frightened confusion.

"You aren't going anywhere," Delphinia told her, crossing the chamber to close the drawing-room door.

Isabelle whirled around. "You cannot keep me prisoner here."

"Sit down, Your Grace," William Grimsby ordered in a deceptively quiet voice. "We intend to detain you only until your husband arrives."

Hoping to escape, Isabelle sat in the chair nearest the door. Then she remembered that Lily was downstairs with Pebbles, and all thoughts of fleeing Montgomery House vanished. She couldn't very well leave her daughter with these three.

"This wasn't part of our plan," Nicholas deJewell

whined. "What will we do when Saint-Germain arrives?"

"What plan are you referring to?" Isabelle asked.

"Our plan to get what we want," Delphinia answered.

Isabelle narrowed her gaze on her stepmother. "And that would be?"

"I want revenge for my sister's death," William Grimsby spoke up, drawing her attention. "They want the Montgomery fortune."

"Don't be absurd," Isabelle said. "Your sister died miscarrying a child."

"Saint-Germain murdered Lenore," Grimsby insisted, his voice and his eyes filled with an unholy hatred.

Staring at him, Isabelle realized that the Earl of Ripon was beyond reason. His hatred had festered for so long it had poisoned his mind.

"How can you gain the Montgomery fortune?" Isabelle asked her stepmother. "Miles is alive, and if something happened to John, his brothers would inherit the Saint-Germain fortune."

"The child you carry will inherit the Saint-Germain fortune," Nicholas deJewell told her. "As for your brother, Miles won't live to see London again."

Shocked, Isabelle felt as though someone had kicked her in the stomach. She fell back against the chair, but kept herself from fainting through sheer force of will. Seeking a few hours' refuge at Montgomery House was proving to be a fatal mistake. How could she have been so stupid to lead her husband into this trap? She would never forgive herself if something happened to him.

* * *

While Isabelle was silently cursing her own stupidity, John stood inside the foyer of Lisette Dupre's town house. With him were Ross and Matthews.

"Alice, fetch your mistress," John ordered. "I have urgent business with her."

"I am here," said a voice from the top of the stairs. "I have business with you too."

The three men turned to see Lisette Dupre descending the stairs. When the raven-haired beauty crossed the foyer toward them, John recognized the angry glint in his former mistress's emerald eyes.

John held up an official-looking document. "I have the magistrate's order granting me temporary custody of Lily," he informed her. "Send Alice to fetch the child."

"You are too late," Lisette said, surprising him.

"What do you mean?" John asked, a twinge of panic shooting through him. If she'd harmed Lily . . .

"Your wife, your mother, and your aunt abducted my daughter at gunpoint," Lisette said, shocking all three men. "I intend to file charges and see them imprisoned."

Bull's pizzle, John thought angrily. He turned to the housekeeper and said, "Alice, you are dismissed."

This time the woman didn't bother to glance at her mistress for permission. She hurried down the corridor and disappeared from sight.

"Let's negotiate," John said, turning to Lisette.

"You have nothing I want except my daughter," she replied.

"Oh, I think I do have a great deal of what you want," John said, and gave her a cold smile. "How much will it cost me to keep you from pressing charges?"

"One hundred thousand pounds."

"That's highway robbery," Ross exclaimed.

"That is my price," Lisette said. "Take it or leave it."

"Write out a document stating the terms," John instructed, turning to his solicitor. "We'll sign it immediately."

"Each," Lisette added.

John snapped his gaze to hers. "I beg your pardon?"

"I want one hundred thousand pounds for each of the abductors," Lisette said.

John felt the muscle in his left cheek begin twitching, protesting his former mistress's greed, but there was nothing he could do. Lisette had him where she wanted, and she knew it.

John nodded. "How much will it cost for you to give Lily to me permanently and never see her again?"

"Lily is my only child," Lisette said with a feline smile.

"How much?" John snapped.

"Two hundred thousand pounds."

John felt the muscle in his right cheek begin twitching as well. He glanced at his solicitor and nodded.

Heavy silence reigned in the foyer while Matthews wrote the terms of the agreement and a promissory note. After Lisette signed the agreement, John signed both documents and then handed her the promissory note.

Following his brother and his solicitor, John turned to leave, but heard Lisette say, "Doing business with you has been my pleasure, Your Grace."

"Invest it wisely, Lisette," John said, pausing at the door. "You will get no more out of me." With those parting words, John left the town house.

Chapter 19

God's knob, but his wife's stupidity had cost him five hundred thousand pounds, John thought, staring out the coach's window as they drove down Park Lane toward Saint-Germain Court.

He didn't mind paying Lisette the two hundred thousand pounds to keep her permanently out of Lily's life, but giving her three hundred thousand pounds to keep the Saint-Germain women out of prison or scandal had been unnecessary. If Isabelle had stayed put instead of rushing off to his mother's . . . How would he punish her?

First John intended to give all three of them a stinging lecture. And then? Why, he would deduct money from his wife's monthly allowance until the three hundred thousand pounds had been paid in full, which should take the next forty years or so.

"Will there be anything else, Your Grace?" Matthews was asking.

"No," John answered curtly, his angry thoughts fixed on his wife and his mother. He alighted from his coach outside Saint-Germain Court and then called to Gallagher, "Drive Mr. Matthews home."

John watched his coach pull into the traffic on Park Lane and then asked his brother, "Would you care to come inside?"

"I don't wish to be present for this," Ross refused, his gaze sliding to the dowager's coach parked outside Saint-Germain Court. He gave his brother a lopsided grin and started down the street, where his own coach was waiting.

John hurried up the mansion's front steps. The door opened before he could reach for the knocker.

"Where are they?" John growled, marching into the foyer like an invading general.

"The ladies are waiting in your office," Dobbs answered.

John took the stairs two at a time and walked down the long corridor. He burst into his office, and the door crashed open with a loud bang.

His mother and his aunt were seated in the chairs in front of his desk, but his wife was missing. Probably soothing Lily's fears from having passed the better part of the day with Lisette.

John fixed his angry gaze on his mother, who leveled a scathing look at him. "Your stupidity has cost me a great deal of money," he said, crossing the chamber toward them.

"Do not be impertinent," the dowager replied, narrowing her gaze on him.

"Johnny, no matter how old you get," Aunt Hester began, "showing parental respect is—"

"Be quiet," the dowager ordered.

Aunt Hester clamped her lips together.

"Son, you are a jackass," the dowager informed him. "Lily Dupre is your natural daughter."

Her statement caught him off guard. "Mother, you cannot possibly know what I do not."

"Have you seen that tiny, heart-shaped birthmark on her buttocks?" she asked.

"Yes."

"I carry the same mark on my posterior, as does Hester," the dowager told him. "Don't bother to ask to see it, for I refuse to drop my drawers for my son."

"That you carry the same mark as Lily is pure coincidence," John replied.

"Johnny, you couldn't be more wrong," Aunt Hester piped up. "Though I do admit that you are hardly ever—"

"Silence!" the dowager ordered. "That tiny heart comes down through my Scottish side and appears every other generation on the females only. Hester and I carry it on our backsides, as did our grandmother. Now Lily has inherited it. I guarantee if Isabelle delivers a girl the babe will carry one too."

This theory was beyond belief. "Why didn't you tell me this before?"

"Would you have believed me?" his mother asked, arching a brow at him.

John smiled in spite of his anger. "No, and I don't believe you now." The dowager opened her mouth to argue, but John cut off whatever she would have said. "Who sired Lily is unimportant at the moment. Lisette extorted three hundred thousand pounds from me in order to prevent her from pressing charges against the lot of you. Now, if you will excuse me I have several things I'd like to say to my wife." John marched across the chamber toward the door, but his mother's next words stopped him in his tracks.

"Isabelle and Lily have taken up residence at Montgomery House," she informed him.

Ever so slowly, John turned to his mother and leveled a deadly look at her. Without saying a word he yanked the door open. His majordomo nearly fell across the open threshold.

"What the bloody hell?" John swore. "Have you been eavesdropping?"

"No, Your Grace." Dobbs stood proudly erect and lied in a haughty voice. "I simply wondered if you'd be requiring refreshment for your guests."

"Refreshments, my arse," John growled. "What I want is my carriage."

"Yes, Your Grace." The man turned away.

"Never mind. I'll walk," John said, remembering that Gallagher was driving his solicitor home. Before leaving he gifted his mother with a thunderous glare and then walked briskly down the corridor to the main staircase.

With her hands folded neatly in her lap, Isabelle sat in the drawing room at Montgomery House. She reached up and fingered her locket nervously. Silently, she called to Giselle for help, but no guardian angel appeared to rescue her.

"What if he doesn't show?" Nicholas deJewell whined as he paced back and forth across the drawing room.

"Saint-Germain will be here," William Grimsby assured him, sitting in the chair near the hearth.

"But what if—"

"Shut up, Nicky," Delphinia snapped, effectively silencing him.

Nicholas deJewell clamped his lips together and continued his pacing. As he passed her chair, Isabelle laughed derisively.

"Tell her to stop laughing at me," deJewell complained. "She's making me nervous."

"Laugh at Nicky again and you will regret it," Delphinia threatened.

"Who remains within the house?" Grimsby asked.

"The upstairs maid, guarding the child," Delphinia answered. "Possibly Pebbles and a few of the downstairs servants."

Giselle, help me, Isabelle called silently to her guardian angel. *You promised to be here whenever I needed you.*

"You are wasting your time," Isabelle whispered as deJewell passed her chair again. "My husband doesn't love me enough to come for me."

"Isabelle says that—" deJewell began.

"For God's sake, Nicky, she's lying." Delphinia cut off his words. She turned to Isabelle and said, "Lying won't do you any good. I've seen the way Saint-Germain looks at you. He'll arrive any moment now, and we'll be ready."

Isabelle made no reply. Could her stepmother be correct? Did John love her? He'd never given voice to harboring such a tender emotion for her.

Suddenly, the drawing room door crashed open, and the four of them snapped their gazes in that direction. Dark and dangerous and forbidding, John Saint-Germain seemed to fill the doorway with his presence.

"Get Lily," John ordered, marching into the room. "I'm taking you home."

Before anyone could stop her, Isabelle leapt out of her chair and threw herself into his arms, exclaiming, "You shouldn't have come here."

Both John and Isabelle heard the distinct sound of a trigger being cocked. They looked across the chamber to see Grimsby with a pistol raised and aimed in their direction.

"Have you gone mad?" John said in a surprised voice. "Lower that pistol or someone will be injured."

"Correct, Your Grace," Grimsby said, an unholy smile lighting his eyes. "Unfortunately, you will be the injured party."

"He's going to get us caught," deJewell complained, turning to his aunt.

"William, Nicky is correct," Delphinia said. "If you shoot him in my house, we will hang at Tyburn."

"I don't care about that," Grimsby replied. "As long as I—"

"I do care." Delphinia cut his words off. "I want no violence done in this house."

"William, why do you want to murder me?" John asked, his gaze fixed on his former brother-in-law.

"You murdered Lenore!"

"I never—"

"My sister died miscarrying your child," Grimsby said. "I blame you for her untimely death."

Staring up at her husband, Isabelle read the anguish in his dark gaze. His pain was her pain.

After a long moment when he seemed to be struggling with himself, John spoke in a harsh whisper. "Lenore bled to death trying to rid herself of the baby."

"I don't believe you," Grimsby shouted. "Lenore would never do such a thing, and if she did, you placed her in that position."

"The babe wasn't mine," John said in an anguished voice, shocking everyone in the chamber.

"Lying won't save you," Grimsby said, aiming the pistol at him.

Delphinia reached out and touched the earl's arm,

saying, "I'm warning you. Do not even consider pulling that trigger in my drawing room."

Isabelle gasped and swayed on her feet. She felt her heart breaking for her husband. He'd carried this secret burden around with him for years in order to spare others the pain and the shame.

"Did you try to have me run over by a carriage?" John asked.

"Yes, of course," Grimsby said in an arrogant tone of voice. "I also paid Lisette Dupre to create that scene at the wedding reception."

"And the shots fired at Isabelle and me on the evening of our betrothal?"

Grimsby inclined his head in the affirmative.

"Why are you doing this?" Isabelle cried, turning in her husband's arms to look at her stepmother, her hand sliding to her stomach to protect her baby.

"Dear Isabelle, you have nothing to fear," Delphinia told her. "You will die an old woman. Unfortunately, your main residence will be Bedlam."

Isabelle stared at her blankly. "I don't understand."

"Do I need to draw you a map?" Delphinia snapped at her. "Once His Grace is dead, you will elope with Nicky, and then we will control both the Saint-Germain and Montgomery fortunes."

"If my husband dies, I'll need my brother's permission to remarry," Isabelle reminded her stepmother.

"You came of age on your last birthday," Delphinia replied. "You need no one's permission to marry."

Isabelle felt the fight drain out of her. There just had to be a way to dissuade them from doing this.

"Besides, Miles won't be around to complain," deJewell added, his weasel's face contorting into a smirk. "We've arranged an untimely accident for Miles before he reaches London."

"I'll shout your guilt to the world," she threatened.

"Do that and the child upstairs will die," Delphinia returned the threat.

"God mend your blackened souls," Isabelle said. And then, surprising everyone, she called, "Giselle, where the bloody hell are you?"

Again, no guardian angel came to rescue her.

"I told you she was crazy," Delphinia said, turning to Grimsby.

"I love you," John said, tilting her chin up and smiling at her.

"And I love you," Isabelle vowed, returning his smile as if they hadn't a care in the world.

"Spare us this sickening sentimentality," Delphinia said.

"Where is everyone?" a voice called unexpectedly. "I'm home from America." Miles Montgomery walked into the drawing room, but stopped short at the sight that greeted him.

"You are supposed to be dead," Nicholas deJewell exclaimed.

"Miles," Isabelle cried, moving to go to him.

"Be easy, Belle," John whispered, holding her tightly lest any movement draw pistol fire. "Do not give him a reason to pull that trigger."

"What is happening in my home?" Miles asked in obvious confusion.

"John and I married last June," Isabelle told him, uncertain of where to begin. "Grimsby wants to kill John, and Delphinia and Nicholas want to steal the Montgomery fortune. They want you dead too."

Isabelle watched her brother slide his gaze to her husband's. Almost imperceptibly, John shook his head to warn him against rash action.

"Delphinia, I don't understand," Miles argued reasonably. "You have always enjoyed whatever you wanted and have no need to commit murder for money."

"Begging for gowns and trinkets has become a trifle stale," her stepmother replied.

"Two bodies are a lot to dispose of and remain free," John said. "No crime has been committed yet. Give up this insane idea, and I'll see that the magistrates show leniency."

Delphinia and Nicholas exchanged glances as if seeing the sense in what he said.

"We're taking them to those lime kilns at the quarries in Essex," Grimsby announced, moving across the chamber to the door. "We can dissolve their bodies there."

Giselle, I need you now, Isabelle thought.

"Patience, child. Trust me."

With his pistol pointed at them, Grimsby gestured them out of the drawing room. Slowly, they walked down the stairs to the foyer and crossed to the front door.

Just as they reached it, the door swung open. Rue rushed inside the mansion, shrieking in excitement, "Charles has offered for me! I'm going to be Rue Hancock, Baroness Keswick."

The interruption was distraction enough. Miles easily overpowered deJewell, while John struggled with Grimsby for the gun. The pistol flew out of Grimsby's hand and slid across the foyer.

"Child, the pistol."

Isabelle snatched the pistol before her stepmother

could reach it. Holding it in her badly shaking hands, she pointed it at Delphinia, who stopped short. "Come closer and I'll shoot you," Isabelle warned her.

John lifted the pistol out of her trembling hand and aimed it at the men. "Lie down on the floor," John ordered. "Delphinia, sit on the floor beside them."

"What is happening?" Rue cried.

Everyone ignored her.

It was then that Charles Hancock marched into the foyer. He glanced around and said to John, "Rue has agreed to become my wife."

"Congratulations," John said dryly. "Now, please be so kind as to fetch the authorities."

Hancock focused on the pistol. "Is this a new kind of game?"

"No, you blockhead," John answered, his patience gone. "These three tried to kill us. Fetch the authorities now."

Rue screamed and fainted at that shocking announcement. Hancock caught her before she hit the floor and gently laid her down.

"This changes everything," Hancock said. "I cannot have scandal attached to my name."

John rolled his eyes at Miles Montgomery and then spied the aging majordomo hurrying down the corridor toward the foyer. "Pebbles, fetch the authorities."

"With pleasure, Your Grace," Pebbles said, casting Delphinia and her nephew a contemptuous look as he passed them on his way out the front door.

"I shall always be indebted to Rue, who saved our lives this night," John announced, flicking a glance at Hancock. "You will marry her or suffer the consequences."

"Very well, but I shan't like it," Hancock replied.

John arched a dark brow at him. "You will like it."

"As you wish, Your Grace, I will like it too."

Ten minutes later Pebbles returned with several Bow Street runners. Seeing who had called for them, the men instantly handcuffed the three criminals.

"Your Grace, we'll need you to file the complaint with the magistrate tomorrow," one of them said.

"The Earl of Stratford and I will be there first thing in the morning," John agreed. When they'd gone, he turned to Isabelle and said, "And now, Your Grace."

John yanked her into his arms and crushed her against his body as if he would never let her go. He lowered his head, and his mouth captured hers in a demanding, earth-shattering kiss.

"I meant what I said about loving you," he told her.

"I love you too."

"Thank you, darling, for not giving up on me," John said, a smile lighting his expression.

Isabelle gifted her dark prince with an enchanting grin. "And thank you, my lord, for putting up with me."

Isabelle rested her head against the solidness of his chest, and John rested his chin on the crown of her blond head. They stood as one for a long, long time. . . .

Epilogue

The wheel of the year turned. Michaelmas daisies faded into autumn's misty mornings and golden afternoons, winter's barren and frost-feathered trees, and early spring's crocuses and forsythia.

On the twenty-third day of April, the feast day of Saint George, powdery snowflakes coated the grounds of Avon Park. The whiteness of those snowflakes accentuated the purple violets adorning the ducal garden while it awaited the blossoming of summer's flowers.

The Saint-Germain heir arrived early that morning. John decided to name him Adam, in honor of his wife's father.

Ten minutes later Adam's sister made her debut into the world. Isabelle decided to name her Elizabeth Giselle, in honor of her mother and her guardian angel.

That afternoon, when the excitement over Avon Park's newest residents had eased, the new parents rested in the ducal bedchamber. Leaning against the bed's headboard, Isabelle cradled her son in her arms, while John sat beside her and nestled his daughter against his chest.

Glancing sidelong at her husband, Isabelle watched him carefully unwrap their daughter's swaddling and lift her tiny buttocks up. "What are you doing?" she asked.

Ignoring her question, John inspected their daughter's buttocks. "Well, I'll be a rat's arse," he said. "Mother was correct."

Isabelle giggled. "What are you talking about?"

"Elizabeth carries the same heart-shaped birthmark that Lily does," he told her.

"Don't forget about your mother and Aunt Hester," she reminded him.

"I've been trying for months to erase that particular image from my mind," John said, and then heard the knock on the door. "Are you ready for company?"

Isabelle nodded. "Let her come in."

"Enter," he called.

The door swung open. Ross and Jamie Saint-Germain, accompanied by Miles Montgomery, filed into the ducal bedchamber to inspect their new nephew and niece. All three men smiled at the heartwarming sight of the Duke and Duchess of Avon cradling their firstborns.

"Where's Lily?" Isabelle asked.

"She's still napping," Ross answered, stepping closer to inspect the babies. "Juniper will bring her down as soon as she awakens."

"Adam is as handsome as his father," Jamie said.

"Yes, and Elizabeth Giselle is as beautiful as her mother," Miles agreed.

Pleased and proud, Isabelle gifted them with a smile. Her husband wasn't fooled though.

"Your compliments positively scream another business proposition," John said dryly. "Wasn't one foolish misadventure enough?"

"We didn't lose a shilling," Jamie countered.

"Traveling to and from America during wartime cost you almost a year of your lives," John replied, and then shifted his gaze away from his youngest brother's disappointed expression.

"Our newest business prospect is in England," Miles said.

John lifted his gaze to his brother's and smiled, saying, "We'll discuss this later when I come downstairs."

"Apparently, I want nothing," Ross drawled. "I think the babies' faces are terribly wizened. Will those unsightly wrinkles smooth out?"

Isabelle giggled. "That really is too bad of you," she teased her brother-in-law.

"The Grimsby family wrote to me," John told them, becoming serious. "William's insanity forced them to place him in Bedlam."

"At least we needn't worry about him again," Ross said.

"And Nicholas deJewell has finally left for Australia," Miles told them.

"I cannot help feeling sorry for Lobelia and Rue," Isabelle remarked, surprising them.

"Why is that, darling? Both enjoy happy marriages," John said, looking at her. "We did manage to avert a scandal by settling this matter without a trial."

"Yes, but they share responsibility for Delphinia's house arrest," Isabelle replied, giving him a mischievous smile. "Imagine what their lives are like with Delphinia as a houseguest for six months each year."

"Living with Delphinia is a fitting punishment for all the years they tormented you," John said, and then leaned close to plant a kiss on her cheek.

"It's time for us to start celebrating the arrival of the newest Saint-Germains," Ross said.

"I'm ready for that," Jamie said.

"Me too," Miles agreed.

"I'll join you later," John told them. "Try to stay sober until I come downstairs."

The three uncles left the chamber, leaving the new parents alone—but not for long. Ten minutes later they heard another knock on the door.

John glanced at his wife.

"Let her come in," Isabelle said.

At John's call the door swung open.

Accompanied by Juniper, Lily raced across the bedchamber toward the bed. "God's knob," Lily cried, sounding like her father. "I see two babies."

"Your father and I couldn't decide if you needed a brother or a sister," Isabelle told her.

"So we made you one of each," John finished.

Lily giggled and clapped her hands together.

"Do you like your brother and your sister?" Isabelle asked her.

"Oh, yes."

"Do you like them more than riding Harmony around the garden?" John asked.

Lily nodded. "I like them even more than rolling down the sides of hills." The little girl turned to her nanny and announced, "Nanny Juniper, I need to talk to God. Will you take me to the chapel?"

"Are you asking or thanking?" John asked, smiling with love at his oldest daughter.

"Thanking Him, of course."

Juniper held out her hand, and the little girl accepted it. Together they left the bedchamber.

"Are you certain you don't want to name her Prudence or Fortitude?" John teased his wife. "She looks more like a Temperance than an Elizabeth."

Isabelle felt her lips twitch with the urge to laugh. "I'm prepared to sacrifice my first three choices as long as you don't name our son Sloth."

When her husband made no reply, Isabelle tore her gaze away from her son to look at him. Wearing a shocked expression, her husband stared at something across the chamber. Isabelle followed his gaze and then smiled when she spied the wizened old crone advancing on them.

"I've missed you," Isabelle said. "Where have you been?"

"Here, there, and everywhere," Giselle answered. "I was always within shouting distance if you needed me." The old woman smiled at the sleeping infants and, reaching out with her gnarled hand, touched each in turn. "May God bless Adam and Elizabeth Giselle with health, prosperity, and everlasting love."

"You aren't leaving me?" Isabelle asked.

"I will be standing in the shadows, but dwelling within your heart," Giselle answered. "I love you, child." She looked at John and asked, "Do you believe in me now?"

With those words a mist enveloped the old woman, swirling around and around her. The shrouding mist evaporated within mere moments. Giselle had disappeared; in her place stood a beautiful blond-haired woman.

"Mother?" Isabelle whispered.

"Death had no power to separate us," the woman said, her smile filled with love and heavenly grace. "Love lives for all of eternity." She leaned close and pressed a kiss on Isabelle's forehead, then vanished in an instant as if she'd never existed.

"I never would have believed it if I hadn't seen it," John said, his voice mirroring his surprise.

Isabelle looked at him through violet eyes glistening with unshed tears. Without saying a word she used her free hand to open her locket, and for the first time she allowed him to see the miniature it contained—the image of the woman who'd stood in their bedchamber, Isabelle's long-dead mother.

"Darling, I'm sorry I ever doubted you," John apologized.

"Giselle was correct; princes don't always wear crowns," Isabelle said, an aching catch in her voice. "Some princes disguise themselves as dukes."

"Thank you, darling." Carefully nestling his daughter against his chest, John leaned close and planted a kiss on her temple, whispering in a voice hoarse with emotion, "*Joy sans fyn,* my love. Joy without end."